Praise for *I'll Be You*

"Her twistiest and tightest work yet . . . *I'll Be You* is a cleverly crafted and psychologically nuanced yin and yang, complete with crackling observations about celebrity, California cults, wellness culture, the fertility industry, and the undertow of addiction."

—*Time*

"An addictive thriller that will keep readers burning through pages . . . sneakily hypnotic."

—*Los Angeles Times*

"Sharply insightful, relentlessly suspenseful and simply unputdownable, *I'll Be You* is Janelle Brown's best novel yet."

—*Bookreporter*

"The perfectly paced emotional reveals of the twins' shared history pull the reader toward fierce investment in Elli's safety and the sisters' reconnection. Brown has upped her game with this one."

—*Publishers Weekly* (starred review)

"A delicious work of intrigue and suspense . . . You won't want to stop reading until you find out what's happened."

—*Kirkus Reviews*

"Brown uses the concept of interchangeable personhood to great effect in this haunting psychological thriller."

—*CrimeReads*

BY JANELLE BROWN

I'LL
BE
YOU

I'LL BE YOU

a novel

JANELLE BROWN

RANDOM HOUSE

New York

2023 Random House Trade Paperback Edition

Copyright © 2022 by Janelle Brown

Published in the United States by Random House, an imprint and division of Penguin Random House LLC, New York.

RANDOM HOUSE and the HOUSE colophon are registered trademarks of Penguin Random House LLC.

Originally published in hardcover in the United States by Random House, an imprint and division of Penguin Random House LLC, in 2022.

LIBRARY OF CONGRESS CATALOGING-IN-PUBLICATION DATA
Names: Brown, Janelle, author.
Title: I'll be you: a novel / Janelle Brown.
Other titles: I will be you
Description: First edition. | New York: Random House, [2022]
Identifiers: LCCN 2021039043 (print) | LCCN 2021039044 (ebook) |
ISBN 9780525479284 (paperback) | ISBN 9780525479215 (ebook)
Subjects: LCGFT: Novels.
Classification: LCC PS3602.R698 I45 2022 (print) |
LCC PS3602.R698 (ebook) | DDC 813/.6—dc23
LC record available at https://lccn.loc.gov/2021039043
LC ebook record available at https://lccn.loc.gov/2021039044

Printed in the United States of America on acid-free paper

randomhousebooks.com

9 8 7 6 5 4 3 2 1

Designed by Debbie Glasserman

For Jodi
This one's for you, sis.

SAM

part one

"YOU BE ME, AND I'll be you," I whispered.

She looked back at me, wide eyes blinking under dense mascara. "We can do that?"

The three dark flecks swimming in the blue of her iris, the freckle beside her right ear, the tilt of her top incisor: These I knew as "not mine" from the hours that we'd spent comparing, but who else would notice? Who else had ever studied her as closely as I had? Who had ever seen me the way that she did?

"Of course we can," I said. "Don't you want to?"

There, in our trailer—amid the drifts of training bras and forgotten scripts and the tarot cards that our mother studied during the long days on set—we turned as one to gaze into our shared mirror. Elli hesitated, examining herself in that foggy way of hers. "I don't know."

Then her eyes slid into mine, and I felt her take me—the strong one, the sharp one, the wild one—into herself with a hot, quick gasp, as if suddenly coming alert. I could smell the mint of her gum; I could taste it in my mouth, the taste of fresh possibility.

"Yes," she finally breathed. "Yes, I do."

I didn't feel a bit guilty about how much she trusted me—not then, at least. We were only thirteen, and it was already the beginning of the end.

ON A THURSDAY NIGHT in July, 378 days into my latest bout of sobriety, my father called to tell me that my twin sister had gone AWOL. My sister and I hadn't spoken in 379 days, so this came as news to me.

"She told us that she was going to a spa of some kind," my father explained. "But she's been gone a week already, and she's not answering her phone. It all seems very strange."

I found this unlikely. My sister had never done anything strange in her life. Elli—married to a real estate lawyer, owner of a two-story Spanish Revival just blocks away from the Santa Barbara beach where we played as children, a woman who coordinated her purse with her heels—was the very definition of conventionality. Last time I was at her house I opened a drawer in the kitchen and found a banana slicer.

As for me: I was living in a near-empty studio apartment in Hollywood, so close to the boulevard that I woke up most nights to the sounds of people vomiting in the bushes underneath my window. I was thirty-two years old and slept on a futon, still crawling my way back from losing most everything I owned or loved in the years before. Fortunately, I still had my looks, some interesting tattoos, and a generous AA sponsor; and with these I'd found employment at a trendy café popular on social media for its latte art.

From semi-famous child actress to milk-foam Instagram model. That had been my life trajectory in a nutshell, a downward parabola precipitously accelerated by the excessive use of intoxicants.

When my father called, I was watching cooking show reruns and eating day-old green curry straight out of the takeout container. It was nine o'clock and eighty degrees out, the air in my apartment still flaccid from the day's heat. I stood by the air-conditioning unit and ducked my head to let the whisper of coolant dry the sweat on the back of my neck.

"Let's be real, Dad. This is *Elli*. She probably just got a bad facial peel and is hiding out until her skin heals. Nothing strange about it."

"That's what your mom said, too, but I can't help worrying." I heard a familiar note of concern and disdain in my father's voice, a tone that was usually reserved for me. I'll confess, I derived some perverse delight in drawing that out of my father: that I—*I*—might be the functional twin for once.

"What about Chuck? What does he think about all this?"

"Ah, well. He moved out a while back. They're getting divorced."

"Divorced?" I stood up abruptly, slamming my head against the edge of the air conditioner. Something squeezed tight in my chest, compressing my lungs.

"You still haven't spoken, then, I take it." Something had shifted in his voice, the pendulum of judgment swinging back toward me.

"No," I said, squirming. "Not in a while." Why was my father calling me anyway? My mother was usually the one who rang me up when something was amiss. Typically, I got a tentative quarterly voicemail, left at a time when I was most likely to be at work, though I noticed that she followed the café on Instagram and "liked" every photo of me.

A moment of hesitation. "And you—you're still . . . *OK*?"

"You mean, am I still sober? Yes. More than a year now." The silence on the other end of the phone was stiff with disbelief. "Look, do you want me to text you a photo of my latest recovery medallion to prove it?"

"No, no, I trust you. We're proud of you, honey."

Was he? I didn't quite believe it, and I couldn't blame him for that, either, given the number of times that I had betrayed their pride in the past. We lapsed into silence, the bitter failures of the last two decades—parenting and childing, alike—leaking into the crack in our conversation.

It dawned on me then that there was a reason for my father's phone call. "Wait, are you asking for my *help* with something?"

My father coughed lightly. "I don't want to inconvenience you," he said.

I had to stifle my laugh. I looked around the minuscule apartment that I called a home, barren of personal effects. My possessions these days consisted primarily of emotional baggage. My social life consisted of AA meetings, with an occasional foray into NA meetings. I had been treading water for so long that I relished the idea of having something—*anything*—to swim toward. It didn't occur to me to legitimately worry about my sister; not yet.

"Not at all," I offered graciously. "So what do you want me to do about Elli?"

"It's not Elli, actually. What we need—what your *mom* needs, really—is for you to come help out with Charlotte. Your mother's struggling a bit, physically I mean, and she's been doing her best but Charlotte's just starting to be too much for her to handle."

This gave me pause. When you've spent the better part of a decade in various states of inebriation, it's easy to forget names and faces. I ran this name through my spotty mental Rolodex, and came up empty-handed. "I give up," I said. "Who's Charlotte?"

My father sighed, his patience with me finally at its end. "She's your *niece*," he said.

THE NEXT MORNING I asked my boss at the café for a week off. "I need to go home and help my parents take care of my niece," I told Tamar, all trembly lips and damp eyes. The tears were probably unnecessary—Tamar was also my AA sponsor, and had spent much of the last year listening to me rehash my family estrangement—but I wasn't about to leave anything to chance. It's a neat trick, to cry on cue. Not all actors can do it.

I still missed being on set.

Tamar flicked a clot of coffee grounds from the front of her apron and gave me a hard look. "Is that such a good idea? That's going to be triggering and you know it," she said. Tamar was ten years older than me and composed entirely of sharp angles and visible tendons. Her eyes constantly darted around the room as she noted dirty tables, monitored the length of the line, judged the crema on a macchiato. She'd been a cokehead, a decade back, and old habits die hard. Or maybe we just choose the drugs that amplify the instincts we already have, that let us be our unedited selves: paranoid, slothful, amped-up, wild. Our ids cranked up to one hundred.

Tamar turned her focus to me, noting something in my eyes that made her squint suspiciously. "Maybe someone should go with you. I don't think you're ready."

"You offering?"

"Point taken." She gave me the time off and told me to go find a meeting when I got to Santa Barbara.

My parents lived ninety minutes away up the coast, in a tile-roofed Mediterranean in the hills, not far from Rattlesnake Canyon. It was not the house that I'd been born in—that had been a far more modest two-bedroom bungalow in a neighborhood where you didn't find hiking trails outside your back door. This particular home had materialized in high school, not long after my sister and I were cast as the stars of a middling Nickelodeon TV series. My mother had done quite well for herself, for a while, as manager of her daughters' acting careers; better than I had done, it had to be said. Then again, any money she might have made off my career was probably better spent by her than by me, because she at least had a house to show for her percentage, while all I had for mine was an empty rental apartment and the scars on my psyche.

My mother was already standing in the garden when I pulled into the driveway. She wore a caftan printed with palm trees that billowed around her stout legs. A straw visor shaded her eyes, bright red curls neatly puffed into place. She waved both arms at me with an eagerness that bordered on aggressiveness. I hadn't seen her since Christmas, which had mostly been fine, except for all the weeping.

"Darling!" She waited for me to approach and then threw her arms around me.

"Hi, Mom," I said, and let her hug me for longer than felt necessary, considering. I guess she was relieved that at least one of her daughters wasn't currently running rogue. She sniffled a little into my shoulder. She had grown smaller, I noticed, more askew. And when she turned to walk with me up the garden path I realized that she was limping a little.

"Osteoarthritis," she said, noticing me noticing. "Just like your grandmother. You'll have it, too, someday, I'm sure. It's how all the women in our family go."

I'd spent so many years skating right to the edge of death and then leaping back that it was strange to imagine my demise as a slow natural decline. Our parents' bodies mirror our eventual mortality, unless we divert the paths ourselves. God knows I'd tried.

"Does it hurt?" I asked.

She lifted her chin, a plucky little display of bravery. "Of course. But I take CBD oil, and that helps. And Belva at Om Chakra gave me some aventurine and blue chalcedony, which are supposed to be good for pain and inflammation, so I carry those in my pockets all the time now."

What I thought was *What would really help you is some oxycodone,* but of course I knew better than to say this out loud since it was only three years back that she caught me crushing up oxy pills and snorting them in the guest bath. The ensuing fight ruined her sixtieth birthday party completely. So, yeah, too soon to make jokes.

"Where's the baby?" I asked.

"She's napping," my mother said. "And she's not a baby, she's a toddler. Two years old."

I did the math—I hadn't seen my sister in a while, but surely it hadn't been *that* long. "Wait, how can Elli possibly have a two-year-old?"

"She's adopted." She bit her lip. "Maybe you know, Elli and Chuck had been trying for so long, and . . ." Her voice trailed off a bit. "Anyway, it's been a big year. You heard that Chuck left? Just bailed out five months ago, only weeks before the adoption came through. Quite a surprise. Both Charlotte's arrival and Chuck's departure." She practically spat out his name. Gone was the dulcet awe of *Chuck who can do no wrong* or *Chuck the successful son-in-law, why don't you find yourself someone like him, Sam, hmmmm?* "Anyway, Charlotte has been a real consolation, a welcome distraction for all of us throughout that whole mess. She's a blessing, really."

She turned to me and smiled, hands clutched tight to her chest, having already shaken off the bad news and moved on to the good. That was my mother: conflict averse. When Elli and I were children and used to fight, my mother would just close the door to our bedroom as if shutting the door might mean our fight wasn't happening at all. If one of us went to her to tattle, she would stick her fingers in her ears and say, *I can't hear you.* She lived in terror that the tiniest crack in her world might let a river of woe come pouring through. This approach hadn't done much good when it came to me.

I thought about the baby—*toddler.* I wasn't sure what a two-year-old even looked like. "Two years old. So—she can walk and talk?"

My mother opened the front door and a blast of cool air hit me in the face. "For God's sake, Samantha. Yes, she can walk. That child is constantly in motion, and with my hips the way they are, you understand why I just can't keep up. She needs someone quick and young to keep an eye on her. To take her places—to the park, or the beach—and wear her out so she actually sleeps."

"Sounds easy enough."

"You'd think so, wouldn't you?" I couldn't tell whether this was a hypothetical, or a jab at me. But she was smiling, at least. We stood in the foyer of the quiet house, the sounds from outside sucked up by the beige carpet and slip-covered couches. I could see a purple crayon streak on the hallway wall, only partially rubbed away. There was an animal cracker under the console. It looked like the house hadn't been vacuumed in at least a week. My mother was clearly losing it.

She looked at me, tiny muscles tightening around her lips. "Elli . . . Well, I'm not going to text her to let her know that you're here. She might not—" She hesitated. "Your sister never explained what happened. Why you haven't spoken in so long. I wasn't sure . . ." Her voice trailed off again and I knew what she was thinking, that Elli might not *want* me taking care of her child. I felt a rush of blood to my cheeks; considering last year's debacle, it was possible my mother wasn't so wrong.

"It was all just a misunderstanding," I said. "We're going to work it out eventually."

"I'm sure you will." She reached out, took my hand, and squeezed it, a nervous smile on her face. "You'll let me know if you don't think you're up for this after all, right?"

"I'm doing *great,* Mom. It's all behind me. Promise." I smiled a radiantly toothy smile that I'd perfected with my acting coach at fifteen, a smile that exuded *trust me. I'm going to take the best fucking care of this child,* I thought. *They are going to be blown away by what a good aunt I am, how much I've changed. It's going to be all ice cream and candyfloss around here.* I pushed past the inconvenient fact that I had never spent any time with children, never paid close attention to them at all. I made a point not to coo at the babies who came into the café strapped to their fathers' chests in BabyBjörns and getting latte foam dripped on their downy heads. A baby, a family—it was so far from the world that I'd built for myself (correction: the hole I'd dug for myself) that it was easier to just fling that notion even further away and to think of reproduction as a monetizable bodily function, rather than an emotional imperative. I'd seen what that desperate need had done to my sister. It wasn't pretty.

Better to want nothing at all, and then you'll never be disappointed.

So here's the sum total of what I knew about kids: They spilled cocoa on the café floor and left pee on the bathroom seats and fingerprints on the pastry display case. They were cute but destructive and seemed to demand a lot of attention. But I didn't *not* like them. So surely I could handle one single kid.

As I was imagining this, my mother looked back through the

front door and eyed my Mini Cooper with trepidation. "Can you fit a car seat in that thing? What's the safety rating? Charlotte's still rear-facing, you know."

"I don't even know what that means."

"It means the car seat faces the rear, darling." My mother turned to study me, trying to figure out if I was really this dim. I offered her a reassuring smile: *Just kidding.*

"It's not like I have another car sitting around. Can I just borrow yours?" My mother drove a silver SUV, all five-foot-one of her hoisted up as high as the front seat would go. I figured she felt safe up there in her tank, looking down at all the people for once.

My mother sighed again. "I guess yours will be fine. It won't be long until your sister gets back anyway."

My flip-flops sank into the carpet as I stepped down into the living room, assailed by a sudden wash of memories of this house. Elli lying on the living room rug, a square of sun on her face, as I lacquered her toes with glitter polish. Myself, coming to on the guest bathroom floor, pills spilling from my purse. I felt my heart settle low in my chest, a precipitous plunge of panic. What had I done?

"I can only stay for a long weekend. Three days. Maybe four," I lied.

"Oh, Elli will be back home by then," my mother said cheerfully. "I'm sure of it. She'll get what she needed from that place and return. She always does the right thing. You know your sister."

Did I? I knew I had, once. Now I wasn't so sure.

3 MY PARENTS' HOUSE WAS starting to smell like old people, which alarmed me: like furniture that had been collecting dust mites for too many decades, ancient cooking smells trapped in the brocade curtains. My niece was asleep in one of the two guest bedrooms—the bedroom that had once been my own—so I headed to the other to drop my bag.

There, I flopped down on rose-print sheets that I remembered from my childhood, now soft from decades of washing. I hadn't slept in this house in at least five years, during a failed attempt at a self-detox. I wondered if my mother had forgiven me yet for ruining her favorite quilt during that stay.

"Mama?"

I sat up and there was a child in the doorway, staring at me. Dark curls tangled around her ears, and she blinked at me with sober brown eyes set into a soft, puffy face. I found myself looking for my sister in her, before reminding myself that, of course, she was adopted. She was wearing a Pull-Up diaper and a T-shirt with a cartoon giraffe on the front, and her skin was still pink with sleep.

"I'm not . . ." I began, but the little girl had already run into the room and toward the bed, her arms flung out at me as if expecting me to pick her up. I stared at her, unsure what to do; and then, hearing the lopsided gait of my mother coming down the hall, grabbed her and lifted her up.

She was hot in my arms, steaming and sticky, and heavier than I expected. She pressed her face into the skin of my neck, leaving something troublesomely damp there. I wrapped my arms around her and then sat motionless on the edge of the bed, terrified of dropping her.

Suddenly she pulled back, as if startled, and looked up at me with a strange expression: studying me, hard. She must have understood, somehow, that I was not my sister. Maybe the way my shampoo smelled, or the texture of my skin. What was my sister's hair like these days? Last time I'd seen her it had been long and shiny and gold, usually pulled back in a ponytail. My own blond hair was shoulder-length, grown out from a pixie crop I'd ended up with a few years back after I sold my hair for cash. *Your crowning glory,* my mother had sobbed when she saw me, as if I were Jo from *Little Women.* I think she was more upset about that than anything else I'd done to myself.

Anyway, Charlotte was still clutching me, staring up at me with wide unblinking eyes, when my mother appeared at the door. I met her gaze over the little girl's curls.

"Did you tell her I was coming?" I asked.

"No." My mother cringed in the doorway. "We didn't want to until you got here. Just in case . . ."

In case you didn't show up at all was what she was thinking. I frowned. "Does she even know that her mom has a twin sister who looks exactly like her but *isn't* her?"

My mother looked panicky. "Well, not exactly? She's seen family photos around our house, but I'm not exactly sure what your sister told her. Maybe nothing? She's only two, after all. These things are hard to explain." We were whispering, as if the child sitting right there between us couldn't understand a thing, but when I looked down at the little girl she was squinting at me as if she knew exactly what was being discussed.

"I am your aunt, not your mother," I said loudly, enunciating every syllable. "I am your mother's sister. We are *identical twins.*

Do you know what that means?" Charlotte nodded, but there was a dark squint in her eyes as she dug very hard for the answer and came up empty. "It means we look exactly the same. So I know I look like your mama, but I am not your mama."

The little girl in my arms took this in for a minute, and then burst into tears. "Waaannn maaamaaaa," she wailed. She flung herself sideways, so that I had to clutch her tight in order to keep her from falling off the bed, which of course just made her cry harder.

My mother backed slowly out of the doorway. "Why don't I go make her a sippy cup of warm milk?" She fled down the hall.

"Hey, shhh, shhh. It's OK." She was rigid in my arms, still trying to throw herself to the ground, inconsolable. What are you supposed to do with a crying two-year-old? Wasn't this when you put the pacifier in their mouth to quiet them? I looked around the guest bedroom but of course there was no pacifier, not even any toys, just some ornamental ceramic orbs in a big wicker bowl on the dresser. I dug in my jeans pockets for something, anything, that might distract the child from her grief. A metal hair pin—perhaps not advisable. A set of keys. She slapped them away when I jingled them in her face. Maybe that kind of thing was for babies, not toddlers.

I jiggled the girl in my lap, bouncing her on my knee until her teeth were rattling in her mouth. The wailing grew louder. My mother had vanished into the kitchen at the far end of the house and I was fairly sure she had no plans to return with warm milk.

Desperate, I dug deeper into my pocket and turned up the sobriety coin I'd been given at my year anniversary, two weeks back. A bright bronze thing, embossed with words Charlotte would not yet understand: *UNITY—SERVICE—RECOVERY*. It was just the right size to clutch in your hand instead of reaching for that drink. It glinted in the light from the window. Charlotte paused from crying to stare at it.

"Tweasure?" she asked, her eyes pink and wet.

She was smarter than I thought.

"Treasure," I agreed. "I stole it from a pirate in the faraway land of Los Angeles, sailed all the way here to give it to you. Should we go bury it in the garden and make a treasure map, so that the pirates don't come and steal it back?"

She gazed gravely up at me, tiny tears still clinging to her flushed cheeks. I could still see the confusion in her face, that two things could look so alike and familiar and yet also be so completely different. I understood how she felt. I often felt the same way myself when I looked at my sister.

"We bewy it," she repeated. Her voice was tentative and reedy. It made me think of bunny rabbits and warm beaches, of the sunny days of my own childhood. A strange wave of nostalgia hit me, a residual memory of a time long ago when my mother used to carry Elli and me on her hips, like bookends. How safe that felt.

I stood and hoisted Charlotte up onto my own hip, which was harder than it looked. "I'm your aunt Samantha. You can call me Sam, or Sammy."

"Mimi?" She looked confused.

"Sure, if that's easier. I know I'm not your mom, but I'm going to try my best to take care of you while she's gone. OK?"

"'Kay," she whispered. And even though she still wasn't smiling, I could feel her body go slack, releasing itself to this new, semi-familiar adult.

"We're going to be just fine," I murmured into her hair.

I wasn't sure if I was talking to the kid or to myself.

4 WE BURIED THE SOBRIETY badge in my parents' backyard, along with a pocketful of baubles that I fished
out of my mother's costume jewelry box. I gave Charlotte a trowel that I found in the gardening shed and then followed her around the garden as she dug holes. While she carefully
placed each rhinestone earring in its own little grave and covered
it with dirt, I dutifully marked its location on a map that I'd
sketched on the back of an old health food flyer I'd found in the
kitchen.

After we'd finished burying everything, I gave Charlotte a hi-
biscus Popsicle from my parents' freezer and we sat side by side
on the porch looking out at the garden. My mother had planted
Mexican sage, lavender, and bougainvillea, and in the full bloom
of summer the yard was a sea of purple. After our acting careers
imploded and our mother's career as our manager fizzled, she had
started a little business in landscape design; so most of the homes
on the street now featured "Linda Logan yards," with burbling
fountains and thickets of drought-tolerant flowers. As a result,
their neighborhood seemed to have an unusually high per capita
number of hummingbirds, butterflies, and bumblebees. I had to
give my mother credit for that.

I smiled at Charlotte. "How is your mama?" I asked her softly.
"I miss her."

Charlotte was busy chasing a melting slab of Popsicle with a neon pink tongue. She cocked her head and slurped. "Why?"

"Why? Because I screwed up a while back, and now she's mad at me."

"Why?"

I didn't know how to answer this. The child stared gravely back at me, unable to compute. I supposed this wasn't an appropriate conversation to have with someone who didn't even know the alphabet yet, but how was I to know how to speak to a toddler? Charlotte seemed unperturbed. She ate the last melting bit of pink sludge and let the naked stick drop to the porch. Then she grabbed the trowel and the map and scampered back off into the garden to dig her treasure back up.

My father came out to join me on the deck, his joints popping as he sat next to me on the bench. He still wore the coat and tie that he'd worn to work—he had been an accountant at a paper supply company for the last three decades—and they tugged at the buttons where his body now sagged in the middle. He looked tired, I thought, and a little diminished, as if someone had put a giant thumb on his head and pushed him right back down into himself. It was five-thirty, time for his nightly G&T, but he was drinking a can of lime sparkling water, because of me, surely. I couldn't decide if I was touched by this gesture or insulted by his lack of faith in my self-control.

He lit up when he saw Charlotte out digging under the giant oak that enveloped the back of the yard. He waved, and she waved back at him. "Tweasure!" she called, jewels sparkling in her fist.

"Is that your mother's earring she's holding?" he asked me. "For God's sake, don't let Linda see that. She'll lose her mind."

But my mother was already standing there behind him, drinking a glass of chardonnay. (Apparently *she* was unconcerned about testing my sobriety.) "It's fine," she said. "They're paste." She dimpled at the little girl in the garden. She'd really lowered her standards for this kid.

I turned to face them. "So, let's talk. What's the story with Elli? What's going on? Where is she?"

My mother stuffed her nose into the mouth of her wineglass. "I think single motherhood was turning out to be a bit much for her, that's all," she said breezily. "It's a lot to have a small child all by yourself, you know? When I had you two there were certainly months when I just wanted to disappear and leave your father to take care of things for a while." She gulped some wine, licked her teeth. "Plus with the whole divorce debacle . . . She just wanted some downtime and she went to a spa. She said it was in Ojai."

"What's the name of the spa? Is it that fancy golf place? Ojai Valley Inn?" I imagined my sister swaddled in terry cloth, mud cracking on her face, the cucumber slices on her eyes conveniently blinding her to any memory of her responsibilities back home. A vision that was hard to reconcile with the sister I knew. And yet who knew what I'd missed over the last year? Apparently, quite a lot.

"I don't think so. But I'm not sure what it's called. Did she say the name to you?" My mother looked inquisitively at my father, who shook his head. "Actually, I think she might have called it a 'healing retreat.' So maybe not a 'spa,' exactly, but some kind of wellness destination."

"Taking an awful long time to get well," my father grumbled. "Seems like it should have taken a weekend, tops."

"The heart and mind need what they need." My mother puffed herself up, her hair a nimbus of hennaed curls. She looked like an indignant dandelion. "Just because *you* don't feel the need for personal growth, Frank, you shouldn't judge others who want to find themselves a little. *I'm* just glad she's finally doing some self-care after such a trying year."

"I just think she should have at least answered your texts. Seems to me that something might not be right with her. Maybe she's having a breakdown. Maybe she's sick." My father frowned at his can of fizzy water, as if unsure why he was holding it and not a G&T at this unpleasant moment in time.

My father tended toward cynicism and my mother toward blind optimism. It was a miracle, frankly, that they were still married; but apparently opposites really do attract. Our childhood had been a tug-of-war between them, with my mother usually winning. My father had wanted to send me to rehab when I was seventeen but my mother insisted I was just "going through a phase." And although I was thrilled at the time that my mother won that particular argument, in retrospect I was the real loser in that battle.

"Elli sent me a text a few days ago, she seemed to be fine. The last thing she needs is us intruding on her emotional life." She sipped at her wine. "Anyway, your father's just being dramatic, as always."

"Pretty selfish of her, don't you think?" My mom gave me a sharp look. *Who are you to judge?* "I mean, it's not very Elli-like behavior, don't you think?"

"And how would you know, Sam? You've been absent all year. Longer than that, to be honest."

I flushed at the rebuke. She was right. "Can I at least see the text she sent?"

She pulled her cellphone out of her pocket. The home screen photo was a snapshot of Charlotte squinting into the sun. Something small and primal inside me stung at this tiny rejection: that I, her daughter, no longer qualified for my mother's landing screen. But, of course, I was in my thirties now. I'd outgrown that primacy a long time ago.

I looked over my mother's shoulder as she pulled up her text history with Elli and handed the phone to me. Curious, I scrolled back through my sister's old messages to my mom. *There in 10.* And *Stopping at Vons, need anything?* And *Charlotte's got a cold, we're staying in.* And *Turn on GMA, that chef you love is on.*

The mundane intimacy between my sister and my mother took my breath away: Is this what I'd been missing all these years? Did I want it, too? Or would I have found this claustrophobic?

My mother must have noticed my curiosity because she grabbed the phone and quickly scrolled down to the last few messages in the chain before handing it back to me. The string began a week earlier, on the previous Thursday, with a *Thanks so much for watching C, back Sunday.* This was followed up, over the next seventy-two hours, by some unanswered texts from my mother to Elli: *Hope retreat is going well. OK to give her M&Ms?* And *Don't want to interrupt your me time but how long is C supposed to nap?* And *She's not allergic to bees, is she?*

Then Sunday—five days ago, now—there was a text from my mother to my sister: *What time are you picking her up today? Dad and I were thinking about going out to dinner if you can get here before six.*

There was a long gap of time after my mother's message, with no response. I could imagine my mother's blood pressure rising by the hour, as the phone remained adamantly silent. It wasn't until seven o'clock that night that my sister finally responded. *Can you handle Charlotte for a few more days? I'm not ready to come home yet.*

My mother replied immediately. *How many days are we talking? Are you OK?*

I'm doing fine. Finding the answers I've been looking for.

By this point, my mother had seemingly lost interest in her daughter's journey to self-discovery. Mostly, she seemed peeved.

You know I love Charlotte but this is a lot. My osteoarthritis is flaring up.

There was a two-minute pause after this. I imagined my sister staring at the blank text message field, thinking her options through. My mother's furious blinking while she waited for my sister's inevitable apology, her promise to return *so very soon.* It wasn't like Elli to ask for favors.

But there was no apology, just a terse final text, more command than atonement: *Get Sam to help you. She'll know what to do. She'll get it.*

And then: nothing.

I looked at Charlotte, scampering back toward us now, her palms black with dirt and bejeweled rings drooping from every finger. What, exactly, was I supposed to "get"? The child? How to help my mom take care of her? My sister's cryptic journey to make sense of things?

Or was it the impulse to bail out of your life that my sister knew I'd understand?

A TALENT AGENT NAMED Harriet Sunday discovered Elli and me on the beach in Santa Barbara when we were nine years old. Towheaded little girls, freckled and sandy, sun-faded bikinis, identical down to the dimples in our left cheeks. We had wide-set blue eyes, which lent us a hypnotic baby-doll quality, both alien and appealing. When we walked down the street in perfect syncopation, blond waves swinging about our shoulders, people would stop in their tracks and stare.

Harriet must have known right away that she'd hit the jackpot.

I remember Harriet's arrival in my life as a shadow falling over us, while we sat there at the high-water line, digging in the sand. She wore a vintage YSL smoking jacket, cropped black hair tucked under a Dodgers baseball cap, and cat-eye sunglasses. "Are you building a sandcastle?" she asked, her voice smoked and husky.

Elli was frozen, our mother's admonishments written across her face—*never talk to strangers*—but I, since birth, had never followed the rules. "A jail," I said. "A jail for crabs."

Harriet liked this. She crouched down and studied us, hard, in a way that most adults didn't bother to do: not as circus freaks, a double novelty act, but as if she was looking for something of particular value that existed underneath the dimples and blond hair.

"Do you girls like the movies?" she asked. Even though her tone was casual I could hear the intensity behind her words, as if

my entire life hinged on the answer to this question. Which, looking back, it did.

Something about this emboldened me. "Duh," I said. "That's
a stupid question."

"*Samantha.*" Elli hit me in the shoulder, horrified. But Harriet
just laughed, deep and long. Ten years later she'd be dead of lung
cancer but that laugh—a raspy rumble that seemed to start somewhere deep in her stomach—made me trust her, because only a
good person could have a laugh that sounded that honest.

Sometimes I wonder what would have become of me if Harriet
hadn't come to the beach that day. (Not a beach person, Harriet.
She was coerced to attend a beloved goddaughter's birthday
party.) Had we not been discovered by Harriet, would I have found
my way to Hollywood on my own? Was acting in my genes or was
it inserted there only through Harriet's suggestion?

And—if Harriet hadn't died a horrible early death when I was
nineteen and still only half-formed, would things have gone so
sideways for me later?

There are moments in life when you collide with something
that sends you careening down a path from which you can never
return. We are ping-pong balls, paddled about by fate and coincidence, doing our best to wrestle back some agency from the forces
that move our lives. On our deathbeds, our last thoughts a faint
echo: *what if, what if, what if.*

My mother materialized then, having looked up from her book
long enough to register the presence of the curious stranger
crouching by her little girls. Towel wrapped tightly around cellu-
lite thighs, zinc oxide on her nose, her fists already clenched at the
ready: "Can I help you?"

Harriet stood, her voice going solicitous. A business card was
suddenly in her hand and she thrust it at my mother. "I'm an
agent," she said. "TV and film. I'm interested in your girls."

"Well, we're *not* interested," my mother responded. She put a
protective hand on each of our shoulders.

"*I* am!" I objected, shaking my mother's hand off.

Harriet's gaze flickered across my mother's drugstore sunglasses, the threadbare towel with sunscreen stains across the logo. "There's a significant amount of money to be made. No pressure, though. I totally understand your concerns."

My mother's face twitched. She tightened her grip on Elli's shoulder with one hand, while the other slowly reached for the business card, almost as if being pulled by marionette strings.

I could have sworn that Harriet winked at me then. "Give me a call and I'll turn your girls into stars," she said before walking off down the shore.

Stars.

The wind picked up, blowing sand across the beach and into our faces. Elli cried out, rubbing her fists in her eyes—tears falling that my mother hurried to wipe away. As for me, I didn't feel anything. I was already blinded, already lost.

I was not a complete stranger to acting. Our suburban elementary school had a serviceable performing arts program and I'd participated in productions of *Mary Poppins* and *Peter Pan*. I loved it: the cardboard props used so many times that they were soft along the edges, the way backstage smelled of dirty socks and spilled soda, the shocking heat of the stage lights against your skin. But most of all, I loved having an audience. Onstage, I could be simultaneously the center of attention and totally invisible. *Here I am, look at me. Here I am, you can't see me at all.*

Maybe this was a result of being a twin, of feeling like I was always only a part of a whole, never a main character in my own right. People look at you a lot when you're a twin, but they never really see you. Their eyes are always flicking away and over your shoulder, scanning for the presence of your other half. As matching children, you are objects of fascination, but almost never complete human beings.

Often, no one can tell exactly who you are anyway.

Onstage, I could be whole. I could be whole *and* I could be anyone I chose to be: a fairy, a witch, a pauper, any flight of fancy I could temporarily inhabit and bring to life. I lived for that moment of stepping into someone else's skin, the excitement of putting it on and feeling what it was like to be them for a while.

All these years of group therapy later, I've come to understand how my twindom drove me toward a career of pretending to be someone else entirely. With my sister, I may only have been half of a whole; but without her, who was Samantha at all?

That was the summer that my sister built us a dollhouse out of scavenged boxes and old wallpaper samples. Elli had a creative eye even then. She meticulously crafted furniture out of bottle caps and bits of cardboard, and painted miniature art for the dollhouse walls. She fashioned a tiny Sam and a tiny Elli out of paper, and our proxies took up residence there alone: no parents, no friends or neighbors or other children, just the two of us in a world of Elli's creation.

The dollhouse had grown to take up most of our room, each new shoebox expanding our domain: an elementary school and an ice cream stand, a hospital for when the dolls got hurt, an amusement park with a Tinkertoy merry-go-round that spun. Our mother had offered us summer camp and gymnastics classes, but we weren't interested. Instead, we spent our days blissfully imagining a life with just the two of us, and everything we had ever desired, in it.

But something broke open after we met Harriet. That night, as we played with the dollhouse—Elli had just built us a swimming pool, and our paper twins were learning the backstroke—my mind kept drifting to other things, bigger places, a life I hadn't imagined wanting before. Through the vents, I could hear our parents talking furtively in the kitchen. Phrases like *Sam has tal-*

ent and *pay for a college education* and *it just seems karmic* echoed through the heating ducts, until finally some consensus was murmured and I could tell that they were going to cave. Elli's gaze kept drifting over to me, even as she cut our dolls' swimsuits out of old wrapping paper. For the first time, I couldn't quite meet her eyes.

Later, as Elli and I lay in our twin beds, the ceiling fan lazily churning the humid summer air, I felt my sister's hand reaching for me across the gap. There was a hot smack as her sweaty palm met mine.

"Sam?" she whispered. "Are you OK?"

"What do you mean?"

"I just thought for a second that maybe you weren't."

I wondered how she knew. That under my giddiness—*we're going to be stars*—I felt some thrilling dread, like when Elli and I went hiking with our parents in Rattlesnake Canyon and got to the part where the path crumbled off into a precipice and I'd feel a terrifying tug compelling me to step over the edge. But Elli *always* knew things, even when I didn't tell her. I'd wake up from a nightmare and find that she'd already crawled in bed with me. I'd touch my forehead because I was hot and discover that she'd already walked in the room with a cold washcloth. Did she know these things because she felt them, too, or just because she could read me so well?

"I don't know how I am. I feel strange."

Her hand let go of mine, and I heard her rustling in the dark and then she was in bed with me, her body in its cotton nightgown paired to mine. "Let's imagine all the fun things we can do once we're Hollywood stars," she said. The enthusiasm in her voice was a little overly bright. It occurred to me that she had never once expressed interest in doing theater with me before; but of course, this was *Hollywood*, why wouldn't she love that? "Like, we can meet other stars. Britney Spears."

"Stay up as late as we want."

"Eat dessert for breakfast."

"Quit school."

"I like school." Elli pondered this a little. "Maybe just quit math."

"Travel around the world. Like Japan, and France."

"Africa. I want to see elephants!" A long silence, the sound of her sucking on the ends of her hair. "I can't think of anything else. I never thought much about anything outside of Santa Barbara."

I hadn't, either, and maybe that's why the vast unfurling vista—the world beyond our dollhouse life—suddenly terrified me. Considering what was to come, I probably should have been even more scared than I was. But at that moment, with Elli's breath in my face, her body so close that it was hard to tell where she ended and I began, I felt safe. Elli would take care of me. Everything would be fine as long as we were together.

How was I to know what was to come?

Harriet labored for months to get us ready for the screen—prescribing haircuts, headshots, acting classes—and then, once we'd been deemed acceptable, our mother took time off from her job as a dental assistant to drive us to auditions down in Los Angeles. It took almost no time at all for us to book a Cheerios commercial. A few months later, we were cast in a tiny role on a children's variety show, followed by an even smaller role in a comedy movie starring Mark Wahlberg. Two months before Elli and I turned ten, we hit the jackpot: a regular supporting role on a detective series that was premiering on network TV.

The thing that Harriet knew, and that we were quickly learning, was that identical twins are a precious commodity in Hollywood. Strict labor laws prevent child actors from working more than a few hours a day. But with identical twins, you can get two actors to play the same role, and voilà, you suddenly have twice as many shoot hours. Thanks to our big break, my sister and I were to inhabit the same character: that of little Jenny Maxx, the beleaguered daughter of hard-talking detective Marci Maxx, on the primetime TV show *To the Maxx*.

Elli typically played sensitive Jenny—the scenes where she got tucked into bed by her mother or cried when she got a bad report card. I liked to be Jenny when she was tough and resourceful, like the time she was kidnapped by her mother's criminal nemesis and had to escape by crawling out an air-conditioning vent, or when she shot a serial killer with her mother's gun. *To the Maxx* ran on network TV for six years, just long enough to make it into syndication, winning a handful of Emmys in the process. For four of those years, my sister and I moved in and out of Jenny's singular body, and only those people who paid close attention to the show's end credits would have noticed that "Jenny" was played by two identical child actresses, not one. But there were bulletin boards, in the deep recesses of the Web, where the show's superfans argued about which twin was in which scene, debating the exact shape of our ears and whether Elli and I could be identified by the quarter-inch difference in our height.

Nearly two decades later, *To the Maxx* still played in reruns on a third-tier cable channel. Sometimes, on those sober nights when I couldn't sleep because I'd had one macchiato too many and I felt on the edge of damage—my eyes vibrating and dry, a bitter chew in my jaw—I would turn on the TV to watch myself. I'd sit there in the dark, feeling my pulse slacken as the familiar theme music washed over me. Watching myself was like Xanax for my soul: that pretty flaxen child, staring brightly into the camera, full of so much confidence as she shaped her mouth around her lines. All the possibility of my youth, frozen forever in time.

Sometimes I'd even find myself saying the words along with the me on the screen: *Mommy! Watch out behind you!*

Then again, I was never really sure if it *was* me I was seeing on the screen, or if it was Elli. Sure, I could blame the passage of time—so many years had passed since the show first aired, how was I to be expected to remember every scene I had ever shot? But really, I knew that my fuzzy recollection was my own fault. I'd spent the last fifteen years of my life brutally bludgeoning my own brain, so of course my memories were going to be wobbly.

And yet, wasn't this the way Elli and I had liked it to be, back then? The edges of *me* blurring into the beginnings of *her*?

Almost exactly a year after Harriet discovered us on the beach, my sister and I moved to Los Angeles with our mother to start production on *To the Maxx*. Our mother had rented us a furnished apartment near the La Brea Tar Pits, a generic two-bedroom box that would be our home base for the next few years. Most weekends—and every summer—we would return to Santa Barbara, where our father had remained, to try to cobble together some semblance of a normal family life.

I loved Los Angeles. I loved how the city went on and on, a river of buildings that flowed in all directions. I loved the wild mix of colors and cultures and cuisines, the way Koreatown fused into Little Armenia and Historic Filipinotown. I loved how there was so much to buy, endless shop windows loaded with things that sparkled in the dazzling coastal sun. The world felt big here, full of unimaginable potential, surreal and exciting.

And yet *my* world here was so small. Each morning my mother drove us to the studio backlot in Burbank where our "home" had been constructed on an enormous stage, and where we would spend our days sitting in dark corners, awaiting our scenes. Even the location days were mostly spent sitting in our trailer, perpetually waiting to be called. When we weren't performing, there was "school," with a retired schoolteacher who joylessly hammered us with times tables and spelling tests. Evenings were spent back at the apartment, eating takeout with our mom and memorizing our lines. Our mother had read enough magazine stories about the tragic lives of child actors and she wasn't about to take any chances. (My problems would start a few years later, after her grip on me had started to slip.)

That first year, most of what Elli and I saw of Los Angeles was through the windows of our mother's car, on our way to set and back.

This seemed to suit Elli just fine. Los Angeles intimidated her. In order to get to the backlot, we had to drive through Hollywood, where homeless teens panhandled on the streets and hustlers in superhero costumes hassled the tourists who marched up and down the Walk of Fame. The air there smelled like a party that was on the verge of veering out of control, like urine and sugar and French fries and vomit.

The first day that we made this drive, I put my window down and stuck my head out, trying to take in everything at once: the looming billboards selling handbags that cost as much as cars, the neon signs advertising wax museums and Scientology exhibits, the drag queens in platform heels who stomped their way against the traffic lights.

"Can we stop?" I said. "I want to see the Walk of Fame."

No one answered. My mother's hands were tight on the steering wheel; driving in city traffic made her nervous. From the other side of the back seat, I heard a click. When I looked over, I realized that my sister had locked her door.

"It's not dangerous, silly," I said. "Look at all the tourists."

"It smells," she said softly.

I reached across and took her hand. "Hold your breath."

She stared at me, her eyes huge, her palm gluing itself to mine with the jammy remnants of our breakfast toast. "How long are we going to do this for, do you think? Be here, in L.A.?"

I thought *forever* but I didn't say it because it looked like she might cry. I knew without having to ask that she was frightened of the scene outside the car, but also of this new life on which we were embarking. Of a life that was going to be spent onstage, with all eyes on her. For the first time, I felt a pang of self-doubt about what I had talked my sister into doing. What if she *didn't* like Hollywood as much as I did? What if she was only doing this because I wanted to?

"It's going to be fun." I slid across the seat until I was beside her, our thighs touching through our brand-new jeans. Our mom had bought us identical outfits at Macy's for this first day on set, and although I'd objected to it at the time—we hadn't dressed the same for a while—I now felt a familiar comfort in our armored uniformity. The power of being two instead of one. A double force to contend with.

I put my arm around Elli, and together we watched Los Angeles slide past in all its gritty glory as we headed toward our new future.

Elli soldiered through production. She'd always been a better student than me, finishing her homework with plenty of time to do the extra credit *and* coach me through my math problems; and now she applied the same diligence to studying her part and hitting her marks on set. She dutifully served up her lines, her wooden delivery masked by the charm of her dimples and her ability to smile on cue. She was incapable of playing anyone but herself, but fortunately the scripts she received never demanded much more of her than that.

Was I the only one who noticed that her performances always felt vaguely colored by panic, as if she were terrified that she was going to disappoint? I hoped I was the only one who could see this, even as I studiously looked away.

I was the better actress, the one who knew how to disappear into the persona of Jenny Maxx. I couldn't wait to get to set every day, where the crew buzzed around us, the hot lights illuminating me from the inside, the aperture of the camera like the world's eyes fixed on me. I loved how complete acting made me feel, as if I were twice as interesting as I'd been before. I loved the way the grown-up actors treated us like little ingenues, bringing us pow-dered donuts from craft services and braiding our hair during breaks in production.

To the Maxx was a show for adults. There were never any other kids around. As a result, my sister and I were always to-gether, more than we ever had been before. In Santa Barbara, over our objections, our elementary school had placed us in separate homerooms; but here, we were always within shouting distance. We sat together in the back of the set every day, snickering over the nonsense Mad Libs that we used to fill the time, or folding our scripts into miniature origami boxes that we would present to each other. At night, in the apartment bedroom that we shared, I would reach across the space between our beds and find my sister's hand there, reaching for mine. We fell asleep like this most nights, our hands linked across the void, a defense against the dark.

We turned eleven six weeks after To the Maxx premiered on net-work television, five months after our arrival in town. To cele-brate, our mother took us to an anodyne open-air shopping mall where the stores—Gap, Nordstrom, Crate & Barrel, Barnes & Noble—were reassuringly identical to the ones we'd left back in Santa Barbara. We watched a talking-animal movie starring an-other one of Harriet's clients and then ate Häagen-Dazs by the synchronized fountains. Teenagers walked by in groups, loaded down with shiny bags from stores that we weren't yet wealthy enough to shop at, gripping phones that our mother said we were too young to own. Who was there to call anyway? The only per-son I really cared about was always with me.

While we sat there, waiting for our mother to return from the restroom, a woman walked by and did a double take. She skidded to a stop, turned to stare at us. She was my mother's age but looked nothing like her, in a gold-and-black tracksuit with *Fendi* printed across the front. The thick blond stripes in her hair made her look like an exotic cat.

The woman pointed a finger at me. Her fingernail had a rhinestone glued to the tip. "I know who you are. I've been watching your show." This observation felt almost belligerent, like we were criminals she'd identified out of a lineup. "I didn't realize there were *two* of you."

Beside me, I felt Elli shrinking into the bench, trying to make herself invisible; but I fully intended to make the most out of this moment, the first time I'd been recognized. "We're twins," I offered brightly, as if this wasn't already obvious.

The woman's eyes were doing that familiar dance, jumping from Elli to me and back again, looking for differences and coming up empty-handed. "Which one of you is the one on the show?" she demanded. "Which one's the actress?"

"We both are," I said. But even as I said it, I noticed my sister pointing at me. I turned to stare at her, and she shrugged.

The woman was fishing a camera out of the baguette-shaped purse that dangled from one wrist. "Can I take your photo?"

Before either of us could respond, she'd snapped a picture.

A family of tourists—parents in identical muscle tees, a sullen teenage daughter—had been sitting on an adjacent bench, studying a star map while they drank their Ice Blended drinks. Now they turned to gape at us. The teen, thinking she'd sniffed out the presence of celebrity, reached into her backpack and pulled out a camera.

A few shoppers slowed as they walked by, their internal antennas registering a developing spectacle.

Harriet's words came back to me, suddenly prophetic. *I'll turn your girls into stars.* I felt enormous, so completely *seen.* I instinctively dimpled at the pushy woman's camera, turned my head at the angle that the director of photography of *To the Maxx* had informed me was my most flattering. I scooted a little closer to my sister, found her hand, and squeezed it.

She didn't squeeze back. When I turned to look at her, I realized that she was about to cry. Her liquid eyes met mine, and I suddenly understood with devastating certainty exactly what she was thinking. *I don't want this, Sam. I don't want strangers thinking they own a piece of me.*

I stood up abruptly, blocking Elli from the woman's camera. "Hey," I said. "We didn't say yes."

The camera drooped in her hand. Her mascara-ringed eyes blinked at me in surprise. "*Excuse* me?"

"Delete the photos," I said. "Please."

The woman looked down at her camera, mentally quantifying the value of what she'd just snapped, the bragging rights she could claim. When she didn't move, I reached out and snatched her camera away. It was warm from being clutched so tight, greasy from her hand lotion. The woman just stood there, mouth agape, as I clicked the trash icon on three successive photos. Me, smiling and puff-chested; Elli, stunned, half-hidden behind me. Delete. Delete. Delete.

The woman snatched her camera back, glaring at us. "You have no right." Her voice quavered, a hoarse bark. "This is a mall. It's a *public* place."

"We're minors. It's an invasion of privacy," I responded. "And my sister doesn't like it."

The nearby tourists had edged away, the teenage girl discreetly pocketing her camera without snapping a photo at all. The shoppers who had slowed down to watch the show now hurried away, eyes averted. In the distance, I saw our mother returning from the bathroom, racing across the trampled lawn with murder in her eyes. Backlit by the sun, her sundress was nearly see-through, her legs pumping against the rainbow fabric.

"Well then," the woman sniffed. Behind us, the fountain had

begun its hourly dance, and she stepped away from its misty halo. She stuffed the camera back in her purse, fixed her gaze on me, and dropped one last prophetic observation before rushing off to Nordstrom.

"Your sister is clearly in the wrong business."

6 THAT FIRST NIGHT BACK in Santa Barbara, after helping my parents wrestle Charlotte into bed—a process involving repeated readings of a book called *Llama Llama Red Pajama*—I called my sister. Her phone went straight to voicemail. I hadn't spoken to Elli in over a year, and the soft lilt of her voice hit me like a punch to the esophagus. Her voice was still an echo of my own, but without the rough edges that came from too many cigarettes and cheap tequila shots.

"This is Elli, so sorry I missed you. Leave a message and I'll call you back." I would never have thought of apologizing for failing to answer my phone. I would never promise to return the call, either. For that matter, I hadn't even bothered to record a message for my own voicemail; lately I'd just let it default to the robot lady. The idea of figuring out what to say to a stranger felt far too momentous.

No one called me anymore anyway.

"Hey," I said to the empty air on the other end of the line. "I'm at our parents'. I'm with your daughter. What the fuck, Elli? You couldn't even let me know that you adopted a little girl? I mean, I know that things haven't been great between us, but Jesus, not even an *email*?" I heard something creeping into my voice, anger and panic, and took a breath. "She's beautiful, by the way. I'm weirded out that I'm an aunt now. But you need to call me, let me know what's going on. Don't you think your spa vacation has gone on long enough? Dad's convinced you're having a breakdown and Mom thinks that you're just cleansing Chuck from your system with colonics." I immediately regretted having said all this. I swallowed it back almost as soon as it came out of my mouth and ended up making a strange squeaking noise into the phone. This wasn't going to help my case.

"Anyway, I don't know what's going on with you but . . ." I couldn't quite finish this sentence. *But I wish I did? But I know it's my fault that I don't? But I want to convince you that I'm OK now, that you don't have to hide from me anymore? But I miss us? But I'm sorry?*

"Just call me," I said, and hung up.

Now what?

In the other room, I could hear the sound of a wineglass being set on a coffee table, the murmur of my parents' voices, the television clicking on. The sounds of my childhood. The evening looming ahead of me now—sitting on the sagging sofa with my parents, making small talk over *America's Got Talent*—made me want a drink so badly I thought my skull might crack in two.

Was my invitation to come home a reward for good behavior, or was it punishment for bad? Suddenly, I couldn't tell anymore.

I found myself an AA meeting. It was in the community room of a Mission-style church in downtown Santa Barbara, a stone's throw from the hotels that sprawled lazily along the oceanfront. Santa Barbara likes to sell itself as an upscale Mediterranean resort—all red tile roofs, Mexican fan palms, and beachfront promenades, open-air fish restaurants and a harbor full of sailboats—but the local population is heavy on college students who surf and retirees who golf and Hispanic families who do all the heavy lifting. The truly rich residents live up in Montecito, where the views are spectacular and your neighbor might go by one name, like Oprah or Ellen or JLo.

Not surprisingly, then, the AA setup here was fancier than my regular meeting in Los Angeles: a Nespresso machine instead of instant coffee, cookies that came from a bakery and not a supermarket, chairs with built-in cushions. The rear wall of the room featured a giant mural, likely painted by a parishioner, of a Day-Glo Jesus with his arms wrapped around a multicultural collection of children with weirdly elongated torsos. Jesus was looking straight out of the mural, an alarming gleam in one eye that suggested he did not have the purest of intentions for these children.

I sat in the back row and sniffed gingerly at my coffee as the two dozen or so attendees stood up and shared their tales of woe: custody lost, finances fallen to pieces, mysterious bruises and broken noses and swaths of lost time. I liked these stories, I always had. They made me feel less alone, yes. But I particularly liked how they almost ended with a note of hope; because you had to have *some* hope in order to end up at one of these meetings. Otherwise, you'd already be dead.

You might say it's naive to hope, to feint toward optimism instead of cynicism. Just look at the world we live in now, at the pain and despair, at the fools running the place who dig us deeper into a hole each day. And yet without hope, there is no reason to live at all. Even if you're only hoping for small things—a nice meal to share with a friend, a mild summer, a day at the beach—this can be the difference between waking up to face the world and taking that second sleeping pill and staying in bed. Believe me, if you want to know how vital hope is, ask a recovered addict; they are the most hopeful people in the world, because they know what it means to be so low that there are only two viable paths left: up, or death. If you're at a meeting, you've chosen *up*. And what is hope but this: the blind, naive belief that things might someday be a tiny bit better than they are now.

Most days, hope still felt foreign to me. Maybe that's why I was so drawn to the meetings and the people who spoke so fervently and optimistically, despite their missing teeth and regrettable face tattoos and permanently damaged livers. One day, maybe all that hope would rub off on me, and my life would improve because of it.

After a stringy-haired folk music guitarist finished speaking (nineteen months sober, he'd just reconciled with his dying mother, which brought the room to tears), the meeting leader surveyed the rows of seats and caught my eye.

"Looks like we have someone new today. You interested in telling your story?"

I brushed cookie crumbs from my jeans and stood.

"Hi, I'm Sam." I looked out at the group, who gazed back at me with mild curiosity. Mostly middle-aged and life-worn, per usual; but Santa Barbara's conservative affluence made for a more clean-cut group of addicts than your average Hollywood AA meeting. In the second row, a blue-eyed man about my age stared at me keenly through tortoiseshell glasses. He was nondescript, just a wiry guy in a plain white T-shirt, although his curly hair was choppy and uneven, as if he'd cut it himself in the mirror with a pair of garden shears. He smiled encouragingly at me.

"I'm three-hundred-seventy-nine days sober and I'm in town visiting my parents for a few days. I'm not going to go into my long and sordid history here today—I've done that plenty at my regular meeting in Los Angeles. I'll just say that I'm aware that staying with them is a trigger. My mother—" I didn't even have to finish the sentence as heads around me started to nod vigorously.

"I haven't actually slept under the same roof as my parents in about five years and it's making me think a lot about my childhood. Wondering where things went so wrong, you know?" More nodding. "Anyway. Maybe it's not such a great idea for me to be here, dwelling on all this. But the thing is—my parents asked me to come and help them out with something, and that's the first time they've done that in . . . decades? And so, even though I know that stepping out of my regular routine in Los Angeles is a recipe for falling off the wagon, I'm trying to hold on to this: that my family is counting on me for once. And I'm not going to let them down."

I took my seat again and let the applause wash over me. That little hit of dopamine that I got from public approval—the same lift of joy that I'd chased all those years as an actress, and then later tried to replicate with a shot of vodka or a line of coke—was the other thing that kept me coming to these meetings and standing up to speak.

I'd lost a lot, but I had this, at least; this, and caffeine; so I sipped at my second cup of watery Nespresso and smiled happily at the faces that smiled back at me.

After the last speaker had finished and we'd folded up all the chairs and moved them against the wall, the tortoiseshell-glasses man found me. Up close, he was more attractive than I'd first thought. He looked like a character from a movie about a midcentury boys' boarding school: the kid who's the beleaguered misfit but grows into his body and returns triumphantly to his high school reunion as a bestselling novelist.

There was something about him that compelled me despite myself, something about the deep lines around his eyes, the wiry muscles under his T-shirt, and the flush of a tan that suggested he spent a lot of time running on the beach. He held out a hand for me to shake and I grasped it without thinking, finding his grip pleasantly strong.

"Sam Logan, right?"

I braced myself. Fifteen years after *On the Double* was canceled, I still got recognized on occasion, but it was usually only by obsessives and oddballs, people who had encyclopedic knowledge of vintage television or who spent a lot of time on Reddit. Sometimes I'd get a sharp-eyed young woman with a good memory of her childhood idols. The men who recognized me were typically the worst: Often it was because they'd fetishized my sister and me as teens, masturbating to our Nickelodeon sitcom. Now they wanted to fuck me just so they could tell their friends, *Hey, remember that actress from that old show about the twins? She gave me a blow job. Boy, she really screwed up her life.*

I quickly released his hand and stepped backward, hitting the wall with my sneaker. There was no escape.

"Caleb!" he went on, triumphantly. His eyes searched mine behind his glasses, looking for something that he clearly didn't find, because his expression of excitement began to fade. "Oh shit, you don't remember me, do you?"

I paused. "Should I?"

"Caleb Stowe. We were in class together, back in grammar school." I stared at him, looking for something that I might remember, but could dredge up nothing. Or wait, there *was* a whisper: a heavyset kid with coke-bottle glasses and lashes so long that they pressed against the lenses. Was that him? "Now that I think of it, there's no reason you'd remember me. I mean, I remember *you* because you got famous and that really ingrained you in my memories, obviously. But why would you remember me?" His face was turning pink, and I could tell that he wanted to quit talking but couldn't quite stop himself. "You kicked me in the shin on the school playground once. Said I was a bully because I wouldn't give up the swing to your sister after she'd been waiting for her turn. And you were right, you know? I was being a selfish dick. I always remembered that later, when I saw you on TV. Anyway, I'm sorry to babble on like this. I'm not a freak or a stalker, I promise. I just wanted to say hi."

"Hi," I said. The moment grew awkward, and I could tell that he was looking for an escape. I took pity on him. "I'm sorry I don't remember you, but you know. I did a lot of drugs. Which probably doesn't come as a surprise because I'm here."

He laughed at this and nodded, running a hand through his hair; and then he got a funny expression on his face as he felt something there he didn't expect. "Oh God, and I look like a crazy person today, too. I let my daughter give me a haircut, and I haven't had a chance to go to the barber to get it evened up yet."

"Oh yeah?" I felt myself perking up. "How old is your daughter?"

"Seven."

"You let a seven-year-old give you a haircut? Are they even allowed to hold scissors at that age?"

He shrugged. "Sometimes you do things that seem crazy just to give your kid a *yes* instead of a *no*. I figured no matter how bad it was going to look, it was still something that I'd be able to fix. And she really wanted to do it."

Suddenly I liked this guy, Caleb, with his wonky haircut and his tendency to overshare and his willingness to do stupid things to make his kid happy. "You know a lot about kids, huh?"

"I know a lot about *one* kid, but sure. If that counts?" He smiled nervously at me. "Why, you have a kid of your own?"

"No," I said. "But I'm borrowing one for the time being and could probably use some childcare advice."

He put his hands on his hips and thrust his chest forward a bit, an exaggerated swagger of confidence that I suspected was intended to redeem himself from his earlier fumbling. "Well, I'm your guy," he said. "Just let me know how I can help."

7 A TERRIBLE SOUND SPLIT my sleep apart, shattering the pleasant void into a thousand nerve-jangling pieces. I lay in the dark, disoriented, as it came again: a wail of utter despair. Was it a dying junkie, a betrayed girlfriend, the victim of a car accident down on Hollywood Boulevard?

My nose registered the soft must of an unfamiliar comforter, and everything suddenly came back to me: I was at my parents' house. Charlotte was asleep on the other side of the wall. Or, rather, she wasn't asleep anymore. Either something horrific had just happened to her or I was hearing the primal howl of a little girl who no longer wanted to be in bed.

I waited for the sound of footsteps in the hall, someone coming to quiet her, until I remembered that *I* was supposed to be the footsteps. I stumbled into Charlotte's room and plucked her from the portable crib where she lay, sweaty in her footie pajamas. The blankets were tangled around her feet and her Pull-Up was sodden, so heavy that it sagged when I picked her up. She clung to me, tearful and dream-tossed.

I changed her Pull-Up and brought her into bed with me. I had visions of us snuggling up together spoon-style, her warm baby skin pressed against mine as we drifted gently back to sleep. Apparently she did not share this vision. She was awake and required entertainment. We lay there in the dark, Charlotte squirming against me, fighting me as if I were her jailer.

She sat up and tugged at my hair, clenched her fists, and yanked until my eyes watered. "Wan' puffs," she said insistently.

"Puffs?" Was this some sort of breakfast cereal I'd never heard of?

"Hungwy," she said, her voice serious.

I puzzled through this for a moment. "Good idea, let's go out for breakfast," I said. "No way am I drinking your grandma's coffee."

There was a café not far from my parents' house that served a decent pour-over and fresh croissants. We were the first in line when they opened the door at seven A.M., Charlotte wedged on my hip, greedily studying the pastry case. I bought a chocolate croissant for her and a coffee for me and we sat at an empty table, eyeing each other blearily, near-strangers.

What did one *do* all day with a two-year-old? My first instinct was to watch cartoons, but I'd already been warned off this path. "Elli doesn't allow her to look at screens," my mother had informed me the previous evening. I'd seen something in her eyes, a glint of sadistic delight. "Bad for brain development."

I wanted to say, *Elli and I spent most of our early years planted in front of a television set, and we turned out just fine,* but then I reconsidered. After all, one of us ended up a junkie and the other one was currently choosing spa treatments over childcare.

Without TV to fall back on, what else was I supposed to do with Charlotte? The day stretched out before us, an empty horizon. My mother had helpfully provided me with Charlotte's daily schedule the day before, an overwhelming grid of meals and naps and snacks and "activity hours" that I'd promptly tossed in the trash. Was this what parenting was supposed to be? The utter abdication of a personal schedule, the day instead dissected into individual units of time that had to be occupied with someone else's food and entertainment?

"What do you want to do today?" I asked.

She stared at me with those big brown eyes, as if she hadn't understood the question.

"The zoo? The park? Go for a walk?"

She stuck a finger in the center of her croissant and hooked out a chunk of chocolate goo, examining it before wiping it on the edge of the table. The expression on her face made me feel like she'd already sussed out my incompetence and had given up hope.

I thought of the one successful card I had played already: "How about the beach? We can bury more treasure? In a sand-castle!"

This got her attention. She bounced up and down in her chair. Her face was smeared with chocolate, brown fingermarks down the front of her strawberry-print T-shirt. "Tweasure!" she announced, as if she'd come up with the idea herself. I wondered how many times I could use the same ruse before she'd get tired by the repetition.

A woman in a jogging suit walked by our table and smiled meaningfully at me, eyes lingering a little too long on mine. I smiled back stiffly, assuming that she had recognized me from television; but then her eyes slid to Charlotte's crumb-covered face and back to me, and then I noticed the diaper bag on her arm, and I realized that hers was actually a grin of solidarity. I had been initiated into a new club without realizing it: the sister-hood of caregivers. I wasn't sure how I felt about this.

"Lala go poopoo," Charlotte announced.

"Shit," I said.

The beach had seemed like a good idea at the time, but as I wedged Charlotte into the car seat, I realized that I hadn't thought it through. The kid would need a swimsuit, presumably, and a beach towel, and sunscreen. A pail and shovel. Sand toys. Floaties? Could she swim? A hat. So much to consider.

My sister had deposited Charlotte at my parents' house with only a weekend bag, and in my foraging through the piles of toddler clothes that morning I hadn't noticed a child-sized swimsuit. But surely my sister owned one. It dawned on me that we were only a few miles from my sister's house. I knew where she kept the key, under a ledge near the garage; or that's where she *had* kept it, back in the days when I had carte blanche to let myself into her house when I was in town or needed a place to crash. It had been a long time since she'd trusted me that way, though, and so as I drove up to her home I was mostly thinking that the presence of the key would be a referendum on my sister's current state of mind vis-à-vis me.

My sister lived in a tile-roofed Spanish Revival, just like half the homes in Santa Barbara, except that hers had red trim and a red front door and a garden planted with matchy-matchy red roses. Mexican fan palms lined the street out front, looming up between the shaggy eucalyptuses and the orange-barked manzanitas. You could see the ocean from her house, just a fifteen-minute walk down the hill.

The house looked exactly as it always had, the curtains drawn open for the light, a trio of sparrows bathing in the fountain that burbled in the front yard.

I glanced in the back seat of my car, where Charlotte was squirming against her straps and whining to be released. I got out and unlatched her and watched as she ran across the front garden, weaving and wobbling like a drunk stumbling toward the bar for last call. She got to the portico and turned and looked expectantly at me, eyes bright with anticipation.

The key was no longer under the ledge. Its absence was a slap.

Feeling vaguely queasy, I walked the gravel path around the perimeter of the house, looking for a likely hiding spot for a key. It wasn't under the entry mat, or above the door, or under the potted lavender on the rear patio. I grabbed the handle of the back door and wiggled it, but it was locked tight. The windows refused to budge. I peered through one and into the empty kitchen, where dead tulips flopped woozily in a vase on the counter.

"I think we gotta go back home, kiddo," I said to Charlotte, but she'd found a sun-faded water table that was set up on the back patio and was splashing in it with a shovel. When I tried to take her hand and steer her away she flung herself backward, yearning back toward the toy. Already I could see the heat building inside, her neck going red with fury. I had a feeling this wasn't going to go well.

I heard the sound of a window sash opening and turned around to look at the house next door, a shingled Cape Cod that had been recently renovated. There was a woman in an upstairs window, looking down at me. She waved frantically. "Elli! Where've you been?!" she called.

"Sam," I called back.

"What?"

"I'm not Elli, I'm Sam. Her sister. I'm babysitting Charlotte."

The face vanished from the window. A moment later, the woman appeared in her backyard and waddled over to the fence, stepping through her own flower plantings in order to get a better look at me. She was a young brunette, and so pregnant that the silk bathrobe around her waist wouldn't stay tied over the mound of her belly. Underneath it she wore a T-shirt with an arrow that pointed to her stomach and read *Spoiler Alert: I'm Pregnant*.

She leaned on the fence and watched as I tried to wrestle Charlotte away from the toys, with little success.

"So you're the twin sister," she said, glee flavoring her words. She looked me up and down, hunting for the details that would differentiate me from my sister. "I'm Alice. I've heard all about you."

"I'm not going to pretend that means good things," I said. "You don't have to be polite."

She laughed. "She said you were fearless and way more obnoxious than her. She also said you weren't talking. So you made up? She's letting you babysit?"

"It's kind of complicated." Charlotte had broken from my grip and was back at the water table, up to her elbows in stagnant water. "Hey, do you happen to have a spare key? I got locked out and I need to get some of Charlotte's swim stuff."

Alice pointed at an outdoor kitchen right behind me, with a sink and an enormous barbecue. "There's a hide-a-key inside the barbecue cabinet," she said. She leaned over the fence, watching me with a look of naked curiosity. "So where's Elli? I was wondering if we could use her pool, but she hasn't been answering any of my texts and I noticed her lights weren't on."

I fished around inside the barbecue, a dark space that smelled of grease and charcoal. "She's been at some spa in Ojai all week," I said.

A wail went up from inside Alice's house. "Shoot, that one's mine. Gotta run." She turned toward the house, hurrying back across the grass and bracing her belly with one hand. It wasn't until she got to her own back door that she hesitated and turned around to look at me. She called across the garden, "The spa—it's not related to that group she's in, is it? GenFem?"

"GenFem?" I looked at her blankly. The word in my mouth felt ungainly, unfamiliar, vaguely vaginal. It rang no bells at all.

Alice nodded. "She took me to a meeting a few months ago. Something about it . . . it was weird. Culty."

"Culty?" Inside the barbecue my hands had closed around a small metal box and I fished it out, forearms streaked with black. I stood up straight, a faint alarm bell ringing in my mind. "I'm sorry, what are you talking about? What's this group?"

Alice hesitated. She seemed about to say something further, but then her child wailed again and she blinked and swallowed. I could tell she was measuring the time it would take to fill me in with the amount of time she had left before her baby had a complete meltdown. The baby won.

"Nothing. I'm sure it's nothing," she said. She flashed me a tight smile and disappeared inside, leaving me ashy and unsettled in my sister's abandoned yard.

Inside, my sister's house smelled like sweet soft rot, as if something was festering in the garbage cans. On the console by the front door, an arrangement of lilies had disintegrated into green goo, desiccated petals scattered beneath it on the parquet floor. The air in the house felt perfectly still, like a stopped clock waiting to be wound again.

Charlotte ran straight through the living room and toward the kitchen. "Mama!" she called. In the empty kitchen, she turned to look at me, her face contorting with confusion. "Mama here?" she asked, her voice tremulous.

I suddenly realized my mistake. "Sorry, baby. She's not here."

A low wail began in her throat. What had I been thinking? Of course she thought we'd find her mother at the house; I had been setting her up for disappointment. She collapsed to the floor of the kitchen, grinding her fists in the floor, shrieking at a decibel so loud that I could feel it in my teeth. Snot dripped down her face, dirt trapped in the translucent rivulets. I tried to spatula her off the floor and into my arms, but she went limp and slipped out of my grasp.

I threw open cupboards, looking for a treat to distract her, and found a tube of what looked like strawberry-flavored Cheerios. *Puffs,* the label said. I crouched by Charlotte and rattled the tube by her ear, so that she could hear it over her own screams. "I found puffs," I announced.

The screams stopped. She sat up and shoved a fistful of the puffs in her mouth, her mood instantly improved. It felt like a miracle. I wished that adults could forgive that easily, that wounds could be so easily healed with sugared cereal.

The kitchen looked like it had been hastily abandoned mid-breakfast. A cup of milky coffee was growing mold near the sink; and a crusted plate of dried eggs still sat on the tray of a high chair pulled up to the table. Someone had spilled pretzels all over the floor. I put dishes in the dishwasher, hesitated, and then grabbed a broom to sweep up the floor. Then I scrubbed the counters with a damp sponge, for good measure. My sister had always been compulsively neat—it was one trait we both shared—and it bothered me that she would leave her kitchen like this. Maybe motherhood had made her more tolerant of a mess, but to leave for vacation like this? It felt discordant.

I kept thinking about what Alice had said—the word *culty* clutching at my brain like a sock with static cling. Culty? What did that mean? I'd heard people say that AA was "culty." So was Esalen, where my mother annually went on a solo trip to meditate and soak naked in hot tubs. You could use the word to describe anyone from red-hat-wearing MAGA types to rabid Kanye West fans to the people you'd find in a hot yoga class. *The world fetishizes intense devotion and charismatic celebrity; it's almost impossible to live in the twenty-first century and entirely avoid doing anything cultlike,* I told myself.

Culty: It could mean anything. It could mean nothing at all.

Other than the dirty kitchen, nothing else about Elli's house looked remotely out of the ordinary. The catchall dish by the back door was still full of seashells and spare keys; the notes on the fridge were just shopping lists and grocery receipts; the mail on the counter was still shelter magazines and solicitations from liberal nonprofits. Over a year had passed since I'd been here last, but it might as well have been a day. On a cursory glance, I didn't even see any evidence that Chuck had moved out, except maybe the lack of Gatorade in the fridge. Though that just showed how little his presence had registered on the house in the first place: This had always been my sister's domain.

A neat stack of invoices sat on the kitchen table, each with my sister's business logo stamped on the top: *Eleanor Hart Floral Design*. In her mid-twenties, Elli had reinvented herself as an event florist who specialized in weddings and baby showers, giant sprays of flowers in elegantly pale colors. "It's really the perfect job for me," she'd once told me. "I work with beautiful things all day and I get to be a part of people's happiest days." Eleanor Hart Floral Design was a one-woman show, its focus far more heavily on arrangements than profitability. I riffled through the invoices. Most were stamped *past due*, but she hadn't bothered to mail them.

Once the kitchen was clean, I headed upstairs to Charlotte's room. Last time I was here—just a little more than a year ago—it had been a guest bedroom, done in cerulean and yellow; it was the room where I'd slept off my last rehab recovery. Now it was a pink and white temple of female toddlerdom, all frills and lace. It was Elli's dream childhood bedroom, I realized, the one she'd painstakingly designed for our dollhouse back when we were nine, now re-created in full size. One wall was covered with shelves of collectible dolls that Charlotte was still too young to play with; the other contained a crib that was tented in a lace canopy. A shag carpet in pale pink was littered with pristine stuffed animals.

Charlotte, delighted to see her toys, toddled over to a play kitchen and began to cook herself a wooden meal, burbling to herself under her breath. I dug through her closet, sweeping aside the hangers where embroidered dresses with French labels hung in pristine array, until I found a pile of swimsuits. The location of my sister's beach towels eluded me, so I took a stack of fluffy towels from the bathroom and shoved them in a tote bag that I found in a hallway closet.

At the far end of the hallway, the door to my sister's bedroom stood half ajar. The room itself was dark, the blackout curtains drawn tight. I couldn't resist. I pushed the door open and peered in, my toes sinking into the pale blue wall-to-wall carpeting. I could smell my sister in the air, a lingering must of sleep sweat and vanilla-scented deodorant. Despite the gloom I could see that her bed had been left unmade, a satin robe abandoned on the floor. Stepping inside the room felt unbearably intimate: If Elli wouldn't have wanted me to let myself into her house, she definitely wouldn't want me in her bedroom. I wavered on the threshold.

But there was something sitting on the table next to my sister's side of the bed: a black binder, thick with documents, bristling with sticky notes. Was it divorce papers? Financial statements? Had my sister decided to go back to school? Curiosity got the better of me. I stepped into the room and picked up the binder. Despite the dim light I could see that the cover was embossed with a single word in gold: *GenFem*.

I took the binder out into the light of the hallway and flipped through it. It was full of worksheets, like a college student's study binder. The printouts had titles like "Conquering Fear Structures" and "Emotional Control Systems" and "Powershifting P-A Relationships" and "Excising Toxicity." The typeface was small, paragraph after paragraph of dense text, followed by pages of empty lines for notes. Some of the printouts had diagrams, rivers of arrows flowing from one stick figure to the next. I could make no sense of any of it at a glance, but clearly my sister knew what it all meant. Each page had been carefully inked up in my sister's neat cursive, salient phrases highlighted, edges carefully marked with stickies.

So this was what Alice had been talking about. GenFem was some kind of self-help group. A little culty, yes; then again, so were most self-help groups. I glanced at some of the phrases that my sister had highlighted: *If it's not painful it means that you're taking the easy route. Growth hurts. Ignore the pain.* And: *You can have a redo, all it takes is reinvention.* And: *You can't wait for someone else to give you the things you desire most. You must take them for yourself.*

This last line gave me pause. Something about it felt off, utterly unlike the Elli I knew. She didn't "take" the things that she desired; that was the kind of selfishness *I'd* embraced, but that had always been anathema to her. Then again, maybe that was exactly why Elli felt that she needed this kind of a lesson plan. She'd never been strong on agency. Still, something about these sentiments struck me as stringent, clinical, cold. Was my sister really trying to reinvent herself? Why would she even want to do that? She was so perfect already.

If it's not painful it means that you're taking the easy route . . . Ignore the pain. A mandate to ignore your instincts. Which, when your instincts were wrong (as mine so often had been), was excellent advice. But what about when your instincts were warning you that something was wrong? If you set yourself on fire, the pain is the first thing that alerts you to potential damage.

As I flipped through the pages, a printed Excel spreadsheet slipped out from between two pages and fell to the floor. I picked it up and studied it. It was a list of prices:

Level One—$3,000

Reenactment 10-Story Series—$5,000

Weekend PSS Workshop—$4,500

Level Two—$5,000

Individual with Dr. Cindy—$4,250

The spreadsheet went on and on, most of the items on it neatly ticked off and highlighted in yellow. I skimmed it, all the way to the bottom of the list, where there was a sum total: *$112,475.00.*

I stared at this figure. It seemed impossible. Had my sister really just spent six figures on a self-help regimen? Putting aside the sheer luxury of that—Elli had that much money just sitting around?—there was something strongly not right about a group that charged that much for advice. I felt a sharp twist at my sternum. *Culty.* The neighbor's word gripped me tighter now, less benign, more poisonous. What *was* this group?

Charlotte was barreling down the hallway at me from her bedroom, her eyes wild, a plastic Disney princess tiara in one hand and a matching wand in the other. She lifted these over her head, triumphant. "Tweasure!" she shouted. "Bewy tweasure now!"

I shoved the spreadsheet back in the binder, but not before my eye drifted back to the last item on the list.

Upper-Level Ojai Retreat—$12,500.

So that's where my sister was: a GenFem retreat of some sort. Knowing this should have made me feel better. Instead, an amorphous unease pressed down, a black blot threading through my mind. I knew, without being able to say why, that something was terribly wrong.

That night, after we'd wrestled Charlotte into bed, I looked up GenFem on my phone. The organization's website was reassuringly normal—slick and professional, with modern fonts and a gray, gold, and pink color palette. *Inspiration—Transformation—Reclamation,* it read. *Lose "Yourself" and Find Your "Self" with GenFem's Personal Success Method.* I had no idea what this meant, but apparently the "system" involved sitting in circles with other women and laughing, doing stretches against a sunset backdrop, typing soberly on laptops while talking on the phone. The women in the photos—and they *were* all women, though in a wide variety of ages and ethnicities—had a roseate glow to them, as if lit by God herself.

They didn't look like any cult members I'd ever seen. Nor did the woman on the site's founder page—*Dr. Cindy Medina, PhD, LMFT, CHT*—bear any resemblance to a cult leader. She was probably mid-fifties, and looked attractive and well groomed—I sensed she'd had some work done around her chin and eyes—with her hair in a smart graying bob and a gold silk scarf tossed around her neck. She wore wire-rimmed glasses that she peered over with a cryptic, all-knowing smile. There were photos of her standing next to Hillary Clinton and Greta Thunberg, her name listed on the roster of international women's conferences in Dubai and Iceland. I skimmed her biography: *Dr. Cindy Medina, a world-renowned clinical psychologist and motivational speaker, developed the GenFem Method to empower women to achieve their best selves, free of the structures that have thwarted their achievements.*

So my sister had felt thwarted. I wondered what "structure" was thwarting her, and then I wondered whether that structure had been me.

I clicked through the rest of the website, looking for information about GenFem's Ojai retreat. The organization's contact page had four addresses on it—centers in Santa Barbara, Sausalito, Toronto, and New Jersey—but nothing in Ojai; although I did find mention of a *private healing retreat in the Topatopa Mountains* on a page titled "Advantages of Becoming a Senior-Level Member." (Other advantages: round-the-clock life Mentors, one-on-one Reenactment sessions, and a customized GenFem license plate holder.)

I dialed the phone number of the Santa Barbara center but it went straight to voicemail. "Hi, I'm trying to locate my sister. Her name's Elli Hart, and she's apparently at your retreat in Ojai. I'm wondering if you could call me back with some information about how to get in touch with her there." I left my phone number and hung up. I had a feeling I wasn't going to be getting a call back anytime soon.

This accomplished, I went back out to the living room and

confronted my parents where they sat watching *The Bachelorette*. "Did you know that Elli had joined some sort of self-help group?"

My mother muted the show and gave my father a sidelong glance. "GenFem?"

"You know it?"

My mother shook her head. "Not really. She mentioned it a few times. She invited me to come to a meeting with her once but, you know, I'm already stretched so thin." She waved a hand, her wrist thick with clattering energy beads.

"Is it a legitimate organization?"

"They have some kind of . . . educational center, I think they call it, over in Samarkand. Kathy from my yoga class says her daughter went a few times and it was a kind of feminist group. Classes in how to be more centered and assertive. Things like that."

I didn't find this very reassuring. "Well, I met Elli's neighbor and she said it was very culty."

My mother laughed. "Culty? That's ridiculous."

I looked to my father. "Do you know anything about it, Dad?"

My father remained staring resolutely at the television set, as if determined not to weigh in on the situation. He gave a half-hearted shrug. I supposed he'd been burned by similar conversations in the past.

"Oh, you know your father," my mother interjected. "The Catholic in him still thinks that anything that isn't old-fashioned is a cult. That's why he refuses to go to Esalen with me."

"I never said Esalen was a cult," my father muttered. "I just don't like getting naked with strangers."

"Anyway—I think that's where Elli is right now," I said. "Not at a spa. At some kind of retreat run by GenFem. And I think she's given them over a hundred thousand dollars."

This finally got my father's attention. He looked away from the screen and frowned at me. I noticed an ancient mustard stain on his top, which made me ineffably sad. "That's a lot of money."

"Right? Don't you think we should look into this? I could go to the center and scope it out, maybe."

My mother sank back into the couch. A furrow settled in between her eyes as she surveyed me with a sudden mistrust. "I asked you here to help with Charlotte, not to play detective. I'm sure that's not necessary. You saw the text Elli sent me. She's been looking for answers and she apparently is finding them, and that's a *good thing*. The last thing she needs is us intruding on that. *I* can certainly relate, Sam, even if you don't find that kind of thing important."

Was that judgment in her voice? Of course it was, a dark little singe of snark underlining her words: Who was I to take issue with my mother's golden child, the good twin, the one she could brag about in her yoga classes?

What I wanted to say was *I have no issue with finding answers, but I know that when it costs a small fortune it's probably a scam;* but then I remembered that Elli had spent a small fortune on *my* personal growth (because what was rehab but a kind of personal growth?) so I figured I had no leg to stand on.

I left my parents watching *The Bachelorette* and drove back to the church for another AA meeting, where I sat in the back and barely listened to a word that was said, not even the hopeful ones.

When I got home later that night, my parents were asleep. They'd left a light on in the hallway and in the semi-gloom I wandered through the rooms of my childhood, looking at the familiar knickknacks that my parents had accumulated over the years. A set of painted porcelain boxes that had once belonged to my maternal grandmother. An amethyst cluster the size of a goose egg on display in the fancy china cabinet. The silver tea set that my parents had received for their wedding. A bronze Buddha. A jade incense burner.

My mother had been an aspiring hippie for a time, before she met my father. She was the eighth and final child of a middle-class Catholic family, and had decided the best way to get her exhausted mother's attention was to drop out of college and follow the Grateful Dead to Southern California. Her tour ended abruptly when she ran out of money just two months later. She ended up finding work as a receptionist at an accounting firm, which is where she met my father, a nice Catholic boy just like all the ones she'd left behind. They were married within a year, much to my grandmother's delight. It's impossible to fully escape the world in which you were raised; it beats inside you, a muted pulse, always waiting for the opportunity to rush back to the surface.

All throughout our childhood my mother dabbled in spiritual movements—Buddhism and goddess studies and a brief flirtation with transcendentalism—before settling on her current mélange, a sort of New Age suburbanism: crystal energy and casseroles. Her friends found her quirky; my father seemed amused by it, even as he refused to let himself get dragged into each new obsession. My sister and I had mostly found her exhausting. It was as if she were trying to grasp something she couldn't quite see, some hidden meaning that could only be found in an elusive arrangement of constantly evolving patterns. Our mother was never quite *there*, never quite capable of addressing what was right in front of her face; there were always more compelling abstracts to be pondered, things that were much further away and therefore far less scary than confronting her daily truth.

Now I wondered whether all that seeking had somehow seeped into my sister, too. Whether the same impulse that compelled my mother to get hugged by Saint Amma and do group meditations at Esalen had sent my sister looking for emotional guidance from someone named Dr. Cindy Medina. Maybe this was the legacy Elli and I had inherited, the pulse that thrummed silently within us: the desire to look beyond ourselves for meaning.

And yet I mostly felt compelled to close my eyes, to not look at all. I had always preferred oblivion, blankness—even now that I was sober. I didn't want to *see* at all. Because what if I looked and there was no greater meaning to find? No God, no inner peace, no miraculous epiphany that knitted life together into something far greater than each individual thread. How disappointing would that be?

I reached for the china cabinet latch, wanting to feel the heft of that amethyst in my hand, wondering if it would impart some of the healing power my mother so willingly believed in. But the key to the hutch was not in the latch. The cabinet with all my parents' valuables—the silver and the china, my grandmother's pearls and a gold commemorative coin my father had had since he was a child—was locked for the first time that I could remember.

I knew, with a sickening pit in my stomach, that they'd locked it against *me*. Even now, I wasn't to be trusted.

I wondered if they were right.

I spent the next two days ferrying Charlotte to the beach, to the park, to the ice cream shop. I changed diapers, cut avocados into cubes, read and reread *Llama Llama Red Pajama* until I could recite the book by heart. *Llama llama red pajama, in the dark without his mama. Eyes wide open, covers drawn . . . What if Mama Llama's GONE?* It was all a little morbid for a kid's book, and perhaps a bit too on point, considering.

My mother made herself scarce. She was attending a multiday chakra-balancing workshop and she came home every night greasy with essential oils and smelling like sandalwood. She'd kiss Charlotte on the head and then sink into a bath with a glass of wine, tunelessly humming Tori Amos songs.

As my first babysitting charge, Charlotte wasn't so bad. She encountered each new scenario—the tall slide on the playground, the lizard that crawled across her toe, the little boy who grabbed the shovel from her hand—with a wrinkled brow and an assessing silence. She was, in general, not a shrieker or a crier, except when she was *really* upset and then all hell would break loose.

Things that made her smile: strawberry ice cream, digging up objects that she'd just buried, anything that was the color of a banana ("Lello!" she would scream with delight), when I did a handstand or a cartwheel and then pretended to get dizzy and fall down.

She did not like vegetables of any kind. She was wary of dogs. She hated being tickled. She was begrudging about hugs, unless she was sleepy or upset.

Her entire life was a primal binary of *yes* and *no,* with no *maybe*s or *sorta*s or *it's-complicated*s, and something about this was soothing to me. The simplicity of it was a balm after so many years of living in the gray areas, in which every decision I had ever made seemed to require hours of explanation and analysis.

But childcare, it turned out, was exhausting. Mind-numbingly dull and repetitive, and yet requiring a heightened consciousness at all times. I wasn't used to being so alert. Charlotte's plump little legs were remarkably fast—she could cover a football field before I'd registered that she was gone—and I spent most of my time with her worried that she might accidentally get washed away by a wave or fall off a concrete ledge or get run over by a car.

At the end of each day I'd hit up an AA meeting and then collapse into bed with a low-grade stress headache and nerves that still jangled. No wonder my mother needed her chakras realigned after a week of this, I thought; no wonder my sister had run off to Ojai and didn't want to come home.

I took photos of Charlotte and texted the most charming ones—Charlotte digging in the sand, Charlotte eating a cupcake—to my sister. If Elli was going to run off to a dubious retreat, there was no point in tiptoeing around the fact that I was now taking care of Charlotte. Sometimes I'd add a message: *When should I tell her you're coming home?* Or *If you're not home by Friday I'm going to let Charlotte watch Breaking Bad with me.* And *Are you at a GenFem retreat? What the hell have you gotten yourself involved with?* The blue check marks let me know that Elli had read my texts, but she never answered them. I took this as a mildly promising sign: If she didn't think I was trustworthy enough to watch her daughter, surely she would be racing home by now.

Maybe it even meant she'd forgiven me.

Then again, maybe there was a decidedly more upsetting reason that she hadn't come back to save Charlotte from me.

Maybe she wasn't allowed to leave.

On my fourth morning home, another day looming bright and endless before us, I decided to give Caleb a call. I hadn't seen him at an AA meeting since that first night; each evening I'd scanned the heads, looking for badly chopped curls, and felt a twinge of disappointment when I realized he hadn't come.

That morning, I left Charlotte eating toast in her high chair while I stood on my parents' stoop and called the number that he'd typed into my phone. His voice on the other end of the line was still thick with sleep when he answered.

"Not that I'm not happy to hear from you, but it's a bit early, don't you think?"

I glanced at the time. It was 7:30 A.M. "I've been up for two hours. Isn't this when parents usually get up?"

"Not me. My daughter is a night owl. I can barely drag her out of bed before lunch."

"Sorry. I'll call back later."

"No, no. It's OK, I was just getting up anyway." I heard him rustling around, water running in a sink. "You need childcare advice? Suggestions of things to do with a two-year-old?"

Through the window I could see my father enter the kitchen, already dressed for work in his suit. He sat down next to Charlotte and peeled a banana with one hand as he read the newspaper, placing the fruit on the tray of her high chair. She proceeded to drop the banana on the ground, then soberly peered over the edge of her chair at the mess she'd made. Her tiny mouth formed a word I could read from here: *Lello*.

"I need adult company," I said. "Someone I'm not related to. Someone who speaks in complete sentences. Maybe we could meet somewhere? A playground, maybe? Assuming you don't have work today. Actually I have no idea what you do for a living." I realized that I was the one babbling this time.

He laughed. "I'm a high school English teacher. I'm on summer break. And so is my daughter, so you'll get two for the price of one. Cool?"

"Very."

We met at a playground that he suggested, with an elaborate, castle-like play structure that sprawled under the shade of an enormous oak. Charlotte took an immediate shine to Caleb's daughter, Mae, a gamine little girl with paint in her hair and scabs on her knees. The two took off for the fort, Mae holding Charlotte's hand as they wobbled across the swinging bridge and toward the fortress tower.

"She loves little girls," Caleb said. "She keeps asking when she'll be allowed to start babysitting."

"How grown-up."

"She's a ruthless capitalist. She goes through my pockets every night and takes all the change. She tells me that she's saving up to buy a helicopter."

"Much more useful than a plane, if you ask me. Easier to land."

We sat on a bench with a view across the playground. I studied him as I drank my coffee. He was wearing track pants and a battered T-shirt that read *Cedar Forest Ultramarathon 2018*. His hair had been repaired since I saw him last, trimmed into a severe symmetrical cut, almost military in length, that revealed a disarmingly delicate bone structure. The fabric of his T-shirt was so thin that I could see the wiry muscles in his shoulders, bunching and flexing.

I pointed at his chest. "You run ultramarathons? Aren't those, like, a hundred miles?"

"Not all of them. I've never run farther than fifty."

"Still. Sounds awfully time-consuming."

"It keeps me busy, but I need that. Plus, you know what they say. Addictive personalities always need *something* to fixate on. So I run until I collapse. Endorphins are a much healthier high." He gave me a sideways glance. "You? Do you have a vice?"

I lifted my coffee cup. "Caffeine and self-flagellation."

He laughed at this, and then we fell silent, watching the children that swarmed over the play structure like locusts. It was ten A.M. on a summery Tuesday morning and every swing was full, children were jostling for a turn at the slides, and every bench was claimed by a diaper bag or an abandoned sippy cup. I'd wondered if meeting Caleb here would feel awkward, like a particularly G-rated Tinder date, but he exuded a kind of meditative calmness that was in sharp contrast to the mothers and nannies who surrounded us. They circled the play structure like sheepdogs, herding their charges away from danger as they wielded tissues and fish crackers and Band-Aids and disinfecting wipes. Caleb was one of the only men in the park, but he didn't seem particularly bothered by his minority status.

"Is Mae's mom"—I wasn't quite sure how to phrase this delicately—"around?"

"Yes and no. We've been divorced since Mae was two. We split custody for a while but now Mae's mostly with me. Her mom is . . . unstable." He studied his hands, and I noticed that his cuticles were bitten to the quick. "It's why I got sober. Mae needed *someone* who could be responsible. So." He shrugged.

"How long have you been sober?"

"Six years, more or less." Ah. So he was *really* sober. "You?"

"A year."

He gave me a smile that I had grown familiar with, one of encouraging approval mixed with faint trepidation. A year was long enough to prove admirable commitment, but not long enough to be out of the woods. "You stopped acting," he said abruptly.

I flushed. "I didn't know that anyone had noticed. What, you looked me up on IMDB?"

Now it was his turn to flush. "I don't know any other famous actors. So I paid attention, and yeah, I'd check IMDB to see if you'd been in something and then I'd watch it."

"Even the horror movies?"

"Even the horror movies."

"Yikes." Something twisted in my stomach: Embarrassment, yes, but was it my own embarrassment at the state of my career, or embarrassment for him, for revealing his hand so quickly? What kind of person would stalk me like that and admit it?

I snuck a look at his face, trying to decide if he was a creep. He smiled back at me. "I'm not a creep," he said. "I swear."

"I'm not one to judge," I lied, judging.

"Plus, I thought you were a good actress. You always elevated anything you were in."

"As long as I was sober enough to make it to set. Which was never a given."

"For what it's worth, I used to be a pretty good journalist," he said. "Until the *L.A. Times* fired me for showing up high to work too many times. So I'm not in a position to judge, either."

An awkward silence fell over us. Over on the play structure, Mae and Charlotte were hopelessly entangled on the tire swing. Finally, he cleared his throat. "Anyway, what brings you back to Santa Barbara?"

"My sister has gone MIA. I'm helping my parents out and watching Charlotte until my sister comes back."

"Of course, Elli. I'd heard she still lived in town." Then, with a mild furrow of his brow: "MIA? What's that mean?"

"She checked into some sort of self-help retreat in Ojai about ten days ago and hasn't come back." I sounded more nonchalant about this than I felt.

But Caleb was looking at me with blatant concern. "That doesn't sound good. Is she OK?"

"I have no clue." That unwelcome word—*culty*—clutched at me again. I thought of the black GenFem binder. "All I know is that she's reading my text messages but isn't answering them. But that's par for the course. She hasn't answered a text message from me in over a year."

"Still. Aren't you worried? What are you doing about it?"

Was that accusation in his face? "Nothing," I said defensively. I pointed at Charlotte, running across the playground with Mae in mock pursuit. "I'm a full-time entertainment and catering service for a two-year-old. No time to play detective."

"No reason you can't do both. How do you think parents survive? Kids get dragged around on errands all the time," he said. "Where's the retreat? You should go check it out."

"That's the thing. I have no clue where it is. This self-help group she joined, something about it feels really off. Its website lists centers in Santa Barbara and a few other cities, but it doesn't say anything about Ojai. I've tried calling the Santa Barbara office a half dozen times but no one ever answers. They don't return my messages." I swallowed.

"Just go there in person, then they can't blow you off." He hesitated. "I'll keep you company, if you like?"

The girls had found a life-sized whale sculpture, rising like a colossus from the sand, and little Mae was trying to boost Charlotte up its smooth flanks. She kept sliding down to the ground and shrieking with hilarity, not in the least bit defeated by the Sisyphean nature of their endeavor.

There was a lesson to be learned from this, but I wasn't exactly sure what it was.

From the outside, GenFem's center wasn't nearly as impressive as its website. The group occupied a space in a strip mall, between a dry cleaner and a frozen yogurt shop. Judging by the faded paint above the door, the space had once been occupied by a pet supply shop. Now its windows were covered with opaque shades, preventing a clear view inside. The glass door read *GenFem* in gold letters.

Caleb and I parked side by side in the parking lot and extricated the kids from their car seats. "We're getting frozen yogurt? In the morning?" Mae asked her father, looking confused. She gripped his hand. She'd put on a cat-ear headband with red sequins that glittered in the sun.

"Special treat. But first we need to do an errand, to help Sam."

Charlotte lolled sleepily on my hip—I vaguely recalled that she was supposed to be taking a nap around now—as I pushed open the door to GenFem. I was greeted by an arctic blast of air-conditioning and a thick fog of vanilla candle, so strong that it made my eyes sting. A small decorative fountain burbled just inside the door, catching Charlotte's attention. She slid from my hip and stuck a hand in the water, grabbing for the pennies that someone had dropped in the bottom of the basin.

"Gross," I said. "Dirty."

"Tweasure!" she crowed, holding up a dime.

The room was empty. At the far end of the space, a podium was set in front of purple velvet curtains; and before this was an array of couches and armchairs in bright candy colors. Closer to the window a row of desks displayed a half dozen shiny new laptops. A young woman in an oatmeal-colored dress was sitting at one of these workstations. She jumped up when we entered, and then she scurried toward us.

"The center is closed," she said. "Our next meeting isn't until two P.M." She eyed Caleb, lips parting to reveal a tight line of perfectly straight teeth. "Women only, I'm so sorry. We do have a men's group, if you're interested, but it meets elsewhere."

"Actually, we're not here for a meeting," I said.

"Are you familiar with GenFem? Did a member refer you?" She kept her eyes locked on mine, pupils huge in the dim room, the smile fixed on her lips, while her hand clawed for a stack of pamphlets on a nearby table. "Maybe you'd like to take some literature about our founder's patented method. You could read it and we could set up an information session? Take one of our assessments?"

"Thank you, but really, I'm just trying to get the address of your Ojai retreat." The woman's hand, still clutching the pamphlets, wavered.

"Oh! Hmm." The woman took a step away from us. "Let me get—" She abruptly turned and scurried toward the back of the room, disappearing behind the purple curtains. Caleb and I waited, the children weaving impatiently around our legs. Charlotte had now fished at least two dollars' worth of change from the fountain. Maybe she'd buy a helicopter for her new friend.

I was expecting the psychologist from the website to appear—*Dr. Cindy Medina*—but the curtains disgorged a regal Black woman, her hair cropped short to expose a finely shaped skull. She approached us with a look of welcoming dismay on her face.

"Hi, I'm Roni. I'm told you are interested in joining us in Ojai?" She had a faint British accent. "I'm sorry, but that's a private retreat, the personal property of our founder. It's invite only."

"Oh, I'm not interested in checking in to the retreat myself. I just need the address."

She shook her head. "We can't share the address. Can you tell me how you learned about it?"

Roni was smiling, all solicitous concern, but something about the naked smoothness of her face put me on edge. I thought of a doll denuded of its hair, perpetually grinning. "My sister is there. I was hoping to go speak to her. We want to make sure she's OK."

The woman gave me a sharper look then, as if seeing me for the first time. The smile faded as she took me in, recognizing something in my face. "Sorry, your sister's name is . . . ?"

"Eleanor—Elli—Hart."

I waited for understanding to dawn across her face—*I'm speaking to Elli's twin*—but Roni's face twitched only once before settling back into its unnervingly smooth mask. "Hmmm. I can't say I recognize the name."

She turned to walk over to one of the laptops, where she typed a few words into a search field. In the back of the room, the young woman was standing at the edge of the curtains, her hands clenching and unclenching the velvet. The room was silent except for the *tip-tap* of the keyboard. Finally, Roni spoke. "I'm not finding her in our database. You're sure she's part of GenFem?"

"Try Logan," I said. "That's her maiden name."

Roni typed again, clicked a few buttons, let out a little sigh. She turned back to face us with an apologetic smile. "I'm sorry," she said, and gave a tiny little shrug. "We have no record of your sister at all. She's never been here."

I was about to protest but I felt Caleb's hand on my back, pinching the fabric of my T-shirt, tugging me back toward the door. "Our mistake," he said. He reached down and extricated Charlotte's damp hand from the fountain, folded it into his own, and then reached for Mae. "Thank you for your time."

Outside, the girls raced toward the frozen yogurt shop, Charlotte dripping a trail of pennies behind her. Once we were out of eyeshot of the GenFem center, Caleb turned to look at me, a deep line splitting his forehead in two.

"They're lying," he said. "They don't want us to know that she's a member."

"I know."

"They clearly don't want to tell you how to find her, either."

"They acknowledged the existence of the retreat in Ojai, though. She's there, I'm sure of it," I said. "I just don't know exactly where it is."

He looked at me and frowned. "Ojai's a small town," he said. "How hard can it really be to find?"

THE FIRST TIME ELLI and I switched places, we were thirteen years old. We were a few months into the fourth season of *To the Maxx* and I had watched Elli grow more wan and apathetic by the day. It was late spring and she wanted to go back to Santa Barbara, to spend long days with her books and her iPod in the sun. "Wouldn't you rather be at the beach than sitting on set every day?" she'd ask me, and when I said no, not at all, she would get petulant and pick at the tiny zits on her nose until Bettina, the makeup artist, swatted her hand away.

The director had noticed the change in her, too.

"Hey, you," he barked at her on set one afternoon. *Hey, you* was what the crew fell back on when they couldn't remember which one of us they were looking at, when the call sheet was misplaced and all they knew was that they had a twin in front of them. "Can we talk about how you're playing this scene? You're supposed to be happy that your mom is taking you to visit New York and instead you look like someone killed your cat."

Elli sat glumly on the white shag rug of our mock bedroom. The plane ticket she was supposed to be clutching to her chest instead hung limply from her fist. The walls of the set ended just yards above her head; if you looked up past the lights, all you could see was the dark void of the backlot warehouse, the ceiling invisible in the gloom. It felt like we were on a spaceship, in the middle of a black hole, flying off into nowhere.

Paige Bart, who played Marci Maxx, gave Elli an encouraging little pat on her head. "It's OK, honey, let's go again."

Elli smiled tremulously at Paige and tried her line again. "Oh, Mummy. You shouldn't have done this. I know we can't afford it." The words caught in her throat and came out as a peevish whine. Paige flicked her eyes at the camera and raised an eyebrow.

"Cut!" the director screamed. From where I sat, in a chair just behind him, I could hear him murmur to the assistant director. "This one's gotta be Elli, right? Can we get Samantha back?"

"We used up Sam's hours already today. We're stuck with Elli unless you want to strike and run it again with Sam tomorrow morning."

The director swore under his breath, and then stood up. "OK, half-hour break, let's regroup and try this again in a bit. Elli, go grab a Coke, get your blood sugar up, whatever it takes, OK, kid?"

My mother materialized out of the darkness behind me, a look of grim concern on her face as she stepped into the lights of the set. Elli saw her coming. She stood up and bolted for the exit, moving fast. I followed my sister out, blinking in the sudden flood of daylight, and chased her across the parking lot to our trailer. I could hear our mother behind us, calling our names.

Elli ran up the stairs of the trailer and threw the door open, but I managed to slip in behind her before she could get it shut again. Once I was inside, I locked the handle and turned to face my sister. She was crying now, black rivulets of mascara worming grooves through the beige pancake makeup that continually clogged our pores.

"You're fucking up your face. Bettina is going to kill you."

She swiped at her face, leaving a black smear across her cheek. "He's so mean. I'm not going back."

Behind us, our mother was banging on the door to the trailer.

"Girls? What's going on in there? Elli? Do you want to do a meditation with me? Would that help?"

"Not right now, Mom!" Elli screamed through the door. She turned to me, desperation in her eyes. "I can't do this anymore."

"What? You mean this scene? Or you can't do *this*, like . . . act?"

"I don't know." Her eyes were rimmed with pink. She looked like a crazed raccoon. She hesitated. "Can't we just . . . take a week off?"

"We can't. It doesn't work that way." I stared at her destroyed face, an anguished echo of my own, and thought hard. How could I save her? How could I save *us*?

"But what if *you* took a week off?" I heard myself say.

"What do you mean?"

I leaned in close. "You be me," I whispered, "and I'll be you."

It didn't take much to become her that first time. I still had my stage makeup on from my scenes that morning; a few quick swipes with the hairbrush and my hair was hers, too. I donned the costume that Elli had been wearing and she put on my sweats, washed her face, and put a compress over her eyes until the redness vanished. Half an hour later, we exited our trailer quietly and found my mother sitting on the bottom of the stairs, reading a book by Pema Chödrön.

She jumped up, her cheeks flushed from the sun, sweat spreading in rings under her armpits. She'd already started on the natural deodorant by then and I could smell her, musky and sharp. "I don't like being locked out," she said, peevish. Already, the balance between us was shifting; paying the bills had given us power, and she no longer knew quite how to shut us down.

"I'm OK now, I just needed to relax for a bit," I said to her, letting a faint tremor creep into my voice. I softened my step as I walked down the stairs and behind me I could hear Elli's feet landing with a thud. *Is that how I walk?* I thought, perturbed and delighted. I was chewing Elli's gum and Elli was sucking on one of the cinnamon Altoids I liked, clicking it against her teeth the way I did. It felt like we were performing cartoon versions of each other; and yet maybe this was how the world saw us, as oversized caricatures of the smaller people we believed ourselves to be inside.

I remember that I felt a vague thrill as my eyes met my mother's, lashes trembling. I willed my face into a mask of weary obedience, the face of a good girl who was determined to try her best just to make everyone happy. The face of my sister, so similar to mine and yet so different underneath. This was the ultimate test of my acting abilities: If anyone was going to catch us, it was going to be our mother.

"You sure?" Her eyes snapped from me to Elli and back again and I saw something cross her face, a faint question mark. And then, just as quickly, it disappeared. Her eyes shot away, as if the question had been answered and she was uninterested in considering it any further.

"OK, then," she said. "If you're ready, then let's get back to set. We're three minutes late."

And so for the next eight weeks, until we finished shooting the season, I played two roles: Elli's and my own. No one ever suspected that when Elli and I disappeared into the bathroom at lunchtimes or in between scenes, we were swapping places. As far as the crew was concerned we were just teenagers, spending too much time preening in the bathroom; and if we sometimes came out a little backward, our hair not quite right and costumes awry—well, no one looked that closely at kids anyway. No one paid close enough attention to note that "Sam" was a little less assertive than usual or that "Elli" seemed to have developed Sam's swagger. Who would it benefit anyway, to sniff out our ruse? The director was happy to finally be getting strong performances out of Elli; he wasn't about to question how he'd gotten them.

Maybe our mother knew what was going on; how could she not? But maybe she also understood why we did what we did—that this was a matter of my sister's survival, and my own. That was how our mother had always been: willfully blind, stubbornly optimistic. It was easier for her to believe that our problems had seamlessly resolved themselves.

So Elli spent her days being me, reading gossip magazines and playing Tomb Raider on my Game Boy. I got to perform in double the scenes—as well as playing Elli, a role inside a role—and I loved it. By the time we finished shooting the rest of the season, Elli had stopped looking so haunted and I had honed my acting skills to a fine point, and the production was even ahead of schedule. Everyone was happy, so how could what we were doing possibly be wrong?

Only one person ever found us out: Bettina. Our gum-cracking makeup person, the bird tattoos flying off her arms as she puffed our faces with powder and brushed gloss over our lips. She studied our faces so closely, knew every contour of our cheekbones and crooked lash in our brows: Of course she would have been the one to notice.

The first morning when I sat in her chair as Elli, she paused for just a moment and caught my eyes in the mirror.

"Elli?" she asked, the *l*'s drawing out languidly on her tongue.

"Yes," I said, perhaps a little more firmly than Elli might have said it, because this caused Bettina's eyebrow to arch upward.

"Sure." She gave me a tiny, knowing smile. Then she gripped my chin with a gentle hand and tilted it up so that she could eradicate my face with a layer of thick foundation.

She said nothing further, not that week or the next. She remained silent until three weeks in, when the strain of playing so many parts—staying up late to learn two sets of lines, getting up early to do my schoolwork before we went to the studio lot, and then doing a double shift on set—began to show on my face. "You're going to wear yourself out, kiddo," she murmured to me one afternoon as she patted concealer on the circles under my eyes. "You look exhausted."

"I can handle it," I said. "I'm fine on only a few hours of sleep."

She glanced over at my sister, who was happily napping on the couch of our trailer. "How long do you plan to keep this up?" she asked.

I thought about this. "Forever, if I have to."

She stared at me for a long minute, her thin face twitching. Then she reached into her purse and pulled out a prescription bottle. She opened it and shook a few small orange capsules into my hand.

"Adderall," she said. "It helps with focus, energy. Try just a half. But if you like it, I can get you more."

I stared at the capsules in my palm. I was thirteen years old and fearless—already high with the deception that I'd managed to achieve—so of course I barely even hesitated before popping one in my mouth. Not just a half, but the whole thing, as Bettina watched with a wry smile.

She was right. It helped. Adderall made me feel quick and sharp; it made my lines rise up in my mouth almost as if I'd conjured them myself; it gave my performances a little edge that made the asshole director sit up and look at me as if seeing me for the first time. I finished off Bettina's entire bottle before we'd wrapped the season. And then she sold me two more.

And that, my friends, was how I started down the long, slow road to addiction; and how Bettina became my very first drug dealer.

———

Fans of the show sometimes said that Elli and I should have been nominated for an Emmy that season, that something about the performances that year felt elevated and sparkling.

At the end of the season, they killed us off anyway. For the ratings, they said. We'd been murdered, at the tender age of fourteen.

On the drive back to Santa Barbara that June—the open sunroof baking the back seat of our mother's new Mercedes with sun, the ocean glittering on our left and the shrubby bluffs looming on our right—Elli leaned across the seat and rested her head on my shoulder. She whispered in my ear, so our mother couldn't hear: "We won't do it again, OK? I'm glad you did that for me, but it doesn't seem right. I don't feel good about it."

"Never again," I whispered back.

But of course, we did.

THE TEMPERATURE GAUGE IN my car clicked up and up as I drove inland, away from the cooling ocean breezes of the coast and into the heat sink of the Ojai Valley. Over the winding hills and through the dusty oak groves, until the rolling peaks of the Topatopa Mountains came into view. By the time I reached the valley floor, the thermometer read 102 degrees. Horses stood listlessly in their pastures, seeking the shade of the shedding eucalyptuses. Orange groves shimmered like a mirage on either side of the car. Even the migrant workers who worked the farms were inside right now, out of the midday sun.

Four years earlier, I had stayed at a high-end rehab center not far from town, the kind of place where pop stars with substance abuse problems go to dry out after they collapse onstage. It cost forty thousand dollars a month, and since my own savings were completely gone by then, Elli footed the bill. I bailed out a week early with a talent manager that I met there, a handsome huckster who had convinced me that we weren't addicts "like the rest of these losers." We snuck out after dark one night and headed to Los Angeles, where we checked into the Beverly Hills Hotel with a gram of cocaine and spent three days screwing our brains out and toasting our newly discovered "sobriety." When I woke up on the fourth day, he was gone and had left me with a six-thousand-dollar hotel room bill.

Elli drove down from Santa Barbara and paid the hotel bill. She tried to convince me to check back into rehab and finish out my stint, but I couldn't. I'd broken the rules and had been banned for life. I got pancakes with her at Norms and apologized for being the worst sister in the world and we both cried; and then after she left I took an Uber straight to a bar and got obliterated. I was a terrible human.

Point is—I hadn't been back to Ojai since.

It hadn't changed much. The town, once a home to Chumash Indians, was now a destination for affluent bohemians with eagle feather tattoos on their shoulder blades. Signs advertised Reiki treatments, energy alchemists, crystal healers, and food harmonics. Faded Tibetan prayer flags fluttered on fences outside of farmhouses that had been converted to massage centers. Even the fruit that fueled the town—citrus picked by a working-class population that was invisible to the weekending Hollywood crowd—suggested an underlying health.

Downtown Ojai consisted of a modest strip of stores under a Spanish Mission colonnade, a clutch of wine tasting rooms and boutiques selling sun hats and rope sandals, a single-screen movie theater with a crumbling façade. Women in athleisure walked the streets, carrying reusable bags full of leafy vegetables. I felt pale and pasty and weak. I desperately wanted a macchiato but the signs all advertised vegan elixirs.

Caleb had offered to come with me today and I'd said no, concerned how my sister might react if I showed up at her retreat with a strange man in tow. Or maybe I just thought that I could handle this one myself. *I don't need no man.* But as I drove through the streets of Ojai, I regretted leaving him behind. I had no clue where I was going. I could have used an extra set of eyes.

I cruised slowly through town, into the quieter side streets and back again, looking for a sign for GenFem. I saw a dozen other spas and retreats and centers, but none that fit the bill. The woman at the center had called it Dr. Cindy's "personal property," though, so perhaps there wouldn't be a sign at all. Maybe it was just a house, indistinguishable from any other. How would I even know?

Charlotte had slept most of the way to Ojai but now she woke up and began to cry at the misery of still being strapped in place. I pulled over on the main street where there was a playground and pushed her on the swing for a few minutes, but the midday sun was unrelenting and soon Charlotte's face was the color of a raspberry. I'd forgotten sunscreen. I didn't have water, either. She swung listlessly in the heat as I cursed myself for not planning better. I was a shitty aunt.

We aborted the mission. Instead, we made a beeline for an ice cream shop across the street. I got her a double scoop of strawberry and we walked down the colonnade in the shade, until I found a crystal shop with a giant pink quartz in the window for twelve hundred dollars. Positive energy is not cheap. The crystal made me think of my mother, which made me think of my sister; it seemed as good a place as any to find a healing-oriented local.

The room was lined with glass shelves displaying glittering rocks on tiny stands. Charlotte immediately lunged for the first one she saw, fat fingers outstretched. "Tweasure," she informed me, as I yanked her backward. The woman behind the counter— black curls to her waist, harem pants—watched nervously.

"Please don't let the baby kill the crystals," she offered, not unkindly.

I gripped Charlotte to my side as she squirmed unhappily. "I'm wondering if you can help me," I began. "I'm looking for a wellness retreat, run by a group called GenFem?"

The woman looked at me blankly. "Huh. I don't think I know that one."

I pulled out my phone and pulled up the GenFem website, then thrust it toward her. "This? Recognize it?"

She took the phone from me and scrolled through the site, frowning a little. "No. But hang on." She turned and yelled toward the back of the store. "Jessa? Heard of GenFem?"

Another woman appeared from behind a bead curtain that led to a back room. She was gray-haired, slight. She looked at us and frowned. "They're the ones with the funny place up by Maisie's avocado farm."

"Some kind of spiritual retreat, right?" I asked.

"Spiritual? I don't know about that. At least it's not *my* kind of spiritual. They're going for a different kind of energy."

"What kind of energy?"

She thought this over for a beat, fingering the stone necklace draped over her collarbone. "More Narcissus, less Gaia."

I had no idea what that meant. "OK. But you know where I can find their spa?"

"Spa?" The woman laughed. "I wouldn't call it that."

"What would you call it?"

"More like . . . a compound."

This was unsettling. The word conjured up wartime bunkers, armed guards. I tried to reconcile this with the benign-looking strip mall storefront I'd visited the day before. Nothing was adding up neatly at all. "Have you been inside?"

She shook her head. "I really don't know anything about the group. I've seen the members at the grocery store, but they don't spend much time in town. Why do you want to go there?"

"My sister is there. Can you tell me where it is?"

She walked to the front window of the store and pointed out to the road. "Take this to the far edge of town, where it starts to climb up over the hill. Turn right at the pizza place and follow the road up past the avocado farm. The compound is gated; there's no sign but there's a big iron entrance. You'll know it when you see it."

"Thank you." I tugged Charlotte toward the door.

"Wait."

The older woman approached us and crouched down in front of Charlotte. She took the little girl's free hand and pried it open, then placed a small, polished rock on her palm. The rock was green and black, a dark light glowing from its depths. Charlotte went still, silent with awe.

"Labradorite." The woman stood up and smiled tightly at me. "For safety and protection."

I followed the woman's directions out to a pizza shack on the edge of town, and then turned off the main highway and up toward the hills. Wildfires had almost devastated the town a while back. In places the hills had been scorched right down to the road, and the blackened skeletons of trees still stood sentry over the devastation, although a green carpet of new shrubs had already thrust their way up around them. I found myself on a narrow road, driving past an avocado grove with an empty fruit stand out front and a sign that read *Take one leave a buck*. There was no farmer to be seen, although the avocados hung heavy on the trees, and lay rotting in piles in the brush. Thousands of dollars of spoiled superfoods.

Somewhere, a dog was barking an alert at our presence.

I kept winding up the hill, coming into a thick section of chaparral, dense with sumac and scrub oak. One more hairpin turn and I knew immediately that I'd found it: A long wooden fence, at least eight feet high, stretched along the road for as far as I could see. The fence was imposing, but it also wasn't topped by barbed wire or protected by armed guards. I drove past an abstract sculpture of a woman, life-sized, made of bicycle parts and rusted scrap metal; and then another, of driftwood, painted pale pink; and then one more, twisted out of frayed and knotted rope. The vibe was less military compound and more hippie commune with a rather intense sense of privacy.

In the back seat, Charlotte had grown quiet; she craned her neck to stare at the curious sculptures as we bumped slowly up the road.

And then suddenly we were at the gates of the compound: two

iron doors, topped with curious metal spikes. No, not spikes—small metal circles, each one topped with a cross. I puzzled over these for a minute before realizing what they were: the sex symbol for woman. The symbol, the amateurish sculptures, the quasi-feminist name—I laughed out loud, startling Charlotte in the back seat. It all looked so . . . harmless. Downright hokey. When you leave gaps in information, people fill the space with misunderstanding, imagining worst-case scenarios as hard reality. I don't know what I'd imagined I'd find, but now that I was here the place looked as benign as my mother had protested it must be.

I felt something ease inside me, the tension slipping loose. Maybe I *was* just overreacting; maybe GenFem was just a women's group with an overdeveloped sense of privacy and an extremely high price tag. Maybe Roni at the Santa Barbara center really *didn't* find my sister's name in their database, not because my sister was lying or because of some sinister disinformation plan but simply because they were disorganized.

The gates were locked, and there was no guardhouse, just a call box off to the side of the road. I pulled over in front of the gate, got out of the car, and pressed the button.

Nothing happened. The air was hot and still. A faint buzz sawed at my temples: the drone of cicadas hidden somewhere in the shrubbery. If there was human life on the other side of that fence, I couldn't hear it.

I looked around, noticed a security camera, and jumped up and down, waving my hands. Maybe the buzzer was broken? Still—nothing. The minutes passed as I stood there stupidly, unsure what to do. Had it all been a wild-goose chase? Was this even the right spot? A mourning dove called out from the brush nearby, plaintive. I banged on the gate with my fist, sweat dripping down the back of my T-shirt, until the side of my hand began to ache. Charlotte stared soberly at me through the open car window, still gripping the labradorite stone in her fist.

Just as I was about to give up and go back to the car, the call box suddenly crackled to life, startling me.

"May I help you?" It was a young woman's voice, friendly enough.

The sound of her voice filled me with relief. "Hi! Yes, I'm looking for my sister. Elli Logan?"

A momentary silence, then: "I've never heard that name before."

"She also goes by Eleanor. Eleanor Logan. Or Hart, actually."

"So many names!" The voice laughed gently. "I'm not familiar with any of them, I'm sorry."

I leaned closer to the call box, confusion rising in me. "But you are a wellness retreat, right? Affiliated with GenFem? She's a guest."

The voice was infuriatingly placid. "I don't know all of our guests by name, I'm afraid."

"Look, I'm just trying to visit my sister. I know she's here. She told my family she was here. Can I just come in, please?"

The call box went dead. A moment later, it crackled back to life. "I'm sorry, but even if she is staying here, I can't let you in. Our guests come here for study and contemplation. We find visitors disruptive. They're not allowed without advance approval."

"How do I get approved?"

"You can submit a request through our website."

I couldn't recall seeing anything on the website about the retreat at all, let alone a visitation request form. I pulled my phone out of my pocket and tried to pull up the website for GenFem, but cell reception in the hills was spotty at best. "Can't you page her or something, and ask for her approval? I drove an hour to get here. This is ridiculous."

"I'm really very sorry, but we have protocols."

I stared up at the security camera and decided to play my trump card. "I have her daughter with me. Charlotte. She's only two and she really wants to see her mother. Plus, she needs to pee." I turned to point at Charlotte in the car, right behind me. *This would be a good moment to cry or throw a tantrum,* I thought, willing her to make herself seen. But Charlotte just stared placidly at me through the window, turning the labradorite stone in her palm, holding it up to the light.

"I'm going to have to ask you to leave now." The voice had grown cold. "If I come across her, I'll tell her you came by. It'll be up to her to contact you. Thank you."

The call box went dead. I jabbed at the button, pressing it over and over, imagining it ringing in some invisible office, but there was no response. I pressed a hand on the iron of the gate. The metal was hot under my hand.

Just then there was a rattling at the gate, the faint sound of voices rising from the other side. I jumped backward as the gate suddenly swung open toward me and two bodies appeared in the gap.

Two women stepped through the gate, opening it just enough to squeeze through before quickly closing it shut behind them. I stumbled backward, disoriented, as an unexpected thought sprang into my head: *Wait, twins?*

The women who'd materialized from the other side were identical. They both had hair cropped short to the scalp—not quite shaved, but close—and skin that was tanned from too much direct sun. They both wore white linen sack dresses that hung loose around their torsos, with practical canvas tennis shoes that were brown with dust. Twins—except that they weren't twins at all. As I recovered from my surprise, I realized that one was older, with crepey skin on her neck and stubble that was threaded with gray; and the other was young, and heavier set, her unplucked eyebrows as thick as caterpillars. The women didn't look a bit alike, probably weren't even related, which made the matching outfits that much more alarming.

They gave me only a glance as they passed by me, their eyes

instead glued to the asphalt in front of them as they headed off down the road. They had canvas tote bags over their arms and I wondered if they were off to do some shopping in town. Or maybe they were going to the orchard down the road to forage for avocados? But in this heat, and without a car? The nearest store was at least a two-mile-walk away.

What kind of wellness retreat *was* this?

Or was it a wellness retreat at all?

Culty, I thought, as it sank in for real. *My sister has joined a cult.*

"Hey!" I called after them. "Hey, can I talk to you?"

They didn't stop. If anything, they walked faster, the older woman hunching her shoulders, as Caterpillar Brows placed a reassuring hand between her shoulder blades. It was almost as if they were *afraid* of me. Or maybe they were afraid of being punished for speaking to me? Had they taken a vow of silence? Was GenFem some sort of monastic retreat?

I tried again, softening my voice until it was friendly and nonthreatening. "Please? I just want to know if you know my sister! Her name's Elli. It's possible that she's going by Eleanor. She looks like . . . well, she's my identical twin so she looks just like me. Is she in there?"

It was as if they hadn't heard me at all.

"Look. You can just nod yes or no, you don't need to even speak! Just let me know if she's there, and if she's OK."

The younger woman stopped abruptly. She slowly turned to face me. A scowl had darkened her face, those impressive eyebrows drawing a sharp line across her brow.

"She's not your sister anymore. You're toxic." The words were a low growl, a challenge. "She's *ours.*"

I reared back with surprise. She bared her teeth at me and then jerked back around, grabbing the hand of the older woman and dragging her away from me, down the road.

So Elli *was* inside.

I thought of chasing them and demanding more information, but Charlotte was still in the car, and I couldn't abandon her. Instead, I helplessly watched them turn the corner and disappear.

I turned to face the gate again, wondering why this fence needed to be so high, why the gate needed to be so heavily fortified. What, exactly, was behind it that I wasn't supposed to see? I craned my neck up at the security camera, which was still pointed down at me, and saw my own reflection mirrored back at me. I wondered if that disembodied voice was still watching me. I wondered, too, if it was possible that my sister was also standing with that invisible woman, watching me on the monitor. Watching her own daughter, locked out on the other side of the gate. My God—could she be sitting there staring at the monitor, waiting for me to leave with her child? The Elli I'd known would never do that. It was unfathomable.

Who were these people, and what had they done to my sister? Was it possible that she had no intention of ever coming home at all?

I slowly raised my fists up above my head and then, with an exaggerated grimace, I extended both my middle fingers up in a silent *Screw you*.

I turned to see Charlotte still staring at me through the open window, her brow wrinkled with worry. I offered her a reassuring smile. "OK, Charlotte! Time to go home," I chirped.

Then I got in my car and we drove away. My ears buzzed with the sound of cicadas, stirring up into a violent whirring swarm, blocking any clarity of my thoughts. This was not a good place, or a benign one, I could feel it in my nerves; but what *was* it? What exactly was GenFem, and how was I going to get my sister back?

10   RIBBONS OF CARS SNAKED up the coast to Santa Barbara, threading past the salt marshes and the polo club and the beaches where slick surfers bobbed in the water like seals. Last week, a surfer had been bitten by a shark. I had watched an interview on TV where he said the first thing he was going to do after he healed was get back in the water, because now the odds were in his favor. "No one ever gets bitten twice," he said with a laugh from his hospital bed. And I'd thought to myself, *You'd be surprised.*

We sat in traffic for half an hour, the stop-and-go lulling Charlotte to sleep. Back at my parents' house, I deposited Charlotte in her portable crib before going to look for my mother.

I found her sitting in the back garden on a meditation cushion, eyes closed, legs splayed out before her. Sage smoked on a brass plate by her knee, filling the air with a thick cloud of bitter smoke. She wore a Japanese kimono that she'd arranged around her like an altar cloth.

I stood on the back porch, watching. "I can feel you breathing, you know," she said, eyes still closed. "It makes it hard to focus." She sighed and rose stiffly, wiping dust from her rear.

"If your hips are so bad, maybe you should be sitting in a chair instead," I observed.

"I like to be closer to the earth," she said, waggling her fingertips toward the dirt, and gave me a significant look. "I can feel it on a deeper level there. The osmosis, the exchange with the elements, everything linked together through our interconnected root systems." She came up the stairs, wobbling with each step, and grabbed my wrist to steady herself. "I think I was a tree in one of my past lives."

I tried to imagine my mother as a tree. I saw something big and colorful and messy: a jacaranda maybe, or a pepper tree, scattering sticky seeds underfoot. "Is reincarnation your new thing?"

The beatific smile faded from her face. "What do you mean, *new thing?*"

I laughed. "C'mon, Mom. You've always got something new you're into. Last time I was here it was kundalini yoga. The time before that you were trying to convince Dad to give all your retirement savings to Sai Maa."

"Stop being so dramatic. It wasn't *all* of our savings." She snatched her hand away from my wrist and smoothed her curls into place, clearly miffed. I'd gone too far. "Laugh if you like, but *I* believe in the power of continually seeking knowledge."

Or, you're a spiritual dilettante, believing everything and nothing, never pausing long enough to let an informed opinion take shape, I thought. But who was I to judge? I had found my spiritual meaning in the bottom of a bottle and now, with that gone, I was too worried about my continued sober existence to spend time thinking about enlightenment at all. "I'm not laughing, promise. Tell me about your past lives. I'm interested, honest."

She shot me a look, trying to figure out if I was teasing her. "Our cells are never destroyed. They just get recycled into new living things. So who's to say our souls aren't, too? I mean, it makes more sense than *heaven,* doesn't it? There's actual science in it!"

"I'm not sure that a scientist would agree with you, Mom."

She shook her head, disappointed in my pragmatism. "Well,

it's nicer than believing that you die and nothing happens at all. It's much more pleasant to know that making the right decisions in *this* life will set you up for an even better life next time around."

"And you made the right decisions, I take it?" I couldn't prevent a wry note of skepticism from creeping into my voice.

She didn't answer that. She reached for a bottle of rosé that was sitting on the table and poured herself a glass. The bottle sweated, prisms of sun caught in the condensation, whispering a lewd invitation to me. How good it would feel right now, I thought, to let myself sink into that comfortable obliteration. After a year of honing my mind—letting sobriety sharpen it slowly back into consciousness—I missed the soft blanket of a buzz.

A drop of moisture collected near the neck, slipped down the bottle toward the label. I reached out and collected it with a finger, put it on my tongue. It tasted like nothing at all. I thought about telling my mother about what I'd found in Ojai, about the shaved heads and the belligerent twins and the gatekeeper who pretended not to know my sister, but when I opened my mouth something else entirely came out. The question I knew I shouldn't be asking at all.

"Mom? What happened between Elli and Chuck?"

The wineglass stopped halfway to my mother's mouth.

"Elli said it was the infertility," she said thoughtfully. "Which is why I assumed that adopting Charlotte would help patch them up, but it didn't. Maybe it was all too broken by then."

"Huh," I said, a flush of discomfort warming my cheeks. "Where is Chuck now?"

"Tokyo. Believe it or not." She took another sip, fuming to herself. "You know I called him? Just to try to leave a bridge open. And he never called me back. We really misjudged him." She sniffed, hiccuped. "The whole thing broke Elli's heart. Thank God for Charlotte showing up so soon afterward. Charlotte really saved her."

And yet Charlotte hadn't really saved her, I thought to myself. Because apparently Elli still felt compelled to join some kind of cult. Something about the timeline of Chuck's departure and Charlotte's arrival nagged at me, something I couldn't quite put into words. "Mom, where did Charlotte come from?"

She put the glass of wine down on the table. "An adoption agency."

"Which one?"

"How would I know?"

"Did you know Elli and Chuck were trying to adopt?"

She shrugged. "She'd said they were looking into it as an option. They were doing everything. Looked into IVF, surrogates, everything. You know that, right?" She said this casually, not knowing that her words felt like needles under my skin. I reached instinctively for the wine bottle, then pulled my hand back. "She said the call came out of the blue, not long after Chuck left. Like an answer to her prayers."

I thought about this. "How old was Charlotte when Elli adopted her?"

"Twenty months, I think?"

"And she didn't come from a foreign country?" My mother shook her head. "So she must have come from foster care, right? Otherwise, who puts up a child that age for adoption?" Something else occurred to me. "And if a couple breaks up, wouldn't the adoption agency put a hold on the adoption? Why would they give the baby to just one parent? Or was Elli pretending she and Chuck were still married?"

My mother suddenly looked less at ease. "Oh. Right. I suppose so. I don't really know that much about the adoption industry."

It was beginning to dawn on me that my mother and Elli hadn't been as close as I thought, that my mother had not been my sister's confidante after all. My mother's lack of curiosity was infuriating. "You *suppose*? Did you not talk at all about where Charlotte came from?"

"We just never got into the logistics." The wine in my mother's glass had vanished at an alarming rate. She poured herself another. "And honestly we didn't see Elli a lot this spring. Once Chuck left she spent a lot of time by herself. We babysat for her one or two evenings a week so that she could have time to herself. But we didn't chat a lot. She was always going to her meetings. So, no. I did not get into the nitty-gritty with her." She gave me a funny look. "I'm not sure why this is important?"

"I'm just wondering—if Charlotte came from foster care, is there some agency that's supposed to be checking in on her? Is someone going to be worried if they can't get in touch with Elli? Is it possible Elli was just fostering her, and she isn't formally adopted yet?"

My mother stared into the wine in her glass. "I don't *know*."

"Nana." We both turned to see Charlotte standing in the doorway of the house, one thumb in her mouth, the other hand clutching a filthy stuffed rabbit to her chest. Dark curls tumbled around her head, stuck in the sleep-sweat on her temples.

My mother stood. "Now how on earth did you get out of that crib by yourself?" she tutted, as she knelt down and swept Charlotte into her arms. She buried her face in the little girl's neck.

"Mom," I said gently. "I'm going to go to Elli's house and look around a little. Just to be sure."

"If you think that's necessary." She lifted Charlotte up with a grunt, stumbling a little under the girl's weight. Charlotte looked at me, a little alarmed, and reached her arms out for me to take her. I could see how much this hurt my mother, so I took a small step back and shook my head at Charlotte, even though she couldn't possibly understand the peculiar sensitivities of adults. We spend our lives saying no to our mothers, rejecting their love when it's inconvenient, but that doesn't mean the sting ever gets less sharp.

———

After dinner, I drove back to my sister's house to see if I could find Charlotte's adoption paperwork, but also, secretly, to get another look at my sister's GenFem binder. I'd left the binder exactly where I'd found it by the side of my sister's bed, imagining Elli coming home and missing it and blaming me and the whole thing driving a deeper wedge between us. Now I was willing to take that chance, and I wanted to examine the binder more closely. Those pages, with all their inscrutable psychobabble, were presumably a map that could explain what kind of lunacy, exactly, GenFem was feeding my sister.

It wasn't until I pulled into the empty driveway to park that I noticed the For Sale sign hanging off the front gate. It hadn't been there before. I wondered why my mother hadn't told me that Elli was putting her house up for sale.

Maybe she didn't know.

It crossed my mind for the first time to wonder who was taking care of Elli's floral shop while she was gone. Was my sister getting texts from furious brides missing their bouquets while bins of flowers rotted in her warehouse? Or had she sold her business, too? I thought of those past-due invoices sitting in a pile in the kitchen, which my sister had left unsent, as if she'd just given up entirely.

I had the uncomfortable feeling that my sister was purging her life in Santa Barbara altogether.

A house too long unoccupied starts to feel like a tomb, a space taken out of time, lifeless. It had been only a few days since Charlotte and I were inside Elli's house, but now the feeling of the still air inside my sister's living room gave me goosebumps. I felt eyes on me, as if there were ghosts in the woodwork, watching.

I didn't linger downstairs but headed straight up to my sister's bedroom. The curtains were still closed, the bed still unmade, the robe still abandoned on the floor, but the binder that I'd left by the side of her bed was gone.

I stared at the empty surface of the side table: Was it possible that I'd put the binder somewhere else? But I remembered setting it carefully where I'd found it, squaring it neatly with the edges of the table, the way my sister would. Someone else had been in the house and taken it.

Was there something in it that I wasn't supposed to see?

My sister kept her files in the desk in the upstairs office, a room that had always been Chuck's domain. I headed down the hall and peered inside. The office had apparently been untouched since Chuck left. The bookshelves were still carefully dressed with his college sports trophies and books by James Patterson and paperweights from his business trips to China and Germany. The desk itself was a big wooden boat that reeked of male vanity, far too outsized for a home office. A half dozen framed photos lined one edge of the desk.

I picked one of these up—their wedding photo—and then another, surprised to see my own face alongside Elli's. It was a photo shoot from our teenage years, not long after we got our Nickelodeon show. Two blond heads pressed against each other, our hair intermingling, our smiles identical; although I could tell from the faint curve of a lip, a slight baring of another tooth, that the one on the right was me. I put it back and examined the rest—they were all of Elli and Chuck. There were no photos of Charlotte at all.

In fact, I realized, I hadn't seen a single photo of Charlotte in the entire house. Of course, Chuck had left only weeks before Charlotte arrived; a lot had been going on. And, of course, people don't have nearly as many framed photos anymore, now that snapshots so easily lived on your smartphone. But still, it struck me as odd that in four months, my sister hadn't found time to frame a single picture of her daughter.

I walked around the desk and began to throw open drawers, not exactly sure what I was looking for but hoping that whatever it was that I needed would reveal itself.

Chuck and Elli had meticulously organized files. *Mortgage / Health / Investments / Utilities.* Neatly labeled tabs marched in perfect symmetry across the span of the file drawers. Everything was color coded and organized by date. But there were no folders labeled *Adoption* or *Charlotte* or *Foster care.*

I closed the file drawers and quickly riffled through the rest: rubber bands and paper clips and neon sticky notes, a few loose keys rattling around, but nothing of interest. Most looked half-empty, as if Chuck had removed everything of value on his way out five months back.

Where else might my sister keep valuable documents? There were others missing, too, I realized: Elli's birth certificate and the title to her car and the deed to her home and her passport. Maybe this was all together in another file cabinet. There was a small closet on the opposite side of the office; I walked over and flung it open. Winter coats, sports equipment, no more cabinets but—on an upper shelf, tucked behind a box of snow boots and a can of tennis balls, there was a small gray fireproof lockbox.

I pulled this down—something inside was heavy, rattling—and brought it back to the desk. I collected the loose keys from the desk and tried them, one by one, in the lock. It opened on the third try.

Inside was a handgun.

This, I hadn't expected.

I stared at it for a long time, afraid to touch it. I'd never held a real gun before, though I'd held a convincing fake. On our second-to-last season of *To the Maxx,* Jenny had confronted a serial killer, shooting him in the stomach and killing him before her mother could arrive to help her. The scene was mine, and before I went on set they sent me down to the prop master to fit me with a handgun. What the prop master dug up for me looked just like a real gun; it even had the same heft. When he urged me to pull the trigger and give it a try, I balked, because it felt so realistic. But eventually, with his coaxing, I picked it up, pointed it at a wall, and pulled the trigger.

I could still remember how heavy the gun was in my hand, and the surprising backward kick when I pulled the trigger. The power in it made me feel like something hot inside me was trying to crawl out of my skin. I almost dropped it.

The prop master laughed, clearly delighted by the sight of a twelve-year-old girl wielding a Smith & Wesson. "And that's not nearly as intense as the real thing," he informed me.

This gun could have been a twin of that gun. Maybe it *was* the same gun, and my sister had saved it as a souvenir? Except that my sister had never even touched that gun—the scenes were mine, and I couldn't fathom Elli being nostalgic for an episode she hadn't performed.

I closed the lid of the lockbox, feeling oddly shaken. I couldn't imagine why Elli would own a gun. What was she trying to arm herself against? Thieves, roving marauders, the zombie apocalypse?

Or—Jesus—was she trying to protect herself against *me*?

Something broke open inside me at this thought, my heart flipping back and forth in my chest. I couldn't stand to be in my sister's house anymore. The hushed silence felt like judgment, the lifeless rooms an indictment. With shaky hands, I shoved the lockbox back up on the shelf where I'd found it. I made my way back down the stairs and to the front door, past the vases of rotting flowers and the spill of junk mail that had carpeted the parquet floor under the mail slot.

I had my hand on the doorknob when, just on the other side of the wood, I heard the sound of movement on the front porch. A key rattled in the lock.

Elli came home, I thought with relief as the door swung open.

But it wasn't Elli. Instead, it was a young brunette woman in a slim blue suit and sky-high heels, who stared at me with shock as she stood in the doorway, a key dangling from her fist. "Oh my God, Elli, I didn't realize you guys were here or I would have rung the doorbell."

"I'm not Elli," I said. "I'm her sister."

"Oh, *right*. Of course. I used to watch your show." She blushed, then looked down at a folder she was holding in her hand. "I'm working with your sister's listing agent. I don't want to bother you, but—she asked me to leave some documents inside the house for her."

Something tightened in me. "You've spoken to her recently?"

The woman slid a foot out of her stiletto, flexed it painfully, and offered me a crooked smile. "Well, *I* haven't. But my boss has. We're doing our first open house this Sunday."

My relief—*so I guess she's OK after all*—was quickly chased off by a swell of unexpected anger. Apparently my sister was talking to her real estate broker, even as she was avoiding her family entirely. Clearly, then, she wasn't being held at GenFem against her will—and wasn't in mortal danger, either—so what was her issue with *us*? Not a single call to check on her daughter, even as she was arranging the staging of her house?

The woman couldn't stop gaping at me. She thrust the folder out to me, almost as if it were a defensive shield. "Do you want to just take these? I'm supposed to leave them in the upper drawer of the console in the living room."

I took the folder from her hand. "What is it?"

"Comps, mostly. An inspection report. Some documents for her to sign." She hesitated. "You're not staying here, are you? Because we need it vacant for the open house . . ."

"I'm not staying here."

She looked relieved. "Oh good. We're hoping to be in escrow by this time next week. Move while the market's hot."

This sounded awfully hasty to me, but then again I wasn't exactly a real estate expert. "When did she decide to list the house?" I asked.

She shrugged. "I was told on Monday a week ago."

I did the math: This was just after she texted our mother that she was planning to stay at the retreat "a few more days." Now I had to wonder if she ever intended to come back.

I thanked the real estate agent and closed the door, a tight headache coming on, the *wrongness* of everything pulsing at my temples. I looked down at the sheaf of papers in my hand: What was I supposed to do with these? Right, the console in the living room.

The console was a marble-topped mahogany chest, carved with flowering vines, with a big drawer that locked with an old-fashioned key. I opened this and discovered that the drawer already held a pile of folders labeled in my sister's handwriting. I picked up the stack and flipped through them. Here were the important documents that had been missing from the file drawer upstairs. The folders held her birth certificate, the deed to the house, her passport and immunization records, and the title to her BMW.

Why here, and not in the desk? It was as if she'd pulled them out from the drawers up there and left them here for someone else to find.

I riffled through the pile again, realizing that the most important folder, the one I'd been looking for in the first place, was the only one that was still missing. Where were Charlotte's adoption papers? Why was there nothing at all documenting her existence in Elli's life? Surely there would have been reams of paperwork, a trail leading back to the very first point of contact, even if she was just being fostered. Had someone already removed this folder?

There was one last file folder on the bottom of the stack, this one unlabeled and seemingly empty. I flipped it open, just to check, and out fell a yellow piece of paper, torn from a lined notepad. It drifted to the floor, and I picked it up to examine it. The page contained a list of addresses, scribbled in hasty handwriting that I recognized as my sister's.

17344 Catalpa Way
Burbank, CA

72 Buena Vista Ave
Laguna Beach, CA

825 Joshua Tree Drive
Scottsdale, AZ

Why had my sister written these addresses down, and why were they here among her most important documents? I examined the addresses again; nothing about them struck a note of familiarity. None of them local to Santa Barbara, I noticed, and none with names attached.

The list could be nothing at all—a folder she thought was empty, mixed in here by accident. Still, something about its presence felt significant.

An arc of small red droplets fanned out across the top of the page, like the splatter from a miniature garden hose. I scratched at the biggest splotch with my fingernail, but it had soaked into the paper long ago. It looked suspiciously like dried blood.

This time, I wasn't taking chances. I took the pile of folders and shoved them all in my purse. Maybe the person who had taken the GenFem binder and Charlotte's adoption paperwork was planning to come back for these, too. If so, I sure as hell wasn't going to let her have them.

ELLI AND I DIDN'T return to Hollywood until we were fifteen years old, more than a year after we were killed off *To the Maxx*. Instead, we spent our freshman year of high school playing at "normal," attending a public school in Santa Barbara down the hill from our house, alongside kids who lived in the neighboring homes but were mostly strangers to us. My mother insisted this was her idea. "It would be good for you girls to take a break from acting, have a normal life," she'd said, as she filled out the registration packets. But I knew that Elli had begged her for this behind my back. I'd seen how, whenever we visited Santa Barbara, Elli would eye the girls who walked past our house in the morning—backpacks slung over their shoulders, giggling behind open palms, flicking their ponytails into the sun. I could see how much she wanted this, and so when my mother suggested, "Maybe we give high school a try for a while," I shrugged and said, "Fine."

I tried—I really did—to be OK with it.

My sister threw herself into high school with a fervor I'd never before witnessed in her. She went out for cheerleading. She joined the student council. She tried out for the soccer team and volunteered for school fundraisers and even attended homecoming with an exchange student from Sweden.

Meanwhile, I sulked. Santa Barbara didn't feel normal to me anymore. "Normal" was the life we'd left behind in L.A.: our tiny trailer and the Hollywood sets we knew by heart, the catering wagons that fed us Caesar salad and chicken skewers, the sterile apartment building full of aspiring actors with symmetrical faces. I hadn't had friends my own age in years. Outside of Elli, my friends were the middle-aged grips and the woman who patted concealer on my pimples every day and fed me Adderall. How was I supposed to go sit in a classroom with a bunch of strange kids and pretend I was suddenly interested in Shakespeare and passing notes when I had already lived in the sophisticated world of grown-ups, gone to the Emmys, shopped for designer dresses at Barneys, and gotten a paycheck with five figures on it?

And worse, now that I wasn't Jenny Maxx anymore—or even Sam Logan, Actress—did that mean I was going to have to figure out how to be someone else? Who *was* Samantha Logan, Normal Kid, anyway?

My only concession to a social life in Santa Barbara was joining the film club, where I was the solitary girl among a group of kindly male geeks who spent their weekends debating the merits of assorted Criterion Collection films and gaping at me. When I was with them, I felt like I was onstage. I liked that.

To placate me—and to keep our résumés current—Harriet booked Elli and me a few small parts in big movies and guest appearances in network dramas, jobs that pulled us out of school for a week at a time. Our absences were forgiven by the high school principal, who liked to brag about his celebrity students to incoming parents. But this probably didn't help our situation when it came to our peers. Our recurring absences and special treatment just reminded the other students that we weren't like them, no matter how much my sister pretended otherwise.

I hated it in Santa Barbara. I hated how different I felt from the other girls in the school. Worse, I hated how much Elli wanted to be like them; it was as if she'd spent the last four years living on

Mars and now was studying at the feet of earthlings, trying to pass as one even though she and I were (I knew!) creatures of the stars.

But most of all, I hated how I could feel her slipping away from me. Different homerooms, different class schedules, different after-school activities. Elli's weekends were filled with soccer games and sleepovers; only rarely could I talk her into going on a hike with me in Rattlesnake Canyon or taking the bus to Starbucks. When I saw her in the hallways at school, she was always trailing after the group of popular girls she'd befriended; and even though she'd wave at me, beckon me into her circle, I knew I wasn't welcome. One twin was already too much spectacle for them; if I hung on, too, I'd doom my sister's chances.

In my parents' brand-new house, paid for with their proceeds from *To the Maxx,* we each had our own bedroom, something we hadn't requested but that had been presented to us as if it was a gift. To me, it felt like a punishment. I hated not being able to hear Elli's breath when I woke up in the middle of the night. I missed the stuffy intimacy of our tiny set trailer, ripe with our shared stink. Even the epic dollhouse that Elli had built for the two of us, all those years ago, had ended up in the trash when we moved.

Most of that year I felt like half of me had been ripped away and I was standing there, exposed and raw, hoping that Elli would come back to complete me.

One afternoon, as I sat in a bathroom stall killing time between classes, I overheard two of Elli's new friends talking about us.

"They're not even that good. I mean, that show they were on is so cheesy, right? My *grandma* watches it. And they got killed off, which means that the audience didn't like them very much." I recognized the sharp crystal tones of the voice lifting over the stall door. It was a pretty redhead named Annika, a cheerleader who doodled lists of her best friends' names on her binder during class. I sat behind her in math and I could see over her shoulder. Elli had never made Annika's list. "You're a much better actress."

"I mean, *thank you*. But yes, right?" I could hear the faint pop of lip gloss being uncorked, the sound of smacking lips. This was Brittany, a bulimic brunette who, until we showed up, had considered herself the class thespian. She was currently playing the role of Red Riding Hood in the school production of *Into the Woods*—a production I'd carefully stayed far away from, not only because I couldn't sing but because I didn't want to come off as attention-seeking and damage Elli's efforts at friendship.

I'd gone to the opening night with Elli, though. Brittany's performance was pitchy and overwrought.

"They think they're *so* special. I mean, they didn't even go out for the musical; like, they think they're better than us?"

The sandpaper rattle of paper towels being yanked from a dispenser, then, "Sam does. Elli is just kind of a fake, so nicey-nice all the time. It's so obvious that she wants so *badly* for us to like her."

"She's the one who follows me around like a puppy dog, right?" Annika snickered. "Honestly, I can't really tell them apart."

A squeak of the door hinges and they were gone. I sat on the toilet seat, enraged; not because their assessments of us were so wrong (Elli *was* nicey-nice, and I *did* think myself better than Brittany), but because of their unwillingness to be generous about it. The ego of a teenage girl is a vicious thing; it relies on manufactured superiority to counteract all that rampant insecurity. We intimidated these girls, Elli and I, with our Hollywood polish and our knowledge of a life they only read about in magazines. We were never going to fit in.

I moved through the rest of that year like an unmoored sleepwalker, popping Adderall just so that I could feel alive, the way I had on set when I was playing two parts. It didn't help.

And so, when Harriet came to us at the end of that school year with a dream role—starring as twins in a new Nickelodeon series—I pushed Elli to take the job. No, that's not quite true: I *manipulated* her. I wept on her bed as she stared at me with alarm, my tears only slightly enhanced—even then, I was good at crying on cue—wailing, "I hate it here, the girls are so mean, we don't fit in."

"They're not that bad." She sounded crumpled, like a wad of discarded Kleenex. "They all grew up together and we're strangers to them. We intimidate them. We need to prove ourselves. You need to put some effort in. It'll just take time."

I could tell that the idea of going back to Hollywood panicked her. I was panicked, too. In her fearful blue eyes I saw my own future drying up and blowing away, like dead leaves scattered by a fall wind. If I let Elli win this time, I knew that it meant we would never act together again. Instead, I would be stuck here, in Santa Barbara, watching my sister drift further and further away, having lost not just one of the things I loved the most but *all* of them.

I let selfishness win.

"I don't *want* to waste any more time." I swallowed, dredged up the ammunition I'd been saving up since the day I first put on Elli's face and walked on set: "You *owe* me. For when I pretended to be you. I did that for you. It's your turn to do something for me. I *want* this."

Her throat moved up and down; she was swallowing back her tears. "I know, but—"

But I hate acting. She didn't have to say it, because I knew it already. Even then, I understood that *performance* went against my sister's instincts. I thought I could find myself in a character; she was afraid of losing herself. She didn't want to be onstage, pretending to be someone else. She mostly wanted to be left alone.

Maybe that scared me. Maybe that's why I pulled out the big cudgel, the one I knew would make her do what I wanted.

"Don't do this to us," I said. "Don't ruin our relationship. Because you will if you say no."

She pushed the palm of her hand into an eye, smeared away a tear. She sighed. "Fine."

"Thank you." I hugged her, feeling her soften and grow limp in my arms. As toddlers, we'd slept in the same bed, our arms wrapped around each other, breathing in time. These days, I realized, we rarely touched each other. As I pressed my face into her hair, the smell of her came as a shock to me. There was the shampoo we both used, and the citrus of our mother's detergent, and the familiar sweet tang of our identical body odor; but there was something new underneath this now, something dangerously unfamiliar to me. A sour tang, like a frightened animal: the scent of our growing difference.

I pushed this aside. We were going back to Hollywood. We were going to be together again.

Before, on *To the Maxx,* we'd been token children on a show for and about adults. There were rarely any other kids on set. This time, we were teenagers doing a show on a kids' network with a whole portfolio of fresh-faced young stars. It was a whole new ball game.

Finally, *finally,* my sister and I had each been given our own part. She was Jamie and I was Jessie, twins separated at birth who end up at the same high school by accident. The parts had been written to fit our personalities—Jessie the bold one, Jamie the straitlaced one—which suited Elli just fine, as it didn't require much of a stretch on her part. And if I chafed a little at the corny dialogue the writers put in our mouths, or the ludicrous scenarios they imagined for us—well, at least I was being treated like the main event now, instead of a footnote in someone else's story.

The television executives imagined they had a new pair of Olsen twins on their hands—and I, for one, was prepared to believe them—but in retrospect nothing about our show was ever going to launch us toward that level of stardom. *On the Double* was totally mediocre. No one beyond a subset of eleven- to sixteen-year-old girls watched it. And yet, in the small world that we inhabited, we felt enormous. The tweens that did tune in were rabid fans. We couldn't get a pedicure without a shrieking pubescent accosting us for an autograph.

There were promotional events, so many obligatory appearances at mall openings and amusement parks and morning shows. Often, we did these with the other teens in our network's lineup: the four girls who played members of a teen rock band, the boy in a wheelchair who played a detective in a teen mystery show, the two kids who played sibling ghosts. We were part of a family of teen stars now. We attended set school with them; we got invited to the same brand-sponsored pool parties; we ate lunch together in the backlot cafeteria and complained about the executives who controlled our every move and the stylists who chose our clothes. For the first time, it felt like we had real peers, and I could tell that made my sister happier.

I'd believed that being back in Hollywood would bring my sister and me close again: a return to the swampy intimacy of trailer living and shared moisturizer, our own little world of two. And for a while, it did. The moments when we weren't in each other's company were rare. Most days we were on the studio lot, standing side by side under the hot lights, all eyes on us as we built a *show* together. At night, we whispered each other to sleep: gossip from the set, who we had crushes on and who we disliked. I did my homework with my head in Elli's lap. She popped the zits on my back.

But being close again presented issues of its own. Because I had secrets now, and while I was adept at hiding them from my mother and the crew on our show (if nothing else, acting had taught me the art of deception), it was much harder to conceal them from my sister.

Elli found the Adderall one night, late in our first season. We were back at the apartment, studying the next day's scenes while our mother made dinner. She'd gone fishing for a stick of gum in my purse and came up with the half-empty bottle instead. She held it up to the light, jiggled it, frowned. "What the hell are these, Sam?"

I looked up from my script. Elli thrust the pill bottle toward me, shook it like a rattle. In the kitchen, my mother was warming up takeout ramen; I heard the beep of the microwave and the faint murmur of her voice on the phone with our father, reporting in on our day.

"Shhh," I hushed my sister. I jumped up and snatched the bottle from Elli's hand. "They're for concentrating."

Elli looked confused. "You never had a problem concentrating before."

"I was taking these before."

"Oh." She wrapped a strand of hair around her finger, twisted it tight. It was brittle from the highlights and hairspray they used on it. "Where do you even get it?"

I was getting it from a wardrobe assistant. Bettina was long gone, but it turned out that prescription pills of all varieties are easy to find on a set staffed by twentysomethings otherwise paid minimum wage. "The set doctor," I lied. I popped open the pill bottle, poured a few capsules into my palm and thrust them toward her. "Here, try one. You'll see. It's no big deal. It's kind of like coffee."

I wanted her to take one. I wanted her to join me inside its pleasant penumbra, for the pill to wake her up and make her feel alive the way it made me. I wanted the pills to be another thing that we shared, a circle we could draw around our secret world. Maybe I already knew then that our differences were starting to be greater than our similarities, that the shared face that bound us together was being overpowered by the disparities in our personalities.

She made a face and drew back. "Coffee makes me jittery."

Our mother appeared in the doorframe, steaming bowls in her hand. "Don't tell Mom, OK?" I whispered.

And she didn't—not that year, at least—but I could tell that the pills were a wedge that had been pushed between us. I saw how she would stare at me sometimes, when she thought I wasn't paying attention: As if she were trying to see something hidden underneath my skin. As if I were a puzzle she didn't know how to piece together anymore.

A year passed, and part of another, and we were turning seventeen as B-list stars. The studio threw us a birthday party at a Mexican restaurant in West Hollywood, with a cake that featured our faces rendered in frosting and a phalanx of photographers from the gossip websites and magazines that fed our teenage fans. Because it was a promotional event, the studio sent a stylist out with our outfits: identical silver dresses, with our characters' signatures scrawled across the front in pink sequins. *Jessie* and *Jamie* were apparently turning seventeen, not Elli and Sam.

All of young Hollywood was there. I'd recently acquired my first boyfriend. Nick was two years older than me, possessed a fatal set of dimples and a whoosh of curly black hair, and was the star of his own eponymous game show on the same network as us. Nick had 429,010 followers on Facebook, mostly underage girls who cropped me out of the paparazzi photos of us that appeared online. Nick liked me, and he also liked to party, so he had recently introduced me to tequila and pot. I was on the verge of losing my virginity, though I'd held off out of a sense of allegiance to my sister.

Elli still had never been kissed. The erstwhile fame that I used to boost my self-confidence did the opposite to her: She constantly questioned the motivations of the people around us. As a result, boys who found us attractive seemed to gravitate to me—*Sam the fun one, always ready for a good time*—instead of her. And this felt like another wedge that was being driven between us, a widening gap that I was starting to worry we might never be able to close.

The night of our birthday party, I talked Elli into drinking a Long Island Iced Tea—*Iced tea! It's practically a soft drink!*—and she got tipsy enough to join me on the light-up dance floor that the studio had installed under the stars. We danced together to the Black Eyed Peas as the crowd watched, camera flashes popping like comets in the night sky, our hands on each other's silvered hips, laughing as we stared with mock intensity into each other's eyes. Purple and yellow patches of light blinked on and off beneath our feet.

I noticed a boy standing on the edge of the dance floor, too nervous to step out and join us: an actor who had just joined the cast of *On the Double* in a supporting role. "Dale's staring at you," I murmured in her ear, over the thump of the bass. "You should kiss him."

She glanced over her shoulder to look at him. He was soft-chinned, wearing a plaid shirt that was buttoned slightly too high, as if his mother had dressed him. "Ew," she whispered. "He's a dork."

"He's cute!"

"He's not nearly as cute as Nick and you know it."

I pulled back to look at her face. She was flushed. Maybe it was just the alcohol, but she wouldn't meet my eyes. "Oh my God, you like Nick?"

She shook her head woozily, blond hair whipping around and catching on her lips. "Nooo!" She stumbled a little in the kitten heels the stylists had picked out for us, a half size too big. I looked around the patio and finally located Nick. He was lounging at a table in the far corner of the restaurant, smoking a cigarette and holding court with a group of girls I didn't recognize. He looked smeary. He saw me staring at him and raised his glass in a mock toast. *Cheers.* Even then, I knew he was temporary.

But Elli wasn't.

"Come with me," I whispered, and grabbed my sister's hand, dragging her off the dance floor and toward the bathroom. Once we were inside, I locked the door and began pulling off my dress.

Elli watched with confusion as I stripped down to my underwear. "What are you *doing*?"

"Put this on." I shoved the dress at her. *Jessie* in scrawled cursive on the front. "Be me. Go kiss him."

"Kiss Dale? I told you—"

"Kiss *Nick*."

She laughed, a nervous snort that ended in a hiccup. "But he's your boyfriend!"

I gripped her shoulders, turned her around, began unzipping the *Jamie* dress. "Consider it my birthday present to you."

She stood there in her bra and panties, pale eyelet, her skin a milky blue in the fluorescent bathroom light. "*Sam*. I can't."

"You can. It's just acting. You're an *actor*, remember?" I pushed my cup into her hand, with the salty remains of my half-drunk margarita. "Drink this. Then go out there and sit in his lap and just kiss him. He won't know the difference. He's loaded."

She gazed into my drink, a watery smile on her face. "You're sure?" She tipped the glass to her mouth, grimaced, licked salt from the rim.

"I don't want anything if you can't have it, too," I said, and I yanked my dress over her head.

Was it cruel of me to send her out like that, my alter ego's name written across her body? Was I testing my new boyfriend—to see how well he really knew me? Or was I testing *her*, with the same question in mind? Elli and I had been each other before; were we still close enough to pull it off now?

Or was the whole setup with Nick just a ruse to claw her back over the gap that had formed between us? Was I forcing her into another secret in order to bind her to me?

And so I watched her, from the far side of the restaurant, as she made her way to my boyfriend. I noted the split second of hesitation, the wobble in those oversized heels, before she let herself sink into his lap. I saw her eyes blink once, in apparent surprise, as he slid his unsuspecting arms around her, still chatting with the girl beside him. And I didn't turn away when she turned sideways in Nick's embrace, tipped her face down, and pressed her lips to his.

I didn't turn away; I watched. It was like I was watching myself in a mirror, and I was fascinated by my own reflection. The way my sister's jaw moved up and down, the lump of his tongue in her mouth, how her hand slid up his back. Was that what I looked like when I was with him, too? I could almost feel him, his hard muscles bunching underneath her palm, his lips liquid under hers. It was as if I were with her in his lap, as if my sister and I had suddenly slid into one body. I felt a strange kind of joy, coupled with a pang of pain that I hadn't anticipated: Did he not even notice? Were we truly *that* interchangeable?

And then her eyes flew open and she jerked up and out of his lap, flying away from him as if he'd electrocuted her. She stumbled toward the edge of the patio, ringed with potted palms.

I waited for her to look over at me. I waited for her to meet my eyes with implicit acknowledgment: *Now I know what it feels like to kiss a boy. I get it. We can be closer again, now that we've shared the same experience.*

But she wouldn't look at me at all. Instead, she gripped the edge of a planter, bent over, and threw up in the dirt. Camera flashes bloomed bright all around her.

———

The photos ended up on a gossip website—"Sam Logan Pukes at Her Own Party"—and minted my new reputation as a Hollywood bad girl.

Our mother was the one who rescued Elli that night, spiriting her through the restaurant kitchen to clean her up and then out to our waiting Town Car. I never knew whether Elli told her or my mother figured out what had happened all on her own. But she found me hiding out in the bathroom and forced me to put back on my own vomit-crusted dress before marching me back through my own party.

"You can't do that to other people, tricking them like that. And you *cannot* do that to Elli." She yanked the zipper so hard that it bit into the skin of my back. "Maybe you think you can handle it, but she definitely can't."

"But she wanted to do it."

My mother spun me around and looked at me, smoothing my hair away from my face. "She *wants* to make people happy. She wants to make *you* happy. She'll do anything that someone tells her to do if she thinks that it will eliminate conflict. And that means that you have to be the smart one here, for the both of you."

"Why is that on *me*?"

"Because." My mother pressed her hand gently on my jaw. It was cool against my skin, but firm, as if she was holding my chin upright. There was a sadness in her face that I'd never seen before. Since we'd come back to L.A. and grown up so quickly, I'd taken our mother for granted—treated her like an employee, a manager, a chauffeur, a nuisance, an embarrassment. I'd forgotten what it felt like to have a mother who treats you like a child.

"Because you're her twin sister and you love her," she said. "And you need to watch out for her when she isn't watching out for herself. If she ever really gets herself in trouble, you have to be capable of helping her. Just like she'll help you." She patted my face once, before withdrawing her hand. "You're lucky, you have each other. Not all of us get that. So for God's sake, darling, don't throw it away."

We graduated from high school toward the end of the third season of our show. Elli and I had applied for college at our parents' insistence—my father put his foot down on that one, the tuition money being the primary reason he'd said yes to our acting in the first place—and managed to get admitted to the University of Southern California, University of California Santa Barbara, and New York University. I thought our destination was obvious: We would go to the film program at USC so that we could stay in town and continue working on our show.

Elli waited until the deadline had almost passed to tell me that she wouldn't be joining me at USC.

"I'm moving back home," she said. "I'm going to go to UC Santa Barbara."

We were in our bedroom in our Los Angeles apartment, just home from production, our hair still sticky with product and makeup ringing our jawlines. Elli perched on the edge of her bed as I sat across from her on mine. Just a few feet divided us but it felt like a world. "So, you're going to come in from Santa Barbara every time we need you on set? That's a lot of driving."

She twisted the bedsheet between her hands, balled it up in tightened fists. "That's the thing. Our contract for the show is up for renewal, right? And I think . . . I think I don't want to do it anymore. Now's the time to bow out, before we sign another contract."

I couldn't breathe. I'd just taken two Valium to come down from performing all day and it felt like my heart was beating out of time, a jarring arrhythmia. "But—Harriet was going to renegotiate. She said we can double, maybe triple, our rate."

"But then we have to commit to another two years." A knot rose and fell in her throat; I could see how much effort this conversation was taking. Had our mother put her up to this? *You have to be capable of helping her.*

"OK." My drug-loosened mind grappled at the strands of our conversation, tried to tie them back together. "OK. So we bail on this show, we use their offer as leverage to get cast on a better show. A . . . a prime-time show. Not a children's network. Harriet could do that! She'll get someone to write a pilot for us. Or . . . or . . . we write it ourselves! I was going to take screenwriting courses at USC anyway."

"You're not listening to me." Elli smoothed the sheet down again, tried to iron out the wrinkles she'd just twisted into the linen. "I don't want to perform anymore. I never really did. I only ever did it for you. Because you loved it and I knew you needed me to do it with you. But I'm done now. It's not my world."

"But it's mine," I whispered.

She stood and crossed over to sit next to me, pressed her knee against mine. I'd grown skinnier than her, I noticed; the pills I was taking were suppressing my appetite. "So *you* keep doing it. We don't need to do everything together, you know. You can go out there and be your own star. Not just one-half of a pair. You can be *you*."

We killed our contract a few weeks later, much to Harriet's dismay. *On the Double* died its untimely death, immediately relegated to the ash bin of forgotten kids' TV series. I helped my sister pack her things and drove her and my mother back to Santa Barbara. I even spent the summer with them there, tanning on the beach and getting pedicures and going to bonfires with some of Elli's old high school friends. They were nicer to us now that we were legitimate stars.

When the school year began, I drove back to Los Angeles,

started college, and began going out for auditions alone. I ran around the city like a madwoman, juggling scripts and home-work, using Adderall and Ritalin and the occasional line of co-caine to stay focused, then relying on booze and Valium to relax at the end of the day. I was finally living alone, far from the watch-ful eyes of my family, which meant that I could party as much as I wanted without getting the side-eye from my sister. And since I didn't have to hide my habits anymore, I let them balloon to fill up the empty space in my life where Elli had once been.

Before I was even legally old enough to drink, I'd become a full-blown addict.

The thing about addiction stories is that they are all the same, and they are boring. God knows I've heard enough of them to know. I've heard them at AA meetings and NA meetings, in group ther-apy circles at residential rehab centers and in books that my rehab counselors gave me to read. I've sat over cups of coffee in dark-ened cafés and let my new recovery friends spill their tales of woe to me, just as I've spilled mine, both of us hoping that our confes-sions might cement a new intimacy that would somehow keep us both sober.

It rarely did. And then when we found each other again, on the other side of yet another relapse, mostly what I'd feel was shame, to be repeating the same sad story that everyone had already heard before, hoping that this time it might finally culminate in a happy ending.

So, at the risk of boring you utterly, I will make my own addic-tion story brief.

At thirteen, as you already know, I took my first Adderall.

At fifteen, at a Grammy preparty, I had my first drink (a mar-garita, puckery and sweet, which remained my go-to cocktail for the next fifteen years).

At sixteen, with Nick, I smoked pot for the first time.

At eighteen, now in college, I turned to ecstasy and coke, which I consumed at the nightclubs that turned a blind eye to the under-age stars who drank themselves into stupors on their dance floors every weekend.

After that, there was some trendy dabbling with hallucinogens—acid and mushrooms, mostly—but these were never my thing. I didn't like the way they made me turn inward.

I tried heroin only once. Needles scared me, and something about the idea of heroin felt desperate to me. Heroin was the treacherous terrain of addicts and street dwellers; the drug that would end with me dead or living under a bridge, I told myself. As long as I didn't touch *that,* I had nothing to worry about. (Irony, rich.)

Instead, in my twenties, as my career started to go into free fall, I turned back to my original love: pills.

This time around, instead of pills that woke me up and made me feel alert, I turned to pills that blunted me and made me feel dreamy. I preferred opioids: Oxycontin, Vicodin, Percocet. I washed these down with vast quantities of alcohol, a daily roller-coaster ride that began each morning with a wash of euphoric calm, ascended into a giddy high, and then brought me crashing down into total obliteration. Most days I woke up not remember-ing most of what had happened after ten the previous evening. I didn't mind that one bit.

My career, you see, had not survived the Great Cleaving. No one had warned me that twins, while a valuable commodity as chil-dren, stop being so appealing as grown-ups. (Unless you're a porn star. There's no shortage of demand for twincest vids, judging by the producers who approached me.) As adults, acting twins are a freak show, doomed to supporting roles in fantasy films and family comedies. Even when there *is* a dramatic role for identical twins, they're usually just played by the same actor, a famous name making a play for that Oscar trophy.

There are even fewer parts for an actress whose main claim to fame is that she *was* a twin but isn't anymore. You are essentially half a person.

Harriet took me out to lunch at Barney Greengrass not long after I came back to Los Angeles alone that fall. "I'm not going to lie to you, it's going to be tough," she warned me. She picked at her smoked fish, moving it left and right across the plate. "We need to rebrand you. Make everyone forget that Elli ever existed. It's going to be like your career up until this point didn't really happen."

"I can change my name if that helps. I'll be Samantha instead of Sam." I looked at her hopefully. If anyone could figure out the situation, it was Harriet, who in her four decades in Hollywood had surely seen it all.

Harriet sighed, pushed her reading glasses back up onto her nose. She'd grown thin, dark circles under her eyes, her signature smoking jacket billowing around her torso. "We need to go deeper than that. Who are you as an actress, if you're not playing opposite your sister? You can't play *adorable twin* anymore. So what's the story you plan to sell instead? Girl next door? Intellectual smarty-pants? Strong-willed badass?" She eyed me over the rims of her glasses. "Party girl?"

I blushed. The previous weekend, I'd gotten obliterated at a nightclub with a group of young actors and had been papped falling down on a sidewalk in Hollywood, my lace underwear visible under my hiked-up miniskirt. The photos showed up on TMZ, with the caption "Logan Twin Loses It Again." "That was a one-time thing," I lied.

"No it wasn't." Harriet coughed, an alarming wheeze that escalated into an uncontrollable hack. She pressed a napkin to her lips, and it came away pink. "I'm not your mother, so I'm not going to tell you what to do. I'm not even going to get into the addiction question of it all, though I'll tell you I know what's at the end of this road you're going down, and it's not pretty. But practically speaking, you should know that casting agents pay attention to these things. They read the gossip pages, precisely so they know what they're up against. Reliability is an asset, Sam. You want me to help you do this, you're going to have to help yourself."

I tried to follow her advice, I really did. I went home after that meeting determined to sober up, stop going out, stay straight and focused on my career. I stayed away from nightclubs, buckled down on homework, doubled up on auditions.

Who did I want to be as an actress? Harriet's question clung to me. A star, of course, but maybe one who did the occasional theater stint. A Scarlett Johansson, or a Natalie Portman—the kind of actress who would open a blockbuster movie and also get an arty black-and-white portrait in *The New York Times Magazine* Great Performers issue. I signed up for a Shakespeare class and a course about silent-film Hollywood, thinking to myself that Harriet would be impressed with how serious I was becoming.

I never got a chance to tell her. Seven weeks after our lunch, I woke up to a headline in *Variety:* "Legendary Agent Harriet Sunday Dies of Complications from Lung Cancer." It had been a fatal pulmonary thromboembolism. She hadn't even told her clients she was sick.

Elli came down for the funeral and we clung to each other at Harriet's grave, and then she went back to Santa Barbara to take finals and I completely fell apart. I felt untethered, as if all the responsible eyes on me had vanished, and now that I was unobserved, I didn't have a clue who I should be anymore.

I began doing a tequila shot with my coffee in the morning,

and by the time the end of my freshman year rolled around I was generally loaded by midafternoon.

I found a new agent, a thirtysomething guy who wore ironic socks, drove a Porsche, and talked a good game but kept calling me Sammy on our phone calls. Without a true champion, the auditions started to shrivel up almost immediately. I was a good actress, but not so good that I stood out; and my reputation—as a twin, as a child actor, as a party girl—preceded me, an anchor I couldn't unlodge without the goodwill granted to one of "Harriet's girls." I booked the occasional part, mostly in indie films that never made it past the film festival circuit, or guest appearances in short-lived television comedies. I even managed to get a sizable "best friend" role in a superhero franchise film, which seemed like it might be my big breakthrough, except that the movie bombed at the box office and ended up being a liability on my résumé.

I managed a few years at USC, but all those years of low-demand school on set of our shows had left me with lackluster study habits; plus, I missed too many classes for jobs and auditions, so my grades were dismal. Eventually I just gave up and dropped out to "focus on my career," as I told my family. But there wasn't much of a career to focus on, just an endless parade of auditions that seemed to lead nowhere even as I watched my acting peers sprint past me and off into the distance.

It's hard to describe the humiliation that comes with the dawning awareness that you have already peaked by your early twenties; that, in fact, your career high had come and gone before you even graduated high school. Your ego shrinks with each fresh rejection, until all that's left is a peanut of hard, bitter self-doubt. As the jobs got smaller and smaller, I could see the endgame, and it was no longer black-and-white portraiture. It was obsolescence.

I filled the void with alcohol and pills, which took the sting out of my empty days. But that meant I was partying too much, and the wicked hangovers (combined with a growing sense of futility) led to a few too many missed auditions. I was blackballed by casting agents because of this, and by twenty-six my career was essentially over other than the occasional role in a low-budget horror film.

Somehow I'd eked out a living without having to think much about the state of my bank account. Even if the indies and the bit parts didn't pay well, I still had the syndication checks from *To the Maxx* trickling in every few months. But as the years passed, the four-figure check I'd come to count on became a three-figure check, and then two, as the reruns dried up. Elli and I had been paid generously for *On the Double,* but even a seven-figure bank account dwindles quickly when you're not replenishing it.

Especially with a habit like mine.

By my mid-twenties, I was spending six figures a year on this habit—pills for twenty to forty dollars a pop, a dozen a day, plus a similar number of fifteen-dollar cocktails when I went barhopping each night. An average day might cost me five hundred dollars. Add in the cost of an upscale residential rehab program—four rounds, at thirty to forty thousand per stay—plus the two-hundred-an-hour counselors and therapists to help me get to "the root of my dependencies," and I spent a cool million dollars on my addictions over the course of the decade.

By the time I realized that I was broke, I was in a hole so deep that it felt like I might never climb out again. Instead of curbing my habit—or doing something logical, like considering a whole new career trajectory—I started selling everything of value that I owned to supplement my increasingly meager acting income. First, the small condo that I'd bought in West Hollywood at age nineteen. Then my designer clothes—straight to consignment. My Porsche, my midcentury modern furniture, a portrait that a now-famous photographer once took of me and my sister: all gone. I sold everything I had, right down to my plasma and my hair, stopping just shy of selling my body on the streets of Holly-wood.

The big question for any addict is *why*. Yes, there are biological factors, genes passed down, an ancestral weakness in the DNA, and in my case these were easy to pinpoint: I had alcoholic grand-parents on both sides, and my mother always *did* love her wine a bit more than she probably should. Addiction can also be blamed on the neurodevelopmental damage that comes from childhood experiences; and surely becoming a child actor so young—living my life as a performance for adult approval while divorced from "normal" friendships with my peers—did its psychological dam-age on me. The therapists that I went to told me that I had be-come addicted to being the center of attention, and when that disappeared I looked for other ways to replicate the high that I'd once gotten from fame.

In other words, I'd destroyed myself by trying to perpetually remain the teenage ingenue in the silver dress, flashbulbs popping, the star of my own life.

If you ask me, though, I turned to intoxicants because I was lonely. Because the most essential part of me had been severed from me—my Elli, my twin, my other half—and there was no one to replace her with. I'd never had real friends, only transients and sycophants and employees, or the kids who passed through my set on their way to their own. I'd never much bothered with them because I had Elli; I didn't *need* them. So by the time I struck out on my own, I'd honestly forgotten how to make friends. I still felt an itchy need for companionship, like a phantom limb—I *knew* I was too alone—but mostly what I wanted was Elli. Opioids and alcohol paved over that hole, smoothed it out until it was shallow, a barely noticeable dent. As long as I remained high, following the party crowd from bar to nightclub to afterparty, I was fine.

I didn't blame my sister for the path that my life had taken without her. Would things have been any different if she'd stayed, and we'd watched our novelty twin act fade away into bit parts in children's movies? Probably not. Maybe, though . . . maybe if she'd been there to prop me up, I wouldn't have fallen so low.

But that kind of conjecture is pointless. If I've learned nothing else from years of rehab, it's that the person responsible for your addiction is ultimately always yourself.

12 IT HAD NOW BEEN six days since I arrived in Santa Barbara and I'd said I was only going to stay a long weekend, but no one seemed particularly concerned about the fact that I was still there. Probably because the minute I left they would have to start changing Charlotte's Pull-Ups themselves. The way I saw it, my ongoing presence was a sign that things with my sister were decidedly *not right*—that she had not, as my mother insisted she would, figured out her shit and come back to retrieve her daughter. And yet my mother's capacity for intentional blindness was breathtaking. Behind his morning newspaper, my father was looking more gray and drawn by the day—*he* understood, surely, that something had gone sideways—but my mother's chirpy positivity was like a bulldozer, paving him under.

"So what do my girls have planned today?" My mother was buzzing around the kitchen, spooning chia seeds into coconut milk, squeezing lemon into her green tea. I sat next to Charlotte at the breakfast table, cutting bananas into coins that the toddler shoved into her mouth with slimy fists.

"First the park," I said. "Then maybe we'll go to the aquarium."

My mom brightened. "Doesn't *that* sound nice?"

It did sound nice. It was also not at all what I had planned for the day.

I'd spent the previous evening, after my return from my sister's house, doing deeper internet searches on GenFem. There wasn't much to be found. I started with their website, searching for clues, but the pages offered no insights about what I'd seen at that Ojai compound. None of the photos featured women with shaved heads or identical dresses, just ones that looked like people you might run into in the Whole Foods produce aisle. The group's website copy didn't help, either: It could have been taken from a corporate marketing newsletter, full of anodyne promises about building *internal strength strategies* and *reenacting critical moments in order to transcend past choices* and *building an international matriarchal sisterhood.*

I read it over and over, trying to figure out how this generic pabulum had convinced my sister to walk out of her life. Then I plugged *GenFem* and *cult* into Google, just to see what came up.

It spit out a few results, most of them posts from a subreddit titled "r/cults." I clicked on a post by a woman who identified herself only as "a former member."

> *I'm not putting my name here bc GenFem is litigious AF and I don't want to end up being sued but I spent $67,000 over the course of a year on "seminars" and one-on-one sessions that were supposed to launch me up some ladder to enlightenment & success and instead all I ended up was broke. Dr. Cindy just kind of . . . gets into your head. And not in a good way. The women do whatever she tells them to do out of fear of pissing her off and getting a Sufferance. Like, she thought my boyfriend was holding me back and when I told her that I didn't want to dump him, she told me that I was just insecure because I was overweight and didn't have any self-confidence. And maybe she was a little bit right but it all felt so intimidating. My punishment was losing 20 pounds so fast that my hair started falling out. Oh, and she encouraged me to do all kinds of vengeance shit to*

him that was borderline illegal, too. All in the name of
some kind of perverse female power. STAY AWAY.

I found a few other mentions of the group online, primarily on self-help bulletin boards where members attested to positive life changes that they attributed to their membership in GenFem— *I'm so much happier and more confident! I was bankrupt and now I'm a millionaire!* A Yelp page for the Canadian center had a few one-star reviews, mostly from people who complained the program didn't produce the miracles they'd expected, especially considering the cost. But these had been drowned out by a deluge of five-star reviews, all suspiciously similar.

A little further digging and I learned that Dr. Cindy Medina had previously owned a therapy practice in Connecticut, but had abruptly shut it down a decade back. A local Connecticut court website listed a lawsuit that had been filed against her by three former clients, but there were no details. GenFem had sprung up a few years later, thousands of miles away on the opposite coast. Dr. Medina *did* have a degree in psychiatry, and a PhD in psychology, from colleges I'd heard of; but she also had certification in hypnotherapy and "neurolinguistic programming," which Wikipedia categorized as a pseudoscience.

After that, the well ran dry. GenFem had managed to exist under the radar, as far as the internet was concerned.

I wondered if I should enlist Caleb's help he'd been a reporter once, maybe he knew more about detective work than I did. And then I wondered if I was just trying to come up with an excuse to call him because I liked him. And since I could already count all the ways *that* might spin out badly and lead to further disappointment, I froze up entirely. Instead, our last correspondence had been a shrug emoji, which I'd sent as a cryptic response to a text he'd sent: *How's it going? Any news from Ojai?*

Even sober, I was the queen of self-sabotage.

Anyway—this was what I had to work with: a missing binder,

a bizarre-seeming compound in Ojai, an eye-popping list of expenses, and a sister who wouldn't return my texts. It didn't add up to anything concrete. It didn't give me anywhere to start looking for answers.

Except for those three addresses.

I pulled the list out from the pile of folders I'd stolen and studied them. Perhaps the list was a clue to understanding my sister's situation. Then again, it could also be an irrelevant memo that was intended for the trash: an aborted Christmas card list, the addresses of former clients, people she'd met in an internet forum. Desperation and paranoia often manifest patterns where there are none: We think we see meaning in scraps. But I had nothing else to go on, and two of the addresses were a reasonable drive from Santa Barbara. Why not go check them out, at the very least?

It wasn't much of a plan, but it was something.

I'd stayed up past midnight, reading up on cults and mind control, and then woken up early with Charlotte; so now I downed a third cup of coffee as I shoved Puffs and sippy cups into the diaper bag. I had no intention of telling my mother what I was up to. *Stirring up trouble,* she'd call it. That's what I remained, even now: the troublemaker. I wondered how long Elli would have to remain missing before my mother would start to question her trust in my sister's good sense. Better to wait until I had firm proof that my sister was involved in something unsavory.

Instead I left my mother marinating in her own blind optimism, limping back and forth across the kitchen while the healing crystals clacked in her robe pockets. I figured, let her be happy for one more day.

Charlotte and I headed south, toward Burbank and the first address on Elli's list. Ninety minutes later, we descended into the hot haze of the San Fernando Valley, turning off Interstate 5 and up into the sun-parched hills that loomed over the suburban sprawl below. The house at 17344 Catalpa Way was an enormous Mediterranean, a modern beige salute to a villa in the Riviera, but with a three-car garage and a pool with a waterslide out back. Below, in the valley, a procession of airplanes took off from the Burbank airport, banking right and over the green belt of Forest Lawn cemetery, before disappearing out toward the sea.

I parked, extricated Charlotte from her car seat, and carried her up to the front door. When I rang the bell, I could hear chimes echoing in the hall beyond, and then, moments later, the tumble of footsteps, a voice shouting, and finally a fumbling at the door.

When it opened, chaos erupted. First a small white dog with a leopard-print collar came bursting through, barking shrilly at me, nipping at my ankle. This was followed by a little girl in a cropped T-shirt that spelled *Mommy's Superstar* over a protruding round belly, her blond hair caught up in a rhinestone tiara. She clutched at the dog's tail with dirty fingers while the dog snarled and whirled around.

Holding up the rear of this parade was a college-aged girl who pursued dog and child with her arms outstretched.

"Bella, *no*! You know you're not allowed to open the door! Leave the dog alone!" She burst past us and grabbed the dog's collar in one hand, the little girl's shirt in the other. She took a few steps backward into house, dragging her charges with her. I got a glimpse of a long hallway, tiled in shiny black stone, and a spiral staircase carpeted in red. Only once the girl had the dog and child stashed safely behind her in the foyer, the door half-closed to block them from leaving again, did she turn her attention to me.

"Can I help you?" she asked suspiciously. Her eyes settled on Charlotte's face and softened. "Oh, what a doll," she cooed. "Don't worry. The dog is friendly; he's just a big noise in a small body." Behind her, the little girl was trying to press herself through the open crack in the door, staring up at Charlotte in my arms. The babysitter put a hand on the crown of the girl's head and gently pushed her back; her foot hovered in the crack, barring the dog's path out.

"Can she come in and play?" the little girl said. "I'm booooooored."

Charlotte craned her head to look at the girl, suddenly interested. She blinked at her, then turned to me. "Lala play?" she asked, eyes big as nickels.

"We're not here to play, kiddo." I turned to the babysitter. "Sorry, but do you live here?"

The girl shook her head and took a tiny step backward, narrowing the gap in the door even more. "I work here. The owner's not home." The dog surged at her feet, yipping so loudly that she had to raise her voice to be heard. "What's this about?"

"This may sound strange but . . . do you know a woman named Eleanor Logan? Or Hart. She looks just like me? I'm"—I realized that I wasn't quite sure how to describe *what* I was doing—"looking for her."

"You think she's here?" She seemed perplexed.

"Well, no—I just found this address in her things. Maybe she was the owner's florist? Did they get married in the last few years?"

The friendly expression on the babysitter's face was fading fast. Quite possibly she was debating whether or not I was insane.

"I wouldn't know, I haven't worked for them that long."

"Can you tell me their name?"

Her eyes narrowed into a squint of mistrust. She took yet another step backward, pushing the door farther closed until she was just speaking through the crack. "I'm sorry but I think you should go now," she said. "You'll have to come back when the owners are here. They get home at six."

Behind her, the little girl wailed in protest. The dog gave one last yelp—a high-pitched whimper, as if it had just been squeezed—and then fell quiet. The crack shrank until all I could see was the babysitter's nose.

I shoved my sneaker into the doorjamb, trying to stop her. "Can I just leave a message for the owner? Can you have them call me?"

The door banged against my foot, hard, and I yelped and pulled it back, giving the babysitter her opportunity to slam it shut entirely. I kicked the wood, and then yelped again as pain shot through my toe. Charlotte looked up at me with alarm.

"I shouldn't have kicked the door. The situation wasn't that girl's fault at all, and I took my frustration out on her," I told her. "That was poor impulse control on my part. Don't do what I did." Charlotte stared at me blankly.

I trudged lopsidedly back to my car, Charlotte fighting me to get down. I deposited her in the car seat with a fistful of Puffs and then fished through the console until I found a solitary sticky note that had lost most of its stick. No pen, but I did find the stub of an eyebrow pencil swimming in the bottom of my purse.

I scrawled on the Post-it as neatly as I could: "Looking for info about Elli Logan. Can you call me?—Sam Logan." I added my phone number and examined the results. It looked like a ransom note written by a psychopath, but it was the best I could do.

I walked back to the front door. There was a brass slot by the entrance, jammed with the day's mail; a fat Restoration Hardware catalog jutted out of the gap. I tugged this out and looked for the name on the label: *Michaela Blackwell*. The name didn't ring a bell.

I shoved the catalog back in the slot and added my smeared sticky note on top.

As we drove away, the front door flew open once more and the little girl came charging out, with an armful of stuffed animals. She stopped at the end of the driveway and watched us go, her face slack with disappointment. A plush unicorn fell from her arms to the concrete as she raised her arm and waved once— goodbye, or come back, I couldn't quite tell.

Then we turned the corner, and she was gone.

The second address on my sister's list was an hour farther south, in the ocean town of Laguna Beach. Almost as soon as we got on the freeway, I realized that Charlotte's tolerance for our expedition had already expired. Five hours in the car was too much to ask of a toddler. She squirmed and whined no matter how many strawberry Puffs I tossed over my shoulder at her, no matter how many times I tried to get her to sing "The Wheels on the Bus." She flung herself against the straps of her car seat until her face turned the color of a tomato.

"Lala play!" she shrieked, as if it had finally occurred to her that she'd missed a critical opportunity back in Burbank, a potential new friend.

"We'll play when we get to Laguna Beach," I promised her. "Just hang in there a little while longer."

"No."

"You have to, kiddo. I promise we'll go to the beach when we're done."

She burst into tears. Any previous happiness or future happiness had been utterly trumped by the perpetual Now, a Now in which she was straitjacketed in a car seat in a Pull-Up that was growing increasingly damp. Something about the expression on her face felt familiar to me, an echo of the neediness I used to feel as I popped an Oxy-Vicodin cocktail and washed it down with a G&T. Perhaps addiction is just a grown-up variation of a toddler compulsion: the constant need for instant gratification.

"Play," she whimpered.

"Puffs?" I offered.

She wailed from Burbank to Anaheim, finally passing out from exhaustion as we got close to Disneyland. I drove in merciful silence as the tip of the Matterhorn passed by on our right, squeezed between the hotel towers. A pop of memory: our ninth birthday, first time at Disneyland, parents fretting over the cost of the souvenirs. Elli wanted to go on the teacups but I insisted on Splash Mountain, promising that I'd hold her hand the whole time; but then it turned out that we couldn't sit together, and instead I listened to her scream in terror in the seat just behind mine. I knew that it was my fault that my sister was alone with her fear; I had done that to her. I spent the rest of the day doing penance in Fantasyland—riding Dumbo in lazy circles—and even though Elli moved on from the trauma, I remained convinced I had broken something critical inside her.

A random thought popped into my head: *I'll take Charlotte to Disneyland someday, when she's older.* A funny idea, but I liked it. And suddenly I could imagine us there, aunt and niece, standing in line for a roller coaster holding cotton candy fluff and wearing plastic mouse ears while Elli remained at home, not wanting her daughter to know that she was afraid of Splash Mountain. I'd get to be the cool aunt, the one Charlotte would confide in when her mother was behaving like a control freak, the one who would take her shopping on Melrose and go to rock concerts with her and buy her beer for the first time and . . . Oh. No. Maybe not the beer. But still, I liked this vision of our future together. It was, I realized, the first clear vision of *any* future I'd had in some time, particularly one with the anchor of a familiar human being.

It had been so long since I felt beloved, I realized, and my heart swelled with affection for the sticky little girl whose sleeping head swung and bobbed with each bump in the asphalt.

Charlotte was still asleep when I pulled up in front of the next address on my sister's list, a home on a street just two blocks inland in the seaside village of Laguna Beach. The houses in this neighborhood were built close together—real estate here was too valuable to waste on lawns—with socially oriented front patios festooned with American flags and planter boxes full of impatiens. A clapboard beach cottage stood at 72 Buena Vista; it had been enlarged and expanded at some point in recent years, and now boasted a two-story addition and a rooftop deck that had views out to the ocean.

It was another expensive-looking house, I noted; perhaps the common thread for these people on my sister's list was their income? My suspicion that these were former customers—that this whole thing was a pointless wild-goose chase—grew stronger.

I didn't have to ring the doorbell at this house. The owners—a well-groomed elderly couple—were already sitting on their front patio, just beyond a low wall covered with Fourth of July bunting. They were drinking iced tea and playing cards. I circled the block, looking for parking, but there was none to be had, and Charlotte was starting to stir in the back, rustling every time the car drifted to a stop. I couldn't imagine what I would do if she woke up again. If I took her out of her car seat, would I ever get her back in again? So finally I gave up and double-parked in front of the house. I left the motor running and climbed out of the front seat to stand just outside of the car.

"Hi," I called, softly, over the hood of the car. "Can you help me?"

The couple turned to stare in unison, startled from their game. They were silver-haired, the woman in a striped cotton pantsuit and the man in a polo shirt the color of strawberry sherbet. Their skin was sun-weathered, preserved like dried apricots.

The man patted his wife's hand and half stood to squint at me over the wall. "Why are you whispering?" he asked.

I pointed at the car. "Sleeping baby," I said.

His wife stood up now, craning to see through the window. "You lost?" she asked.

"No, that's not it. I'm just wondering . . . I'm trying to track down my sister, and this address was in her things. I know this is a long shot, but do you happen to know her? Elli Logan, goes by Eleanor sometimes. Or even Eleanor Hart."

"Elli Logan?" Something lit up in the woman's face, her dried-fruit skin crinkling as she smiled with surprised delight. She approached the dividing wall, grasped it as if she might leap right over, and peered closer at me. "And you must be Sam, right? Oh my goodness."

"You know my sister, then?" The relief made me wobbly. *Finally. Answers.*

"Well, yes!" She blinked, almost shyly. "I was such a fan of *To the Maxx*. Watched every episode! So I feel like I watched you grow up! And then my daughter, she just loved that show of yours on Nickelodeon, what was it called?"

"*On the Double*," I said, as something inside me deflated. "Wait. Do you *know* my sister, as in know her personally? Or do you just know *of* her?"

She laughed, lightly touched her hand to her silver hair as if to check that it was still properly coiffed. "Well, I would certainly be shocked if she knew of *me*." She smiled. "You said something about this address? She had it? You're looking for her here?" Her lips pursed together now, and her eyes grew wide. "Wait, is something wrong? Did I miss a story in the tabloids?"

I realized that I'd made a terrible mistake. I imagined this woman calling her friends, the story leaking out through the social networks of the Southland, the calls from the local gossip press. "Forgotten Child Star Elli Logan Goes Missing." It had been well over a decade since I last showed up in the pages of a gossip magazine—a wild night that had resulted in a paparazzi shot of me passed out in the passenger seat of a rap star's car. My sister had been absent from the news even longer. Would we still merit a story?

If my sister has joined a cult, absolutely, I realized. There is no expiration date when it comes to scandal.

"No! No. My sister is fine." I straightened, flashed a look from my old playbook: an *On the Double* smile, one part *girl next door*, one part *charming rogue*. "I think you misheard me. I'm just trying to locate an old friend for her. Maybe I got the address wrong."

"Oh." The woman's face fell. "Well, we've lived here only a few months. Are you looking for the family who used to live here? The Millers? We bought the house from them."

"Yes," I said, grasping. "You know them?"

"Oh, no. You never get to *meet* the people you buy from these days. We get their mail sometimes, though. Tom and Carrie. They're your sister's friends?"

"Yes," I lied. "Elli and Carrie were very close. She'll be so disappointed. Did they leave a forwarding address?"

The woman frowned. "No . . . I think they moved their family out to the East Coast, though? New Jersey? Connecticut? I can't remember, sorry. Do you want me to call my real estate agent and see if she can track them down for you?"

Through the window, I could see Charlotte stirring. A solitary Puff clung to her lower lip, which quivered tremulously; her nostrils flared with a sudden intake of breath. Shit. I felt a sudden lurch of desperation. *Get in the car. Get her home. There's no information for you here.*

"Thank you, but no . . . my baby is—" I clambered back into the car, gunning the engine as the woman stared at me, dismay on her face.

"But wait!" I heard her call as I drove away, Charlotte blinking with disorientation in the back seat. "I didn't get your autograph!"

Charlotte and I drove north along the coast until we found a beach that wasn't jammed with teenagers and tourists. I showed her how to dig for mole crabs, scooping them from the wet sand as they tried to burrow away. We made a collection in an abandoned pail, counting to ten and back since Charlotte couldn't count any higher. When the pail was half-full, she put a fat fist in the water and stirred it around and looked at me with amazement as the mole crabs burst into a frenzy. I could tell that my niece was the kind of girl who wouldn't be afraid of bugs, and that filled me with a strange sort of pride.

The sun was in its midsummer glory, high and unrelenting, only a whisper of a breeze blowing off the ocean. The curls at Charlotte's temples had pasted themselves to her head with sweat. I took her gritty hand in mine and we went down to the water to splash in the surf, stomping in the yellow foam that the waves left behind. She found a stick of driftwood almost as tall as she was and we dragged it in the wet sand, spelling out our names. *MIMI + LALA.*

Eventually I sat down on the sand while Charlotte poked around the waterline with her giant stick. My sister was missing and the day's expedition had been a waste of time and, really, my entire life was barely sputtering along—and yet, sitting there watching her, a strange emotion settled over me. I looked out at the cloudless horizon, past the oil platforms and the cargo ships hauling Chinese electronics toward San Pedro, and instead of feeling a sense of dread at the emptiness out there—the doom of a world in slow decay, dying oceans and islands of plastic trash— I felt something else entirely. The openness of possibility: a little girl poking at kelp with a stick. A bucket full of mole crabs. Our names in the sand and a promise of ice cream and a future filled with the unexpected. A curious, abstract feeling: hope.

A question floated into my head: What if my sister never came back? What if I took care of Charlotte forever? What if *this* was my shot at parenthood?

The dog came out of nowhere just then: black and shaggy, hair matted with sand, mouth foaming with seawater. His eyes wild with beastly excitement at the sight of the giant stick in Charlotte's hands. He leapt and grabbed the stick in his bared canines, giving it a firm shake.

Charlotte's jaw went hard. She dug her toes into the sand and yanked back.

But the dog outweighed her by a good thirty pounds. He

whipped his head back and forth as Charlotte hung on to the driftwood, flung about like a rag.

"Mine," she wailed.

I was on my feet and running, and down the beach I saw the dog's owner sprinting toward us, too. We both arrived at the exact instant that momentum got the better of Charlotte and she went flying across the sand. She screamed like she'd broken something essential.

I had her in my arms before I could stop to think, brushing away the sand, feeling for lumps. She wasn't badly hurt—sandpaper scrapes on her knees, a lump on a thigh—but a scratch across her cheek was oozing a thin line of blood. The dog's owner dragged him away, apologetic, as I rocked Charlotte in my lap. I didn't have a Band-Aid or Neosporin, just a bottle of tepid water and the hem of my T-shirt. Her tears felt like an accusation, that I hadn't been diligent enough, that I hadn't been watching her when it really counted, that I wasn't prepared for this at all.

She pushed her face into my chest, leaving a smear of snot and blood and sand across my front. A biplane cruised by overhead, towing a banner that advertised a marijuana delivery service called High Supply. I wanted to hide Charlotte's eyes from it even though she couldn't read yet. Someday she would, though, and by then it would be far too late to protect her from dogs and drugs and things she didn't yet understand. All the diligence in the world can't keep a child from harm. My mother could have warned me about that.

"Lala go *home*," she said tearfully.

"Time to go home," I agreed, even as I wondered where, exactly, home was supposed to be for each of us.

We arrived back in Santa Barbara to find my mother working in the front garden, pruning back the lavender along the path with a pair of garden shears. I extracted a tearstained and sticky Charlotte from the back seat, and she wobbled onto her feet and charged across the yard to her grandmother. She flung her arms around my mother's veined legs and my mother wobbled a little with the impact, a painful smile on her face.

"Ouch," she said softly, and stuck her fingers in Charlotte's soft curls, holding her tightly against her body. She lifted Charlotte's head with a cupped palm and traced a finger down the bloody scratch.

"Oh my God. What happened?"

"It's just a scratch. She had a little fall."

Charlotte looked up at my mother, sober as a judge. "*Bad* dog."

My mother looked over Charlotte's head at me. Her voice was hot with accusation: "She was attacked by a *dog*? How did this happen?"

"We were at the beach. And she wasn't attacked. The dog wanted her stick and Charlotte wouldn't let go and she got knocked down. That's it."

"What were you doing during all this? Just sitting there letting her be attacked by a dog?" My mother approached me and pushed her face so close to mine that I could smell the lemongrass oil she used for her joints. She sniffed.

I leapt backward. "Jesus, Mom. Are you trying to tell if I'm drunk?"

My mom's hands flew up in mock defense. "I just don't understand. Dogs aren't allowed on the beach in Santa Barbara."

"We weren't in Santa Barbara. We were near Laguna Beach."

My mother frowned. "Laguna Beach? Why all the way down there? I thought you had gone to the aquarium?"

I realized I'd screwed myself. "I found a list of addresses at Elli's house and I thought they might belong to people who would know more about what she's gotten herself into in Ojai. So we went to check it out."

I saw something flicker behind my mother's eyes, a momentary bump, before she was able to smooth it away. She *was* worried, I realized. "And? Did you learn anything?"

"Not yet," I said. "There's still one more address, but it's in Arizona."

The muscles around her mouth twitched, turning her lips into tight little raisins. "I appreciate that you're concerned about your sister," she said carefully. "But, Sam, didn't we decide that we were going to give Elli some personal space? She's on her own journey. It's not our place to judge." She tilted Charlotte's head up, examined her crusted face. She curled her nose, as the vinegar scent of Charlotte's sodden Pull-Up wafted up. "Poor baby, spending the whole day in the car. And then getting attacked by a dog! Did you take a break to do *anything* for her? Or was it all about you?"

"About me? This is about figuring out what's going on with Charlotte's mother. It's *all* for her."

My mom shook her head forlornly at Charlotte, as if the child shared her disbelief. "So you say."

"Mom, just stop." I walked past her toward the front door.

She untangled Charlotte from her legs and followed me up the steps. "I don't understand what you think you're doing. We asked you to come stay with us to help with Charlotte—to take her to the park, push her on a swing—not to drag her around Southern California while you play at detective."

I stopped. "Is that what you think I'm doing? Playing some sort of game?"

"Honestly? I can't help but wonder if you're on some holier-than-thou quest to prove that your sister is just as lost as you are." Her eyes met mine, and I could see her recalculating, realizing her mistake. "As you *were,* I mean."

Was she wrong? I felt a small twitch of dismay; maybe this whole endeavor *was* just an attempt to drag Elli down with me into the muck. And yet, something whispered at me that this was not normal. GenFem wasn't just a benign self-help group, like an extended stay at Esalen. "OK, so I hang out and push Charlotte on a swing for a few hours. And then what? Just sit back and hope that Elli will come home and fetch her? Because it's been two weeks since she left, Mom. And Elli has shown no sign whatsoever that she plans to return. She's *missing*. Can you honestly tell me you're not worried? What are you going to do when I have to leave?"

This elicited a sharp "shhh" from my mother. Her eyes followed Charlotte as she toddled up and down the garden path, chasing a butterfly. "You don't need to be so melodramatic," she said, her voice low. "This is what Elli has always struggled with, you realize. You turning everything into a performance, even when you aren't onstage. You want all the attention on *you,* all the time. You can't just let things be, you can't just sit on the sidelines and let someone else have their moment."

Something hard and hot had lodged in my throat. "Elli isn't having a *moment,* she's joined some kind of cult. And I don't think it's wrong to try to get her back home."

"It's *not* a cult. Stop being so judgmental."

"Mom—I went to Ojai. She's staying in a locked compound in the middle of nowhere and they wouldn't let me in to talk to her. The women who came out of the place were wearing identical outfits and had shaved heads."

Uncertainty flashed in my mother's eyes. "It sounds like a monastery." She brightened. "Maybe that explains why she's been so out of touch—she's on some kind of a silent retreat!"

"Mom—Elli's selling her house. She put it on the market last week. Does that sound like just a *moment* to you?"

She studied the gardening shears in her hand. "*Of course* she's selling the house. That's what happens when you get divorced. There doesn't have to be a nefarious reason for everything."

I threw up my hands. "Why are you making me out to be the bad guy? I'm trying to help."

"Then *help*. Make Charlotte some dinner. Take her to a mu-

seum. Teach her to swim. Just don't make my life any more stress-
ful than it already is." She picked up the shears and lopped a
waving lavender tendril off the shrub in front of her. Charlotte
picked it up and ran out into the garden, waving it like a wand.
Her leggings sagged from the weight of her Pull-Up.

"I'll change her diaper." I was about to give Charlotte chase
across the yard, but inside the back pocket of my jeans my phone
began to trill loudly. I froze in place, hand hovering over the
pocket, unsure what to do.

My mother made a face. "Oh for God's sake, just answer your
phone. I'll change her." She started after her, but then stopped
and turned to look back at me. "I *knew* this was a bad idea. I told
your father, *Sam's not ready yet*. I was just going to hire some help
but he thought . . ." She didn't finish but I already knew exactly
what he thought: that twenty-five dollars an hour for a babysitter
is ridiculous when you have an underemployed daughter who fits
the bill. "He insisted we give you a chance, against my better judgment. And so here we are. I just don't know if I can trust you,
Sam. I don't know that I trust your motivations. I don't think
you're aware enough to even know what they are."

At that, she turned and swept across the yard, in pursuit of my
niece.

I couldn't remember the last time I'd wanted a drink so badly.

The phone was still ringing. I ducked inside the house, where
the air-conditioning hit my skin and transformed the sheen of
sweat into a blanket of goosebumps. The caller ID showed an 818
number that I didn't recognize. It wasn't until I'd hit the Answer
button and lifted the phone to my ear that it clicked into place.

818. *Burbank.*

"Hello?"

The voice on the other end of the line was a woman's voice,
high-pitched and ragged and breathy, as if she'd just run a race.
"Is that—Sam Logan?"

"Yes. Is this . . . Michaela? Michaela Blackwell?" I dropped the diaper bag, leaned up against the cool stucco wall. "Thank you so much for calling me. I know that note must have seemed . . . strange."

"Did you think I *wouldn't* call?" Incredulity dripped from her words, stopping me short. I didn't know how to answer this. I could hear the rush of her breath into the mouthpiece, so loud I had to hold the phone away from my ear. "How did you find us?" she asked.

This was not the question I'd anticipated. "I found your address and I thought Elli—" I began, a little flustered.

She interrupted me before I could find a way to finish my sentence. "*Don't* call her Elli. She's *not* Elli. How *dare* you name her?" Her voice had ascended several octaves and was so loud that I had to hold the phone away from my ear. "You are not allowed to call! We were *told*. Do it again and I'll call someone, the liaison, the authorities. Stay *away* from us."

The line went dead. She'd hung up.

Fuck. I scrambled with the phone, hit Redial, but it went straight to voicemail. "Hi, it's Sam Logan, I'm sorry, but I don't understand what's going on. Maybe you could just call when you're a little calmer and we can discuss it?" I regretted this as soon as I uttered the words. What if she *did* call the police? Had my sister done something wrong? "Actually, forget it. I'll leave you alone."

I hung up, the woman's words—*She's not Elli*—still echoing in my ears. It reminded me of something, something that nibbled at me as I stood in my parents' foyer, listening to the sounds of Charlotte laughing in the garden. Through the front window, I could see my mother, calling after my niece, demanding that Charlotte "stay away from that bee," "come out of the sun," "we need to change your diaper" as the little girl squealed and ran through the lavender, lopping off flowers with her hands.

She's not Elli. It reminded me of what that woman had said to me in Ojai, the day before. *She's not your sister anymore. She's ours.*

That was when it struck me, the possible common thread linking Michaela Blackwell and Carrie Miller and the Arizona address to my sister.

What if *they* were GenFem members, too?

13 I DIDN'T STAY FOR dinner that night. I couldn't handle making small talk over chicken curry, knowing what my mother was *really* thinking underneath that tight, beatific smile. I would never redeem myself in her eyes, I realized; no matter what I did, I was always going to be the bad twin. Not to be trusted. To be kept at arm's length. Well—*fuck her*.

I told my parents I was meeting an old friend for dinner and drove off into the night, heading toward Old Town. I found an Italian restaurant not far off State Street and settled in at a corner table. A waitress took my order while I fumed and a few minutes later a plate of ravioli materialized in front of me, cheesy pillows floating in a fragrant puddle of oil.

The smell made me queasy.

"You sure you don't want something to drink with that?" the waitress asked. Her pen hovered over her pad, the tip quivering in anticipation. I stared at the ravioli, wavering. I thought of all the excellent reasons I had to not order a glass of wine, all the progress I'd made. I heard a strangled sound from somewhere deep in my throat. A voice in my mind whispered, *Just one glass. You had a terrible day. You can handle one glass.* I instinctively reached into my pocket for the sobriety medallion, but it was still buried somewhere in my parents' garden, a treasure map fail.

"A bottle of pinot," I said.

After the waitress walked away I picked up my phone and dialed Tamar. She'd talk me out of doing anything regrettable, I thought, just as she'd done a half dozen times over the last year. Tamar could always see what I never could. She'd warned me, hadn't she, that this trip was a bad idea. That I wasn't ready. All I needed was for her to talk some logic into me and I'd get up from this table and walk right out the door, get in my car, and drive back to the (relative) safety of my small life in Los Angeles.

But Tamar didn't answer her phone. She was probably still at the café, working the evening shift. When her voicemail picked up, I found myself leaving an entirely different message than I'd intended.

"Hey, Tamar. I know I'm supposed to be back at work on Friday, but I could use a few more days." The waitress was walking back toward me, wine in one hand, corkscrew displayed like an offering in her palm. "There's a lot going on here and I just feel like I'm . . . needed." *Even if my mother doesn't agree,* I thought. I hung up.

I let the waitress pour me a glass.

The wine tasted like cherries and leather on my tongue. My whole mouth was on fire, every taste bud lighting up, awakened from a year of dull dormancy. I pushed aside the nagging voice— *what are you doing, you've been triggered, you were doing so well, you're proving that your mother was right not to trust you, show some self-control*—and took another sip. And then another, until the smooth oblivion of a wine buzz pushed the self-doubt further and further under the surface and all that was left was *This is fine. You've earned this. It's just a little wine.*

A few glasses in, it occurred to me that I was drinking alone, which was the most dangerous kind of drinking—the kind of drinking that had, in the past, led to regrettable acts of pathetic desperation. If I was going to fall off the wagon tonight, I wanted it to be *fun*. I needed a companion, and the only one I could think of was Caleb. Which seemed like a great idea until I remembered that he was supposed to be sober.

I called him anyway. He answered on the first ring, and sounded happy enough to hear from me, until I told him where I was.

"I'm at an Italian restaurant by myself and I'm about to order another bottle of wine," I said to him.

There was silence on the other end of the line. *"Another?"*

"The last bottle was pinot. Not sure what this one's going to be. A cabernet. Maybe something with bubbles."

"I see." He sounded amused. Or maybe he sounded concerned. I couldn't quite tell. "Are you going to drink it?"

"No, I'm just going to stare at it for a while, I think." The words slid on my tongue, fuzzed with tannins. My flippant act wasn't at all convincing.

"I think I should come join you," he said, which of course was what I'd been hoping for all along.

By the time Caleb walked in the door, I had finished off the pinot and the waitress was returning with a Lambrusco that she'd advertised as having "perfect effervescence." He stood in the front of the restaurant, studying the tables, jiggling up and down in his shoes. The shoes were leather, and he was wearing a button-down shirt with fresh iron marks in it. He'd dressed up for me, which made me feel warm in my fingertips, although maybe that was just the alcohol.

I waved him over. "You clean up nice," I said.

His ears went pink as he slid into the chair across from me. "Sorry it took me so long. I had to hunt down a sitter."

"You were with Mae tonight?" A mix of emotions knocked at my chest. Guilt, that I'd dragged him away from his daughter. Delight, that he'd go through the effort for me. Concern, that perhaps his reason for going through the effort was not that he wanted to hang out with me but because he thought it was his duty.

He shrugged. "It sounded like you needed company."

I arched an eyebrow. "Are you here to save me from myself?"

The waitress had arrived with the bottle of wine and he let her pour him a glass. "So, *not* here to save me from myself, apparently."

"It looks like that ship has sailed."

I twirled the stem of the glass of wine in my hand, sloshing Lambrusco across the tablecloth. "Ah, but how far will it sail is the question?"

"I'm not here to lecture you," he said. "I'm here to make sure you don't get yourself into too much trouble."

I pointed at his glass of wine. "And are you going to get *yourself* into trouble? I thought you'd been sober for years. I didn't realize it would be so easy to knock you off your pedestal."

"I still drink a glass of wine on occasion. The difference is that now I know how to stop."

I took a sip of the Lambrusco, which *was* perfectly effervescent. It lit up one side of my brain, even as the other was starting to feel troublesomely fuzzy. "And how do you know when to stop?"

"God tells me."

He said it so simply that I assumed he was deadpanning, but he looked back at me with clear blue eyes and the laughter died in my throat. "You believe in all that higher power stuff in AA? Because I always skipped over that step."

"My sponsor was a believer. At first I just did the prayers with him because that's what you're supposed to do, right? Go through the motions until it sticks? But then I realized that it was really helping." He took a modest sip of his wine. "The thing is, I like to believe that there's something out there keeping me company as I go through my life, nudging me in the right direction. It's a lot less lonely than believing you're all by yourself, right? It makes me feel responsible to something bigger than me."

"As in God, the supernatural authority figure in the sky?"

"I don't think of God quite *that* literally. More like, a spiritual power. The force that helps me when I'm trying to help myself. I don't know what that is, exactly, but why not call it God? Everyone needs a reason to keep carrying on when it feels like the world is falling down. To persevere against *this*." His hand did a sweep across the table, taking in the empty wine bottle and the spots of grease on the tablecloth, and then landed—oh so casually—on mine. "You have one, right? Something that keeps you hopeful, that makes you keep trying? Something to believe in, even if you don't name your reason God?"

Did I? I couldn't pinpoint anything. The wine and the weight of his hand on mine were making it hard to think. "Can we table this conversation until a time when I'm not already drunk?" I used my free hand to lift the glass of Lambrusco and drain it. I felt dizzy. "I've clearly fallen off the wagon tonight and am now clinging to the moving cart with my fingernails so talking about my reasons for staying sober is kind of beside the point."

His hand tightened over my fingers. I knew so little about him, really, and yet his presence across the table made me feel safer than I'd felt in some time. I felt an urge to bite the corded muscles along the sides of his neck. "Do you want to talk about something else?" he asked. "Like, what happened today that set you off?"

"Not really," I said. The edges of the room had grown round and soft, shapes blurring in the candlelight, and I wanted them to stay that way for a while longer. This was what alcohol had always done for me: It sanded away the sharp corners of my life, made it possible not to focus too hard on what remained. Was this why I'd never stayed sober for longer than a year? That I didn't have a *reason* that felt as strong as this compulsion toward blindness? I wobbled in my seat, felt my head—unbearably heavy—dip and sway on my neck.

"Well, what do you want to talk about?"

I let myself succumb to gravity then, my body lifting forward over the grease marks and breadcrumbs that marked the distance between us. "Honestly, I don't want to talk at all," I said, as I fell across the table to kiss him.

14 MY SLEEP WAS SUGAR-TOSSED, the residue from the wine sour in my mouth, a sharp ache throbbing in some central lobe of my brain. I drifted in and out and under and finally dreamed of Elli as a child. She was standing on the beach watching me, motionless, as I was pulled out to sea by the tide, choking on the salt water. Or was I the one on the beach, watching her as she drowned? Then we were *both* in the water together, pummeled by the rolling waves, clinging to each other with slippery limbs and eventually dragging ourselves under with our combined weight.

I woke up, coughing on the saliva that had pooled in my cheek while I slept.

The pillow under my head was strange, a corded velvet. When I sat up to look around—a stab of pain accompanying the movement—I realized that I was lying on a couch in an unfamiliar living room. Someone had put a chenille blanket over me and left a glass of water sitting on the coffee table just a few feet away.

The couch was large and worn and full of crumbs, with a water-stained Malcolm Gladwell paperback left open on the arm. The IKEA rug below my feet was scattered with puzzle pieces and art supplies; instead of framed photographs, the walls boasted construction paper artwork taped at a child's height.

I was in Caleb's apartment. Presumably. I didn't remember arriving here.

Where was Caleb? Why had I slept on the couch and not with him? Was that my choice, or his? A familiar void at the center of my memories, the muddy shape of a midnight binge. Once, I had been happy to wake up oblivious; the emptiness had felt like a blindfold that kept me from witnessing my own misdeeds. Now my cluelessness made me feel ill.

I had blacked out. Of course I had—I'd drunk two bottles of wine, which once might have felt like nothing at all, but after a year of sobriety was guaranteed to knock me right out. I recalled exactly how long it had been since I *last* got blackout drunk— 386 days—and that uncomfortable memory was what finally shook me alert.

From the open door at the end of the dark living room I could hear the faint sound of a child's snore. Jesus, had Mae seen me like this? I needed to leave, before they both woke up. But when I looked at the clock on my phone I discovered that it was still only 3:45 A.M. I couldn't go back to my parents' house, not like this, not at this time of night. I imagined my mother standing in the doorway of her bedroom, watching me creep down the hall in yesterday's clothes, smelling of booze. Shame shattered me.

I had been so close to being OK, to proving her wrong, and instead I fucked it all up, yet again.

I gathered my shoes and purse, which were neatly arranged beside the couch. I imagined Caleb watching me sleep, taking off my shoes and aligning them on the floor, filling the glass of water and putting it within arm's reach of the couch. At least I was fully dressed and clean, which suggested that I hadn't done anything *too* embarrassing—hadn't thrown up on myself or jumped in a pool fully dressed or shed my clothes in the street somewhere.

I'd kissed him, though, hadn't I? Yes, I remembered that much. Had I slept with him, too? That, I couldn't answer.

I found a purple crayon among the art supplies on the floor and scribbled a note for him. *Thank you for taking care of me. I owe you.* I stuck it to his fridge with an alphabet magnet—*S* for Sam, *S* for Sorry, *S* for So Ashamed, *S* for Not Sure I'll Ever See You Again.

And then I let myself out.

The night was mild, with a faint breeze that lifted the hair on my arms. My car was parked right out front—presumably Caleb had driven it for me? It seemed unlikely that he would have let me drive myself. I got in it and then sat there for a long time as I surveyed the street: stucco apartment buildings painted in pastel colors, sturdy sedans parked out front, fairy lights hanging from balconies. A pale gray sky, washed with moon.

What was I going to do now?

I wondered, fleetingly, if any bars were still open.

Call Tamar. Tell her what's going on. She'll help you. But it struck me how selfish that would be, to ruin someone's sleep so that they could make you feel better about yourself. If I really wanted to feel better, *I* should do something to make myself feel better.

I remembered Caleb's words about God at dinner last night: *The force that helps me when I'm trying to help myself.* What was my reason for pushing forward, for trying to find the light inside a darkness of my own making?

And suddenly, through the murk of my hangover, I saw that I didn't want to be Charlotte's alcoholic aunt.

I closed my eyes and remembered Charlotte looking up at me, a mole crab crawling across her palm, wonder in her eyes. I'd disappointed everyone else in my family, but not her. Not yet. I could still be her hero. I could even bring her mother back to her.

I looked at the keys in my hand and a thought flashed into my head. *Drive back to Ojai and break into the compound and kidnap Elli by force.* But this seemed like a terrible idea, too.

Instead, I started the car and drove aimlessly down the block.

I turned left, then right, then left again, unsure exactly what neighborhood I'd landed in, until I saw a freeway on-ramp looming ahead. An invitation to drive somewhere farther away. Flee. To another city. Another state. Somewhere like—

Somewhere like Arizona.

Why not? I still had the list of addresses tucked in a pocket in my purse. Seven hours there, seven hours back, I'd be home by the evening, with a decent excuse for my parents to explain why I'd vanished overnight.

I yanked the steering wheel to the right, and hit the gas hard, accelerating up the ramp onto the deserted late-night highway. The stars twinkled overhead and the date palms shivered in the ocean breeze. I snapped on the radio and the tuner settled on a Chopin étude in a minor key. The highway stretched ahead of me, clear and open, full of promise.

NUMBER 825 JOSHUA TREE DRIVE was a modern Southwestern home in an upscale Scottsdale neighborhood, designed from monumental plinths of pale pink adobe that seemed to hold up the blinding blue of the Arizona sky. It sat on an island of lush grass, which was shockingly green against the sunbaked terrain. A hundred feet past the house, the lawn ended abruptly, as if you'd come to the end of the world. There, the Sonoran Desert began: a stark landscape of desert scrub pierced by saguaro and ocotillo cacti, with occasional shocks of purple sage and bright yellow marigolds that had gone crisp in the heat.

It was another rich person's house. If GenFem was indeed the connective tissue between these three homes, it was clear that they were recruiting members with an abundance of disposable income. Or perhaps they were *responsible* for the disposable income: a manifestation of the success of their "Method." How was I to know.

I pulled over in front and surveyed the neighborhood. The houses were set far apart, with meticulous drought-tolerant landscaping in between. No one was out on the sidewalk—the midday sun was far too severe—and the houses were shuttered against the heat, curtains drawn tight. The few cars parked on the street clearly belonged to the help: beat-up hatchbacks, a plumber's truck leaking oil. The owner's luxury cars, if they weren't parked at their offices, were probably tucked behind the doors of their three-car garages.

My own car's temperature gauge read 109 degrees. Outside, the air shimmered, deceptively soft. I shut off the ignition and within seconds, my car was an oven. I could feel the sweat pooling between my breasts.

My entire body ached from the long drive. All those hours in the car had helped clarify something, bring my focus away from my own solipsistic woes and back to something fundamental: *Help Charlotte. Bring her mother home.* But now that I'd finally stopped, a muddiness began to seep in. The penumbra of last night's drunken petulance, the shame of it all. When I looked in the mirror, I saw a ghoul. My face was puffy, my hair greasy, my shirt covered with cheese dust from the Doritos I'd eaten for breakfast. I still had last night's makeup on, and there were black crescents of smeared mascara in the pockets under my eyes.

I rummaged around until I found a stray container of baby wipes next to the car seat and gave myself a refresh—across the face, under the armpits, between my breasts. A fresh coat of mascara, some lip gloss. *There.* I still looked limp, but at least I no longer resembled a streetwalker. Whoever lived in this house might be cult members, but they were clearly *rich* cult members. And judging by my bizarre phone call with Michaela Blackwell, I might be walking into a confrontation.

I arranged my face into the correct balance of friendliness and concern, looked in the mirror, adjusted it. I prepared to perform.

The heat hit me like a wall once I stepped out of the car, undoing in seconds all the cosmetic fixes of the last few minutes. It felt like the air had sucked all the moisture out of my bones; it was so dry I couldn't even sweat. Sweet Jesus, how could anyone live here?

I walked stiffly along the front path, past a decorative cactus garden, and toward the front door. There was no portico for shade, just a severe slab of concrete jutting out from the wall. I rang the doorbell and then stood there blinking in the sun.

Nothing. I counted to twenty, then rang it again, this time pressing my ear to the door to listen for movement inside. I couldn't hear a sound except the faint metallic chime of the doorbell echoing off a tile floor.

The house was empty. The owners were at work, or on vacation. Maybe this was even their second home.

I looked up and down the street. The homes in this neighborhood were far apart, discreetly positioned for privacy, and showed no signs of life. There wasn't even a gardener in sight.

I stood there wilting, lost. What to do now? Drive all the way back home empty-handed? What a ridiculous waste of time this had been. There wasn't even a mailbox from which I could glean the name of whoever lived here.

My mother had been right all along: My sleuthing was of no use whatsoever. I could have been taking Charlotte to the park today, eating ice cream with her on the pier. Getting to know my niece. *That* would have been more helpful than this, another day of half-assedly pursuing clues that might never have been clues in the first place. A list that meant no more than the scrap of paper it was written on.

And yet. I kept thinking of that bizarre phone call with Michaela Blackwell yesterday afternoon. *She's* not *Elli.* It had to mean something. It had to have some connection to GenFem and my sister's current situation, didn't it? The first name on this list had not only known who Elli was, she'd known that she wasn't herself anymore.

I checked the time—it was only noon. My only shot at salvaging this trip was to wait until the end of the day and come back to see if the owners returned to the house after work. It would mean spending the night in Scottsdale, but perhaps that was better than driving home in this condition anyway. I could feel the previous twenty-four hours starting to weigh me down, a yoke of exhaustion.

I'd noticed a café on my way through town and I headed back

in that direction now, driving until I found myself in a small shopping district. The café was wedged between a gallery displaying oil paintings of stoic Native Americans and a boutique selling alligator cowboy boots, as if standing an awkward sentry between the two conflicting narratives. It was a neighborhood place, the sort of café that compensated for its mediocre coffee with live jazz trios on Fridays and community bulletin boards where you might find yourself a local teenage babysitter.

Inside, the air was so cold that it made my teeth hurt. The café was empty except for a pair of bored-looking teenagers ignoring each other as they tapped on their phones. The barista was wearing a sweater. How strange, to live in a climate of such extremes; how hard it must be to find equilibrium.

I ordered a black coffee and took it to a table in the corner. I sat there, nursing the coffee as it revived me, wishing I'd brought a book. How was I going to kill the next six hours?

I pulled out my phone and texted my sister. *For God's sake just let me know you're not being held hostage. I'm worried.* It joined the rest of the texts and photos I'd sent her over the last few days. *WTF is going on?* And *Is today the day you're going to stop giving us the silent treatment?* And *You need to stop this.* And *Please come home.* And *Do it for Charlotte not for me.* All of them had been marked read. None of them had been answered.

I hit Send and then sat there, sipping my coffee, waiting to see if Elli would respond. A few minutes after I sent it, three dots appeared below my message. She was typing. I sat upright, jerked alert. But the dots hung there, and hung, and after a maddeningly long time they finally just disappeared altogether. Maybe she'd changed her mind about responding, or maybe she wasn't OK and she didn't want to lie. I was too tired to speculate anymore.

I ferried my coffee cup back to the barista, a paper-clip-thin twentysomething with rhinestones glued along her lash line. "Refill?"

Her pour was haphazard; half the coffee ended up in my saucer. "Sorry," she said. "Napkins are over there." She pointed me toward the coffee station.

It was underneath the community bulletin board. As I sopped up the excess coffee, I skimmed the flyers that had been pinned there, wondering if I might find an ad for a GenFem learning center. *Punk band needs drummer.* And *Thai massage $50.* And *Painting lessons by a proffessional Artist.* And that's when I saw it, on a flyer that was barely visible underneath a postcard for a local real estate agent.

It was Charlotte's face.

I yanked the real estate agent's postcard down so I could see it better, to make sure I wasn't hallucinating. But I wasn't. It was her. Younger—still a baby, really—her hair shorter; but the furrow in her forehead, the unsettling sense that she was watching you and thinking something surprisingly adult—*that* was unmistakably Charlotte.

MISSING, the flyer read. *EMMA GONZALEZ.*

I dropped my coffee cup, barely even noticing as the scalding coffee burned the skin of my calf.

The barista was by my side in seconds, wiping off my legs with a damp tea towel. "Fuck," she said. "Was the coffee too hot? Please don't sue the café. I'll get fired."

I ignored her, preoccupied with the flyer that I'd torn off the bulletin board and was now reading.

> *MISSING: EMMA GONZALEZ*
>
> *Last seen: March 13*
>
> *Hair: Brown*
>
> *Eyes: Brown*

Age: 22 months

Weight: 26 pounds

Circumstances: Emma Gonzalez was last seen on Tuesday, March 9 at 12 p.m. in the garden of her home in the 800 block of Joshua Tree Drive in Scottsdale. Family members in attendance believe that she may have wandered into the desert.

A throb of nausea, dank and pulsing, rose in my stomach.

The barista was still dabbing at my leg with the sodden towel, making noises about ice packs and bandages. I nudged her off. "I'm fine, really. Thank you."

She stood and noticed the flyer in my hands. "Oh yeah, that. So awful. Poor kid."

I looked up at her. "You know about this?"

"You don't?" She blinked at me from underneath those disconcerting rhinestones, a fairy trapped in a coffee-stained apron. "Shit, it was all over the local news."

"I'm not local."

She folded the towel in half, and in half again. "So yeah, the grandma is taking care of the little girl, right? They're out in the garden and the little girl falls asleep in the grass and the grandma goes inside to use the bathroom and when she comes back out a few minutes later, the kid is gone. They think she woke up and wandered off into the desert. Or a mountain lion snatched her." She twisted the towel in her hands. "Desert's full of predators. A coyote got my cat last year."

"They searched for her?"

It was a stupid question and the barista gave me a suitably withering look. "Of course. Big search parties. But, no, nothing. Never found her body."

Of course they didn't, I thought. Because there was no body.

Because Emma Gonzalez was now Charlotte Hart, living in Santa Barbara. My sister had her. Or rather, she *had* had her, before she vanished, leaving the missing child in *my* care.

It made no sense whatsoever.

I thought of something. "Was the family part of a cult?" I asked.

The barista looked taken aback. "A *cult*?"

"Or, like, a self-improvement group."

"I mean, who *isn't* in a self-improvement group? My parents were into the Landmark Forum. And my brother worships Tim Ferriss like he's some sort of god." She paused, gave me a closer look. "Why? Do you recognize the kid, or something?"

I realized I was in danger of drawing suspicion to myself. I shook my head and pinned the flyer back on the board. "No. Just thought she was cute."

Another customer came in then, and the barista headed back to her counter. I waited until she was distracted at her espresso machine before pulling my phone out of my pocket and snapping a photo of the flyer.

I waited until I was back outside before texting the photo to my sister.

YOU NEED TO CALL ME BACK NOW, I typed.

This time, there were no dots at all.

The drive from Scottsdale back to Santa Barbara flew past as a smear of desolate landscape and radio static. I pounded Starbucks coffee until my head buzzed so loudly that it almost drowned out the questions that were spinning through my brain. Was it possible there was an innocent explanation for why this little girl had disappeared from her Scottsdale home and materialized in my sister's in Santa Barbara? Could my sister have *rescued* her? Did Elli somehow not know who she was? Or had my sister absconded with the Gonzalez child? If so, why *this* child, all the way out in Scottsdale? Were the Gonzalez parents members of GenFem, friends of my sister? And if so, was Emma/Charlotte's disappearance something that had been engineered by the group—not a disappearance at all, but some sort of smoke screen?

I wanted so badly to believe that Elli hadn't done anything wrong.

It wasn't until I was crossing the border into California that it finally occurred to me that Charlotte wasn't my niece after all. She was someone else's niece. But calling my sister *Mama*. How long had it taken Charlotte to adjust to her new reality? Did she remember her real mother? Did she miss her? She'd been twenty-two months old, still a baby, when all this happened. She didn't seem traumatized to me, these four months later. But still . . . my God.

And the parents.

I couldn't even think of them.

It was growing dark, just past eight, by the time I made it back to Santa Barbara. It had been less than twenty-four hours since my bender landed me on Caleb's living room couch, thirty-six since I'd started visiting the addresses on my sister's list. I'd slept four hours since then, maybe five, and driven for fourteen; and now I was tired, so tired that the road was blurring in front of me. I slapped myself to stay awake, until my face stung and my palm hurt. Now was not the time to die.

When I let myself into my parents' house, I found my father sitting on the couch watching baseball highlights. He saw me standing in the doorway and muted the television, then shifted sideways so that he could take me in. "Well, well. Look who decided to come back." The expression on his face wasn't anger, or even sadness; it was profound resignation, as if he'd expected this of me. "Where have you been?"

"Trying to get some information about Elli."

He shot me a look of disbelief. "Since last night?"

"I had to go to Scottsdale."

Now he didn't look resigned. He looked perplexed, like I'd handed him a lemon and told him it was an orange. "Why Scottsdale?"

"Too complicated to get into now, I'm exhausted." I could tell from his expression of disbelief that this wasn't helping my case. "I swear, Dad."

"Your mother's been worried sick," he said.

"I doubt that. She's probably been saying 'I told you so.'"

He didn't disabuse me of this. "It might have been a good idea to call, Sam," he said mildly.

"I sent her a text this morning! *I have to leave town, back tonight.*"

He shook his head, as if this were entirely irrelevant. He was still wearing his clothes from work but had unbuttoned his shirt to where I could see the top of his undershirt, and a lonely tuft of gray hair in an expanse of pale, puckery skin. I kicked off my sneakers, sat down on the edge of the couch beside him, and stretched my sore legs. The house was utterly silent, all that double-paned glass blocking the sound of the world beyond the windows. I could hear the ticking of the clock in the hallway as we sat there, uncomfortably motionless. My father and I had never been good at talking to each other, even when I was young, and the gulf had only grown with each passing year. I'd never really compensated for all the years that Elli and I had spent on set in Los Angeles, visiting our father only for weekends and summers. Instead, I'd fled the scene entirely. No wonder he felt like a stranger, but it wasn't necessarily his fault for not trying. At least *he'd* believed in me enough to ask me to take care of his grandchild.

I sat up straight. "Where's Charlotte?" I asked.

"With your mother. She's putting her down to bed."

I started to stand up to go to them, but my father put up a hand to stop me. "Sam," he said softly.

I paused. "What?"

"I think you should go back to Los Angeles tomorrow."

A twist in my stomach, like someone had reached inside me and grabbed a fistful of intestines. "But you're the one who asked me to come in the first place! I just asked my work for more time off."

"I know," he said. "But I think it's too hard on your mother. All the ups and downs of having you around. The instability. And while I know you're doing better than you were, the fact is that you can still be . . . unpredictable." He swallowed. I knew how much he hated this conversation. "On top of what's going on with Elli, it's just too much. Your mom is fragile, you know. She's not as strong as you. And sometimes when you're around she feels very . . . judged."

"I'm just trying to help."

"I appreciate that. But it doesn't mean that you're good at it, I'm sorry to say."

I couldn't think of anything to say to this. My father wouldn't look at me. After a moment, he picked up the remote and unmuted the television. A chorus of boos rang out from baseball fans protesting a bad umpire call.

I left him there, watching his hometown team lose to the Dodgers.

My mother was in the guest bedroom with Charlotte. They'd finished reading *Llama Llama Red Pajama* and now they were snuggling in the big armchair, lights low. Charlotte had her thumb in her mouth, her eyes at half-mast. She wore pajamas with bunnies on the feet that broke my heart.

My mother's eyes flew to mine as I tiptoed into the room. She stared at me over Charlotte's hair, her eyes narrowed into question marks. I didn't know how to answer her unspoken queries. Not tonight. Not yet. As I drew close I could see that my mother's face was puffy, her eyes watery. Had she just been crying?

"Sorry," I mouthed at her. She blinked at me and then looked away, resting her cheek atop her granddaughter's head. *Not her granddaughter's,* I thought. How much longer would we have Charlotte? It occurred to me for the first time that this was going to destroy my mother. I tried not to think of what it was going to do to me. Already it felt like the floor was giving way beneath me, and if I looked down I'd see a bottomless abyss. I was trying so hard not to look, but I could sense it there, the familiar black pit of despair.

Charlotte stirred then and opened her eyes, noticed me standing there. She fixed her dark gaze on mine and dropped her thumb from her mouth. Her arms shot out as she heaved herself out of my mother's lap and toward me. "Mimi."

Like a royal edict: *Pick me up.*

I lifted her into my arms and she crumpled against my shoulder, thumb back in her mouth, already half-asleep. My mother, denuded of grandchild, rose from the chair and edged past me. She wouldn't meet my eyes as she walked stiffly toward the bedroom door.

"*Mom,*" I whispered urgently, but she was already gone.

I settled into the warm, rump-shaped spot that my mother had left in the seat. Charlotte nestled into my chest, her breath fast and hot on my neck, her hummingbird heartbeat racing against my slow one. The bunnies on her feet twitched as she slid into sleep. She was so much more alive than I felt, and so vulnerable because of it. I imagined her wandering in the desert all by herself, dwarfed by prickly cacti, stalked by coyotes, lost under an unforgiving sky. I imagined her being swept up into a stranger's arms, crying out with alarm.

I wept into Charlotte's hair, until we both finally fell asleep.

16 EXHAUSTION KNOCKED ME DOWN, and then anxiety woke me up. I lay in bed, listening to the thrum of the compressor pumping cold air through the vent over my head. In the oak tree outside the window, a songbird pierced the dawn with a plaintive cry for companionship. The sky was the color of wet sand.

My bag sat, packed, by the bedroom door.

It would be so easy to leave for Los Angeles. To resume my life there and leave the problem of Charlotte and Elli for my parents to solve. This could even be my parting salvo as I walked out the door: *Goodbye, and by the way, Charlotte's real name is Emma and she's a missing child from Arizona. Good luck with that!* How satisfying it would be to see them realize that they'd been so very wrong about me.

But I just couldn't do it. It was too terrible a redemption. How could I put my parents in that position? It was hard enough to be in it myself, knowing that Charlotte wasn't Charlotte, that Elli had seemingly done something terrible, and that I had some sort of moral obligation to go to the authorities. Of course I could never turn my sister in; I could never live with that. And yet, somewhere in Scottsdale, Charlotte's real parents were quite likely crying themselves to sleep every night wondering what happened to their daughter. I couldn't live with that, either.

The conundrum was a sharp black stone sitting at the center of my chest, pressing down until I couldn't breathe. I knew I couldn't make my parents carry it, too. There was no way I was going to tell them what I knew.

Your mom is fragile. She's not as strong as you.

The unfairness of my father's words sat with me as I lay there, fretting. Since when had I ever been strong? I was an addict, for God's sake, and a freshly relapsed one, too. It didn't get any weaker than that. I would go back to Los Angeles, wash my hands of this unwinnable situation, pretend I never saw the Missing poster or the GenFem compound. I'd focus on something simpler. Like staying sober. Making rent. Finding a better *reason* to keep trying than a kid who wasn't even part of my family, or a sister who wasn't talking to me.

After all, Elli had fled from the mess that she'd made—gone off to hide behind an iron gate and a double-height fence—and if she wasn't capable of handling the situation, why should I be?

On the other side of the wall, Charlotte rustled and then let out a soft moan. I lay there listening, willing myself not to move. She went quiet, waiting for someone to retrieve her. When no one did, she cried again, letting her moan curl up into a wail, at which point something primal lurched inside me, and I found myself running, half-dressed, to soothe her unhappiness away.

Charlotte and I took a last walk around the neighborhood before my parents woke up, looking for ladybugs and lizards, licking the dew off of daisies. I wished I was a photographer, so that I could capture the purity of gesture every time Charlotte pointed and cried out *Bird! Butterfly! Pretty! Lello!* Like a deity dispensing labels on a newly formed world, each word a wonder.

When we returned to the house, my father had already left to run errands but my mother was sitting at the table, nursing her green tea. She held her arms out to Charlotte. Charlotte ran to her grandmother and climbed up into her lap. She began eating the toast off my mother's plate, an entitled little princess.

"Your father tells me you're going back to Los Angeles today," my mother said. Her voice was studiously calm, pretending. "He says they need you back at the café?"

I sat down across from her, grateful to my father for giving me an excuse to hang on to, even as I hated him for kicking me out. "I'm out of vacation time," I said.

She nodded, relieved to have an explanation that made everything feel OK. "So that's where you were yesterday, your father says? You went home for the day?"

I got up to pour myself a cup of coffee. It tasted like cinnamon and charcoal. "I don't want you to worry about me," I said carefully. "But I can't afford to lose this job." It wasn't exactly a lie.

"Well, you could have told me that sooner, your text was so cryptic. I don't know why you don't just tell me the truth," she said tartly. She glanced at the clock. "So will you be heading back early? I thought maybe I'd take Charlotte with me to my aquaballet class. She can wear floaties."

I reached out and smoothed a red curl of my mother's hair. The texture was coarse, frail and brittle from so many years of color. I wondered how gray my mother was underneath it all, how much she hurt. I wondered if all her spiritual seeking had made her feel any more ready for her own death, or if she still needed an explanation that would make the panic go away.

She flinched a little, surprised by my touch.

"You'll be OK, Mom? You can handle this?"

"Oh, *sure*. I'll figure it out. My hip's a little better this week. It'll be nice, a little bonding time with my grandbaby." She pushed her hot tea out of Charlotte's reach. "And I'm sure Elli will be back this weekend."

I couldn't wrap my head around my mother's blindness, I

really couldn't. I dropped my cup in the sink, with a little more force than necessary. "I can come back and babysit on my days off, if you want. Just let me know if you need me." I reached across my mother and patted Charlotte's sticky cheek, blinked hard to push back the tears. I wondered if I would ever see her again.

Charlotte smiled up at me, her teeth full of toast.

I turned to leave but my mother reached out and grabbed my hand to stop me. Her fingers were dry and cracked from the garden, despite the balms she rubbed into them every night. She looked at me with watery eyes.

"Thank you," she said. "I know your father told you it would be a few days and now you've been here a whole week. And you didn't complain at all. So, I'm sorry I questioned you, and your motives. I really do appreciate everything you've done for Charlotte. I know that taking care of kids doesn't necessarily come naturally to you. You've never struck me as very . . ." she hesitated, as if regretting the thought she'd been about to utter.

"Maternal?"

"Well, *no*." Her eyes blinked with relief, as if I'd finally verbalized something that she'd been waiting years to say. As if all the traits typically assigned to mothers—love and nurturance, reliability, protection—were missing from me, and *that* explained why my life had gone so sideways. It stung, in a way that I hadn't expected. I wasn't maternal. I was missing a gene. Elli had it, but I did not: another way in which we weren't identical at all. Another way in which I was flawed.

"Not everyone is meant to be a mother," I said, and I went to get my bag.

I didn't drive to Los Angeles.

Instead, I drove to Caleb's apartment. The day was turning out to be sunny and mild, and I wondered if he might already be out with his daughter, but when I got there his Mazda was parked out front.

Mae answered the door, wearing an old T-shirt of Caleb's that reached down to her knees and had paint stains down the front. *METALLICA MADLY IN ANGER WITH THE WORLD TOUR 2004*, it read.

"Hi . . ." Mae hesitated. "Charlotte's mom?"

"I'm her aunt. Sam. And you really shouldn't open the door to strangers," I admonished her.

"You're not a stranger," she responded. "You slept on the couch the other night."

"But you couldn't see me before you opened the door. So I *could* have been a stranger."

She stuck a hand on her hip and squinted at me. "You're trying to trick me."

I liked her; she was sharp. I bet she'd get herself a helicopter someday.

Caleb appeared in the doorway from the kitchen, wearing a T-shirt and threadbare boxer shorts. He had a pancake flipper in his hand and white flour down his front, and when he saw that it was me he looked flustered.

"Mae, you know you can't open the door without asking me."

"You're just *embarrassed* because you're not wearing pants," Mae sang.

Caleb flushed.

I felt my own face going hot, too. "I can come back later . . ."

"No, it's fine." He wiped at the flour on his shirt, as if this and not the gaping underwear was the issue that most urgently required fixing. "Are you OK? I called you yesterday but it went straight to voicemail. I was worried." He glanced at Mae, then back at me, his eyes telegraphing what he couldn't say aloud. *Why did you leave the other night? Are we OK? I do not understand this situation and I am in over my head but am trying to remain cool about it.* At least that's what I hoped he was saying.

I telegraphed back, *I am not sure if I slept with you or not and I am mortified by this not knowing, but I like you and I hope I didn't screw everything up by being such a mess.*

Maybe he couldn't read my mind but he was, at least, smiling. "Everything's fine," I said. "But I need a favor from you."

He waved me in. "Come on in, we're about to have pancakes."

I stepped inside and Mae closed the door behind me. Caleb and I stood there staring at each other, no hugs or kisses, just an awkwardly polite distance while Mae examined us with obvious suspicion. Surely I would remember *something* if I had slept with him, I thought, but I had nothing, just a memory of the coconut smell of his hair, a faint flash of his arm bracing me upright as I stumbled in his living room. Still, it was possible he was remembering me naked right now.

"So what's the favor?" he asked.

"Do you have an electric razor?"

He laughed and self-consciously touched the week-old stubble on his chin. "Sure, why?"

"I need you to give me a haircut," I said.

"Set it to three."

Caleb's eyes met mine in the mirror. Mae danced in the bathroom doorway, delighted by the spectacle she was about to observe. Their bathroom had cracked peach tile that dated back to the 1970s and a night-light that looked like the moon, and it appeared that both father and daughter used the same bubble-gum-flavored Crest Kid's toothpaste. I wanted to sniff Caleb's breath to see if it smelled like candy.

"That's got to be too short," Caleb said, hesitating as he held the clippers against the back of my head.

"No, it'll be perfect. Those women looked like shorn sheep. I swear."

I could feel it buzzing, a hairsbreadth away from the nape of my neck, an electric tension. "But you have such beautiful hair. It's a shame. Couldn't you just wear a bald cap or something?" He cupped my skull with his palm as he gently lifted my ponytail away from my neck. His hands were warm and strong.

"Just do it," I said.

And he did.

It almost didn't matter, then, if we'd slept together yet or not; *this* felt like an almost unbearable intimacy, the slow reveal of my bare scalp, his palm braced against the side of my head as he carefully worked his way around my ears and past the pulsing vein at my temple. I watched myself in the mirror, the shape of my skull coming into view, fascinated by my transformation into a stranger. Blond hair fell in clouds to the floor as Mae, her eyes huge, squealed with excitement.

Caleb eyed the pile of hair on his bathroom tile. "You could save it, make a wig," he offered.

"No, Mae should have it. She can use it for her art projects."

Mae descended on the hair with a broom and a box, as Caleb walked me to the front door. We stopped there, an awkwardness descending between us. He examined me, running his eyes across my scalp. I felt naked then.

"You look beautiful," he said. "Is it weird to say that? It makes you look . . ."

"Like a cancer patient?"

He shook his head. "I was going to say otherworldly. Like something fallen from the sky. Not quite from here."

I thought about the women I'd seen in Ojai. That wasn't exactly what I'd thought when I'd seen their shorn heads; and yet there had been something alien and strange about the way they looked. I wondered if that was the point that GenFem was making with this haircut: They wanted their members to feel unearthly.

Or—more alarmingly—inhuman.

"Thank you, I guess?" I said. "And I'm sorry about the other night. I really appreciate you taking care of me. It might have been so much worse if you hadn't been there to help."

He looked down at his bare feet, where blond strands of my hair were still tangled between his hairy toes. "I was glad to be the one you called." He shrugged. "Anyway, I've been there, too. You can't do it alone."

"I'd say let's try dinner again, without the wine, but I have to head back to Los Angeles after this," I said.

He smiled. "Well, that's not so terribly far. We could still make it happen."

Mae was watching us so I just kissed him on the cheek, letting my lips linger there for a significant second. The whiskers on his chin were the same length as the stubble on my head, a sandpaper attraction.

He pulled back and smiled at me. "Please be careful," he said.

I found the dress I needed in a shop in Ojai. It took most of the afternoon, walking in and out of boutiques all along the main road through town, looking for the right kind of shapeless white shift. Eventually, on a side street, I came across a small shop with batik scarves fluttering from its awning. In the window was a display of bright saris and shalwar kameez and other garments appropriated from countries on the other side of the planet and brought here, to be sold to professional creatives with six-figure salaries who wanted to look "nonconformist."

I almost walked past the place entirely, deterred by the spangles and color, but as I passed by I glimpsed a flash of something pale and ghostlike through the glass. I stopped and went in, as a trio of overhead bells rang out my presence. The saleswoman behind the counter looked up and smiled. Then she clocked my new haircut, and her smile grew wider, stiffer, falser.

I reached up, ran my hand across my bare scalp, felt the fine

stubble tickling my palm. She knew exactly who I was, I realized—
or rather, who I was *trying* to be.

"You're here for one of these?" she said, already reaching for
the rack of white cotton dresses that hung behind her. She pulled
one out, seemingly at random, her eyes locked nervously on mine.
She had a kombucha glow to her, with long braided hair, tiny bells
chiming off her wrists. It did not appear that she was inclined to
like me.

I nodded, took the dress from her. "You sell these to . . . ?" I
wasn't sure how to finish the sentence. *The women in the compound? GenFem? That cult?* But she was already nodding, eyeing
me like I was a spy from enemy territory.

"You don't really need to try it on. It's one-size-fits-all."

I shook my head, reached for my purse. "What is it?" I said.
"The dress. In real life, I mean."

"It's from Cambodia. For morning."

"Why do you wear it in the morning?"

"*Mourning,*" she corrected me. "As in, death."

She counted change for me, her eyes flicking to the top of my
head and then away again. When she was done, I asked her to
point me to a dressing room, where I swapped my cutoffs and
tank top for the dress. It slid over my head, loose and shapeless, a
cocoon of soft cotton. I stared at the alien creature standing before me in the mirror. Caleb was right: I *did* look otherworldly. It
was something about the effect of the pale head and the billowing
dress, something angelic and deathly at the same time.

A terrible thought struck me: What if Elli *hadn't* shaved her
head? What if she looked exactly the same, and I'd just jumped to
the wrong conclusion? What if *I* was the one who had just donned
cult clothes for no reason?

It was too late to worry. I stood there for a moment more, listening to the saleslady pace back and forth outside the dressing
room door. I practiced rounding my shoulders, a slight sideways

tilt to my neck, a softening of my eyes, until I finally saw *her* in the mirror looking back at me.

Elli.

My performance wasn't perfect; it had been too long since I'd studied my sister closely, and clearly she'd done some changing. But it would have to be good enough.

On the way out of the shop, I hesitated, and turned to the saleslady.

"I'm not one of them," I said. "I'm just acting."

She nodded, eyes big, not believing, wanting me to leave. I shrugged apologetically, then opened the door. The bells chattered overhead, marking my departure with a chilling finality.

I drove to the pizza place at the edge of town, parking in the lot at an angle that allowed me to watch the road that led to the compound. I sat and waited, my rolled-down windows the only defense against the sun that slowly turned my car into a skillet. I flapped the loose sleeves of my dress, directing air toward my dripping armpits. At least my head was cool, an upside of my drastic new cut.

An hour passed, and then another, as the sun began to descend and a breeze kicked up in the orange groves across the way. Customers came and went from the pizzeria, giving me odd looks as they passed by my car with their greasy stacks of cardboard boxes. No one asked me to leave.

It was nearly dinnertime when I finally saw them in the distance: two women with shaved heads wearing white dresses, slowly making their way down the road from the center of town. Their arms sagged under the weight of the grocery bags they were carrying. They were not, thank God, the same women I'd encountered last time.

I waited, slumped out of view below the dashboard, until they passed the pizza place and turned up the road. Once they had their backs toward me, I got out of the car and followed them. I brought nothing but the key to my car, which I tucked into my moist bra.

I caught up to them as they were passing the avocado farm, halfway up the hill. They heard my footsteps and turned to watch me approach. Now that I was closer I could make out their features, beyond the distractingly bald heads. One was a heavyset blond woman, her eyes bloodshot and pale in the sun; and the other was a slight Asian girl, probably just out of her teens, but alarmingly young-looking.

I slowed my walk as I approached, rounded my shoulders, and let a dimple escape. *You be me, and I'll be you.* I smiled benignly.

The Asian girl looked at me and then down the road. "Eleanor?" she asked, her voice a tinny squeak. "Why are you alone?"

The air spun around me, hot and languid and disorienting. I didn't know how to answer this woman's question. "What a lovely evening," I said, trying to be as sweet and anodyne as I imagined my sister would be. Did she still want so much to please? I had to assume that she did. "Nice and balmy."

The heavyset woman was still staring at me, and for a moment I wondered if she'd seen right through me that quickly. I hadn't seen Elli in so long; maybe she had a new tattoo, or a facial scar, a giveaway that I'd missed entirely. Maybe she was angry and abrasive now, not the sweet and pliant sister I was conjuring up. Maybe I just wasn't as good an actress as I thought I was, which explained why my career had tanked.

But this woman had other concerns. "Did they give you dispensation to go into town alone?" she asked accusingly. I nodded, a wild guess, and she frowned. "Christ. I've asked three times and never gotten it." She glanced down at my hands, saw that they were empty. "And no Service, either? Fuck. Cindy really does play favorites." She turned and swerved off down the road, heaving the bags to adjust them, then slouching under their weight with exaggerated annoyance.

"Ruth . . ." the Asian girl squeaked. She threw me a look of commiseration and then dashed after the older woman, her grocery bags thumping against her skinny legs. There were giant sweat stains on the back of her dress.

"Here—let me help." I chased the older woman down the road and took the grocery bags from her grip. The bags were full of sweet potatoes and cans of coconut milk, and the weight of them almost knocked me down. Ruth grumbled, but I could tell she was happy to let go. She flexed her palms, crossed with pink welts from the plastic handles.

The Asian girl gave me a dirty look, as if I'd just kicked her in the shin. "That's *her* Service. You're not supposed to take over someone else's Service. That's defeating the whole purpose. Dr. Cindy says that the Method only works if we push through our own vulnerability and weakness. The best way to help Ruth up is by letting her find her own bottom first."

Ruth rolled her eyes. "Hush, Suzy. It's only for a minute."

"We're supposed to be *warriors*," Suzy persisted. "How are we going to lead a new movement of powerful women if we can't even carry our own groceries?"

I fell into step beside them, unsure of what to say. I wanted to ask these women what this place was about. Was the retreat some sort of psychological boot camp? Was it a punishment or a reward? Was it supposed to be a permanent residence? If not, how long until my sister came home?

But I couldn't ask any of this without giving myself away.

I was sweating now, too, the grocery bags cutting grooves into my palms. We turned a corner, walking single file as the road began to narrow, and when I looked up there was the tall wooden fence. The women both fell silent as we started to walk alongside it, our feet kicking up dust in the road. One by one, we passed the towering female statues that stood guard along the path.

Across the valley, the disappearing sun had set the Topatopas alight with a neon pink glow. It made me think of ice cream, and

I realized I hadn't eaten a thing since breakfast. We entered the shade of the oak trees, passing through pockets of cool air trapped between the shrubs. "We'll be late for dinner," Ruth muttered. "And I'm getting three hundred calories tonight."

"Does that count the apple you ate in town?"

"*Shhh.*" Ruth seemed to have shrunk into herself. The lines around her eyes had grown deeper, and I could see an angry rash on her bare skull. It struck me that she wasn't grumpy; she was scared. And then the shadow of the iron gate fell over us and I suddenly felt frightened, too. What if I was found out? What if Elli was standing right there, on the other side of the gate, and the whole ruse fell apart? Worse—what if she was there and she wanted me to leave? What would I do then?

I'll just go back to L.A., I thought. *Forget any of this ever happened.* But I knew it was too late for that now. I wasn't going to abandon my sister to this, whatever *this* turned out to be.

We stopped just outside the gate. Ruth reached out and pressed the button on the call box and then peered up at the camera. She waved. "It's Ruth and Suzy and Eleanor," she called, speaking less into the call box than to the camera monitoring our presence. I looked up, too, and held my breath.

The red light blinked at us, there was a blast of static from the speaker, and then the gate swung open with a shattering squeal of iron on iron.

And just like that, I was in.

17 IN JUNE OF LAST year, I emerged from yet another rehab stay—my fourth—and found myself living with my sister and Chuck while I "got back on my feet." That mostly meant spending endless hours floating on a raft in their swimming pool and drinking can after can of fizzy water in order to keep my hands occupied while I tried to figure out a new future for myself. I read my way through the novels on my sister's bookshelf, sweet romantic stories about star-crossed lovers who worked through minor character flaws and the occasional bout of cancer in order to find each other again. Nothing on my sister's shelves was dark or twisted; even the tragedy was tear-jerkingly pure, of the Nicholas Sparks variety. It felt like a balm.

After so many years of existing on the opposite side of the divide from my sister, it was strange to be living inside her world. Elli's life trajectory after *On the Double* could not have been more different from mine. It was as if, after a childhood that defied normalcy, every choice she'd made since was a middle finger in the face of her former unconventionality. While I was auditioning for horror films and going to parties in Chinatown warehouses, she was rushing for a sorority and majoring in interdisciplinary studies. While I was fucking my way through an ever-rotating cast of bad-boy actors and musicians and aspiring producers, she was married by twenty-four to her all-American sweetheart. She became a *florist,* of all things, and moved into a pretty house that perfectly matched the pretty houses of all the other affluent white families that populated our pretty hometown.

Most foreign of all to me, she wanted kids. Lots of them.

"We want three kids," she'd told me not long after her wedding to Chuck (a three-hundred-person affair at a beachfront hotel in town). "Maybe four."

I laughed. "You'll need to trade in your BMW for a bus."

"Right? With built-in seatback television sets and a cooler for snacks. A pop-up tent for soccer games and a hanging rack for ballet costumes." She was being sardonic, but there was a shine in her eyes that took me aback, as if she thought this wouldn't be *such* a terrible fate.

Seven years on, I still couldn't figure out the appeal of that life, but I also knew that my sister would make an excellent mother. She cut the crusts off her *own* sandwiches. She went to see *Frozen* in the theater, for fun. I'd once watched her spend an hour patiently teaching an eight-year-old girl how to do a cat's cradle.

And, of course, she was unfailingly reliable. I knew this from personal experience. The night that had kicked off this latest rehab stint had ended with me calling her in tears at four A.M. I'd gone to a bar in Highland Park with a DJ I was dating and had washed down two Valium with a half dozen tequila shots and blacked out. When I woke up, hours later, I was on the floor of an unfamiliar house in Eagle Rock and a strange woman in spangled tights was throwing water in my face while another woman was on the phone with paramedics. My date was nowhere in sight. Apparently, I'd left the bar with these two strangers and proceeded to smoke a joint with them. Then I passed out cold from a standing position and hit my head on a potted ficus. There was puke on the floor and blood on my T-shirt and when the woman gently asked me if there was anyone she could call, I'd said, "My twin sister," and started to bawl.

Elli had driven the hundred miles in exactly eighty-two minutes. When she found me sitting on a dark porch, soaking wet and covered with blood, she went pale. I waited for her to rebuke me, or to remind me of my three previous failed attempts at rehab—one of which she'd paid for herself—and call me a disgrace. But instead, she just retrieved a clean T-shirt and a pair of cashmere sweats from the back of her car. "You'll feel better in this," she said, and began undressing me as I sat there crying, helpless as a baby.

The whole drive back to Santa Barbara she kept up a patter about a "really fantastic program" she'd recently heard about, with a whole new rehab protocol we'd never tried; she'd call as soon as they opened and reserve me a spot. When I wept that this time I was really going to kick it—*really, I was*—she just looked at me with a sanguine smile and said emphatically, "Of *course* you will. You're my Sam. You can do anything, you just have to try."

I tried. I really did.

The rehab stay had gone well, and it seemed to work; of course, it always did until it didn't. But I was hopeful. And now I was back at her house, seven weeks later, waking up every morning to a fresh plate of eggs and the morning paper folded neatly to the arts section. Some days, I'd go with Elli to her workshop and work alongside her, stemming roses and culling the slimy leaves from the peonies. I liked these days the best, working in amiable silence in the cool dark space where she made her arrangements, the air thick with the smell of flowers and fresh dirt. I found the repetitive simplicity of the work calming; more than that, I liked the proximity to *her*. We hadn't spent so much time together since Elli put the kibosh on *On the Double*.

My sister was quieter than I remembered, intently focused on her arrangements, frowning over accounting sheets that seemed to always end in red numbers. Our conversation was frequently stilted, and I wondered if that was because she didn't know how to talk to me anymore, or if something else was bothering her.

The fertility question, maybe? It had been seven years, and there was still no baby, though I'd found a bag full of ovulation kits under my sister's sink. Sometimes, I heard her and Chuck talking in fierce whispers when I wasn't in the room; he'd been sleeping more and more on the couch in the downstairs den, presumably because he was working late, but I had to wonder. The books by the side of her bed had names like *You Are a Badass: How to Stop Doubting Your Greatness and Start Living an Awesome Life* and *Girl, Stop Apologizing: A Shame-Free Plan for Embracing and Achieving Your Goals.*

I asked her, half joking, what those goals were, "because from where I'm sitting it looks like you've achieved most of your goals already." Maybe I was projecting; maybe I just *wanted* her to be OK because I wasn't prepared to deal with the alternative. I was selfish that way.

She smiled, a little wobbly. "You know. I just . . . hit a plateau. And I'm not sure what's next. Don't you ever feel . . ." She blinked and stopped, apparently unsure if she wanted to get into the end-less morass of what I felt. "Anyway. Positive manifestation never hurt anyone, right? Isn't that how you got sober?"

"No, you're right," I said, even though she wasn't. What I'd accomplished was less *positive manifestation* than *last stop be-fore landing in a homeless shelter*. But I smiled and let her hug me, and we both got a little teary as she whispered in my ear, "I'm so glad you're here. I'm so glad you're finally OK."

Maybe she was right, I thought. Maybe I should read her books. Maybe I could use some positive manifestation, too.

I started to toy with the idea of staying in Santa Barbara. Maybe I could convince Elli to bring me on as a business partner. Why *not* be a florist? I had nothing left in Los Angeles—no audi-tions lined up, no career prospects worth mentioning, nothing but a tiny apartment with peeling paint and paltry few belongings. Tamar, my AA sponsor, had offered me a job at the hipster café that she managed, but beyond that, my life in Los Angeles had vanished into a yawning hole of nothingness. Here, I at least had my sister. I could start over again, back in my hometown, like winding my life back to the beginning and giving it another go.

One afternoon, Elli asked me to take over at the workshop while she went to an appointment with a fertility doctor. "We've been looking into IVF," she said. She stood at a utility sink, prepping buckets. "It's been a while, and nothing else is working."

I stopped what I was doing and watched her, red hands plunged in cold water, her face a stone. "Kinda hard to get pregnant when you're sleeping in separate rooms?"

She dropped the buckets to the ground with a clatter and by the time she turned to me she was smiling again. "Oh, that's just because Chuck snores," she said. "It's been keeping me up at night." She grabbed her purse and keys, looking at the wreckage of discarded flowers strewn across the floor of her shop. "You'll clean this up?"

Her face was strained and pale. My sister had never been good at covering her fear. "Of course. You OK?"

"Fine," she said brightly. "I'm still young. We have plenty of time to figure it out."

I spent the afternoon prepping a massive delivery of pink roses destined for a wedding that weekend, and when I got back to the house I found my sister red-eyed in the kitchen, mashing potatoes with alarming vigor. Since my return she'd been vigilant about keeping alcohol out of the house, but now an open bottle of rosé was perched at her right hand, two glasses down. Chuck was puttering around outside, grilling dinosaur-sized steaks on the barbecue. There was an electric tension in the room, a smell of blood and plastic.

I dropped onto a stool with a tube of balm and began to rub it into my chapped palms. "How'd things go today?" I asked warily, sensing already that things had not gone well.

Elli stared deeply into the bowl. "I got some test results back," she said. She stabbed at a potato lump with the masher. "And guess what? I'm infertile. They said there's no point in going ahead with IVF."

She burst into tears. I jumped up from the stool and came around the kitchen island and hugged her. She dropped the masher and it fell to the floor, splattered potato across my bare feet. Her skin under her sundress was hot, as if something had burst into flame inside her. "It's something wrong with me," she sobbed into my shoulder. "They called it primary ovarian insufficiency. My follicles aren't functional. It might be genetic, they weren't sure."

"Oh God. I'm so sorry."

She quivered in my arms, tense and broken. "Sam," she moaned. "I'm never going to have a baby."

"Of course you'll have a baby," I said firmly. "There's more than one way to have a baby. You'll adopt. Millions of people do."

She shook her head, glanced toward the garden, and lowered her voice. "Chuck doesn't want to look into adoption. He's scared he won't be able to bond with a child that didn't come from him. Or me, for that matter. He wants a kid that's a mix of *us*. He thinks it's a biological thing, and he won't love the child properly, you know? He says he'd rather not have a kid at all. That maybe it wouldn't be so bad to be childless." She was crying hard now. "IVF was my last chance."

Fuck Chuck, I thought. He was the kind of person who was used to having life handed to him on a platter, and I'd watched him go stiff and tense when things didn't feel *easy*. A dent in the bumper of the BMW, no milk for his coffee—even little things like that would make his neck go red and the pulse at his temple go wild.

Of course, I freaked him out with my messiness and unpredictability. Whenever I walked in the room I could feel his blood pressure rise, and I was sure he was counting the days until I left. So I could only imagine how he felt about *this,* my sister's infertility, a crack in the foundation of his own home. No wonder they'd been sleeping apart.

"Well, there are still other options." It felt strange to be the one doing the consoling, rather than the one being consoled. "You can get a donor or a surrogate or something." Already, my mind was racing. *What if.*

"Maybe," Elli said. She stepped out of my arms, used the back of her hand to wipe the snot away, and then cleaned it on a nearby towel. "But Sam . . ." She blinked at me, her eyes going soft. "You know this affects you, too, right?"

"Me?" I struggled to locate the connection she meant. "I mean, yes, it would be cool to be an aunt. But it's not . . ."

I trailed off. The expression on her face was so forlorn. "Sam . . . if I have this ovarian insufficiency . . . you might, too. They said it's often genetic. So you may never be able to have children, either."

"Oh!" I felt a little lost. I picked up the balm, squirted more into my palm, began rubbing it into the backs of my hands. I was drawing out the moment, trying to hide the pang of guilt I suddenly felt. "Yeah, that's not a problem."

"You say that now. And I get it; with what you've been through the last few years, you might think you'll never want kids. But you're sober now! And if you stick with it and meet the right person, you might change your mind and want them after all."

I hated this. I hated her unflagging belief in me, which I didn't share. Even more, I hated what I was about to say to her, and the unfairness of it all. Why me and not her? Why was *this* the place where our DNA differed? If one of us couldn't have a baby, why wasn't it me, who didn't want one anyway?

"No, I meant to say, I know I'm not infertile."

She flinched, her face making a tiny shift from sorrow to surprise. "Wait—you've been pregnant? You never told me. Did you have an abortion? Or a miscarriage?"

I hesitated, reluctant to admit an inconvenient fact that I'd been hiding from her. Three years back, I'd emerged from that failed Ojai rehab attempt with my career in tatters, my bank account in negative numbers, and no casting director willing to meet with me. I couldn't ask Elli for cash—not after throwing forty thousand dollars of her money down the drain on my rehab, and then another six thousand for my hotel bill. Instead, in a moment of desperation, I'd sold my eggs for twenty-five grand a pop, plus thousands in bonuses. The shady IVF clinic that paid me to jab myself with hormones was willing to overlook my addiction history because of my winning (if slightly fudged) vital stats: *blond and fit, college educated, and quasi-famous.*

I had never told Elli. Not just because I was afraid of her judgment about my financial desperation but because I had an uncomfortable feeling that her own attempts to get pregnant weren't working out quite the way she'd planned. All those years, but no kids: It didn't take much to figure out what was going on. I knew, somehow, that the news would hurt her.

There was no avoiding it now. "No, no—not pregnant," I said. "I donated my eggs. Actually, sold them. For money. A couple times. So I know"—I struggled for the right words—"they work."

The cords in her neck had gone tight. "You're kidding."

"Not kidding."

"But . . ." Her mouth seemed to be caught in an epic struggle, twisting around words that didn't want to come. "You're a drug addict. And an alcoholic. Who would want your eggs?" Her nose flared, as if horrified by the thought of my tainted eggs, and the flawed children that might come from them.

"Ouch. That's harsh."

I watched her cheeks flush pink. She wouldn't meet my eyes. "But it's true. People are afraid of their kids inheriting lifelong problems like yours."

I stared at her in shock. Is this what she really thought of me?

That I was somehow permanently tainted? A *lifelong problem*? How long had she been secretly judging me like this while pretending to be my champion? It's not that I didn't think she had perfectly legitimate reasons to feel that way about me—I was a fucking mess, and I knew it. And yet there was so much cruelty in the way she said it. *Who would want your eggs?* Was I really incurable? It felt like something noxious and buried had just unexpectedly bubbled to the surface between us.

"Well," I said curtly. "I guess I shouldn't volunteer to donate my fucked-up eggs to *you,* then."

The minute these words came out, I regretted them. It wasn't that I hadn't thought of offering my own eggs to my sister before that moment. All afternoon, as I stripped thorns off roses, I'd wondered if this was where the journey might end. I would have done it. Would even have carried the baby, if they'd asked. I *would* have stayed sober for the sake of her child, I knew it. Maybe it would even have been good for me, the positive motivation I needed to start a new chapter of my life.

But now I regretted putting the idea out there like this: as a backhanded insult, not a real offer at all.

"No, you shouldn't." Her words were flat and dark. It felt like I'd accidentally broken something between us, the fragile connection we'd been rebuilding for the last few weeks.

"Have I done something to offend you? Seriously, what's with the attitude?"

She reached down and picked up the potato masher from the floor and walked it stiffly over to the sink. She wouldn't even look at me now. "I've spent the last decade of my life picking up the messes you've made," she said quietly, her eyes fixed on the drain. "You had everything you wanted and you screwed it all up like it meant *nothing* to you. And now here I am and the only thing I *really* want, you somehow have and you just . . . throw it away."

I didn't know how to respond to this. She wasn't wrong about the first part, but how was the second *my* fault? There were plenty of things to pin on me, I wasn't going to deny that, but her infertility seemed particularly unfair. "Gosh. It must be hard being so *perfect,* living in your safe little world. It must be awfully hard to see from the height of the pedestal you've put yourself on."

She turned around and glared at me. I saw my anger mirrored in hers, the way her eyes went pinched and tight, the hot red spots on her cheeks, the tight line of her lips. I knew my own face must look exactly the same. "God, it's always about you, isn't it? There's never any room for me to struggle because *you* suck all the air out of the room. You always have. Even when we were kids." I tried to interject but she held up a hand, silencing me. "So you know what? If the life I've chosen for myself is so galling to you, why don't you just leave? You don't need to stay here anymore. Go back to L.A. I'm *done* helping you." With that she swept up her wineglass and marched from the room.

It's so easy for good intentions to get undone by unspoken resentments; a history of small bumps piling up until you have an insurmountable mountain of issues. I wanted to rewind the conversation back to the moment when I'd hugged her; if only I hadn't said anything about my own fertility. I never planned to have kids anyway; I could have let her believe we were still identical in this one critical way. It wouldn't have hurt me. Instead, I'd managed to send myself back into exile.

Go back to L.A. I'm done *helping you.* I couldn't catch my breath, as if her words had lodged in my solar plexus.

I heard Chuck clattering around at the patio door, heading back to the kitchen with a platter full of oozing meat. I didn't want to look at him. Instead, I grabbed the half-empty bottle of wine and walked straight out the front door.

———

Of course, I got drunk.

I finished the bottle of wine in a beach parking lot, watching the sun drown itself in the ocean as the last stragglers made their way, sandy and sunburned, back to their cars. And maybe at that point everything would still have been OK if I'd just sucked it up and gone back to my sister's house, only slightly tipsy; but I just couldn't imagine facing her and her judgment—you *suck all the air out of the room . . . you screwed it all up*—so instead I made my way to a beachfront bar where they sold buckets of Coronas and fish tacos to partying UCSB students.

For the first few margaritas, I let myself be furious that my sister had expelled me from her nest for a transgression I couldn't even control. A few drinks after that, I got into a morose phase, in which I felt sorry for myself, feeling helplessly trapped in the fly-wheel trajectory of my life. The usual solipsistic alcoholic pity party. But by drink seven, around the time the walls of the bar began to feel like they were closing in and I stumbled out onto the sand with a double-pour of tequila in a plastic cup, I'd realized that I *was* a terrible sister, that Elli was a saint, and that she was just sad. So sad! Poor Elli was sad. I had to do something about that.

It's hard to explain the logic of intoxication. When your brain is blurred like that, caught in the dimming spiral of your drunkenness, any sudden moment of clarity feels like brilliance. Even if it would be patently ridiculous in the cold, sober light of day. You reach for and grasp anything that feels like it might be something solid: *I need a pizza and a bag of Doritos. Skinny-dipping in this public fountain is a good idea. I should have sex with this guy I just met. I should call my mom and tell her I love her even though it's two* A.M.

Or, in this particular case, *My sister wants a baby and I should make one for her to show her how much I love her and appreciate everything she's done for me.*

The sentiment was fine—noble, even. My solution to the dilemma was . . . not.

It was nearly one by the time I found myself back at Elli's house, not quite clear on how I'd managed to navigate my way home. The house was dark, shuttered tight, the HVAC compressor humming quietly. I let myself in and stumbled around the downstairs, looking for my sister's liquor cabinet. There was a wet bar in the living room, which my sister had thoughtfully cleaned out before my arrival, but surely she had to have stashed the bottles in a cabinet somewhere.

I almost tripped over Chuck, asleep on the couch in the den. I stood weaving over him, trying to bring him into focus in the gloom. The gold hair against the dark blue pillow, the rise and fall of his breath under the thread-worn gray tee he wore to bed: He was handsome as a Greek statue chipped from smooth marble. No wonder he wanted his DNA and my sister's DNA mixed together in a child, I thought. Any child of theirs would be extraordinarily beautiful.

Oh, but Elli's DNA was my DNA, too.

As I stood there, I understood suddenly what I had to do, with an imperativeness that almost knocked me off my feet.

I stumbled out of the room and went to the laundry room, where I found a pile of my sister's clothes in a basket waiting to be folded. I found her favorite perfume in a pocket of her purse in the kitchen. I went to the bathroom, changed, scrubbed my face clean of makeup that might give me away, and pulled my hair up in a messy bun like Elli wore. I looked in the mirror and even though I couldn't quite focus—the room blurred and pulsed with every breath and my eyes were going sideways—I knew I could see my sister in the person looking back at me. Good enough, right? *Men like Chuck don't bother to look hard at women,* I told myself;

they never think to question their privileged realities and wonder just who is adoring them. It had worked on our seventeenth birthday and there was no reason it wouldn't work now.

I'll be you, I thought.

I was ovulating. I'd learned how to identify this pretty easily, during those rounds of egg retrieval over the years—from the number of days in my cycle, from the pang in my side, from the consistency of my mucus. It was now or never. Elli had already turned down my offer to donate an egg, but once it was presented to her as a done deal, a baby already conceived, wouldn't she be thrilled? Wouldn't she forgive me? Wouldn't it bring us close again? Wouldn't it make up for all the ways I'd let her down before?

I was nearly blackout drunk. Which isn't an excuse. But it will hopefully explain why it seemed perfectly logical—selfless, really—to walk back in the den and crawl under the blanket with Chuck and run my hand down his chest and whisper in his ear, "Let's do it."

I was wrong about men being blind to women, apparently, because it took Chuck only a minute—maybe two—to figure out that I was not his wife. At first, he just stirred in the dark, eyes closed, sleepily running his hands up and down my body as I pressed myself against him. He must have connected with something that felt familiar at first: the soft texture of Elli's T-shirt, the rise of her hip, the heft of her hair. And the smell of her perfume, surely that was right.

I lay there for a moment, steeling myself against a sudden wave of revulsion. *Hadn't I screwed plenty of men I didn't like when I was drunk?* I told myself. *Why was this any different?* And then I reached for his sweatpants. He shifted slightly to let me work on the drawstring, which was tied in a tight knot. I fumbled at this, with fingers that didn't know how to obey. I could feel him growing hard and hot below my hand, and he kept trying to kiss me, though I turned my head from his lips, feigning focus. The alarming reality of the situation was quickly setting in—*this is a terrible idea*—but I kept at the knot, tearing at it madly. Eventually, I gave up and tried to tug the sweatpants down without loosening the drawstring.

The room spun in giddy circles around me; I realized that I was dangerously close to throwing up.

The sweatpants lodged on his hips and wouldn't budge. And now he was awake enough that he finally opened his eyes. "Here," he said, "I'll do it." He reached down with his own hand and began to work at the knot and then he suddenly shifted, his eyes going sharp, and he was *looking* at me.

"Elli . . . ?" It wasn't a question so much as an expression of hope. *Please be Elli.*

But he already knew the answer. Maybe it was my breath, still shot with booze, that had given me away. Maybe Elli had a gentler touch, as opposed to my panicky, aggressive fumble. Regardless, he jerked upright, sitting up so quickly that I slid straight off the couch and onto the floor with a loud thump.

He stared at me in disbelief. "What the fuck, Sam."

I lay on the floor, stunned, my head ringing from where I'd made contact with the edge of the coffee table. "I'm sorry— I'm . . . just trying to help."

His voice was awfully loud. "By trying to *have sex* with me?"

Already, I could hear noise overhead, the soft patter of bare footfall on floorboard. I'd woken up my sister. *Shit.*

"I didn't *want* to have sex with you. I was just trying to . . . make a baby, for you guys." The words felt thick and convoluted in my mouth, making no sense even to me. "Because I *love* Elli. Because I want you guys to have what you want because you have been so good to me."

He wrapped his arms protectively around his chest, as if he thought I might fling myself at him again. "That's insane, Sam. You need help."

And suddenly Elli was standing in the doorway, holding a silk bathrobe closed with one fist, her hair wild, eyes swollen into slits. She stared at me, rolling around on the floor, trying and failing to sit upright.

"Are you *drunk*? Seriously? Oh, *Sam*."

The notes of concern and disappointment in her voice—that *this,* my sobriety, was what she was most worried about at this particular moment—nearly broke me in two. A momentary uplift of hope: *She doesn't know what I just did.* Why would she? I was on the floor, drunk. Chuck and I were both dressed. Maybe I'd get away with it. Maybe Chuck would help me sweep it under the rug, a terrible mistake we would pretend never happened, to preserve Elli's feelings.

I think I understood then, for the first time, just how fragile my sister was, and that this might be the moment that would break her.

I rolled on the floor, fumbling my words. "I'm so sorry—it was just a few drinks . . . a onetime thing . . . I'll go back to rehab."

But Chuck was speaking over me, his voice pleading and needy. "I swear, Elli, I didn't do anything. She just climbed under the blanket and . . . nothing happened, I swear."

Now my sister froze, suddenly understanding—or misunderstanding—the situation. "I'm sorry, *what*?"

I finally maneuvered myself into a sitting position, trying to ignore the dangerous heave in my stomach, the bile lifting in my throat. "No—you don't understand . . . It's not what it sounds like."

"You're wearing my clothes." She blinked, took a step backward. "Oh Jesus. Oh my God. Please tell me you didn't."

I had pushed myself to a full stand, but now I slid sideways against the couch. "I was just trying to help you. I want to be your surrogate. Maybe this was a stupid way to do it, but I want to do this for you and I thought"—I was crying now, sober enough to see that I had done something unfathomably stupid, something irrevocably terrible—"I thought you wouldn't let me."

She had gone white, her face a pale moon in the dark.

"Get out," she whispered hoarsely. "Get out *now* and don't come back."

And so I did.

And that was the last time I spoke with my sister: 388 days ago. Not that I was counting.

18

GENFEM HAD ONCE BEEN a summer camp, probably built in the 1950s. The campus stretched out under a canopy of oaks, a sprawl of old clapboard buildings that gripped the hillside. The road on which I entered with Suzy and Ruth wound on through the trees, past an empty swimming pool, and ended at a small parking lot that held a bright red Land Rover, a gold Mercedes, and a cluster of other cars, mostly expensive and European. Just past this lot was the main building, a two-story lodge with a wraparound porch and a flagpole. An old wooden sign on a heavy post lay splintered in the weeds at the edge of the parking lot: *WigWam Woods Christian Youth Camp*. Someone had lodged an axe between the *W* and the *i*.

The rest of the buildings—smaller bunkhouses and bathrooms—nestled farther up the hill, half-hidden between the trees. The bunkhouses had whimsical Hansel and Gretel trim around the windows and doors, which had been painted in a bright collection of rainbow hues, as if a child had come in with a box of crayons and decided to add some color to the scene.

At the center of camp, between the main lodge and the bunk buildings, was a great lawn that had gone brown from too much sun. On the far end was an amphitheater, with benches tiered around a stage; and at the center of this was a small, altar-like platform that looked like it might have once supported a giant cross. Now it held another one of those statues of the naked female form. She was at least seven feet tall and had been constructed out of barbed wire, an arm lifted toward the sky.

Everywhere I looked, there were women in white linen. A half dozen of them sat in a circle on the great lawn, intently listening to another woman who seemed to be giving some sort of lesson. Other women scurried between the bunkhouses, carrying mops and buckets, duffel bags, stacks of books, nothing at all. A few wore red, and the one teaching was in yellow—these women, I noted, had normal hair—and I wondered if these dresses denoted status, or duration of their stay. If you looked past the drastic haircuts and the shapeless garb, these woman didn't *look* particularly brainwashed. They looked . . . happy. A pair of middle-aged women walked past me toward the main lodge, giggling, clutching each other's hands. Another woman sat cross-legged, reading, serene, in a patch of sun under a tree.

The overall effect, with the smiles and the Crayola paint job, was less cultish and more monkish, as if these women were novitiates in some colorful new religion.

One of the women holding hands nodded at me as she passed. "*Shanti shanti,* Eleanor," she said and smiled. Or maybe it was *enchantée*? I felt disoriented, as if I'd found myself in a foreign land where I didn't understand the language.

Once we were inside the gate, Ruth grabbed the groceries from me, her eyes scanning the women in the field, as if someone out there might be watching. I followed the two women up the road toward the main lodge, searching every face that passed me. None was Elli's. Maybe she was out in the group on the lawn? But from a distance everyone looked the same, a blur of naked heads and white forms slipping between the sun-parched trees.

At the lodge, the two women scurried toward the back of the building, disappearing through a door without even bothering to say goodbye. Without them, I felt exposed. What now? It wasn't like I could walk around asking anyone if they'd seen my sister; I *was* my sister.

I could smell something cooking, onions and cumin; and just as it registered that this was dinner hour, a bell began to ring. The inhabitants of the camp shifted and turned almost in unison, their attention moving toward the main lodge. The women sitting on the lawn stood, wiping dead grass from their rears, gathering books and sun hats. In a minute, they would all be upon me, and what would I do then? What if Elli *was* among them and the whole ruse fell apart?

I really hadn't thought this whole thing through.

An adrenaline kick moved my feet before I'd even decided I needed to get out of sight. I walked away from the main lodge, turning up one of the smaller paths that led to the bunkhouses, my head down to avoid the attention of the women who were passing me on their way down the hill.

Halfway up the hill I felt a hand on my arm, stopping me. *Elli,* I thought. But when I looked up I realized that the hand belonged to the woman with the caterpillar eyebrows, the one who'd confronted me on the road during my first visit to the compound. Today she was wearing a yellow dress, and a new air of authority. *She recognizes me,* I thought, but the expression on her face was of consternation, not anger.

"Where are you going?" she whispered, her eyes flicking down the hill.

I thought fast. "Bathroom?"

She frowned. "Use the one in the lodge. Dinner is in five minutes. You'll get a Sufferance again if you're not careful. That'll be three times this week."

I thought fast. "But I have to get a tampon and they don't have any down there."

"You have one in your cabin?" She looked up the hill, her eyes falling on a bunkhouse with orange trim, as if measuring the time it might take to get there and back. "OK. I'll get you dispensation. Ten minutes enough?"

"Sure." The bell in the main lodge rang a second time. Around me, the women picked up their paces, scurried a little faster. Caterpillar Brows let go of my arm and jogged after them.

I turned and raced up the hill toward the bunkhouse with the orange trim, no longer bothering to try to make myself invisible.

And then, like an apparition, I saw her. Standing on the top of the steps just outside the door to the orange-trimmed bunkhouse, her white dress billowing around her, her naked head pink and vulnerable. Slack-jawed and disbelieving as she watched me ascending the stairs: My sister. My twin. My Elli.

"Sam?"

Her voice was tiny, barely a hiccup.

Right away I saw that we weren't at all identical anymore. She'd grown thin since I saw her last, with hollows under her eyes and matchstick legs covered with inflamed bug bites. Her blue eyes protruded slightly from her skull, making her look ravenous and haunted. My poor sister. It seemed impossible that Suzy and Ruth and Caterpillar Brows had seen me as their Eleanor. But so often we see only what we expect to see. We are deceived by our own ingrained assumptions.

I stopped just below her on the stairs, out of breath from the climb. "Elli, what *is* this place? Are you OK?"

She was staring at the telltale dress I was wearing. "I don't understand . . . you joined? And they let you come here already? They didn't tell me."

I touched the fabric of the dress, pulled it away from my body. "No. I just put this on in order to get in here."

Her eyes were glazed, distant. "But your hair . . ."

I stepped closer, grabbed her hand. It felt like a hollow-boned bird, quivering in my grip. "Look. Did they tell you I came by earlier this week? With Charlotte. They wouldn't let us in to see you."

"You did? But . . ." Her voice trailed off and she stared down the steps toward the great lawn, where the last stragglers were racing toward the main lodge. She seemed to wake up then. "We have to get inside." Her hand came to life, gripping mine as she pulled me toward the bunkhouse. Then she hesitated, reconsidered, looked around, her eyes fixing on a small building a little farther up the stairs.

"Let's go to the bathroom. It's got the only door that locks. We'll be safe."

We'll be safe. With those three words I understood, with a sickening finality, that we weren't safe at all.

The bathroom was a cold, concrete box that smelled like mold and bleach. The toilet seat had no lid and the ancient mirror was spotted with rust. Bugs crawled in through the louvered window slats. I imagined the generations of children that had gingerly crouched over that toilet, holding their breath, watching for spiders.

My sister locked the door behind us and then we stood there, motionless, listening for footsteps on the stairs.

"They'll be up soon looking for me," she murmured. "You're not supposed to miss meals."

"I pretended I was you. I told them I needed to get a tampon. They gave you ten minutes."

She seemed to finally understand then; and she laughed, though it was on delay, a terrifyingly empty sound. "God, that's so *you.*" The smile faded, replaced with hollow longing. She leaned in and whispered urgently, "How is Charlotte?"

Suddenly, I was furious with my sister's pretense. "You mean Emma? She's doing fine. Considering that she apparently went missing from Scottsdale four months ago and hasn't seen her parents since."

Elli went still, her eyes huge in her face. "Oh," she said softly.

I waited for her to continue, but she seemed to have lost the ability to string words together.

"Yeah, *oh*. For fuck's sake, Elli. What the hell is going on? What are you doing here? Why haven't you responded to any of my text messages?"

She flinched with each question. "They took my phone," she said. "I haven't earned it back yet. It's my Sufferance."

If she hadn't seen my text with the photo of Charlotte's Missing flyer, hadn't read all those messages I'd sent, then who *had* been reading them? And, oh God, what were they planning to do with the information I'd unintentionally conveyed? I cursed myself for not considering this option. *Of course* they'd been monitoring her communication.

"Let's go step-by-step," I said slowly. "Is this place a cult?"

"A *cult*?" She looked stunned, as if the thought had never occurred to her. "Of course it's not. It's a women's movement. They've been trying to help me with my issues."

"Help you with *what* issues? The fact that you are in possession of a missing child?"

She shook her head. "It's too complicated to get into now." Her eyes met mine, trepidatious, and then darted away. I could tell there was something she was thinking that she wasn't going to tell me.

"Well, are you allowed to leave?"

She struggled against the question. "That would be a bad idea."

"Bad, as in *inadvisable*? Or bad as in *forbidden*?" She shook her head. She was staring at something over my shoulder and I turned to see her looking at herself in the mirror with a look of vague horror. She lifted a hand to her face and gently probed the dark hollows above her cheekbones, before sliding her eyes over to study my face, instinctively comparing the two. I couldn't see the parallels between us today; I could only see the differences. The lines around my eyes from too many years of hard drinking; the thin spots in her eyebrows from overplucking. Her eyes wide and open and desperate where mine were hooded and suspicious. Her dimples gone sharp from weight loss.

"We don't match anymore," I said sadly.

"We haven't matched in a long time." She closed her eyes and turned away from the mirror. "I should go to dinner, and you should go home. There's nothing for you to do here." She reached out and unlocked the latch of the door, but I reached out and stopped her hand.

"Are you serious? You really want to stay in this place? You're just going to . . . ditch me?" There was a wobble in my voice, a stinging behind my eyes.

She flinched. "It's always about you, isn't it?" she said softly.

"This has *nothing* to do with me," I retorted.

Her eyes met mine. "This has *everything* to do with you," she said, her voice cracking.

My hand on her wrist grew tighter. She winced, and I released it, giving up. What a waste this had been. *My sister has become a stranger; she's not my other half anymore,* I thought. And then it occurred to me that this must have been what Elli thought when I showed up at her door, high and incoherent, time and time again; when I threw myself at her husband, in the name of "helping" her; when I took her money and betrayed her trust. All the way back to high school, when I guilt-tripped her into coming back to Los Angeles with me to perform a job she hated. She was right: We hadn't matched in a long time, and that was more my fault than hers.

She was here to work out her issues. Well, hadn't I been her issue since the day we were born? So maybe all this was my fault. I'd broken her—maybe as early as that day on Splash Mountain—and she'd never healed correctly.

I watched helplessly as she opened the door and peered down the steps, preparing to dash to the lodge. "So what am I supposed to do now?" I said to her back. "Just leave you here and go back to Santa Barbara to keep taking care of Charlotte for you? You want *me* to be her mother? Am I supposed to keep pretending that I don't know who Charlotte really is?"

She stopped then, and turned to me, surprise on her face. "So you do know, then? You figured it out?"

"Figured out that you stole her? Yes. I already said that."

"No," she said, frowning. "I mean, who she really is."

"Yes." I was growing frustrated by her willful cluelessness. "Her name is Emma Gonzalez."

"No," she said again. "That's not what I meant."

"Oh for God's sake, stop being so cryptic, Elli. Just spill it."

She looked out the door then, down the steps to the lodge, as if measuring the distance between us and them. Faint voices carried up in the distance, the high soprano hum of women singing in unison. Night had fallen and the oaks rustled overhead, sending a shower of brittle leaves clattering to the stairs. Slowly, my sister closed the door, turning to face me.

"She's yours," Elli said. "Charlotte is your daughter."

ELLI

part two

WHEN WE WERE CHILDREN, *we treated it like a game: You be me, and I'll be you. In the bathroom, when we were brushing our teeth; in school, when our teacher was droning on too long; on set, when we were picking up our lunch paninis, one of us would give the signal, and we would switch. Settling faces, rearranging limbs, changing inflections. By the time we got to high school it had become an art form. We studied each other's mannerisms like a textbook—the way we each held our toothbrushes or doodled in our notebooks or chewed our sandwiches. We even came up with a secret hand signal, a twist of a flattened hand, that meant* Let's switch.

How proud we were that we knew each other so well. How secretly pleased to have two personae to play with, when most kids only had one. We didn't realize how dangerous it was.

I remember eating dinner with my parents one night, our freshman year, and my father looking up just a few moments after my sister had flashed me the signal. He caught me slumping over my plate, idly smashing my spaghetti with a fork, while across the table Sam was neatly cutting her meatball into quarters. My father glanced at me, then at Sam, gave a small frown, then turned back to me: "Sam, pass the salt, please."

Across the table, Sam laughed into her napkin and I thought I might explode with the joy of our secret.

I liked being Sam, more than I liked seeing myself in her. The Elli I saw mirrored back in Sam's face was never quite as interesting, never quite as vivacious. I sometimes wondered why I didn't just step into the Sam persona and stay there, forever. Why couldn't we both be her?

Of course, I didn't know then what lay ahead for her in life, how quickly she would crash.

The game stopped being fun on the night of our seventeenth birthday, the night I became Sam in order to kiss her boyfriend. When my lips met Nick's—when I felt the strange, soft shock of his tongue—I suddenly knew that I'd given some critical piece of myself away to my sister. My first kiss had belonged to her; the desire he felt was for Sam, not me. I would never get that moment back. Some piece of first love was forever lost to me.

How much more of myself was I in danger of losing to our game?

Queasy, my stomach churning with Long Island Iced Tea, I'd leapt from Nick's lap, but not before I'd seen my sister across the illuminated dance floor. She was watching us, her eyes hot with ownership. Not ownership of Nick, ownership of me. But—me as her, or her as me, or me as myself? It was all getting too confusing. Even drunk, I knew that we'd gone too far.

We had to stop, but I knew that if Sam had her way, we never would. And if I broke away—if I ended the game, killed our TV show, put space between us—it was going to tear Sam apart. What would happen to her if I wasn't there to pick her up and set her straight?

Even then, even before she fell into the abyss, I understood where Sam was weak. She thought she was the tough one, the strong one, that she had to protect me from my fears—and she wasn't wrong—but I also knew exactly what would make her fall apart. She was no good at all at being alone.

———

This was a Trigger Moment that I was unwilling to share, not with Iona, not with Dr. Cindy. I was afraid to tell them that I knew that Sam's addiction was my fault, because I was afraid of getting lost in her, and so I sacrificed us in order to save myself. I was afraid of Reenacting this moment with them and changing it forever.

The guilt was all I had left of my sister, and so I clung to it, unwilling to let go.

I WAS IN A cult.

Even now, these many months later, these words feel strange in my mouth. Eleanor Hart, *née* Logan, former child actress, former cult member. Both feel equally antithetical to my vision of myself, and yet both are true.

When I first returned from Ojai, I spent many sleepless nights skimming cult recovery sites with names like Dare to Doubt and The Art of Leaving, reading testimonials and taking quizzes: *Wonder if you are in a cult? Eleven important signs.* I'd take the tests over and over, just in case the calculations might come out differently, absolving me of this particular sin—the sin of cluelessness—but the results were always the same. I could be absolved of nothing.

Like it or not, I had joined a cult.

Although what you also have to understand is that no one *decides* to join a cult. It's something that sneaks up on you, like a frog in a pot with the heat turned up underneath it, swimming complacently in the warming water, until it boils alive.

You do not *join a cult*, because cults don't advertise themselves as cults. They are *self-help groups* or *spiritual movements* or *guru-centric religions*. When you join one, you believe that you are simply being a *proactive person* identifying a *core issue* in your life and using a *success strategy system* to resolve it (this, at least, was the GenFem terminology). And how could that possibly be a bad thing? You weave your way through a world that beats a constant drum of self-improvement—whether through meditation or lip fillers or hypnotherapy, through watching Oprah or reading Deepak—and you believe that joining one of these groups is just another path toward a better you. Toward a brighter, shinier, more self-assured future.

You have to continue believing that, too; even as you find yourself spending hundreds of thousands of dollars to reach this ever-elusive brighter future; even as everyone you love is slowly peeled away from you; even when you find yourself locked inside a gated compound with a shaved head and a case of mild malnutrition. Even when you find yourself committing crimes in the name of self-improvement. Our innate compulsion toward confirmation bias means that until the moment when you feel that water boiling around you—the pain too excruciating to ignore—you will keep telling yourself that it's everyone *else* who is getting it wrong. Because look how much you've already given up for this dream! You have to keep believing that you were right—that this isn't a cult, for God's sake; that your shiny future is still a possibility—because the only other option is to accept that you have made a colossal mistake.

I made a colossal mistake.

Somewhere, deep inside me, I knew this. Even before I left the GenFem compound, I think I was aware. The water had grown too hot to deny. What was happening there, in Ojai—what had happened to me, with my life, with Charlotte, with Sam—had moved beyond the soft boundaries of self-improvement and descended into a world that was downright *bad*.

And yet, when Sam tracked me down at the compound and looked me straight in the eyes and accused me of joining a cult, I still experienced a jolt of rejection. *I* joined a *cult*? Nononono. I did not. It wasn't possible. Samantha was wrong. *She* was the one who would make that kind of mistake, not me. Never me.

But even as I recoiled from her accusation that day, I knew that she was right. Even then, I knew what GenFem was, even if I hadn't yet assigned it this particular label. I'd known it for months by then, hadn't I? The truth I couldn't voice out loud, couldn't even acknowledge as a passing thought, even when the mounting evidence grew undeniable.

Yes, yes you did. You joined a cult. You did, you fool. You did you did you did.

WHEN MY SISTER AND I were nine years old, Sam performed in our elementary school's production of *Mary Poppins*, playing the role of Jane Banks. On opening night, I sat in the second row of the auditorium, sandwiched between my mother and father, the room thick with the scent of Twizzlers and unwashed hair. In the dark, chewing furiously on my cuticle, I watched my sister—her face caked with makeup and the too-big costume hanging loosely off her torso—turn into a complete stranger. Much to my surprise, Sam was *good*, so transfigured that I found myself forgetting that the girl onstage was my twin sister, and not a love-starved child in need of a proper British nanny.

It terrified me.

We were at that stage of twindom when parents start worrying about issues like differentiation and overreliance, and so my mother had recently retired our quasi-identical outfits and was no longer encouraging us to do the same after-school activities. Sam got acting and I got soccer, we had separate homeroom teachers, and if that meant less convenience for my mother—now carting us in two directions instead of one—it also meant that we were going to be developing our own "unique personalities."

This, at least, was what I gleaned from the heavily underlined sections of the parenting books that sat on my mother's nightstand next to her incense and cardamom hand lotion. Sometimes, when she was preoccupied in the kitchen, I'd sneak in and read the notes she'd jotted in the margins. Things like *Elli needs her own confidence instead of relying on Sam's* and *separation = individuality* and, most terrifying of all, *what to do if they end up hating each other.*

I didn't know what to make of all this. But even at nine, I was already aware that the tether between myself and Sam had begun to fray. I had only faint memories of the secret language that we had once spoken, back when we slept in the same crib. My mom described it as our "funny twin babble" but Sam and I couldn't remember the words at all anymore. When we lay in bed at night now—separated by a moat of peach pile carpet—we would still sometimes try out nonsense sounds on each other (*Squenchie! Febabal!*) to see if the other could figure out what it meant. It never worked.

We needed *real* words in order to understand each other now; words, and maybe even more. Even though I'd sometimes still look at Sam and sense exactly what she was thinking, feel this awareness as a warm spot somewhere underneath my belly button and know exactly how to assuage her fears, there were also moments when I gazed into her eyes and saw something frighteningly strange there. A blind being pulled down, flat and blank. I didn't like it at all.

And so, as I sat there that night at *Mary Poppins,* watching Sam the Stranger up onstage, her face red with exhilaration as she took her bows and soaked up the applause, I didn't feel happy for her at all. Instead, I mostly felt sick. I didn't want Sam to be feeling things that I didn't understand. I didn't want us to end up hating each other, like my mother's book warned we might.

This might explain why, when Harriet discovered us building our sandcastle on the beach just a few weeks later and wooed us with her promises of fame—*I'll turn your girls into stars*—I didn't balk. I didn't tell Sam that I had no desire at all to be onstage, with the whole world looking at me, that I didn't want to pretend I was someone else entirely, or to play at being famous. Because *she* wanted it, and so if we were to be close again, I was going to have to want it, too.

So when Harriet walked away from us and Sam grabbed my hands and squealed with excitement—"We're going to be *famous*, Elli! We're going to be in *movies*, together!"—I gripped her hands and squealed right back.

"I'm so excited," I trilled as we swung each other in circles. Our bare feet trampled the castle that we'd so carefully constructed, until it collapsed into soggy piles of sand.

Twenty-two years later, Dr. Cindy Medina and I would reenact that day—one of my Trigger Moments, she called it—over and over and over and over again. I sat with her in one of the curtained rooms at the back of the GenFem center—our knees pressed against each other, eyes closed, fingers woven together—as I recalled out loud every detail that I could remember from that day. The way the elastic in my swimsuit was cutting into my leg, the feeling of the sun against the peeling skin of my shoulders, the stubbornness in my sister's voice as she insisted that our sandcastle be square instead of round.

"We're going to be famous," Dr. Cindy said in a mock little-girl voice that was nothing like Sam's, her face so close to mine that I could smell the lunch on her breath (a scoop of tuna on lettuce, no mayo, black coffee). Her hands gripped mine—it felt like my bones would be crushed—as I took her prompt. This time, instead of saying, "I'm so excited," I responded with the truth.

"I don't want to," I whispered, and Dr. Cindy squeezed my hands harder until I answered more loudly, more assertively. *"I don't want to.* I'm not going to go to Hollywood with you. No."

"Good girl." Dr. Cindy's approval melted over me like warm butter. "So you say that, and then what happens?"

My eyes were closed in the velvet darkness, my nose tickled from the smoke of a vanilla candle burning in the corner. I cast my mind toward an alternative reality, tried to bring it into focus. "The opportunity goes away. We don't call Harriet and we never see her again. Life continues in Santa Barbara and Sam and I drift a little bit—because we are unique individuals—but that's OK. We aren't driven apart by Hollywood or her partying or her neediness. Sam doesn't become an actress, or maybe she does, but later, when she's older and has the emotional tools to resist temptation. She doesn't become an addict. She doesn't end up . . ." I trailed off.

Dr. Cindy whispered, "She doesn't end up *what*? We've discussed this."

"A loser," I whispered. It didn't feel good to say this, it felt like a betrayal. But Dr. Cindy taught us that if you're not uncomfortable, you're not doing the Method right. Comfort is laziness; it's complacency. If you want to grow, it has to hurt.

Dr. Cindy leaned in closer. "Good girl. But we don't care about Sam. This is about you, remember? What happens to *you*? How is *your* life better, beyond your sister? What bold steps do *you* take toward actualizing your true, unacknowledged desires?"

At this, I drew a complete blank. "I don't know," I whispered. "I can't see it."

And this is when Dr. Cindy slapped me, hard. "You *can* see it," she said. "You just haven't mastered the IAS Method yet. Identification, Articulation, Self-Determination. We've identified the Trigger Moment, you're starting to articulate what went wrong, but you haven't yet found your self-determination. You haven't broken the pattern because you're still not strong enough. You haven't let go of Sam yet, and until you do you won't be able to move *past* her."

She gave me an ice pack for my cheek and a Sufferance—six hundred calories a day for the next three days, no sugar, no caffeine—and when I came back on the third day, light-headed and shaky with hunger, we ran the Reenactment again. And again, and again, day after day, until finally one day I saw what *should have happened* after that day at the beach. By this point, I wanted them all gone, all the irritants that lived in my mind: the irresponsible sister who broke my heart, the husband who I'd once loved for his placidity but who now just seemed stubbornly inert, the failing florist business that kept me dependent on him, the parents who expected me to make up for my errant sister by being doubly responsible. Everything that I had annoyed me. Everything that I possessed felt like an onerous weight that was keeping me from lifting off and taking flight. My body already felt half-gone; why not just jettison the rest?

"I say no to Hollywood and then I grow up and cut Sam out of my life because she's toxic for me," I said that day, thinking my bones might snap in Dr. Cindy's grip. "Just because she's my twin doesn't mean that I have to help her. I do not spend the next twenty years bailing her out of trouble. And I have more confidence because of this and so I solve all my own problems. I marry a different husband, who doesn't balk at my infertility; and we adopt a child, or two, or three; and I don't have all these emotional issues about having been famous as a kid. I begin a whole new life that allows me to succeed in ways that I haven't even imagined yet. All because I let go of my sister."

Dr. Cindy's grip loosened. She leaned in and pressed dry lips against my forehead. "Good girl," she said. "I'm so proud of you. You're ready to level up."

I opened my eyes and saw her beaming at me, little fires from the candle flickering in her gray eyes, reflecting off the solitary tear of pride that glistened on her cheek. Outside our velvet space, I could hear the murmurs of the other women, doing their own Reenactments with their own Mentors in the little curtained rooms that lined the back of the GenFem center.

"So now what happens?" I asked Dr. Cindy. I felt weightless, as if the only thing now holding me to the surface of the planet was her hand on mine. *This giddiness must be happiness,* I thought. *The happiness I haven't felt in quite some time. What else could it be?*

"Now we get you those things," she said.

21 WE HAD TRIED TO conceive for four years, Chuck and I. Our attempts to make a baby were an experience that slowly stripped the joy from our marriage, like peeling the petals off a flower until you are left with nothing but a naked stamen. Haphazard optimism—birth control gleefully tossed in the trash—had eventually led to scheduled sex, which then led to ovulation kits and learning terms like *mucus consistency* and *basal temperature*.

By year three, things had grown more serious. But since I was still in my twenties, interventions like IVF felt unnecessary—or so Chuck, always fiscally conservative, argued. "It's such an ordeal, and it's so expensive," he'd mused when I broached the subject. "You still have youth on your side. It'll all work out." Instead, I started in on noninvasive therapies: acupuncture, stress-relieving massages, and aromatic balms for my belly that were prepared by a Chinese herbalist in Ventura. I ate sunflower seeds and drank bone broth and buckets of pomegranate juice.

Eventually I started lurking on fertility message boards, jotting down obscure treatments that other women *swore* had gotten them pregnant. I made an appointment for Mayan abdominal therapy, which was supposed to guide my misaligned organs into their optimal positions, but that mostly just made me feel constipated. I went to a crystal fertility healer that my mother had heard about; the healer placed carnelian and moonstone rocks on my stomach and then left me lying in the dark for two hours, listening to whale songs. A college friend dragged me to a fertility rite at a beach house in Malibu, where a group of panicky-looking women sipped on raspberry leaf tea and swapped phone numbers for their dermatologists.

Nothing worked, of course, and the compounding failures made me feel frail and useless, like a hollow egg missing that essential yolk. Chuck watched me from a distance, unable to relate to my mounting panic. I could feel his eagerness to grow our family waning, in opposition to mine. "I'm not sure all this stress is good for you." "Is it so awful, just the two of us?" "A baby would get in the way of my CrossFit schedule anyway," he'd joke, trying to cheer me up, but I didn't think it was all that funny.

Of course, it turned out that the problem was something that pomegranate juice and massages could never fix, something buried deep in my genes. By the time I finally convinced Chuck that we needed to suck it up and do the IVF, we'd been trying for nearly four years. But in preparation for my first round of progesterone shots, I underwent a barrage of ultrasounds and blood tests that revealed what I wished I'd known on day one: My ovaries were incapable of generating viable eggs.

Four years I had spent single-mindedly pursuing a goal that I never had the slightest chance of meeting. The endgame—a baby of our own—had become the singular driving force of my life, and so the news of my infertility made me feel like Charlie Brown when Lucy pulls the football away from him. A chump, a blindly trusting fool.

No wonder I was so angry when I finally found out: at my own faithless body, at Chuck for his lack of support, at my sister for being able to conceive when I could not. No wonder that when the dam broke that night in the den, and everything finally came flooding out, I found myself so deep underwater.

No wonder I was so primed for GenFem.

———

The important thing about GenFem isn't how I got there the first time (it was a woman in my Pilates class, who noticed me weeping during stretches and suggested I visit her "women's support group"), but that I *joined*. That Dr. Cindy noted my presence from my very first meeting, where I sat in the back with my Pilates friend, and singled me out. "Come up here, new girl, pretty girl, sad girl," she said, gesturing me to the front of the room where she sat on a high stool like an eagle on a perch. "You look like you're in need of a Confrontation."

I didn't know what a Confrontation was and didn't much like the idea of going onstage in front of all those strangers (I had gratefully left all *that* behind when I was eighteen), but something about the way Dr. Cindy was looking at me made me feel like I had no choice in the matter. The pamphlet I'd been handed when I walked through the door said that Dr. Cindy Medina—*but just Dr. Cindy to us!*—was a world-renowned psychologist with ninety-seven international patents for behavioral therapy breakthroughs. She had a PhD plus a string of unrecognizable abbreviations after her name that made me feel stupid and uneducated.

In person, she exuded a friendly gravitas, an aura of success, that demanded you take her seriously. Nearly twice my age, she had finger-wide gray streaks in her black bob, neat wire-rimmed glasses, and a gold silk scarf knotted loosely at her neck. *I will never figure out how to tie a scarf like that,* I thought as I stood up. It looked both effortless and utterly intentional.

Did Dr. Cindy know who I was when she singled me out from the crowd? She pretended she didn't, but looking back on it now, she *must* have known. Dr. Cindy always did her research.

In any case, on that first day, in just half an hour onstage, Dr. Cindy tore my whole life story out of me: from the day I was born eleven minutes after my twin sister to the night when I kicked that sister out of my house, telling her to "get out *now* and don't come back." The whole messy tale of Sam-and-Elli, and by the time I got to the end, I was in tears. The injury of it felt just as raw as it did in the moment—just two weeks earlier!—when I'd caught my sister drunk in the den, dressed as me, trying to get my husband to impregnate her.

I found myself publicly weeping at the unfairness of it all. That I couldn't get pregnant, but *Sam*, my flighty twin? The one who didn't even want a kid? *She* could.

I'd spent my life being the counterweight to Sam, I told Dr. Cindy in that first Confrontation. I was always trying to balance Sam's chaos and destruction, making myself small next to her larger-than-life persona. Always being the hand she could use to steady herself when things got rocky. I'd told myself that I was being a positive role model, and that *Sam* was the one who had things wrong. And yet, as Dr. Cindy pried the story out of me, I began to realize that I'd just been a doormat, letting Sam step on me as she saw fit. I'd done everything "right"—reliable husband, beautiful home, creative job, lots of money, blah blah blah—and yet none of it made me happy because I'd been denied the one thing I wanted the most. A baby of my own.

I was angry, and I didn't know what to do with my anger. I never had.

As I told my story, Dr. Cindy sat across from me on the small GenFem stage. Her eyes held my gaze so tight that I couldn't look away; her breath was in perfect time with mine; her voice like a smooth pond upon which I could trustingly skate. She nodded at the end of each of my sentences, encouraging me, making me open myself wide.

In the audience, two dozen women watched the Confrontation, their damp eyes mirroring my tears, all of us as one in our common understanding that life isn't fair.

"You're right. Life isn't fair," Dr. Cindy said when I was finally done talking. "But so what? We can *make* it fair. We can grab life by the balls and force it to give us what we want the most. That anger you feel? It's time to start using it. So now that you've put a name and face on your pain, I want you to look it right in the eye and tell it to go away. You're going to choose not to be a victim." When I shook my head, laughing a little, she repeated herself, suddenly impatient. "I mean it. Scream it. Be rude."

I hesitated, then I closed my eyes, and let the words pour out of me. "Go away, pain! I choose not to be a victim! Fuck you!" My heart pounded out of my chest. I was a little shocked at myself. It was thrilling.

Dr. Cindy smiled, gripped my hand. "Good girl. That's how we start." She turned to face the room, a stillness emanating from her that made the air electric, brought goosebumps to all of our arms. "Women are taught to be nice," she said. "We are supposed to be kind and gentle and nurturing. We're supposed to gracefully accept the ways that the world has shafted us, put us in positions of vulnerability, while instead giving all the opportunities in life to the loudest, largest voices in the room. Usually that's men, but sometimes it's women, too.

"My patented Method empowers women to reclaim the ability to steer their own destinies, letting go of the restrictions that society has mandated on what is right and wrong for us to do," she continued. "I want to revolutionize the world by teaching women their self-worth, helping them remove all the toxic obstructions from their lives, so that they can take what's rightly theirs. I want *you*"—her finger scanned the room, landing on each of our faces—"to achieve the success you're all seeking." Two dozen shining eyes lifted hopefully to hers. "I can teach you."

I stepped off the tiny stage, shaking, feeling like that hollow-shell place inside me had been filled up with a hot light. She was going to help me get—no, *take*—what I wanted most. I didn't know how, but I wanted in. Of course I did.

After the Confrontation the women in the room made a point of coming over to introduce themselves to me. They carried Kate Spade bags, wore cute floral sundresses, and their hair was blown out and shiny. They all seemed so happy and beautiful and put together. They spontaneously hugged me as if I were a long-lost sister and not a stranger who had just wandered in the door. I felt dizzy and disoriented, but pleasantly so, as if I'd come back to a home that I didn't realize was there.

Before I walked out the door that night, I signed up for a five-day workshop with Dr. Cindy the following week. Limited time offer, a reduced price of only three thousand dollars that night only.

I would achieve Level One by the end of the month.

By the end of the year, five months and fifty thousand dollars later, I'd made it to Level Four. A lot of money, yes, but money well spent, I told myself; I was part of a *revolutionary sisterhood*, changing women's lives for the better (and my own, in the process). Anyway, I had well over a million dollars collecting dust in the bank account that my parents opened for me back when Sam and I cashed our first *To the Maxx* paychecks. There was no child to spend it on, and I wasn't paying for any more of Sam's rehab, so I figured I might as well use it to make myself happier.

Dr. Cindy said the money would come back to me manifold once I'd conquered the Method and achieved Level Ten.

So I went to meeting after meeting, workshop after workshop, letting GenFem hone my pain into a sharp point of rage, with which I felt I could stab the world, poke it wide open, leave a hole through which to climb to the bright, clear air on the other side. A more hopeful place, where I could leave all my disappointments behind.

Women came and went from GenFem over the early months that I was there. Some—like the Pilates friend who brought me in the first place—were just dipping their toes, with no intention of jumping in fully. I quickly learned to recognize these women by the way their eyes never quite met mine, how they shifted back on their heels when they talked, as if preparing to run out the door. The other women, the ones who stuck with the Method, were *Neos,* working their way through the levels. Once you reached Level Ten, you could apply to become a *Mentor,* a full-time Gen-Fem career. Mentors were identifiable by the pink scarves at their necks and the look of serene confidence in their faces. There were three Mentors at the center in Santa Barbara—a Black woman named Roni, who sold real estate; an artist named Shella, known for her enormous statues of women assembled from unconventional materials; and a formidable lesbian ex-lawyer named Iona, who was my assigned Mentor.

Dr. Cindy would come and go, jetting across the country to visit the other centers, giving lectures at foreign universities, and visiting with world leaders. (A photo of her shaking Malala's hand was hung by the doorway.) Word was she owned a stunning Spanish estate in the hills of Montecito, but no one had ever seen it.

When she was in town, I could book special one-on-one sessions with her; they cost extra, but they were always worth it. Dr. Cindy gave off a sizzle of authority, as if she saw and understood everything in the world with just a glance. She seemed so *sure,* where I was not. When I was with her in that velvet Reenactment room it felt like I was so close to seeing things clearly, the entirety of my past and my future, the meaning of life itself. All I needed to do was squint just a little harder (or buy a Reenactment ten-pack series) and I'd *get it,* just like Dr. Cindy did. Maybe then, I'd know what to do to be happy, how to steer my ship toward achievable goals.

The higher-level Neos vanished on occasion. They'd be there one day, their faces flush with some secret that they wouldn't divulge, their eyes damp and wild, then the following week, they'd be gone. A Mentor would inform us that they'd gone to recruit for a center in Toronto or New Jersey, but those of us in the lower levels sometimes speculated that they'd checked into the retreat. The retreat was invitation-only, held at the secret GenFem compound in Ojai, and you couldn't tell who had been because they weren't allowed to tell you that they'd gone. But we could always guess because of the haircuts. When they rematerialized, luminous with suppressed secrets, their heads were almost always shaved, like warrior queens.

Chuck didn't much like GenFem. He didn't like that I was no longer spending my evenings with him, watching ESPN and laugh-track comedies. Instead I was spending them at workshops or doing Reenactments with my Mentor. When he arrived home from work, I was no longer busy cooking us dinner, but deep in GenFem matrix worksheets that diagrammed all the things standing in the way of my success. While I studied he would bang around the kitchen, huffing into the cupboards, asking aloud why no one had bothered to go grocery shopping that week.

GenFem didn't much like Chuck, either.

"Make him cook his own dinner," Iona scoffed when I told her that Chuck thought I was spending too much time at the center. A sinewy blonde ten years my senior—her opinions as sharp as her cheekbones—Iona had been with GenFem since Dr. Cindy started the movement, three years earlier. She used to be a cutthroat corporate lawyer but she gave up her partnership to work at the center full-time as a Mentor, and she told me she'd never been so happy and fulfilled. (Under Dr. Cindy's mentoring, she'd also left her controlling ex-wife and the beachfront mansion they'd occupied together.) I was starting to fantasize about closing my florist shop and working full-time as a GenFem Mentor, too, once I hit Level Ten. After all, my business was barely subsisting, which Dr. Cindy said was part of my pattern of resigning myself to being second best: less interesting than my sister, less successful than my husband.

"Your husband's behavior is pure patriarchal laziness," Iona continued. "He's got you at his beck and call. You shouldn't tolerate it."

"But he makes so much more money than me and works such long hours." I knew how weak this sounded, that this would get me a Sufferance, but I was not strong enough to think otherwise yet. "And I'm usually done with work in time to make dinner, but he never is. Someone has to cook so it kind of makes sense that it would be my job, right?"

"Do you *like* cooking dinner?"

A worm curled inside me, a tight squirming coil. "Not really."

Iona fixed me with a dark stare. "So he gets everything he likes and you get nothing you like. Sounds similar to the logic that is keeping you from getting your baby, too. Because a kid might be too much *hassle* for him, he's afraid he might not love a kid that isn't his biological spawn, and his feelings are more important than yours."

I nodded mutely, seeing the connection.

"That's what we call Devaluation. I think you need a Sufferance until you remember your own self-worth. Let's say, three days of sleeping outside on your pool chaise. No blankets."

It was December by then, with chilly nights, and Chuck thought I was insane, plus I ended up with a terrible cold; but I didn't mind. Sufferances made me feel empowered and disciplined, as if I were a soldier that had pushed past the pain and won a battle. Sufferances made everything else seem achievable, which Dr. Cindy said was the whole point.

After that conversation with Iona I never again openly questioned my value relative to Chuck. Instead, just before Christmas, with Iona's coaching, I gave him an ultimatum: Since we couldn't make a baby on our own, we would instead adopt a baby. He needed to suck it up, stop balking, and start the process with me or else . . . I didn't finish the sentence, didn't want to threaten to throw him out, although that's what Iona had told me might be necessary. I still thought we might be able to resolve our problems, start a family, get a fresh start now that I had GenFem propping me up.

We sat across the dinner table from each other, a platter of cold salmon between us. I watched Chuck push individual grains of rice into a symmetrical row, his gaze fixed on his plate so that he wouldn't have to meet my eyes. "Having a kid is something we *both* have to be really enthusiastic about, don't you think?" He spoke so softly I had to lean in to hear him; I felt an unwelcome surge of empathy at how broken he suddenly sounded. "And the idea of adoption . . . I just can't help but feel ambivalent. I don't want *a* kid. I want *our* kid. Yours and mine. No one else's."

The smell of fish brine and capers was making me queasy. "But we can just start the process. It's so long, I'm sure you'll come around. It's just a mental block, an irrational fear. There are therapists you could talk to, to work through this . . ."

Chuck looked up at me then, baffled. "We haven't even had sex since last July," he said. "We are barely even speaking. I think we need to fix our issues before we bring an adopted kid into the mix, don't you?"

"I *am* fixing my issues," I responded.

He looked at the pink tissue by my hand, the broken capillaries around my nostrils from where I'd blown my nose a thousand times that day. The cold I'd caught from sleeping outside wasn't going away, and I was having persistent nosebleeds. I'd shed twelve pounds since I started GenFem. Some of it was from the Sufferances, but some was just because I was so busy—with meetings and worksheets and Reenactments—that I didn't have time to eat.

"I don't know if *fixing* is what I would call it," Chuck said in a voice choked with sadness. He was crumpled into the chair, as if his whole body were imploding into itself, and I couldn't remember if I'd ever seen him look so defeated.

I'd fallen in love with Chuck in college because he was every-thing my Hollywood childhood had not been: solid and calm and *normal*. He was the anti-Sam. He didn't drink much alcohol be-cause he didn't like losing control; at parties, he would nurse a solitary beer, carrying the bottle around long after it was empty so that he wouldn't come off as a party pooper or a scold. I liked that about him, how concerned he always was about other peo-ple's feelings. When I was around him, it felt like an ocean was calming to a stillness, and everything in my head went suddenly quiet.

But after five months of talking it through with GenFem, I thought I saw a new truth behind this stillness: It wasn't peace, it was *stasis*. I no longer wanted to remain motionless, too. And yet it still hurt me to see the wounded expression on his face. He truly didn't understand why I didn't want to stay where we were, just the two of us, forever together.

I banished him to the guest room until he came to his senses. And as I watched my husband move his pajamas and toothbrush down the hall, looking like a kicked hound, I felt a strange kind of victory. For the first time in my life, I was taking a firm action— a *hard* action—for my own good. All these months of emotional labor with GenFem had shown their worth. I was becoming a strong woman. I thought I was finally on the path toward the life I deserved.

Iona told me that it might take a few weeks before Chuck would see the light, but that he would eventually come around. She was wrong. He would never sleep in the master bedroom with me again.

That first night alone in our big king bed, I dreamed a child into existence: the baby that Chuck and I might have conceived. A lit-tle girl, towheaded like her parents, folds of soft fat at her wrists, thighs like meringue. Green eyes from Chuck, and dimples that revealed themselves when she laughed, just like the ones that Sam and I shared. She would grow up to be creative and a caretaker, like me, or controlled and thoughtful, like her father; or maybe she would deviate from us both and turn out to be funny, or wild, or studious. But for the duration of that dream, she was just a child, with all the potential in the world, waiting to see what fate would choose from all the possibilities that lay before her.

In my fantasy, she toddled in front of me, through a grassy field busy with bumblebees and sunflowers. I called to her, and she turned around so that I could see her face and I lit up with recognition: *It's you, my baby.* And she lifted her arms to me, begging to be picked up, crying "Mama?" When she was in my arms—warm, smelling of soap, sticky with kisses—I suddenly felt all the potential that remained for *me,* for us together, mother and child. A warm yellow light poured through my heart.

And then the dream ended and my child vanished. I found myself alone in a dark, empty room, listening to the sounds of my husband farting in the guest bedroom down the hall. And all that was left inside me was rage, an all-consuming fire, hotter and brighter than the yellow light of hope that had so quickly faded away.

HERE'S ANOTHER TRIGGER MOMENT that I failed to ever share with Dr. Cindy, even though I knew that she'd want me to: the day that I found my sister passed out for the first time.

We were sixteen, back in Hollywood. The second season of our show *On the Double* had recently premiered and we were in the middle of a press tour that seemed to have no end. It was a beautiful sunny weekend. Back in Santa Barbara all of my old friends were swimming or at the beach, but Sam and I were stuck in a suite at the Beverly Hilton for two days of meet and greets with members of the media.

Magazines for teenage girls, entertainment websites, cable TV shows, foreign trade publications—I would imagine my face in their pages and cringe. Acting felt unnatural to me, but I had learned to grin and bear it, to hide behind the character I was playing. Press days, however, made me feel like a bug inside a vitrine, taxidermized and exposed and inhuman.

Our publicist positioned us side by side on a blue mohair couch, in coordinating denim-skirted outfits, our makeup heavy and TV-ready. "Be funny, be upbeat." She smiled at us, her faux friendliness nevertheless laced with a steely disapproval, as if she expected the worst from us. "And remember to be on-brand. This is a family-friendly show, so nothing off-color, nothing racy. Remember your primary audience is girls who are still in training bras. So we show *only* our best behavior, OK?"

She sat in the back of the room as the media entered, one by one, to examine us under their magnifying glasses. The questions were the same every time: "How are the twins on your show different from you two in real life?" "What do you like about working together?" "What's the best part of being a twin?"

I obligingly dimpled and dimpled and dimpled on cue, trying to give every press outlet a different answer even though the questions were identical. I didn't want them to get in trouble for not getting a good interview. Print journalists sat across from us with poised pens and whirring recorders, and when they didn't write my words down I worried that I was being too boring. Behind them, I studied the face of our publicist, looking for the microscopic facial twitches that might reveal that I'd said something *off-brand*. My skirt was too short, the T-shirt made me sweat, and the mohair couch irritated the backs of my legs, but I didn't dare complain.

Sam took center stage, of course. She was impish, a little sassy, delighted to be the center of attention, quick with a witty response. The journalists loved her, which left me mostly off the hook. But by the end of the eighth interview the repetition had gotten to her and she grew surly, short-tempered, monosyllabic with her answers. She kicked the edge of the hotel room coffee table until it scuffed and then she asked to go to the bathroom. When she came back, her pupils were large and her breath smelled like buttered gasoline, but she was loose again, and silly.

I thought I knew why, and I hated it.

Another hour, two more interviews, and we were finally released for lunch. Sam said that she needed to get something from our hotel room, so my mother and I headed down to the restaurant alone. The burger that we ordered for Sam grew cold and congealed; the ice in her root beer melted into a watery syrup. "What on earth could she be doing?" my mother muttered, looking at her watch. "She won't have time to eat before the afternoon session and you know how Sam is when she has low blood sugar. Will you go check on her?"

I made my way up to our hotel room and when I opened the door I knew immediately that something was wrong. The room smelled sour and sweaty, and Sam was lying on the bed, arm splayed across her chest, denim skirt twisted up around her waist. The snowy white pillow sham was smeared with flesh-colored makeup. On the desk, next to a half-pillaged welcome basket, were three empty minibar bottles of rum and a can of Coke.

The girls I knew back in Santa Barbara had been starting to experiment with alcohol before I left, but they mostly drank hard lemonade and cherry-sweet cans of fruit-flavored cider. Annika's brother would buy her a four-pack and they'd drink one each under the bleachers during the football game, and then brag that they were *soooo wasted*. They did not drink hard alcohol. They certainly didn't drink three minibar bottles' worth over the course of an hour, plus whatever my sister might have consumed earlier that morning.

I tiptoed across the room to the bed, which made no sense, because Sam was so comatose that my carpeted footsteps certainly weren't going to wake her up. It didn't occur to me to think that she might be dead, though years later—after Sam had brushed up against death a half dozen times—I would realize that I should have been scared. But on that particular day it was not an overdose, or at least not a dangerous one. She was just sound asleep, a rivulet of drool slipping from her mouth to the makeup-smeared pillow.

"Wake up, Sam." I shook her. She made a groaning sound and flapped a limp hand at me, but didn't open her eyes. "What the hell, Sam," I said loudly, hoping to jolt her into awareness, but she was already dead asleep again.

Sam's purse was on the floor next to the bed. I picked it up and fished through it, remembering the bottle of Adderall pills that I'd found in her things a year back—the ones that she said made her feel like she'd been drinking coffee. I didn't find a bottle this time, just a half-empty cardboard blister packet that said *Diazepam 10mg*. I wasn't sure what this was, but it clearly had the opposite effect, at least when mixed with alcohol.

I thought back to all the times over the previous year that my sister's moods had ricocheted from one extreme to the other, from manic to serene and back again. Of the way she so often kept her purse clutched to her body, as if expecting a bag snatcher to make a lunge for it. And the booze—had she been dipping into our parents' liquor cabinet this whole time, or did the free access to a minibar trigger a sudden loss of control?

How much had I been missing?

I straightened my sister's skirt and wiped the smeared mascara off her face with a tissue, then wrapped the minibar bottles and the blister packet of pills in another tissue and buried them in the bottom of the bathroom trash can. I flushed my sister's vomit down the toilet and lit a scented candle from our welcome basket to chase off the smell. And then I sat on the bed next to Sam and held her hand while she slept. I was dimly aware that this was an Adult Moment and I wanted to live up to it.

Five minutes before Sam and I were due back downstairs in the press suite, I heard a knock on the door. I opened it a crack and saw our mother standing in the hallway. "What on earth are you girls—" Her eyes drifted over my shoulder and stopped when they landed on Sam's inert body. Our mother was rarely silenced but this sight, for once, left her speechless.

"She's asleep," I explained. "I tried to wake her up but she's pretty out of it."

Our mother pushed into the room and stood over Sam's body, her eyebrows knotting, as if she were doing a tricky math problem in her mind. She ran a hand over Sam's forehead, checking for fever. Sam exhaled softly in her sleep, a slow bilious hiss.

"Poor thing," she said. "She must be overtired. It's too much to ask of you girls, this kind of grueling schedule on a weekend after you've already been in production all week. I need to talk to the producers."

Surely our mother's not that naive, I thought. *Surely she smells what I smell, sees what I see.* I was left wondering if she was lying for my sake or for her own; and then I questioned my own interpretation of the situation. Was it possible that Mom was right? That my sister was really suffering from exhaustion, and the alcohol and pills were just a symptom of a different malaise? Did my mother have a more sophisticated understanding that I was missing? I was left confused, reeling, acquiescent.

This would turn out to be a lesson that I'd take forward into the rest of my life: that we are the masters of our own spin, that disaster can be reframed as triumph if only you choose to tell it that way. Say something emphatically enough, and people will believe you despite all evidence to the contrary. Say it emphatically enough, and you'll even convince yourself. *I'm in a happy marriage. We'll have a baby soon. My sister is going to get better. I feel good about my life choices. This is a self-help group, not a dangerous cult.*

Of course, when you finally realize that your life is built on an edifice of lies, and that there's nothing actually holding you up, the fall is precipitous.

My mother lifted the receiver on the phone and started to dial. "I'll tell them that we'll have to cancel the afternoon interviews," she said.

My initial relief at this—*no more interviews!*—was quickly chased away by panic. I imagined how upset the publicist would be, how that might travel up the chain of command to the executives at Nickelodeon, and how my sister and I would get a reputation for being unreliable. The spurned press would be catty and mean. Maybe the producers would start closely monitoring our behavior on set, notice Sam's secret habits, cancel the show. Sam would be devastated, I thought. It might even make her act out *more*.

And so, before I'd even gotten my driver's permit, I made a conscious decision to become my sister's first enabler, thinking that I was helping her; although of course I wasn't. Not at all.

"Don't cancel it," I told my mom. "We'll tell them Sam got food poisoning. And I'll do the rest of the interviews myself."

So why didn't I ever share this story with Dr. Cindy? Because I already knew what I should have done that day, and I didn't need a slap or a Sufferance to remind me. If I hadn't hidden the evidence of my sister's nascent substance abuse, if I'd made my mother confront the truth instead of letting her pretend everything was fine, if I'd only stood up for what I'd known was right—how different Sam's life might have been.

GenFem wanted me to believe that we could rewind the timeline of our lives, try to find the moments that defined us, imagine who we might have become instead, and then go *become* that person. All those months, all that money, spent rewriting my history, in hopes of total reinvention: When I look back now I realize that it was only ever so much speculation. There is only the *here,* the *now,* the *what it is.*

The only thing that we can hope to change is the path forward.

23 FEBRUARY MARKED MY SEVEN-MONTH anniversary with GenFem. I'd achieved Level Five at a record pace, marking it with a ceremony and an orange scarf just before the holidays, but since then I'd plateaued. I couldn't seem to get any further ahead in the levels no matter how many one-on-ones I paid for or workshops I attended. Chuck had been sleeping in the guest bedroom for months and still showed no interest whatsoever in meeting with adoption agencies; in fact, we'd barely spoken since Christmas. My GenFem family was starting to question my commitment to the Method: I hadn't kicked Chuck out yet, hadn't forced the issue, hadn't *taken what I deserved.*

That was a sign of my weakness, Dr. Cindy told me. "You are manifesting your own victimhood."

That month, she organized a day trip to a shooting range in the foothills near Santa Ynez, where a half dozen of us shot at targets in a sandy pit overlooking Lake Cachuma. A "bonding exercise," Dr. Cindy called it, "that can reveal hidden strength of character." I didn't want to go, but felt like I should, to prove my commitment. When I got to the range, though, I found that I enjoyed the weight of the warm steel in my hand, the explosive fury of the handgun's kickback. It made my heart race; it made me feel alive.

I was a good shot, to my surprise—the only one of our group

who consistently hit the center of the target. So when Dr. Cindy whispered in my ear that I should really buy a handgun—"a symbol of the power you contain within yourself, a reminder that you do not have to be the victim"—I found myself handing over $575 for a Smith & Wesson.

I didn't know what to do with it—was I supposed to use it against Chuck? I wondered. But, of course, she'd never suggested *that*. Instead, I hid it in the closet in our office, and sometimes, when I couldn't sleep, I would think of it, gleaming in the dark. A little frightened by what it represented, the secret violence inside me.

One winter afternoon, Iona and I were in one of the velvet cubbies in the GenFem center, working on a Reenactment of my most recent Trigger Moment—the night when I found Chuck with Sam, dressed as me, in the den. After three weeks and four Sufferances, I still couldn't get my response right no matter how many times Iona and I ran through it. Was I too forgiving of Sam's behavior, too slow to see her duplicity? Should I have kicked Chuck out when I found him with her? But every time Iona pretended to be my drunk sister—her voice nothing like Sam's as she slurred, "I was just trying to help you. I just want to be your surrogate"—I burst into tears. An insistent voice in the back of my mind kept questioning what actually happened that night. Yes, what Sam did was horrifying, but was *I* the one who screwed up? Should I have let Sam be our surrogate after all? Would that have been so bad?

Had I been, perhaps, too hard on her?

"Of course not," Iona said sharply, when I asked her these questions. "Remember what we talked about yesterday? About Sam keeping you subservient to her? She's toxic. Do you really think that would have changed if you let her get pregnant with Chuck's kid? It would only have made things worse."

"But . . ." The words choked out of me. "But we're identical twins. We share the same genes. It was a chance to make a baby that was basically half me, right? And now, even if we adopt, I'll never know what a baby of my own would have looked like. And I *could* have. I know that's unimportant in the grand scheme of things, but I can't stop thinking about it." I thought of the blond child in my dreams, the one who always vanished into a blur as soon as I woke up.

Iona leaned in, a dark flash in her eyes. "What about your sister's babies? They might as well be yours, right?"

I felt a sharp prick, like a thorn, in my chest. "My sister's babies?"

"Like you said, same genes. Same DNA. Yes? So those eggs she gave away—sorry, *sold*—are equally *you*. And the babies they produced are half yours. You really want to know what your babies would have looked like? Well, you can."

I stared at my hands, so pale and bony as they twisted uselessly in my lap. "Yes, but it's kind of pointless to think about it, isn't it? They're gone."

Iona dug her fingers into my shoulder and pushed me backward, so that I had to look up at her. She shimmered in front of me, her pale features in vibration, filled with rage on my behalf. "They're not *gone*. You just don't know where they are. It's simple: You need to find those babies. Just to see them. Have a real-life Confrontation. That's what Dr. Cindy would tell you to do, right? Look your pain right in the eye, put a name and a face on it, tell it to go away. Don't let yourself be victim to it."

I let myself sink into this idea. The temptation was strong. Just to *see* them—maybe then I could let go.

"How would I even find them? I can't exactly ask Sam. Dr. Cindy forbade me to talk to her until I reach Level Ten."

Iona shrugged. "The donor agency Sam used would know where they are."

"But they're not going to tell me, though, are they?" I asked.

———

Where is the line between destructive and healthy? I found this question on a website for cult survivors recently, and it made me try to pinpoint the moment when this line was irrevocably crossed. When GenFem stopped being a tool for growth for me, and instead became a weapon of self-destruction.

There were so many moments I might choose—from my very first visit, even—and yet I kept going back to this particular one: my hypothetical question, and Iona's answer. The long hard look she gave me as she studied my features with a frightening intensity, and then the gleeful malice in her voice as she responded.

"You're right, they're never going to tell Eleanor Logan," she said. "But what if they didn't tell *you*?"

24 I LOCATED SAM ON Instagram. She wasn't that hard to find. A few months back my mother had casually dropped the name of the café where Sam worked and of course it had a social presence. Three pictures in, there Sam was, pouring a heart into someone's cappuccino. She had a new tattoo of a bird on her forearm and her hair was a little shorter than the last time I saw her, but otherwise, she looked mostly the same. I studied her face, looking for signs of a relapse, but she appeared healthy enough, no puffiness or dark circles, her hair clean, a bemused smile lifting the corners of her lips.

A hard knot blocked my throat; I could barely breathe. For a minute I forgot that the loss I was *supposed* to be confronting was that of my hypothetical child, not my real sister. I rubbed my eyes, pushing back against the pressure building there, then studied Sam's outfits instead. According to the photos, her wardrobe these days generally consisted of a tatty white T-shirt and tight black jeans, accessorized with a red bandanna that she used to yank her hair out of her face.

If you went by Instagram, my sister could be found at the café most weekday afternoons. So I drove down to Los Angeles on a Tuesday and found the place on a quiet stretch of Third Street, not far from the condo complex where Sam and my mother and I once lived. I parked out front and sat in my car, peering through the plate glass window.

Sam was behind the counter, in conversation with a customer. From that distance, I couldn't quite see her face, but I could tell it was her anyway: the way her body was loose and animated as she looped back and forth across the coffee bar, pouring drinks, making change. She held the stage so easily; she always had. And I'd always hated her for it a little. I'd worshipped her for it, too, of course, but in that moment I homed in on my lingering anger. There she was, my sister, the woman who had given away our babies, tried to sleep with my husband, taken my money and thrown it away like it meant nothing.

Sam suddenly looked up and straight out the window, as if she'd sensed my presence. I shrank a little behind the wheel of my BMW, my heart beating a sharp staccato. But the afternoon sun, with its sideways slant, blinded her. She lifted a hand to shade her face, trying and failing to see past the glass. And then she turned back to her customer.

I left her there, pulling an espresso, and drove to her apartment.

Sam lived in a midsize courtyard building on a side street in Hollywood, a featureless beige cube of indeterminate age. I checked myself in the rearview mirror and adjusted the red bandanna that was tying back my hair, stretched the neck of my T-shirt a little more. I was a pale imitation of my sister—the white T-shirt too tailored, the jeans too loose, everything lacking Sam's effortless *cool*—but it was a close enough resemblance if you didn't look too hard. I got out and stood lingering near the entrance of the building, pretending to text on my phone.

After a few minutes, a man about my age appeared at the door, dragging a geriatric beagle on a leash. When he saw me, he flashed a distracted smile. "Hey there, Sam."

I smiled back, a queasy victory, and grabbed the door for him, waiting until I was safely inside to turn around and call after him. I softened my throat until my voice went laconic and hoarse, then gave a loose cock to my hip. *I'll be you,* I told myself and smiled. "Hey, I'm a moron. Can you remind me of the super's apartment number?"

He frowned. "Three?"

My laugh sounded more manic than relieved. "Oh God, of course!" And I released the door so that it swung shut behind me, leaving him on the other side of the glass, looking vaguely puzzled. I waved, as the beagle conveniently lunged after a passing poodle. The man was jerked away, having already forgotten me.

The super, an older Latino man with a prosthetic leg, didn't question me when I told him that I'd locked myself out of my apartment. He barely even looked at me. He just grumbled *"otra vez"* under his breath and then led me up the courtyard stairs to a door with a rusting mezuzah in the frame. A minute later, I was inside my sister's apartment, no questions asked.

Years had passed since I last visited my sister at home. I knew that she'd been downwardly mobile for the better part of a decade—that once she sold the modernist condo that she bought with her *On the Double* proceeds, her living situation had gone precipitously downhill—but this barren box of a studio was such a comedown that it shocked me. A neatly made bed crouched in one corner, next to a small bureau, with a mountain of novels piled on an IKEA bookshelf that also doubled as a TV stand. A dining table the size of a postage stamp separated the kitchen from the living space. An ancient air-conditioning unit clung precariously to the window frame, just inches from a thrift-store couch.

On top of the bureau, next to a framed photo, was a small pile of metal coins in different colors. I picked one of them up and turned it in my hand. It was an engraved sobriety chip, marking my sister's one-month anniversary of AA. One side read *God grant me the serenity to accept the things I cannot change, cour-age to change the things I can, and wisdom to know the differ-ence.* The other: *To Thine Own Self Be True.*

I scooped the other five chips into my palm and examined them. Each one marked an additional month of sobriety, making a total of six months. I wondered if there was a seventh in her pocket right now. I wondered how long it would be before she fell off the wagon again, because of course she would.

The framed photo, I noticed, was a candid that was taken on the set of *On the Double,* something the assistant director of pho-tography snapped while we were blocking a scene. In it, Sam and I were curled up facing each other on a bed, our noses just inches apart, laughing. We were perfect mirrors of each other, and yet the photo exactly captured our individual distinctness: the pli-ancy in my face and the slyness in Sam's. The photo, I remem-bered, was taken just two days before I told Sam I was quitting the show.

I stared at the picture, waiting for some feeling of loss for the career I'd walked away from, for the fame we might have achieved if I'd stuck it out with Sam. But the truth was that I didn't miss acting at all. I had never been comfortable on a stage. When I was on it, all I could think about was getting off. I had never wanted to stand out. All I had ever wanted was to blend in.

So the only real loss that I felt when I saw the photo was for the ease that I'd felt in that moment: the naive belief that my sister and I would always be that close.

I put the photo facedown on the bureau, and kept looking.

Sam's apartment was so small that I found what I came for almost as soon as I started digging: a solitary cardboard box, tucked at the bottom of her tiny coat closet. When I lifted the lid I found a pile of documents, haphazardly thrown together. My sister's important files.

I dug through the box, pulled out medical records and old car lease forms, unearthed an expired passport and a SAG card that was five years out of date. Finally, toward the bottom of the box, I dredged up a stack of pale pink documents, clipped together, each one emblazoned with a logo for BioCal Donation Center. I unclipped the top form and read it: It was a copy of an egg donor agreement, signed by my sister, dated almost four years earlier. I skimmed through the agreement, looking for the names and addresses of the intended egg recipients, but found nothing of interest, just a lot of legalese.

Two more donor agreements were clipped underneath the first, documenting three donations over the course of twenty-nine months. My sister had been a veritable egg factory. I thought I might be ill. How blasé she had been about her own fertility, even as I was struggling with mine. *Did it never occur to her how much this would hurt me?* I wondered. Then again, how could she have known? I'd never told her about our problems conceiving, never invited her to drink my raspberry leaf tea and talk about my empty uterus. I'd always let her addiction issues fill up the room instead, been a sounding board instead of a person.

I thought back four years, tried to remember what Sam and I had been doing at that point in time, and realized that it was the period following her failed rehab attempt at the Ojai treatment center. She was broke, so I'd paid for the program. "Throwing good money after bad," Chuck had observed, but I'd covered the cost with my own savings, so he had no say in the matter. But then she'd bailed out a week early to go on a cocaine binge at the Beverly Hills Hotel with some sleazy Hollywood manager, proving Chuck right. I'd bailed her out of that, too, found her a local outpatient program in Los Angeles instead, and a sobriety counselor who charged me $150 an hour, because I wasn't about to be the person who gave up on Sam.

I could still remember how I felt so helpless when I rescued Sam from the Beverly Hills Hotel, sweaty and pale and smelling of unwashed scalp. How could she keep doing this to herself? I didn't understand how we could have started as the same person and ended up so very far apart. But I took her to Norms and watched her cry mascara tears into her untouched pancakes—as she repeated, "I'm such a terrible sister, I'm such a bad person, I don't know how you can keep believing in me," over and over again—and thought to myself, *But of course I'd do anything if it will save you.*

Apparently "saving her" that time around had prompted her to do this: sell our shared DNA to strangers.

I picked up the forms again and flipped through them until I found the name of Sam's "donor liaison" at BioCal: Camilla Jackson. There was a phone number listed underneath her name and I dialed it.

A woman answered on the first ring. Before I could think better of what I was doing I heard my sister's voice coming out of my throat.

"Hi, Camilla?" I said. "It's Sam. Samantha Logan."

25 CAMILLA JACKSON WAS MIDDLE-AGED but had undergone so much expensive plastic surgery that her skin was as smooth as the nape of a baby's neck. Her makeup looked professionally applied, with lashes that were dense and black and couldn't possibly be natural. Heavy gold jewelry weighed down her earlobes, her fingers, her wrists.

She wore a pristine white lab coat over her designer wrap dress, presumably to convey doctoral authority, despite the fact that there was no *MD* after the name embroidered in script on her lapel. Not even an *RN*. She was just a glorified broker, trying to coax viable eggs out of one person so she could sell them off to another.

Only an opportunist would take pleasure from this job, I thought as I stepped into her office: pairing up the broke and the childless, matching desperation with desperation.

Camilla Jackson stood up from her desk when she saw me come in, her eyes lighting up with recognition. She reached out and grasped both of my hands in hers, squeezed them, as a stack of gold bracelets jangled merrily against her wrists.

"It's good to see you, Samantha," she said, with a smile wide enough to reveal some equally expensive dental work. "How long has it been? Two years? Three?"

The BioCal Donation Center was in a neighborhood that

wasn't quite Beverly Hills, not quite Century City, not quite posh but close enough not to seem sleazy. Their offices commanded the entire top floor of a gold-mirrored medical building on a strip of Pico Boulevard that was otherwise populated by Jewish delis and wedding dress boutiques. From where she sat, Camilla Jackson had a clear view across the city to the Hollywood Hills.

Her desk was a modern expanse of pale blue glass, the kind that needed to be wiped free of prints at least once a day. Otherwise, the dominant feature of her office was the series of baby photos that hung on the wall behind her: six enormous black-and-white portraits of newborns, blissfully sleeping on top of knitted blankets and furry rugs and cupped palms. I wondered if BioCal was responsible for any of these babies. Then I wondered if any of them were Sam's, and my heart made a funny hiccup.

Camilla noticed me staring at the photos. "They're not BioCal babies," she said briskly, a warning in her voice. "In case you're wondering. The photos were taken by an art photographer in Seattle."

I sat in a chair across from her, tried to settle my sister's expression of nonchalance across my features. I tucked a leg underneath me at an angle that felt uncomfortable to me but always seemed to be second nature to Sam. But I was fifteen years out of practice, and my performance felt so effortful, so false; I couldn't believe this woman didn't immediately see through it. Would she notice that my arm tattoos had gone missing? But then, she hadn't seen Sam in years.

Camilla *was* studying me, though, not as a stranger but as if I were a piece of meat in a butcher's display. She took in the broken capillaries around my nose, the dark hollows under my eyes. I sneezed—that lingering cold was still wreaking havoc on my nasal cavities—and she flinched. I imagined her ticking off a box in her mind: *Donor has weak immune system. Don't put it in her bio.* Then again, Sam's history of addiction apparently hadn't given her much pause.

On Camilla's desk, next to a framed photograph of her own family (three teenage sons, a wall of pimples and braces), was a stack of medical file folders, each one dense with yellow and blue forms. I craned my neck, hoping to see Sam's name on the top folder, but the angle was wrong.

"So are you here to discuss another round of donation?" She smiled. "Because we have several prospective recipients who will be very happy to hear it if you are. We never seem to have enough natural blond donors! And your former celebrity status has proven a real value-add for the families interested in an open donor situation. Though—" She frowned. "How old are you now? Over thirty? I hate to say it, but that might bring your market value down a bit, and you might not command the same compensation as before."

"I'm not here to donate," I jumped in. "I just have some questions about the donations I did in the past."

"Oh?" She leaned back in her seat, her movements measured and deliberate. She pushed the gold bracelets up and down her wrist. "What kinds of questions?"

"I was wondering," I began, ready to edge around my question, before remembering that Sam would just be blunt. "Am I allowed to look at my donor history file? The families that received my eggs, and all that?"

Camilla sat upright again, her chair back popping forward with an urgent snap. "Of course not." She was still smiling, but her disapproval was palpable. "I'm sure we made that clear from your very first interview. Recipients are *always* anonymous. Donors can choose to be fully anonymous, or they can choose to reveal their identities to the family, or just the child when he or she turns eighteen. As you may remember, BioCal prides itself in being a more modern, *flexible* donor agency, and so we are able to help facilitate these decisions with additional monetary compensation. Regardless, it's never 'open' in *both* directions, unless the recipient families decide otherwise. Which is rare."

"Right. Of course. I remember." I could smell myself sweating through the new T-shirt, a sickly jasmine deodorant scent. Panic rose and fluttered inside my chest, like a trapped butterfly. "What I meant to say was—I can't recall if any of my donations were open. And I've been thinking a lot about whether my kid might hunt me down in sixteen years."

Camilla's smile was tight over her teeth. "Not *your kid*. Their child. And yes, that's a possibility though it doesn't always happen."

"So I *did* have an open donation?"

Now she just looked annoyed. She glanced at the Cartier wristwatch on her left wrist. "I seem to recall that at least one of your recipients offered an additional financial incentive to you, in order to have full biographical details, name, photo, all that. But I couldn't say for sure. It's all in your paperwork, though."

"See, that's the problem. I lost my paperwork," I said. I ruffled a hand through my hair, trying to look hapless and forgetful. "My basement flooded and all my files were ruined. And I just can't remember the details of all the donations."

Her face softened. "Oh! You should have told me. We could have just sent you copies." She reached for the pile of folders on her desk and grabbed the one on top. Now I could see the label on the tab: *Samantha Logan*. The butterflies in my chest lifted and took flight. "But let me take a look."

I am not a devious person by nature. I always feel like my lies are as obvious as a neon safety vest, visible from miles away. This was always my excuse for why I was such a stiff actress: I was just too honest. (Really, the only roles I ever felt comfortable playing were Sam and Elli.) So while I was sure Sam could have come up with at least a dozen tricks to pull off what I was about to do, I was able to conjure up only three—and even then, I still needed Iona to help talk me through them beforehand.

One: I would convince Camilla Jackson to hand me Sam's file folder so I could go through it myself. This, obviously, hadn't happened.

Two: I would get *her* to open Sam's file folder in front of me, and take the opportunity to read it over Camilla's shoulder. But now that this scenario was unfolding in front of me, I knew that it was impossible. The typeface on the forms that she was flipping through were far too small, and impossible to read upside down, especially with an expanse of desk between us. Plus, she was turning the pages so fast that I couldn't catch which of the documents might list the recipient families.

Which left me with option three: somehow get this woman to leave me alone with the folder.

So as Camilla skimmed through the paperwork, her eyes rapidly scanning the forms, I tugged a dusty, crumpled tissue out of my jeans pocket. I lifted it to my damaged nose, sniffed loudly, and then blew as hard as I possibly could.

Blood erupted from my left nostril.

I let out a shriek of alarm and Camilla looked up and recoiled. "Oh my God."

"I'm OK," I said. I dabbed at the rivulet of blood trickling down my lip, and then sneezed, spreading a mist of red droplets across Camilla's pristine glass desk. Camilla jumped out of her seat, alarmed. "No, I'm not OK, actually. Do you have any Kleenex? This one is falling apart."

Camilla's gaze swept across the surface of her desk, as if hoping that a box of tissues might materialize before her, but of course there was nothing there except her own pimply sons grinning back at her. "I'll go get you one," she said. She checked the front of her white lab coat for splatter, and then moved cautiously around the chair where I sat with blood dripping down my face.

"And some ice, maybe?" I added, hoping to prolong her absence.

She gave me a wide berth as she headed to her door. "I'll see what I can do."

I waited until the sound of her heels faded away and then I reached across the desk and grabbed the folder. The stack of documents inside it was thick, and I paged through them as fast as I could: psychological screenings (how had my sister passed *those*?) and interview notes (*Donor expressed her honest desire to help a family in need*) and ultrasound charts documenting the contents of my sister's ovaries. I longed to read everything but instead I flipped past them all until I finally came to a photocopied document that read *Recipient Consent Form* across the top.

I scanned to the bottom of the page, past paragraphs of dense legalese, until I got to the signatures. The two names scrawled there were nearly illegible—Blackworth? Backwell?—but the address just beneath the signatures was written in clearly typed letters: *17344 Catalpa Way, Burbank, CA.*

A yellow legal pad sat next to Camilla's computer keyboard. I tore off a piece of paper and scribbled this address down. Then I kept flipping through the folder until I encountered another recipient consent form: *72 Buena Vista Ave, Laguna Beach, CA.* Then another: *825 Joshua Tree Drive, Scottsdale, AZ.*

I didn't bother writing down the names of the people who had bought my sister's eggs. I didn't really want to know who they were. Why humanize the couples that had absconded with our DNA, taken advantage of my sister's vulnerability? I just wanted to know where I should go to find the babies. *I'm only going to look, to confront my loss,* I rationalized, as blood dripped down my chin and left a chain of droplets across the lined yellow paper. *The less I know about the families, the better.*

I had just written down the third address when I heard Camilla Jackson's heels clattering across the travertine at the end of the hallway. But three was good enough. I slammed Sam's folder shut and slid it back across the desk, shoving the scribbled list in my purse. By the time Camilla appeared in the doorway, a cube of ice in one hand and a box of tissues in the other, I was standing up, head tilted backward, nose pinched shut with one hand.

"I feel dizzy," I said. "I think I should go."

She looked puzzled. "Don't you want the information about your donations?"

"I'll just send you my address so you can mail it." I edged past her, toward the door. "I need to get home."

I left her standing there, the ice melting down her wrist, a look of vague bafflement on her face. A trail of tiny blood droplets marked my way as I found the path back out to the elevator and fled.

26 A WEEK AFTER MY visit to BioCal, my mother took me out to lunch at our favorite outdoor café, where the tables are spread out under the oak trees and you can sometimes hear the children's chorus practicing at a nearby church. I hadn't seen her in weeks. We usually met for lunch every few weeks, plus family dinners on the first Sunday of the month, but I hadn't had much bandwidth of late. She looked at me hungrily, as if I were an appetizer she was about to pick off a tray.

"You've gotten so *skinny,* darling," she said and sighed, a bite of jealousy in her voice, as she ordered a bottle of Sancerre. In previous times I would have shared the bottle with her but that day I placed my hand over the glass. I'd lost my taste for alcohol. Lately, when I drank, I could sense something deep inside me starting to ferment, a panicky sourness rising from my gut. Anyway, Dr. Cindy discouraged drinking. "Alcohol is about losing your self-control," she'd say. "And here at GenFem we're trying to *gain* control."

I was finally a Level Six, a promotion given to me after I returned from Los Angeles with the list of egg recipient addresses in my purse pocket. That night, Dr. Cindy had pulled me up onto the stage in the middle of a workshop to give me the yellow scarf that denoted my ascension up the levels. "You've proven your ability to transcend your comfort zone and push into new frontiers," she said as she wrapped the strip of silk fabric around my neck, just a hair too tight. A half dozen fellow Neos applauded in the audience, their faces swollen with pride and envy. "You're well on the path to achieving your best self."

And yet that list still sat in a folder in a drawer in my living room, proof that I wasn't pushing *that* far. I hadn't visited the addresses on it, hadn't even looked them up on a map. When I lay in bed alone at night, I could feel the list in the downstairs console, taunting me with its proof of my transgression. I had pretended to be my sister, I had stolen private information. I couldn't believe I had done these things. The lightness that I had felt during the first few months of GenFem—the giddy feeling that I was discovering something essential about myself—was fading. In its place was something harder, something a little darker and more frightening.

Of course, Dr. Cindy had warned me that the growth would hurt: *If it isn't hard, then you aren't making any progress.* And yet, seven months in, I still mostly felt like I was in limbo, torn between the person that I had been and the person that GenFem told me that I ought to be, somehow managing to be neither.

My mother took a piece of focaccia from the bread basket and tore it into small pieces that she used to sop up a puddle of olive oil. The sight made me feel queasy: I didn't have much of an appetite anymore, even when I wasn't having a Sufferance. She popped a piece in her mouth with relish and looked at me as she chewed, her jaw slowing.

"Are you OK?" she said. "You're not eating."

"I'm just not hungry," I demurred.

"You aren't turning anorexic on me, are you?" The focaccia dangled from her greasy fingers; it looked like she was considering forcing it on me.

"*No.* I'm just . . . a little stressed."

"Is it something to do with Sam?"

I didn't know how to answer her question. Because of course

it was about Sam, though not in any way that our mother could possibly know, since I'd never told her about Sam's donated eggs or her attempted seduction of Chuck. (She assumed our fallout was related to all the money I'd spent on Sam's failed rehab, and I let her believe it, since it just seemed easier.) But it was also about *me*, in a way that felt so much bigger; and I felt an unexpected surge of resentment toward my mother, for never looking past my sister to really *see* me. For always assuming that she didn't have to worry about me.

"It's not about Sam," I said.

"You two made up?" She said this hopefully. A powerful smell of lavender was emanating off her, the essential oils she rubbed into her joints that didn't seem to help her very much.

"No. And I really don't want to talk about her."

She seemed a little relieved by this, as if she didn't *really* want to know anyway. "Of course, I understand. I just hate that you two are having issues. It seems like you should work to patch them up, don't you think? And she *does* seem to be doing OK this time around. Apparently she's stayed sober for half a year now. Maybe longer. She seems happy."

I recalled how Sam had looked in the café the previous week, her silhouette against the coffee bar, the way she tilted her head back and laughed at something the customer had said. It didn't seem fair that she would be happy, I thought bitterly, not when I wasn't. And then I felt terrible for being so vindictive. *I do want my sister to be happy,* I reminded myself, *even if I'm angry at her.* And then I wondered if Dr. Cindy would approve of that sentiment, or if she'd consider it weak.

So much second-guessing. It was getting exhausting. I reached for the bread, and then withdrew my hand. Did I have a Sufferance? I couldn't even remember anymore.

"It's *not* about Sam, Mom," I said, and then added, in a burst of unintended honesty, "It's about Chuck. And me. It's just, the baby situation—it's been really rough on us."

My mother shook her head, *no,* banishing my words from the table. "But I just have a feeling that everything is going to be *fine,* sweetheart." She reached across the table and put her hand on top of mine. "I've been meditating on it, did I tell you that? Channeling my positive energy your way. You two are going to get your baby soon, I just *know it*. I mean, those tests you did, they weren't a-hundred-percent-without-a-doubt conclusive." She patted my hand once, definitively, as if this had settled the question. "Maybe you should come with me to my next meditation group session? It might help with the stress. Maybe stress is the real reason you aren't conceiving!"

It took all my self-control to prevent myself from pushing my chair back and throwing my napkin on the table. *Meditation.* Sitting silently, doing nothing, emptying your mind: exactly the kind of inaction that Dr. Cindy always preached against. How was that going to change my situation?

"No, it's OK, Mom," I said, keeping my voice bright, straightening up and taking a bite of spinach salad to prove to her how OK I was. "I've got something of my own. I joined a new group, a self-help movement for women. It's pretty exciting, actually."

My mom's face lit up. "You did! That's great, darling. What's it called?"

"GenFem." I wondered if it was a bad idea to tell her, if I'd given away the keys to a vault that I should have kept locked. What if my mother wanted to join? Would I want her there with me?

But it didn't matter, because my mother seemed uninterested. "Hmm, don't know it, but I'm glad for you, sweetheart, really glad. You need something to believe in. It's too hard to do this all by yourself." It was unclear what she meant by *this,* but I didn't ask her because she was signaling the waiter for more Pellegrino and clearly didn't want to elaborate, didn't want to know any more about my pain than I'd already told her.

I found myself thinking of my one-on-one session with Dr. Cindy a few weeks back. We'd been discussing my mother and her chronic dabbling with new philosophies, when suddenly Dr. Cindy pressed a knuckle to her cheek and cocked her head at me. "Your mother, a real piece of work," she murmured. "Maybe it would do you both some good to get some space. Have you considered that she might be toxic, just like your sister?"

I stared back at her. "What do you mean?"

"All that New Age stuff she believes in—or *pretends* to believe in, I should say—how has that ever helped her? All it has ever done is enable her to be blind to the reality right in front of her eyes."

"It's true. But she's still my mother," I protested.

"I'd argue that your *real* mother is the person who opens your eyes to yourself," Dr. Cindy pushed back. "Anyone can give birth to and raise a child, yes, but the true maternal figure in a woman's life is the person who helps her learn how to identify her core issues, resolve them, and redirect her life. Be her best self. And only once you've achieved those three critical things are you truly capable of being a good mother yourself."

And so now I wondered, had my mother ever, really, helped me achieve my best self? If anything, hadn't she always avoided taking responsibility for my emotional growth altogether? Would a good mother have moved her twins to Hollywood at age nine, ignoring the signs that one of them hated the whole concept of being an actress? And later, when Sam and I started trading identities, hadn't she just looked the other way and pretended she didn't notice? Surely my mother had known, just as I did, that Sam was flirting with substance abuse; and yet she'd done nothing about that either, until it was far too late.

All those parenting books my mother read, all those books on healing and meditation and spirituality. Why hadn't she spent less time looking inward at herself and a lot more time trying to actually see each of *us*?

If you looked at it this way, Dr. Cindy had been more of a mother to me lately than my actual mother.

Maybe I do need some space, I thought as I stared at my mother across the table. *Maybe I need a clean slate, for a while, just so I can see myself clearly.* And I lifted a forkful of spinach to my mouth, gritting my teeth as I swallowed, thinking of the greens slipping their way through my body, weighing me down like an anchor.

27 I SPENT THAT AFTERNOON working on the center-pieces for a fiftieth birthday party, a thousand dollars' worth of pale pink roses in gold vases. I'd always enjoyed this part of my day—the quiet hours spent patiently pinning flowers into sprays, trying to achieve a balance between delicate and solid, prickly and soft. I created beautiful objects that made people happy on their special occasions, and that had always felt less like a career than a privilege. But that day everything felt off. The roses, despite being delivered just the day before, weren't very fresh, and were curling at the tips despite my best efforts to revive them with sugar water. The paint on the vases was chipping. The centerpieces were several inches shorter than the client's specifications, no matter how I rearranged them.

I headed out in the delivery van nearly an hour late, with no time to address the piles of paperwork that I promised myself I'd attend to. Five years in, and my business was still only barely scraping by. I loved the buckets of flowers brimming with possibility, the blank canvas of a vase, the clouds of sweet fragrance and the dark taint of earth just below, but I was dismal as a business-woman. Dr. Cindy said that I'd undermined myself by choosing a career path at which I was doomed to fail. "You should consider selling your business and becoming a Mentor when you hit Level Ten," she'd suggested, a prospect that both thrilled and terrified me. Was I ready for that kind of a commitment to the Method? (But if not, why was I pursuing it at all?)

I dropped the flowers at a modernist compound up in the Montecito hills, with a vanishing pool that looked out to the sea and a Richard Serra sculpture gracing the front garden. The client, deep in conversation with the caterer, was too distracted to notice the lackluster height of her centerpieces. I left the flowers and then drove back to my house, planning to stop in for just a few minutes before heading back out to a GenFem meeting.

I was in the kitchen, weighing out my carrot sticks, when I heard a thump above me, the sound of something heavy being scraped along the hardwood floor. I followed the sound up the stairs and found Chuck in the office, digging through the closet. Sports equipment and luggage were piled on the floor next to him, golf clubs tangling with duffel bags and tennis gear. A tube of neon green tennis balls rolled drunkenly across the room and stopped just at my feet.

He looked up to see me standing there and startled, a guilty, stricken look on his face. It wasn't even six P.M. but he'd already changed out of his suit into jeans and a faded T-shirt that read *Jackson Hole Ski Team.* He'd bought that shirt on a trip we took nearly five years back, a ski vacation in Wyoming that ended in a snowstorm. The snow was so heavy that they closed down the resort, so instead of skiing we spent most of the trip naked by the fireplace in our hotel suite, having sex and ordering room service champagne. That was the vacation that we decided to throw my birth control in the trash. I remembered Chuck rolling over to me in the flickering light from the fire, his hands cradling my face, as he whispered, "Think of how incredible our babies are going to be. They'll be the best of both of us." I felt like a red carpet was unfurling before me, a plush path toward my future, leading to a perfect baby, our perfect family. When Chuck pushed inside me I whispered, "I've never been so happy" in his ear, and meant it.

When life has yet to disappoint you, you have no reason to

believe it ever will. It's only later, when you've been battered by failed expectations, that you grow cynical. Is it ever possible to find your way back to that initial, blissful optimism? Maybe not. Maybe that's why I was so willing to believe in the other path, the one that GenFem was teaching me: cudgeling your way through life, fueled by self-righteous rage, demanding to be given what you believe you deserve. Less *hope* than *brute force*.

My husband and I stared at each other across the room. "What are you doing?" I asked even though it was obvious, of course it was, from the heap of objects at my husband's feet, the presence of the matching suitcases that his parents gave us for our wedding.

"The company had a sudden opening in our Tokyo office," he said. "I'm taking it."

I almost laughed, because of course he had to be joking, until I realized, with a nauseating twist of the gut, that he wasn't joking at all. "You're moving to *Japan* and you just decided to tell your wife? You never even thought about asking me to come?"

Chuck looked terrible. The skin under his eyes was baggy and bruised, and he'd gained at least ten pounds, probably due to the fact that he'd been living on takeout. "I'm sorry. But we need a break anyway. We both know that this is unsustainable," he said. "Our relationship—it's broken."

"I know," I said. "But it's *fixable*. I've already explained to you exactly what I want. All you need to do is agree to start looking into adoption, and everything will be fine again."

He shook his head. "I'm not going there again, Elli. This isn't even about that anymore, don't you realize? It's about how irrational you've gotten, how single-minded and obsessive. It's your way or it's no way at all. I don't understand what's gotten into you. Marriage is supposed to be a partnership, not a dictatorship."

"Exactly." I sensed that this was one of the moments that Gen-Fem had warned me about, when a Toxic tries to break you down into smaller pieces so that they can make themselves feel bigger. *The important thing is to stand strong in your beliefs and remain whole.* Page twenty-seven of my binder: I'd highlighted that sentence just last week. "And *you* don't get to dictate that we aren't going to have a family just because you suddenly decide you don't want one anymore."

"But I do want a family," he said. His eyes had dropped to the floor and his voice was as low and flat as the pile of our Persian rug. "That's why I'm leaving."

"You're leaving me because I'm infertile?"

"No." He nudged at a golf club with his foot. "I'm leaving you because you aren't *you* anymore. You're not the same person I wanted to start a family with."

"I am me. I'm more *me* than I've ever been."

He was picking his way through his words now, like a child doing its best not to trample on the flowers. "I know it's been a hard year for you, with your diagnosis, and your estrangement from Sam. It's been hard for both of us. And I know that you think this, this . . ."—I coolly watched him struggle—"*group* is helping you heal. But it's not, Elli. GenFem has stripped away everything I used to love about you, and all that's left is this veneer of bravado that's just covering a whole lot of fear and anger. The Elli *I* knew was gentle and kind and patient . . ."

"The Elli *you* knew was an insecure pushover. I think that's why you liked her. You don't like strong women."

He sighed and reached down, stuffing tennis gear into a duffel bag. I kicked the tube of tennis balls at him and it skittered along the rug and then struck him in the shin, hard. He looked up at me, his face reddening.

"If you walk out that door, I'm filing for divorce," I said. I think I still hoped he wouldn't, that this final threat would tip the balance back over to me. But of course, it didn't.

"I'm really sorry, Elli," he said. He sounded so much smaller than he was.

I thought of the gun in the closet just a few feet behind him, *a symbol of the power you contain within yourself, a reminder that you do not have to be the victim*. I imagined pointing it at Chuck, wondered how powerful that would feel. But would it make a difference? Not in a good way. I still had the clarity, then, to understand that.

"I don't need you," I said, and it was hard work to make my voice ice-cube cold and to not break into tears, but I did it, and I knew Dr. Cindy would have applauded me if she could hear me. "I'm reclaiming my own destiny. *I'm* deciding for myself what's right for me. I'm learning my own self-worth. And I'm still going to get what's rightly mine, with or without you."

With that, I whirled around and left the room and drove to my GenFem meeting, where I spent the next two hours crying so hard that I barely registered the leveling ceremony that was happening onstage. At one point, I noticed that Iona was watching me from across the room, with a look of consternation. After the meeting, I went to look for her but she had already disappeared behind the velvet curtain with Dr. Cindy, the two of them talking in low whispers. As the rest of the members trickled out, I waited for someone to come and ask me what happened, to reassure me that I'd done the right thing, that I was going to be OK, but the other women were too distracted, too giddy about the new silk scarves around their necks to notice my emotional state. Eventually the room emptied and I found myself sitting on a threadbare couch, depleted and hungry and alone.

When I got back to my house, Chuck was gone.

28 DAYS PASSED. TWO OR three, maybe more, I wasn't quite sure. I canceled all of my work events and stayed in bed with the curtains closed, drifting in and out of consciousness but never fully asleep. A numb inertia had settled into my limbs, making it impossible to move. I waited and waited for a triumphant swell of energy, the one Dr. Cindy had predicted— *a big step toward achieving a better Me!*—but it never arrived.

I thought of Chuck a lot, running through the course of our failed marriage over and over, but I found myself thinking of Sam even more. I lay in bed and imagined her showing up at the door with a bottle of wine and a tub of ice cream. She'd paint my toenails and tell me outrageous stories about her life until I had a stitch in my side from laughing. She'd have me forgetting about Chuck entirely for hours on end, she'd take me to that happy-sad place where all the emotions mingle together and leave you feeling oddly sanguine about human existence. At least, that's what the old Sam, the addict Sam, would have done. Who was Sam now, this Sam with a half dozen recovery chips piled up on her bureau? I didn't even know and that made me even sadder.

So, of course, the first thought that came to my mind was *Sam* when my doorbell rang at ten A.M. one morning. But when I stumbled down to the entry—still in my pajamas, face puffy and stinging—I found Iona standing in the doorway instead. I tried not to let the disappointment show on my face.

"Oh, Eleanor. You look *awful*. Mind if I—?" She squeezed her way through the door. A faint scent wafted off her, salt and lemons and perspiration, as if she'd come straight from a brisk walk on the beach. Her blond hair was tucked back in a loose ponytail, wisps of gray showing at the roots, and she was dressed in sensible athleisure.

She was carrying a bakery bag and a giant Starbucks coffee. She handed me the coffee and I took a bracing gulp. "I take it Chuck's gone? Did he leave on his own or did you kick him out?"

"I kicked him out," I lied, because it wasn't *so* far from the truth and because I knew it was what Iona would want to hear.

She flung an arm over my shoulder, squeezed me tight. I felt shaky in her grip, on the edge of tears. "I'm proud of you," she whispered. "Dr. Cindy is proud of you. It's a big step but it needed to happen for your growth as an independent woman. I think Level Seven is on the horizon. We see a big future for you at Gen-Fem. Dr. Cindy and I agree, we really do think you could be a great Mentor someday. You're a natural empath and that could really help other women on their journeys."

I managed a wobbly smile and swallowed more coffee. It burned my ravaged throat as it went down.

Iona had never been to my house before. I watched as she drifted away from me and across the living room, picking up objects—a crystal vase, a decorative tray—to examine them with an assessing eye. White sofas from Restoration Hardware, a pair of vintage armchairs that I had reupholstered in leather, a burl wood coffee table that gleamed with polish. She made a beeline for the marble fireplace, where photos were displayed in silver frames on the mantel: a wedding portrait, Sam and me in elementary school, a black-and-white snapshot of our parents on their honeymoon. She studied these with avid curiosity.

"Your home is lovely," she said. "I can tell you've put a lot of work into it. And so big. How many square feet?"

"Thirty-three hundred."

She whistled. "You'll downsize now that Chuck's gone, I assume?"

I hadn't considered that. Yes, my home had become a repository of curdled memories, but I still couldn't imagine *leaving.* "Maybe," I said slowly. "It is a lot of house for one person."

Iona nodded thoughtfully. She pulled a chocolate cupcake out of the bakery bag and held it out to me, then laughed when I hesitated. "Oh, come on. It's a cupcake. Who are you going to get in trouble with? Me?"

I took a hesitant bite, and then I was cramming the whole thing in my mouth, gulping it so fast that crumbs cascaded down my front and scattered across the Persian rug. When was the last time I'd eaten? A wave of dizziness came over me, a queasy sugar shake.

Iona sat down beside me. She had a cupcake, too, and she took a small nibble of it—a token gesture of solidarity—before setting it gently down on a stack of *Elle Decor* magazines on the coffee table.

"Don't you think that today is a good day to get closure on all fronts?" she asked. She was sitting so close to me that her thigh was pressing against mine. I could smell the frosting on her breath.

"What do you mean?"

The look she gave me was a little contemptuous, a little indulgent. "You know what I mean. You never followed up on those addresses. You went to all that trouble to pretend to be your sister, you stepped right out of your comfort zone, and you haven't done anything about it since."

I glanced at the console, where the list was hidden in a manila folder inside a locked drawer. It's easy to pretend that drawers full of ugly things don't exist if you simply refuse to open them. "I guess . . . I just think it might be painful to see those children in person. It's hard enough to know that they exist at all."

"Pain means you're growing. Nothing good ever comes from a life that's easy. Right? *Easy* makes you soft and vulnerable, it makes you lazy. *Painful* is confrontation, it's growth, it's rebirth."

I sucked my teeth, tasting the pasty chocolate still caked on my gums. The old Elli would have spent another week in bed in her bathrobe, eating ice cream and watching Real Housewives reruns. The new Elli was supposed to face her painful new reality, gird herself like a warrior going back into battle to face an even more terrifying foe. It felt exhausting.

"How about this?" Iona said. She put an arm around me and pulled me in close, her wiry forearm—muscle over bone, nothing more—like a clamp on my side. "I'll go with you. We'll do it together. I won't make you confront this alone."

I wavered. Her arm pressed against my back, nudging me forward on the seat. "OK," I said. My voice sounded very small.

"Great!" She jumped up, radiant with victory, the cupcake forgotten on the coffee table. She looked down at me, at my fuzzy bathrobe covered in crumbs, and then grabbed my hands, pulling me upright. "But first, let's get you dressed."

We parked Iona's car just down the street from a Mediterranean McMansion, a hulking home on a quiet street high in the hills of Burbank. A row of wilting begonias lined the home's front drive, the front door framed by stands of white calla lilies going brown with drought. I idly imagined picking the lilies, mixing them with white ranunculus and jasmine, a spray of fern for color and texture. Brainstorming floral arrangements was a pleasant distraction from thinking too hard about what I was actually doing here: monitoring a stranger's front door, waiting for a glimpse of a niece or nephew that I wasn't totally sure even existed.

Stalker. I tried the word on for size. *You're a stalker. A creep.* But mostly I felt alive with a giddy anticipation, one that made my fingers vibrate and my breath come hard. *I was going to see a child that came from my genes.* I couldn't deny that it was exciting to simply give in to that longing, without any concern about logic or consequence. Something wild and transgressive was growing within me—an impulsive id that demanded to be fed— and I wondered if this was what Sam felt like when she went on a bender.

As we sat there, just staring at the house, Iona kept up a distracting patter of instructive encouragement. "Think of this as an emotional stakeout," she said. "We'll just sit in the car until you get a glimpse of the child, enough to bear witness to the emotions that this brings up in you and dispel them."

Iona's car was a heavy Mercedes sedan in pale gold with leather interior, and I wondered just how much GenFem was paying her to be a Mentor. Apparently quite a lot, judging by the buttery scent of the leather. Outside it was so hot that the view of the valley below us shimmered like a mirage, but inside the car the air-conditioning was turned on high, blowing icy Freon straight into my face. I leaned my cheek against the window, feeling the heat of the sun through the cold glass, a disconcerting contrast.

The list of BioCal addresses was propped on the console between us, fluttering slightly in the blast of air from the vent. Iona had come up with a plan before we left my house: We would "witness" Burbank first, and then head to Laguna Beach next, and finally drive out to Arizona for the last address on the list. I was too exhausted to protest that this was too much for one day, and anyway I didn't want to risk any more Sufferances.

Minutes turned into hours as we sat there. The sun beat through the windshield, making me drowsy. I drifted off into a stuporous doze, and dreamed of the child again. This time I was walking down a cracked sidewalk, on a suburban street just like this one, following a toddler who pulled a rolling caterpillar on a string. I thought I heard him cry out, "Mama?" and so I scooped him up and went to kiss his fat cheeks and it wasn't until I got his face close to mine that I could see that his features were strange and distorted, not *my* child's at all but something oozing and monstrous.

I woke with a start because Iona was slapping my leg.

"Look," she said, and pointed.

A white Lexus SUV was pulling into the driveway in front of us. A woman—mid-forties, in leopard-print silk, hair long and streaked pale blond—climbed out of the driver's seat. She walked around the car to the rear passenger door and opened it, leaning in to collect something. The SUV's windows were tinted so I couldn't see what she was retrieving, just the peek of pink lace underwear rising above her white jeans as she craned to get whatever was in the depths of the back seat.

When she came back out, she was holding a child.

A child. My heart seized.

The child was small, blond, wearing a pink sundress, a glittery headband, wispy hair tied up in cherubic pigtails. A girl, then. *A girl.* She was three years old, maybe four—it was hard to tell from where we were parked, fifty feet away. She squirmed and protested and her mother, wobbling in high sandals, gratefully plopped her on the ground and turned back to grab something else from the car. A giant plush bunny almost as big as the girl. The little girl grabbed the stuffed animal and waddled toward the front door, pressing her chin into its fur.

I'd stopped breathing.

But I was too far away to see her face, I realized with frustration. Did she look like me? Had the Logan DNA dominated, or did she look like the father who inseminated my sister's egg? Did she have my voice, my facial expressions? I thought of the photos of myself at that age and remembered enormous eyes, deep dimples, hair so blond that it was almost white. Did the girl have dimples?

Maybe if I got closer to her, I'd feel some instinctive recognition—blood calling out to blood.

Before I realized what I was doing, I'd pushed open the door of Iona's car and was climbing out, prepared to chase them down. I wasn't thinking it through at all, just following a hot impulse.

Iona grabbed my wrist, yanking me back inside the car. "You can't," she whispered.

"I just want a better look."

"No," Iona said. "We don't know the terms of the donation, if it was open or anonymous. What if she saw photos of your sister when they picked her as a donor? She might recognize you. That would only cause problems. We just watch."

But there was nothing to watch anymore, because while we were arguing the mother had wedged the front door open with a foot, and the little girl had scurried under her arm and into the house. The door closed behind them both, and just like that they were gone. The whole encounter was over in ten seconds, before I'd even had a chance to process what I was seeing.

Was that it?

Iona reached out to cup my chin with her palm, then turned my head so that I was looking at her instead of at the house. "What do you feel now?" she asked softly. "Pain?"

"Disorientation." I sent feelers out to test my heart, like pressing on a bruise to see if it hurt. It did, but it was the dull pang of missed opportunity, not the sharp agony of personal loss I'd expected. Maybe if I'd gotten closer to the little girl. Maybe if I'd really seen her face, I'd have more clarity. "It's not what I imagined. I thought I'd feel a connection but instead I mostly feel confused."

Iona turned the key in the ignition and the engine jumped to life. "That's good. You're already letting go of expectation, dropping the fantasies and facing your truth. Let's go do it again, and see what we can turn this into."

She did an abrupt U-turn in the middle of the street, and I

turned in my seat to watch the McMansion disappear behind us. I hoped irrationally to get one last glimpse of a small face in a window but there was no sign of life at all, not even a fluttering curtain, just that wilting front garden and darkened windows that stared back at me, unblinking, as we slowly glided down the hill.

Sam's second child was a little boy, slightly younger. We saw him right away, in the tiny front yard of his family's Laguna Beach cottage, watering pots with a garden hose and the assistance of a much older sister. This time, we couldn't stop to watch. The narrow street was too busy, clogged with cars on the hunt for a parking spot. Instead we had to drive right past the house and then circle back around the block.

On our second pass, Iona slowed so that I could get a better look. The boy's hair was blond under his floppy sun hat, his fair skin was greased up with chalky white sunscreen, and he wore a striped sun shirt down to his wrists. He was chubby, more than my sister and I ever were at that age, with plump folds of skin at his wrists and knees. He laughed as he splashed his sister with the hose; I thought I glimpsed a familiar flash of dimple, and my heart lurched. *There.* But he was intent on his play and didn't look up, not even when Iona's car slowed to a stop across the street.

But his big sister saw us. She was a teenager in a yellow crop top, just out of pubescence but already self-aware enough to notice that two strangers were staring at her just a few feet away. She shaded her face with her hand, trying to figure out who was behind the tinted windows of the idling Mercedes.

Behind us, a car full of teenagers honked in annoyance, making our gawking even more obvious. The sister put a protective hand on her brother and tucked him safely behind her. The dropped hose splattered a torrent of water across her thighs. She held up her other hand and extended her middle finger at us. *Fuck you.*

"Busted," Iona whispered, and kept driving.

"Circle back," I commanded. She shot me a look. "Please? I barely got a glimpse."

She said nothing but obediently turned around the block one last time. When we arrived back at the house, three minutes later, the teenage girl was in the front yard with an older blond woman, and the little boy had disappeared from sight. When the sister saw us coming around again, she jumped up and pointed out our car to her mother. Their heads swiveled in unison as we pulled up in front of their house.

"Dammit," Iona swore, and hit the accelerator. The Mercedes's engine growled and the car leapt forward. In the rearview mirror I could see the mother running out into the street to watch us go, framing our car in her cellphone viewfinder.

"Do you think she saw us? Could she identify us?"

"Not unless she got my license plate number, and then what's she going to do with that? Call the police? We weren't doing anything wrong."

Iona turned right and left, seemingly at random, until we ended up on a commercial street lined with boutiques and restaurants. She gave me a sideways look as we slowed to an idle in the traffic. "And?"

I was silent for a moment. "He had dimples," I said dully. I didn't realize that I'd started crying but when I touched my cheek my hand came away wet.

"*There's* the pain you were looking for," Iona said. "Embrace it. Confront it. What does it make you want? How can you channel that into something positive for yourself?"

I didn't know how to answer this. The feelings I had weren't positive at all. Instead, I looked out the window at the pastel-painted bungalows crowded one on top of another, the surfers thronging the sidewalk with sand-crusted boards under their arms. Convertibles cruised past, packed with teenagers in neon-bright beachwear, blasting pop music by sexy boy bands. The cerulean sky was pierced by an incandescent afternoon sun. Everything in a holiday mood. I blinked and shut my eyes against it all.

I wanted to turn the car around and drive back to those two children, to study their faces and run my hands over their sun-warmed skin and feel the texture of their blond hair. I wanted to hold them in my arms and see if they felt like *mine*. It was an impossibility, of course. A quixotic quest.

I wondered if Sam ever shared this longing. Was she *ever* curious about the children she created? Or was egg donation just like so many decisions she made: impulsive, haphazard, quickly forgotten? She'd always been so good at moving past the things she didn't care to remember. Or blacking out so she wouldn't *have* to remember. Another trait that we didn't share. I supposed she was the lucky one, that way.

This whole endeavor was a terrible idea, I suddenly understood; a masochistic pursuit that was, inevitably, just making everything worse, manifesting my abstract longing for a baby into something frighteningly tangible and visceral. *That baby. Our baby. My baby.*

"Let's go home," I said to Iona. "I'm done."

"But there's just one more address on the list," she protested. Her hands tightly gripped the brown leather padding of the steering wheel. "You should really see this through."

"I'm not sure what else I hope to gain. And it's such a drive to Arizona."

Iona was quiet as we came to a stop at an intersection. A flood of families filled the crosswalk: children with zinc on their noses and sand pails clutched in their fists, parents burdened by the weight of coolers and beach chairs. Then she spoke.

"I was a lot like you three years ago. Just . . . stuck. I was an associate at a big law firm but the work was giving me ulcers and partnership kept not happening because they said I wasn't 'personable enough' with clients. I was married to this woman, an artist type, who was critical of everything I did, angry at how much I worked. She wanted me to be more loving, more attentive, more *present* even as she also expected me to cover all our bills with my high-paying job. Then I met Dr. Cindy and she helped me realize how toxic the whole situation was, how everyone around me was just draining me dry, using me up and giving me nothing back in return. And so I left them both. The job. The relationship." The light changed and she accelerated into the intersection, driving a little too fast considering all the foot traffic. "My wife came from money. She got her father to pay for the best divorce lawyer in Southern California and they took me to the cleaners. She walked away with the beachfront house, the art collection, the condo up in Mammoth." Her face was oddly blank as she remembered this. "She didn't even *need* any of it. She had family money, see? It was just her way of getting revenge for my leaving her. Another way to squeeze me dry.

"The easy thing to do would have been to slink away, nurse my wounds, let my ex win, and be the 'bigger person,' right? But Dr. Cindy talked me into reclaiming my control. We did what you and I are doing right now: confronted my failures of strength. We drove to my old home together and sat outside it, tailed my ex as she drove around, just watching her. Dr. Cindy made me address my emotions straight on and ask myself: *What do I want most right now?* Turns out that my ex was sleeping with her male studio assistant. They'd been fucking for months, apparently. She was bi and didn't even tell me."

"Oh God," I said. "I'm so sorry. That's terrible."

"No." She had an odd expression on her face. "Not terrible, really. Because that knowledge just helped give me permission to do what I *really* wanted to do, deep in my heart—what I hadn't admitted to myself because I was supposed to be *nice* and *nurturing*. I wanted to burn that bitch's house down."

I was a little startled. "You mean, metaphorically?"

"I mean literally." Her smile hardened into a twist. "So I let myself inside when no one was home—she hadn't changed the locks yet, she was too naive to take that kind of precaution. And I set the goddamn house on fire. Made it look like an accident—a gas burner left on. Easy enough. The house was utterly destroyed. But guess what?" She laughed, a sharp little bark of victory. "I was still on the insurance and got half of the settlement. Boy, did that piss her off."

I was stunned. I tried to imagine the Iona I knew—seemingly so cool and controlled—turning on the stove and holding newspaper to the flame, touching the burning paper to a curtain, watching fire devour fabric and rise up to lick the ceiling of her former home. The heat of the act, so irrevocable. "You didn't feel guilty about it?"

"Oh, no. My ex was *fine*. She didn't need that house. She had money. She had everything she wanted. All I did was take back a little of what I was owed. Proved to myself that I wasn't going to let the world walk all over me. I wasn't going to conform to how I was 'supposed' to behave." She made a sharp turn onto the parkway that led to the interstate. "I took back control and I've never been healthier. Dr. Cindy gave that to me, she saw a *leader* in me, instead of a mouse. That's why I've committed myself to the program. It's really a good life, once you make it to Level Ten. Being a Mentor . . . it's great. We get to teach women how to be powerful. We're starting a real movement, one that has the potential to change the world."

Her voice was firm, final; and yet now that I think back on the conversation, knowing what I do, I wonder if there might have been something just underneath her words, a faint quaver of doubt that swallowed the end of her sentences. Was Iona aware of her own complicity in what GenFem was becoming, the devil she'd given her soul to, and did she feel guilty about it?

If she did, she hid it well. She brightened her smile, put a hand on my thigh, patted it twice. "And that's what this process will give you, too. We just need to figure out what *control* looks like for you."

I stared at Iona's face, her pale eyes above blade-like cheek-bones, the fine lines that traced her forehead and fanned out from her eyes. I thought about the beachfront house, consumed by flames. She seemed so clear-eyed about it all. And yet what she did was definitely illegal. Then again, no one was *really* hurt, were they? Maybe it was even deserved, I told myself. And Dr. Cindy had endorsed it. She was there. She was a world-renowned psychologist; wouldn't she call it out if something was wrong?

The exhaustion hit me then, a tangle of conflicting emotions that I was too tired to parse out. So I just let it all go and sank back into the seat, let the rich leather envelop me, released myself to the reliable V-8 engine and Iona's certainty. I was glad *someone* was certain since I was not. Iona steered us onto the highway, due east, toward Arizona, and the last address on my list.

I was already in too deep, past the point where I could save myself from drowning.

29 THERE ARE CERTAIN PIVOTAL moments in your life when you make a decision that will completely change the course of your existence. You might think that you'll recognize those junctures when they arrive—that you'll perceive the importance of the moment, give your choice the proper gravitas and consideration, and then accept the consequences of your decision. And yet, so often, these choices happen unconsciously, unintentionally, a piling on of coincidence and circumstance rather than a moment of thoughtfulness. You aren't even aware they're happening.

This, certainly, is how I made the decision that would derail my entire life. Not with any forethought or intention, but simply by slipping sideways through events as they happened. One step leading to the next, blindly following a path toward the horizon. Only after my choice had come and gone did I even realize that it was a choice at all.

We arrived in Arizona too late to visit the last address on my list, so instead we spent the night at a hotel on the outskirts of Scottsdale with a view over a golf course. I was asleep by nine and wide awake again by one in the morning. I tossed and turned until I finally pulled out my GenFem binder and read a few of Dr. Cindy's lectures on letting go of toxicity and regaining control; this made me feel less tenuous, more grounded. By the time the sun rose— a pale gray gleam over the desert sky, the light cold and dry—I was nauseous from sleep exhaustion and edgy with hunger, but once again I felt hopeful. I was making positive change in my life, I reminded myself. If it was painful, it just meant I was doing something right. *The Method is patented,* I reminded myself. *I'm part of a revolutionary movement.*

At seven in the morning Iona knocked on my hotel room door. We drove, in a sepulchral silence, to the final address on the list: 825 Joshua Tree Drive. We found ourselves at a modern home on the outskirts of town. Its stucco was painted pale pink, a color that mirrored the fading remnants of the sunrise. The curtains over the front windows were drawn, but through the gauzy fabric I could see silhouettes, people moving through rooms. A family, in shadows.

We arrived for our stakeout just as the neighborhood garages were emptying their occupants out into the day. Iona parked the Mercedes in a strategic position, across the street and fifty yards down, which kept us out of eyeshot of the house, which was un-fenced, on a square of lawn that ended abruptly at the desert's edge. From where we were parked, we could see the whole prop-erty. I worried that we might be conspicuous—two women in a giant gold Mercedes, just sitting there—but the homes were far enough apart, the traffic sparse enough, that we didn't draw at-tention.

At 8:30 A.M., a small sports car pulled out of the garage, a middle-aged man behind the wheel. I caught a glimpse of dark hair, a business suit, the glint of a gold watch against the steering wheel. The man drove down the street in the opposite direction from where we were parked, the garage door zipped back down, and all was quiet again.

We kept waiting.

At ten-thirty, an Uber pulled up in front of the house. A heavyset older woman—hair gray and professionally puffed, pearls paired with a crisp button-down—heaved herself out of the back seat, burdened down with shopping bags from a gourmet food shop. She approached the door, extricated a key from her purse, let herself in.

We waited some more.

Fifteen minutes later, the garage door lifted again and disgorged another car, this one a new-model Volvo station wagon. The Volvo drove past us, close enough that I could glimpse yet another middle-aged blond woman behind the wheel. *The mother.* It dawned on me that all three of these women had chosen Sam as their egg donor because of her (*our*) vague resemblance to them: white, blond, skinny, pretty. A younger, more fertile version of themselves. A choice rooted in vanity, perhaps; or maybe they hoped to find some visual connection with the children that wouldn't share their DNA. Maybe it was just a way to avoid uncomfortable questions about a visibly mismatched child.

If I was ever to consider egg donors, I wondered, would I do the same? Probably.

A low winter sun slowly rose over the homes on the street, chasing away the chill of the desert night. The temperature outside was in the low seventies but by hour three the car was getting stuffy and the air-conditioning was in danger of draining the battery.

Iona looked at her watch. "Maybe we take a break, go fill up the gas tank and get a bite, then come back this afternoon," she offered.

But I wasn't listening, because I'd finally caught sight of her. The last child on my list, the littlest of them all. The girl that would become my Charlotte.

The older woman had brought her out into the yard behind the house to play. The woman was obviously a grandparent, enlisted to help for the day while her daughter took a few hours for herself. It was something about the way the woman watched the little girl toddling ahead of her on the garden path: bemused, but a little bored; loving, but low-energy; attentive, but without the obsessive concern of someone whose salary depended on it. She had a cellphone in her hand, and she kept glancing down at it as her grandchild lurched across the grass in pursuit of a white butterfly.

The little girl, to my surprise, was a brunette. She was younger than the other children Iona and I had seen so far—almost two, I guessed. Walking, but with the drunken hitch of a child not yet at ease with her own mobility. She wore a pink cotton T-shirt and striped leggings, her curly hair tumbling across her forehead, held back by an ineffectual barrette.

The grandmother had a blanket and an armful of toys, and she spread these on the grass in the sun and then collapsed on the blanket, seemingly exhausted by this effort. The little girl zoomed back and forth across the yard like a wind-up toy that's just been let go, dragging a mangy stuffed animal behind her. The grandmother's cellphone rang and she answered it, talking animatedly, occasionally casting an eye about to make sure that her granddaughter was still within sight.

It felt like a secret show, just for us. I was riveted, barely breathing. Beside me, Iona studied the tableau in silence, her arms folded over the steering wheel, lost in thought.

Time passed—five minutes, ten, the grandmother still talking and the little girl still adventuring. As I watched, I simmered in a stew of emotions: rage at the haphazard grandmother, melancholic longing for the beautiful child, bitter envy for the whole mundane scenario that I might never be able to replicate myself. Eventually, the little girl staggered back to the blanket and climbed into her grandmother's lap. Her grandmother, still talking on her phone, pressed a packet of pureed fruit into the little girl's hand. The girl drained it, lay down on the blanket, and closed her eyes. The arms clutching the stuffed animal to her chest slackened, and the animal eventually slipped to the grass beside her.

Finally, the older woman hung up her phone. She leaned over the sleeping little girl, her brow puckered, frustration on her face. Then she heaved herself to her feet. She gazed at the house twenty feet away, measuring the distance between them, and then a wave of pain contorted her face. She pressed a hand to her stomach, glanced down at the child again, then turned to survey the empty landscape around them. She seemed to be making a calculation; she frowned again, hunched slightly, and then hurried to the house with a strange, abbreviated step.

The child, sleeping, didn't notice her grandmother's departure. A hushed silence seemed to descend over the yard, an oppressive stillness, the desert holding its breath.

"Jesus," I whispered. "She just left the baby there alone? What if she wakes up? The garden's not even *fenced*."

"It's an opportunity," Iona said quietly. "Don't question it." She leaned across me and opened the car door. "This is your chance for a real Confrontation. Go. Quick. Get a proper look."

I hesitated. "But what if the grandmother finds me there?"

"Judging by the way that woman was moving, you've got a few minutes," Iona said. "And if she comes back out, you were passing by and saw the child all alone in the yard and were concerned. She won't question that. You're an affluent white woman, just like her. You get an automatic pass."

She prodded me and I got out of the car, walked across the road, took a tentative step onto the lawn. *I'll just get a quick look up close*, I told myself as I moved toward the sleeping child. *One glance, and then I can let this go.*

The grass was plush green underfoot, a rebuke to the harsh desert climate and a testament to the wealth of the family that could afford so much extravagant water. I took three steps, then ten, then twenty, and then I was on my knees on the grass, right next to the little girl, watching her as she slept.

Her chest rose and fell, her breathing so shallow that I worried that something was wrong, that she was overheating or hyperventilating or having a terrible nightmare. Or was that normal? I'd never examined a sleeping child that closely.

I leaned in closer. The noontime sun, directly overhead now, cast my shadow over the child's sleeping form. I wondered if it would wake her up, but she didn't stir. Now that I could study her up close, I could see that she didn't obviously resemble me: her hair was curly and brown, for one, her skin tinged with olive where mine was pale, and she didn't have visible dimples. If each of the three children we'd visited so far was half me and half stranger, in this particular case the stranger's genes had clearly dominated.

But there was also something about the shape of her face—her wide-set eyes, the tight point of her chin, the upturned bud of her lip—that I recognized as Sam's and mine. You had to look close for it, but it was there.

An unidentifiable yearning gripped my insides, twisted them until I gasped.

How much time had passed? A minute, maybe less. I glanced at the house behind me. A wall of weather-coated windows reflected the desert landscape back at me; if the grandmother was in there, looking out, I wouldn't be able to see her. But there was no sound of life coming from inside, no shrieks of alarm. The grass was sharp and itchy underneath my knees. The desert air was so dry that it hurt my lungs to breathe. I wanted to run a finger along the curve of the girl's cheeks, press my palms around the soft pudge of her naked arm, but I was too scared. Instead, I tentatively placed my hand on the little girl's chest, right above the pocket of her tee. Just to see if she was OK, because that rapid breath was so alarming. I told myself that I was just being a conscientious observer, because the child was alone out here, and what if she *wasn't* OK? I could feel the frantic quiver of her heartbeat through the thin cotton, and it felt too fast, far too fast.

And then suddenly her eyes were open and looking right at me.

Her gaze was deep and still, not surprised at all but calm, as if she'd recognized me and was relieved to find me there.

I felt it then, that instinctual connection. My DNA, in this child. *My* child.

She blinked a few times, and then—blinded by the midday sun pressing down directly overhead—winched her eyes back shut again. "Mama?" she asked, in a tiny sleepy voice. I realized that, with the sun in her eyes, she'd probably seen a halo of blond hair, nothing more; just enough to give her the impression of *mother*. And yet that single word—an echo of the question I kept hearing in my dreams—sent a sharp needle into my heart.

She lifted her arms to me, letting them hang limply in the air, asking to be held.

Naked instinct kicked in. Before I could second-guess myself, I'd picked her up, pressed her against my chest, and was rubbing my palm along her back. She was so warm, almost hot to the touch. Was she feverish? But she slackened in my grip, put a thumb in her mouth, and let her head loll against my shoulder. Almost immediately, I felt her jaw working against her thumb, soothing herself back to sleep. The heat of her body against mine, the faint strawberry scent of her hair: It was all so visceral—my hallucination come to life—that I felt dizzy.

I heard a voice calling softly behind me, "Let's go."

I turned and Iona was standing there, halfway across the yard, just out of eyeshot of the windows that faced the backyard. She gesticulated wildly, waving me toward her, and, in my dazed stupor, I moved without thinking.

The child in my arms didn't even stir.

When I walked within reach, Iona grabbed my elbow and rapidly steered me toward the car. I let her direct me across the road, afraid to ask what she had in mind, afraid to open my mouth at all, because what if I spoke and the child woke up and started to cry? What if her grandmother heard it and came out and saw me crossing the road with her baby in my arms? What if she called the police? Somehow this was a more terrifying prospect than silently following Iona's lead as she ushered me and the baby across the road. I noticed that the door to the back seat was wide open, a mouth waiting to swallow us. The engine idling, the car gently vibrating, ready to move.

I didn't resist as Iona pressed me into the back seat, her hand firm on my back. I didn't say a word when she climbed in the front seat and put the car in drive. I didn't question the logic of what was happening, I didn't ask myself whether I should be doing what Iona clearly wanted me to do.

Looking back now, it would be easy for me to pin the blame on Iona. It was her encouragement—her *idea* really—that had me climbing into a car with another woman's child in my arms. Would I have done it if she hadn't suggested it? Hadn't grabbed my arm and steered me across the road? Hadn't pressed me into the back seat of the car? I doubt it.

And yet, I can't absolve myself. Of course I can't. Because if I am going to be honest—truly honest with myself—wasn't it exactly what I wanted, too? To climb into the safety of those deep leather seats and clutch the sleeping child against my chest, to hold her there forever and ever, to make her mine?

Iona just saw what my darkest longing was and pushed me to make it a reality.

As we drove away from the house that day, I didn't realize that I'd just made a decision that would change my life. Dazed and overwhelmed, I wouldn't come to this awareness until five minutes later, ten minutes, twenty; not until we'd pulled onto the highway and were already driving back west; not until my heart stopped beating so fast and the adrenaline cloud began to dissipate and logic reinserted itself into the haze of madness. Not until the child in my arms finally stirred and looked up at me and didn't murmur "Mama," but instead started to cry.

Only then would I understand that I had somehow made a choice, and that the choice I'd made was so utterly, irrevocably wrong.

30 AND JUST LIKE THAT, I had a daughter, one that was technically half mine. I called her *Charlotte,* a name that had topped my list for years, and when I called her by this it was like a memory made manifest. I purchased the contents of an entire Pottery Barn Kids catalog and converted the guest bedroom to a nursery. I bought books with names like *The Happiest Toddler on the Block* and studied them for parenting tips. I wooed my new daughter with ice cream and cookies, I took her to the beach and the playground and strapped her on my back for hikes up to Inspiration Point.

In response, Charlotte cried. She sobbed because the sand was too hot. She threw herself out of my arms when I picked her up. She refused the food that I set in front of her. She wailed when I belted her into her brand-new car seat and she screamed when I took her out of it. She pushed her hands against my face and said *NO,* one of the few words she could clearly articulate. I knew, of course, that her tears had nothing to do with anything that I was doing wrong; her malaise was something much bigger, and it was all my fault.

Of course it was—I'd selfishly taken her away from everything she'd ever known.

But eventually, a few weeks in, she stopped crying so much. It was as if she'd accepted some inevitability, realized that her new reality was perhaps not so bad after all. She'd decided I was safe. Perhaps the memory of her life before was already fading away, paved over by the eternal *new* of existence as a fledgling human.

I studied her for signs of long-term trauma, for some evidence that wrenching her away from her parents had caused permanent damage. In retrospect, I'm sure it did; how could it not? But at the time I was reassured when, so quickly, she started eating like a normal child, she played with the toy kitchen that I set up in her bedroom, she made eye contact with me and laughed when I read her Sandra Boynton board books. She started snuggling into my side when I picked her up, and burrowed her head in my neck when a neighbor's dog barked at her, just like I was her real mother.

I discovered that she had more words: *Kitty. Hungry. More.*

And yet sometimes, I would look over and see her watching me with measuring eyes, a worm of worry furrowing her brow. As if she was trying to fully comprehend this new reality she'd found herself in.

Then, a month in, she called me *Mama*. We were at the park, and she'd gotten herself turned around under the play structure. She wandered out into the sun on the wrong side of the sandpit, looked around, saw only strange nannies and unfamiliar diaper bags. She cried out in a tremulous voice, "Mama?"

"I'm right here, honey," I called as I crawled out from underneath the swinging bridge, sand pebbling my shins. The wobble in her lip firmed up, turned into a smile. She lifted her arms out to me and said it again, a command: "Mama, *uppie.*" And I swung her up onto my hip and pressed my lips into her hair, like it was a completely normal thing to do, not a fantasy that just a few weeks earlier felt completely unattainable. I realized that I was crying.

Because I should have been happy, but I wasn't.

———

Of course I wasn't. I'd stolen someone else's child, and all the self-justification in the world couldn't erase that fact. I was a terrible, terrible person. The guilt flooded through me every time I looked at Charlotte, a poison that consumed me from the inside out, seeped out through every pore, a toxic miasma of misery.

I loved Charlotte so much that it hurt, but I wasn't happy. I wasn't happy at all.

I needed to do something to fix the situation. But what?

I had confessed everything to Dr. Cindy just a few days after returning to Santa Barbara with Charlotte. We met in the empty GenFem center on a cold afternoon, and went through a Reenactment. I walked Dr. Cindy through the visit to BioCal and my impersonation of my sister, the stakeouts of the three houses, the snatching of Charlotte from her parents' garden. I waited for the stinging slap on my cheek, for the redirection that would point me toward the correct choice—the path I *should* have taken, the one it was perhaps not too late to take—but this didn't come. Instead, Dr. Cindy smiled indulgently and took my hands in hers.

"You wanted a baby," she said. "Now you have one. You took control."

It sounded as if what I'd done was no worse than taking someone else's lunch from the office fridge. "But I stole someone else's child," I explained. Did she not understand?

Dr. Cindy sat back in her chair. "Indeed you did. You did exactly what you wanted to do. You made it to the last step in the IAS Method—Self-Determination. And now you get to live with that choice."

I didn't think she intended this to sound like a punishment, but it did. Her steady gray eyes, fixed so tightly on mine, made me feel unsettled, uncertain about my own feelings. "I just feel a little lost," I said quietly. "I don't know what to do."

"Don't you think the path forward is quite clear? She's *yours* now. Raise her! What else would you propose to do, take her back to Arizona? You'll be arrested, you know."

It felt like there was a vise around my lungs, slowly squeezing out the air. "But I might be arrested anyway. They're going to be looking for her. They could track her here. Maybe they'll be more forgiving if I bring her back."

"But why would they look for her in Santa Barbara?" Dr. Cindy shook her head. "They have no reason to connect you with the child's disappearance."

"Sam," I explained. "They might see a connection with Sam. Wouldn't the egg donor be an automatic suspect?"

Dr. Cindy shrugged. "Even if they do look into her, they won't find the baby, will they? She had nothing to do with it. And you and your sister are estranged, so the path will end there." She hesitated, then looked at me sharply. "You haven't been talking to Sam, have you?" I shook my head. "Good girl. Look: The grandmother was neglectful and left the baby alone. The child woke up and wandered off into the desert. That's what authorities have assumed. Not that someone drove by and kidnapped her. You have nothing to worry about."

I was silent for a long moment. "But . . . I hurt someone. A lot of people."

Dr. Cindy made a dismissive gesture with her hand, as if swiping a bowl off a table. "Who? The parents? Why does that matter? You don't know them, they're just an abstract concept. People get hurt every day; they feel pain for lots of reasons. Your responsibility is to yourself. Don't fall victim to that kind of weakness. See, this is what women do, this is why we don't run the world yet— because we worry too much about *other people's feelings*. Men just barrel ahead and assume they have the right to anything they want. You need to worry about your *own* needs."

Looking back now, it's obvious that the moral code of GenFem was that there *was* no moral code—just a personal drive toward self-fulfillment. And maybe this was the moment when things started to break for me, when the first doubts started to creep in. Because Dr. Cindy's words didn't sit well with me, as much as I wanted to let them reassure me. *Worry about your own needs.* Just a month or two earlier, Dr. Cindy's dispensation had felt like a kind of freedom, after a lifetime of thinking too much about others; but now that I was claiming someone else's child as my own, the sentiment made me undeniably queasy.

Maybe once I hit Level Ten it would all become easier, I told myself, but at that moment I felt more lost than ever.

"But Charlotte," I persisted. "She's not an abstract concept."

"And she's not hurt. She's a *baby*. She'll have no memory of this whatsoever. Babies that age lose their parents all the time and they don't know the difference." She adjusted her glasses. "Her parents were neglectful, yes? They left her in a situation where she was endangered. And you will *never* do that. Ergo, the child is in a better home now. You've *improved* the child's life."

I tried to let her logic spill over me, like a protective coat of lacquer that might keep the guilt from seeping out. She studied my face, seeing something in it that made her own features stiffen into a point.

"I can tell it's still eating at you. So let's do this: Write everything down, like a confession. Get it off your chest. Put it all on paper and then we can burn it and let it go."

So I did. I wrote it down, the whole affair, from the day when I masqueraded as my sister to get access to her apartment to the moment that I drove away with Charlotte in the back seat of Iona's car. I put it all down in my handwriting and then handed it to Dr. Cindy, who tucked it in a folder and smiled at me and told me that she was proud of me. Identification, Articulation, Self-Determination. Then I went to pick up Charlotte from my parents and I held her so tight that she squirmed in protest, and I felt a little better, though not much.

Dr. Cindy and I never actually burned the paper. And I didn't really let it go. Dr. Cindy never mentioned the confession again, and neither did I, lest I get another Sufferance. The knowledge of the paper's existence was just another thing that festered inside me: more evidence that I shouldn't have left behind.

I brought this up with Iona when I cornered her in the parking lot one day. "Oh, I did that, too—gave Dr. Cindy a written confession after I burned down my ex-wife's house," she said. "It's a sign of our trust in GenFem. Dr. Cindy holds all our secrets, she takes on that burden for us. Don't you see? It allows us to let go of guilt, of any feelings of responsibility to others, and just live for ourselves."

I didn't see, really. I still felt guilty. I still felt responsible. I still felt like there was damage I must undo. But I tried to push that away, to make up for it by being the best possible substitute mother to Charlotte. I smothered her with love so that I could forget that I was the one who couldn't breathe.

Weeks passed. I stopped sleeping. Exhaustion wove itself into the fabric of my existence, my queasy, achy new normal. At night, I sat in the armchair in the nursery and watched Charlotte sleep, my heart beating in time with the rapid rise and fall of her chest. Often, I found myself thinking of Sam. Wondering what she would think of this madness, wondering how shocked she would be to hear what I'd done. Would she be disappointed in me? Would she try to talk me into taking Charlotte back to Arizona? Would she laugh, tell me she didn't think I had it in me?

I wasn't angry at her anymore, I realized. I'd lost that right the minute I crossed the street with someone else's child in my arms. Or maybe once my anger tipped over from emboldening to frightening, I knew it was time to snuff it out. Instead, I once again found myself fantasizing that my doorbell would ring, and I'd open it to see Sam standing there. We'd look at each other and nothing would need to be said, we'd both just *know*. The way we used to, when we were children. She'd help me untangle the mess I'd made.

But of course she wouldn't come, not with the way I'd left things last year. And I couldn't even call to ask for her help: Dr. Cindy had made me delete her number from my phone months earlier. We were so far apart, and I had no clue how I could ever claw my way back.

A few weeks after I wrote out my confession, I was awarded Level Eight, which meant I was officially an "upper-level" member. I was given a pale green scarf, and an admonishment that I needed to start recruiting new members. (But who? I'd once dragged my neighbor Alice along, and she never looked at me the same way again. I could think of no one else to bring.) After the ceremony, Dr. Cindy pulled me into one of the velvet cubbies, and handed me a mug of chamomile tea. She sat down across from me so that our knees were touching.

"I'm so proud of the work that we're doing here. But there's so much *more* to do," she said. "And I really want you to be part of it, Elli. You're one of our brightest stars, you've made leaps and bounds this year. But the thing is—we need funding. We need to expand, to meet the demand of these women who need our help. We want to open a new center in San Francisco, we want to start a scholarship fund for women who don't have the means to pay for workshops, and we have big plans to renovate our Ojai retreat into a state-of-the-art headquarters. And, of course, we need more full-time Mentors. This is where you come in." My stomach flipped—was I being invited into the inner circle, a Level Ten Mentor?—but then she continued. "I'd love to show you our business plan and see if you would be up for an investment."

"Oh," I said, a little flustered. I thought of the amount that I'd already spent on GenFem so far—it had just crossed six figures—

and wondered where, exactly, that money had gone. "How much do you think you need?"

"Three hundred thousand would be a good start."

The tea scalded my throat, and I choked. I still had more than a million dollars in my childhood savings account, but my day-to-day income had dried up. Since Charlotte's arrival, I'd let my florist business wither on the vine, turning down clients and canceling events. I just didn't have the time. And I'd already told Chuck, via his divorce attorney, that I didn't want anything from him except our house. I didn't want to have to deal with lawyers who might dig into my current situation and discover the existence of an undocumented child. I figured I still had a career as a Mentor ahead of me anyway—but when would that materialize?

Dr. Cindy gripped my hands tighter, as if reading my mind. "You look panicky, I can tell what you're thinking. But you're looking at it the wrong way. This is an *investment*. A way to *make* money. You'll double your money in a matter of a few years, I promise. It's a win-win, really."

I told her I'd think about it, she told me she'd get me some spreadsheets, and then I left to retrieve Charlotte from my parents' house.

On the way out, I passed Dr. Cindy's brand-new cherry-red Land Rover parked in the strip mall lot. It shone like a newly minted penny.

31 I STOPPED GOING TO GenFem almost by accident. I just got lost in single motherhood—the constant churn, the soothing repetition, the problems so easily solved. *Lost bunny toy? Here it is! Hungry? Have a snack! Dirty diaper? Let's clean you up!* My mind was too numb, my conscience too conflicted by my day-to-day, to even think about bigger things like mastering the Method or leading a new women's movement.

I found myself attending meetings only once a week, and then every other week, and then I stopped going altogether.

In June, Iona called to ask why I hadn't been to a meeting in twenty-seven days. "Motherhood is a full-time job," I said, a little alarmed that they'd been counting. (*And yet, wasn't it also nice that they'd noticed, and missed me?* I thought. I was still looking for silver linings.) Across the room, Charlotte was smashing chunks of neon-bright Play-Doh into the cracks in the cabinetry.

"I wouldn't know." I registered the disapproval in her voice. "So . . . Dr. Cindy and I were discussing you today. July is the month of our annual upper-level retreat in Ojai. We really think you should attend, for a long weekend at least. We don't want you to lose your momentum." She hesitated. "Frankly, Dr. Cindy is a little upset. She feels like you don't appreciate the work that she's put into you, that you're choosing to abandon us now that you've got what you wanted out of the program. And she had such high hopes for you."

I imagined Dr. Cindy's disapproving eyes fixing on me and felt a little shiver of panic. I remembered my confession, hidden away God knows where. I didn't want Dr. Cindy to be angry at me.

"I swear, I didn't abandon the program. I'm still totally committed."

"Then you'll come to the retreat? It's a guaranteed way to jump a level, maybe even two if you stay long enough. You're so close."

I glanced down at Charlotte, who was trying to wedge a violet ball of Play-Doh into her nose. I gently pried it from her fingers, tossed it in the sink. A few months back, I would have jumped at the opportunity to go to Ojai—that mysterious sanctum, only for the anointed—but now I felt a coil of undefinable dread.

And yet, Iona was right. I'd already invested so much into Gen-Fem. Almost half a million dollars, plus a year of my life and every relationship I valued. How silly it would be to quit before seeing it through to Level Ten, when everything might finally get easy again. "I'd love to go. It's just . . . what would I do with Charlotte?"

"That's what grandparents are for!" Iona crowed. "For God's sake, give yourself a few days off. You're a mom, not a saint. Don't let motherhood obliterate your sense of self. In fact, that's the whole *theme* of this retreat: taking control over yourself by learning how to let go when it matters." She paused, I heard her flipping through papers on the other end of the line. "Look—this retreat is going to be so special. We've got dozens of women flying in from the Toronto and New Jersey centers, women who we really see as the future leaders of GenFem. All the top Mentors will be there. I'll be there—we can even carpool! And I really think it would be good for you right now to remind yourself that you're part of a loving, nurturing community."

Community. This plucked a chord in me. Charlotte and I had

been cloistered in the house for months. We hadn't joined the local mommy-and-me playgroups or taken baby music classes or organized playdates with neighbor kids. When we left the house—for a hike, or to go to the playground—it was always at odd hours, when fewer people were out and about. Because what if she was recognized? The case of Missing Emma Gonzalez had never quite made the national news—I suspected, with dismay, that this had something to do with her Latino surname—but with just a few clicks on Google I'd found the articles in the Arizona newspapers and the Facebook page with her photo. All it would take was some eagle-eyed transplant from Scottsdale to get too close on the playground swings.

I kept telling myself that it was just a matter of time until we could breathe more easily—already, she was a different child from the one I'd picked up off the lawn just a few months back, and soon she would look different again. But until then, being in public made me feel panicky.

If there was any safe place for me, it was GenFem, where my secret was already being held without judgment. Where I was seen as a "future leader," not despite what I'd done but *because* of it.

Maybe Iona was right, I thought, and I'd abandoned the very community that I needed the most. Maybe it would be good to remind myself of the support system that had validated my choices, to recommit myself to the Method, the movement, to Dr. Cindy Medina and a future as a Mentor.

Eleven days later, I was in Ojai.

32 THEY CUT MY HAIR on the very first night.

We had assembled for dinner in the great hall of the main lodge, a cavernous room with spiderwebs drifting from the beams overhead and nails in the wood paneling where decades of Christian summer camp photos once hung. The table where I sat was pitted and scarred with children's initials, hard coins of gum embedded in its underside.

There were nearly two dozen women on the retreat with me, mostly strangers but also a few upper-level Neos that I knew from the Santa Barbara center. One of the latter was Ruth, a mother of four in her late fifties whose husband had dumped her for a Peloton instructor. She had proceeded to gain sixty pounds in a year, a rebuke to her husband and his hardbody girlfriend, which of course just made her more miserable. Since Ruth joined GenFem, Dr. Cindy had given Ruth Sufferance after Sufferance, almost all of them calorie restrictions, in order to teach her self-control. She'd lost much of the weight, but this state of semipermanent starvation had a somewhat detrimental effect on Ruth's mood. As we sat there, listening to a parade of Mentors tell us about the retreat's activities, Ruth grumbled under her breath to me.

"No massages, huh? No hot tub? Not even yoga. Some *retreat*."

"There's daily morning exercise," I offered helpfully. "But I don't think it's *that* kind of retreat. They never said it was. It's mostly about workshops and learning, not relaxation."

"Sure isn't. Did you see that pool? It's got a foot of dirt at the bottom. 'State-of-the-art headquarters,' my ass. I wonder if they actually have a plan to upgrade this dump. God knows they have the money." She adjusted the neckline of the dress they'd given us to wear during our time at the retreat: white for Level Eight, red for Level Nine, yellow for Level Ten Mentors. "And what's up with this shroud we have to wear? I think it's giving me hives."

I liked the dress, frankly. It reminded me of what the bohemian moms in Santa Barbara wore when they shopped for oat milk at Lassens: shapeless sacks that weren't in the least bit sexy. It made me feel invisible. "A uniform helps eliminate distractions from the learning of the weekend," I said. "No one's going to be judging anyone else."

"Yeah, I heard the same lecture," she snapped.

I shifted my chair a few inches away from Ruth. I didn't want her discontent to taint my optimism. Despite my initial trepidation about coming, I was feeling strangely light, almost buoyant. Iona was right—it did feel good to be released from Charlotte for a few days, and to remember what my *own* priorities were. Not that I wasn't experiencing pangs of longing—for the damp heft of her rear, her pancake-sweet breath in my face—but something had lifted off me since I drove away from Santa Barbara. Gone was the boulder of anxiety, the bilious pit in my stomach, the fog of guilt. I felt strangely safe here behind the compound's high iron gates. Off the grid. Forgotten. Untouchable.

I couldn't even call my parents to ask about Charlotte if I'd wanted to: A Mentor had taken away my cellphone when I checked in at the front office of the lodge that morning. "It's a Sufferance, to break you of your addiction to outside validation and constant connection," she'd said as she wrestled the phone from my hand. I could hear my text messages pinging, a sound that filled me with Pavlovian panic—*What if something's wrong with Charlotte?*—

but she shook her head and smiled reassuringly. "Don't worry—just give me your passcode and we can monitor it for you and let you know if there are any emergencies that need to be addressed back home. In a way, it's not a Sufferance at all. We're simply taking the responsibility *off* you. That's what makes it a retreat!"

She turned and tucked the cellphone into the top drawer of a file cabinet. Before she slid the drawer closed, I caught a glimpse of a row of alphabetized file folders, fat with paper, each with a name carefully inked on the top. I wondered if there was a folder with my name on it.

Now Ruth and I consumed our dinner in semi-silence—a scoop of chickpea stew with rice for me, a smaller scoop with no rice for her—and once our plates were cleared, someone clapped for our attention at the front of the room. I looked up to see Roni—the Mentor I knew from the Santa Barbara office—standing on the speaker's platform, holding up a pair of electric hair clippers. Dr. Cindy stood behind her, hands folded behind her back, looking out calmly at her assembled followers. Behind her, a pink banner read *GIVE UP CONTROL IN ORDER TO TAKE CONTROL.*

The women in the dining hall went quiet, looking around at one another with alarmed expressions, even though we had all suspected this was coming. I kept my eyes on Roni, the corners of my mouth tugging artificially upward, because I wanted to please the Mentors with my openness to the GenFem vision. Anyway, why *not* agree to an extreme haircut? There were so many bigger things to be concerned about.

"Vanity is weakness," Roni began. "It means you care *too much* what other people think of you. Why else do we spend so much time—hours upon hours every week—fussing over our hair? All the time wasted on blowouts and flat irons and weaves, thousands spent on cuts and color, all to meet some arbitrary beauty standards set by whom? Men, typically. It's just another way of distracting us, preventing us from taking charge." Roni's head was already shaved short—and had been for as long as I'd known her—revealing a shapely skull, Grace Jones regal. But not all of us had her bone structure. I cast my eyes over to take in Ruth, with her soft chin and an expensive dye job that concealed her gray roots. Her lip wobbled; she blinked at the far wall, refusing eye contact with me.

Roni continued. "And at GenFem do *we* care what people think of us?"

"No . . ." I added my own voice to the tentative chorus. Someone tittered nervously.

She turned the clippers on with a dramatic buzz. "I'm sorry, but that wasn't very convincing. Do we *care* what other people think of us? Do we care about what other people think about what we do, or how we look, or whether we're *quote-unquote* feminine?"

This time, the response reverberated off the walls of the dining hall, rattling the cutlery in the glass jars on the tables. The two fortysomething women in front of me shouted with an urgency that bordered on hysteria. "NO! We don't care!"

I found that I was half-standing, eager to show my enthusiasm, to prove my lack of concern to this dazzling woman. My eyes met Dr. Cindy's, and she tilted her chin in a nod of approval, her lips twitching into a smile, and my heart filled with joy. *This is where I belong. How could I forget that?*

"So you see?" Roni continued. "By temporarily ceding control to GenFem and letting us shave your heads, you're actually proving your *own* control over your self-worth. Your best shot at finding yourself comes when you truly don't care what outside people think. That's why we rid ourselves of Toxics, that's why we focus on tightening our own community so that we can grow within it. The haircut is just a sign of your commitment to our beautiful future together." Roni looked around the room with an encouraging smile. "So then, who's first?"

————

Back in my cabin that night, I stared at myself in the rusting mir-ror that was clipped to the back of the door. The person who stared back at me was unrecognizable, not the winsome blond twin who once charmed TV audiences with her dimples, nor the pretty young coed who did her damnedest to make everyone for-get that fact. I was not the sought-after florist or the respected community member or the devoted twin/daughter/wife, or even the emotionally conflicted new mother.

Instead what I saw was barely a person at all, just skin over skull, my physical existence pared back to the absolute minimum. I wondered what Dr. Cindy planned to rebuild in her place. I won-dered if stripping down so completely really *would* make it easier to grow back as a stronger, more in-control Eleanor. Someone who didn't feel moral conflict and wasn't racked with guilt. At that moment I felt so passive, contentedly sheep-like, waiting for GenFem to show me what my future held.

The cabins were outfitted with squeaky iron bunk beds, thin plastic mattresses, the shadows of crucifixes still visible on the walls. If it hadn't been for the high-thread-count sheets on the lower bunks and the cheery succulent arrangements on each chipped side table, you wouldn't have known that the compound was now being used as a retreat for grown women.

There were a half dozen bunk beds in my cabin but only three residents in the room—myself, Ruth, and a slight young Canadian-Korean girl named Suzy, whose commitment to the Method bor-dered on the fanatical. Nothing that Ruth or I did went without a comment by her, from the amount of toothpaste we put on our brushes ("You know toothpaste has calories, right? Did you count them in your Sufferance, Ruth?") to our reluctance to turn out the lights promptly at ten P.M. ("Lack of sufficient sleep is just an-other reason that women fail to get ahead in the world"). I suspected that Suzy would be more than thrilled to report any of our misdeeds to the Mentors who were running the retreat.

Ruth was furious about her haircut. Roni had taken some pity on her, and her stubble was slightly longer than mine—in a few weeks, it would almost be a pixie cut—but the look was wildly unflattering on her, and she knew it. She stalked around the cabin, getting ready for bed, her pink eyes giving away her anger, though she refused to admit it. Certainly not in front of pious Suzy, who kept running her hands over her head and crying, "I love it so much! It's so freeing!"

We went to bed in silence, Suzy flipping the light switch off at the appointed hour even though I was still smearing night cream on my face. Ten minutes later, I heard her snoring. I lay in the dark, listening to the oak trees whispering outside the cabin, telling one another their wind-secrets. The metal coils of the ancient bunk bed dug into my back. Cold night air seeped under the doorways, through the cracks in the windows. I thought of Charlotte in her crib, splayed in her footie pajamas, the shallow rasp of her night breath. I didn't know how I was ever going to get to sleep.

That's when I heard a voice, disembodied in the dark. It was Ruth, her low whisper echoing off the concrete floor.

"So, what do they have on you?" she asked.

At first I wasn't sure I'd heard her right. "What do you mean?"

The only light in the room was coming through the transom windows, a yellow and sulfurous glow from the floodlights on the path. I saw Ruth roll over so that she was facing me on her side, only the whites of her eyes visible in the dark as she peered across the room toward me. "I mean, did they have you write out a confession?"

"You wrote one, too?"

"Everyone writes one eventually. That's what gets you to Level Eight. You want to be in the inner sanctum, you need to fork over some collateral. Your biggest secret. It's what keeps us in line, right? They would never call it *blackmail,* but that's what it is, of course. They get the confession and then you're beholden to them forever. I gave Dr. Cindy half my alimony settlement, called it a donation. So what was it you did? I bet they *encouraged* you to do whatever it was, didn't they?"

In my stomach, the stew from dinner curdled and threatened to rise up again. I opened my mouth to confess, but the words didn't come. "You first," I managed.

"I paid someone to retake my daughter's college entrance exams for her after she failed them the first time. It was my Mentor's idea, actually. Shella. She said that Izzy—that's my daughter—had also been traumatized by my husband's betrayal of us, and it wasn't fair that she should be punished for his transgressions. And Shella, she knew this girl, a kid in need who could use the cash . . ." Her voice trailed off. "Anyway, Izzy got into Swarthmore, and I never broke it to her how it really happened. But it was a stupid thing to do. If Izzy ever found out, or my husband—or, for God's sake, *Swarthmore*—it would ruin my daughter's entire life." She was quiet for a minute as I digested all this, surprised but also a little relieved (*it wasn't just me!*). "I should have just let Izzy fail. But honestly, it's not like I hadn't thought about cheating before. I thought about it all the time. Izzy never showed much academic aptitude, but I still wanted my kids to have a leg up on life, whatever it took. I just hadn't done anything about it until GenFem encouraged it."

Suzy let out a wet snort and we both went silent, listening to her rustle in her bunk. When she was still again, I whispered, "But Dr. Cindy would never actually *show* your confession to anyone, would she? Iona told me it's just an exercise in letting go of the burden of a secret."

Ruth's laugh was a bitter bark. "She doesn't have to, does she? She just needs you to be afraid that she will. It's leverage, for the other things she wants out of you."

Collateral. I thought of the six-figure check that I'd just written to GenFem, a third of my savings gone with the swipe of a pen. *I want to make Dr. Cindy happy,* I'd told myself when I signed the check. *I believe in GenFem, and I want it to grow. This is my future. It's just an investment.* Now it felt as if a caul had dropped from my face, leaving me with unexpectedly clear vision. Another truth had been right there, if I had chosen to look for it. I just didn't want to admit to myself that I was being blackmailed for my own criminal behavior.

I lay there in the dark, acknowledging what I hadn't wanted to see before. How had Ruth and I both ended up succumbing to our worst instincts? It would be easy to blame GenFem, I thought, but that felt like I would be letting myself off the hook. Yes, Dr. Cindy's Method had unearthed the darkness within us, brought it to the surface, but *we* let it define who we were. We secretly wanted to be like this; GenFem just gave us permission. And now we couldn't escape it.

GenFem was the punishment for the very flaws it unearthed.

"So what do we do?" I whispered.

"Nothing," Ruth said bluntly. "I'll be a Mentor soon and then I'll get my cut of it all, too. That's why I'm sticking it out. Top leadership has to be making mid six figures, don't you think? I mean, Dr. Cindy flies *private.*"

Something in me protested at this. "But that's not really the point of being a Mentor, is it? It's about wisdom and self-knowledge. It's about being the leader of a new women's movement."

Ruth snorted. "*Movement.* Please. There's no real *movement;* we're not changing the world. It's just a concept that they spoon-feed us to get us to feel like we're in the service of something bigger than ourselves instead of doing something that's innately selfish." She laughed softly. "I mean, the point of the whole Method is to get you what you want most, isn't it? I wanted to lose sixty pounds, I wanted to be *stronger.* And I did. I'm skinnier and I'm not the emotional weakling that I was and I hate *him* instead of hating myself." She paused. "I bet you got what you wanted, too, or else you wouldn't be at Level Eight, right?"

I thought of Charlotte, the soft give of her cheek pressed against mine. "Yes," I said.

"So, wasn't it worth it?"

Suzy's snore caught in her throat. I wondered whether she might be feigning sleep, listening in, eager to report on our conversation. Ruth, too—how was I to know whether or not she was a spy, spinning yarns to get me to admit that I wasn't as committed to the Method as I should be?

"Of course it was," I lied.

"Like I said." She sounded triumphant. "So what'd you do? It's your turn. No judgment."

I turned to lie on my side, facing away from Ruth, so that I was staring into the blank void of the cabin wall. The night chill had seeped into the concrete floor, the metal coils of the bunk bed, until it penetrated deep into my core. I didn't answer and I didn't answer and eventually I heard Ruth sigh and roll over. I waited until her snores had joined Suzy's before I let myself cry.

A bell woke us at dawn the next morning. Before breakfast, a Mentor from Toronto took us on a nine-mile hike up Matilija Canyon, through the poppy-strewn valley and past the scorch on the fire-blackened hills, then up into the mountains, until we reached a modest waterfall. The women chattered and perspired, sharing complaints about politics and the patriarchy and treacherous ex-husbands. We all seem to have exes. It was all reassuringly normal compared to the previous evening—*just a women's retreat!*—which made it easier to convince myself that my conversation with Ruth had been a fever dream, nothing of great concern. Ruth was paranoid, that's it.

The hike was followed by cold showers, and then a morning of workshops on subjects like "Summoning the Warrior Woman

Within" and "Childhood Perceptual Distortions: Letting Go and Growing Up" and "Mastering Your Own Life: No Victims, Only Choices." A light lunch was followed by reading and then one-on-one Reenactments with the Mentors. In the afternoon, we did Service, which was glorified camp upkeep: cleaning the bathrooms, walking to town for groceries, washing dishes in the kitchen. In the evening we had study sessions with Dr. Cindy, Confrontations, and a new exercise called Circle of Confidence where we all yelled trigger words at a member until she found her inner strength to scream back at us.

Despite everything, I found myself enjoying it. (Or: Maybe I am just my mother's daughter, and the impulse for denial was still too strong.) I enjoyed the camaraderie of the other women as we combed through Dr. Cindy's patented words in search of the secrets to a better life, as we sweated our way through our hikes and cried through our Circles and laughed over the near-inedible meals we were served. I teared up when Kelly—a Level Nine cancer survivor with alarming eyebrows and a gruff demeanor—was promoted to Mentor and burst out crying. I even started to feel tenderness for poor Suzy, who admitted in a Confrontation that her parents' wildly unrealistic expectations for her had led her to self-harm. (But thanks to the Method, she'd finally stopped cutting herself.) We were all in this together, exhausted and dizzy with hunger and light with the freedom of letting go. I remembered that this was part of what drew me to GenFem in the first place: the camaraderie that comes from feeling seen and understood.

On my third morning, I was headed up the stairs to shower after the hike when Roni stopped me. She was nearly a foot taller than me, her back ramrod straight under her loose yellow dress, her hand cool and dry on my sweat-sticky arm.

"Iona told me about your house," she said.

"What did she tell you?" And why was my house a topic of conversation? I wondered.

"That you think it's just too much house for you right now." She smiled knowingly. "She said you want to unburden yourself so that you can move forward in your life."

Had I said that? I reached my mind back to Iona's one visit to my house a few months back, tried to figure out if she might have misheard me. "Oh, I don't know—"

Roni stepped in closer, so close that I had to tilt my head up to meet her eyes. She lowered her voice conspiratorially. "It makes sense, honestly. To start fresh. Move somewhere new. Considering your current circumstances."

Your current circumstances. I wondered what current circumstances she was referring to, and then realized, with a sinking awareness, that she was referring to Charlotte. Roni knew, too. Did everyone? She was smiling with so many teeth visible that it was hard not to read a veiled threat in her words, a wolfish hunger. I thought of Ruth's word—*collateral*—and wanted to cry. It wasn't just paranoia; Ruth was right. How many more pieces of myself was I going to be asked to give away?

Roni rubbed her hand up and down my arm, as if I were a nervous child who needed to be soothed. I had to stop myself from twitching away from her touch. "You know I'm a real estate agent, right?" Roni continued. "All you'll need to do is give me your keys, sign a few papers, tell me where your important documents are kept, and I can take care of everything else for you. Remember, *Give up control in order to take control!*"

By then, I understood exactly what would happen after my house was sold. Roni would take her cut, and Dr. Cindy would ask for the rest—another "investment," perhaps—and somehow I'd end up with nothing at all.

I gave Roni the keys anyway. Because I didn't have a choice. And—if I'm going to be honest—part of me wondered whether she was right, and it wasn't such a bad idea to start fresh. To run away. I imagined moving somewhere far away with Charlotte, someplace where no one—not my family, not Chuck, not the Arizona police—would ever find us. A place where I wouldn't have to explain myself to anyone. Maybe, once I hit Level Ten, I could go be a Mentor in New Jersey. Charlotte and I would be safer there.

I'll happily sell everything I own, give it all to GenFem, if that's what it takes to protect us, I told myself. And for a few minutes after I handed Roni the keys to my life, I almost convinced myself that it was possible.

My final evening at the retreat, not long before I was supposed to return to Santa Barbara, Iona came to find me. She was my ride back home, and I assumed she was coming to plan our departure. But instead, she led me down to the field, where we sat in the shade of the oak trees and sipped on canned seltzer. It was coming toward evening but the heat of the day was still crushing. Sweat trickled down my stomach underneath the loose tent of my dress. Beside me—her pale bare legs stretched out before her, flip-flops kicked aside—Iona gazed out across the grass. On the other side of the field, in the rustic amphitheater, Dr. Cindy was giving a lecture on "memory distortion" to a group of women who had just arrived the previous evening.

"You've done great work this weekend," Iona told me. "But I think you have more to do."

"*More?*" *But I shaved my head!* I thought. *I smiled and I wore the dress, I took the workshops, I am letting Roni sell my house. Is that not enough?*

"Dr. Cindy feels like you have some block that we need to keep working on. She can feel your resistance to fully embracing the Method, which makes us all concerned about how prepared you are for life back in Santa Barbara. You have made choices"—she said this with a waggle of her eyebrow, as if she hadn't steered me toward those *choices* in the first place—"which require *commit-*

ments and I worry that you haven't mastered the control and strength you'll need to face these. You're not ready to go home."

I thought of Charlotte with a pang. "How long do you think I should stay?"

Iona frowned. "Another week, at least, I think. It would be another twelve thousand, of course, but I think it would be worth it. You'd get a lot of one-on-one time with Dr. Cindy. Maybe we could get you to Level Nine, which, you know, is just a step away from becoming a Mentor yourself."

I was silent, mulling this over. I wondered what would happen if I just *left*, cut ties completely. How long before the Arizona police got an anonymous call about the whereabouts of Emma Gonzalez? Would that be my punishment for letting GenFem down, for denying my fealty and finances to Dr. Cindy's cause?

Of course it would. The vengeance would be swift.

In the distance, the sun was fading from the tops of the Topa-topa mountain range, the evening shadows creeping up to steal the light. The air smelled like Mexican sage and eucalyptus and a faint whiff of charcoal. On the other side of the field, the women sitting with Dr. Cindy assiduously scribbled in notebooks, their foreheads buckled with intent. I tried to imagine this as my future, a never-ending string of workshops until I was finally the one standing in the middle of the circle, dispensing advice. A steel-spined Mentor.

Even without the threat of exposure, I *wasn't* ready to go home, I realized. I wasn't ready to face my disemboweled existence in Santa Barbara—business dying, relationships severed, house for sale, constantly living in fear of getting caught. Nor was I ready to try to reimagine a new one with Charlotte, somewhere far away.

But I also wasn't prepared to stay there in Ojai, living in exile from Charlotte while I let GenFem continue to drain me, pretending I had never heard what Ruth had told me. Maybe remaining there longer was the punishment that I deserved. But it mostly felt

like a form of avoidance—a way of staying where it was compara-
tively safe, hoping that everything in the outside world would
somehow fix itself before my return.

And it *wouldn't* fix itself. I knew that. As I looked at Iona, who
was staring back at me expectantly, I thought that she was right: I
didn't have the control and the strength necessary to live a lie. I
didn't want to spend life on the run. I couldn't imagine raising
Charlotte to believe that she was truly my child. Maybe Dr. Cindy
believed that she was going to turn me into the kind of person
that *could* be that selfishly cruel, but I knew better.

I was never going to make Level Ten, and frankly, I didn't want
to anymore.

The last of the sun disappeared from the mountains as I
chewed over this dilemma. There was no way I could continue to
pretend that Charlotte belonged to me, and yet I also didn't feel
strong enough to take her back and face the consequences. And as
long as Charlotte was in my possession, GenFem would have an
iron grip on my life. We were tied together, irrevocably: the child,
the cult, and me.

I now understand that this is what cults do. They cut you off
from the rest of the world, encourage you to sever all your ties to
the people that you love so that you have no one left to rely on.
They make themselves your entire family, the only ones who you
think can see you as you really are. You are bonded together by
the unconventional beliefs you've all chosen, too difficult to explain to the outside world, so you might as well not even try. We
women of GenFem were bound together in a sticky web of our
own making.

And yet, despite all that, I still felt a faint silvery connection to
someone in the real world, a strand that couldn't quite be severed
no matter how hard GenFem had tried. A person to whom I would
forever hold a bond, if only because we shared a common genetic
code. A tougher, bolder, more fearless version of *me*—one that

might be strong enough to do the things I was too scared to do myself.

My mirror. My twin. My Sam.

Iona was still watching me, growing suspicious of my long silence. "So, are you going to stay?" she asked.

And I suddenly thought I could glimpse a path out of this situation—an unlikely one, but better than none at all. I dusted the dead grass off my lap, smoothed the fabric of the dress across my bare knees. "Will I be allowed to send a text to my parents if I stay?"

Iona had the presence of mind to look mildly offended by this. "Of course," she sniffed. "You're not a *prisoner*."

part three

SAM

ONCE, WE WERE ONE. *I was her and she was me.*

Then, floating in our mother's womb, we doubled ourselves: two new lives, identical in every way.

But then, at some point, we weren't exact mirrors of each other anymore: We became her *and* me. *Environment—or was it circumstance?—put its thumbprint on each of us, pressed us into a unique form. Handed us each a personality of our own. Gave us foibles, diseases, hang-ups. Thrust us apart.*

I grew up wondering about how this had happened: How Elli became Elli and I became Sam. How far back would we have to rewind until we found the first moment of differentiation? Was it because of our relative positions in our mother's womb, or the fact that I was born first and Elli came eleven minutes later, or was it something else—something utterly inconsequential, like a mosquito bite or a diaper that didn't get changed—that first set us off on divergent paths? Was it possible to go back, fix the rift, and reconverge?

In my late twenties, a boyfriend gave me a book about an adoption program that had intentionally separated identical twins at birth, handing them off to different families, and then studied them. The twins never even knew they had an "other." The researchers thought that, by monitoring these split-apart sets, they might solve the nature versus nurture debate once and for all. It sounded barbarous to me, but the doctor behind the study insisted that it was actually good for the children. "Identical twins must be raised separately if they are to truly become who they really are," he argued.

I stopped reading after this quote, as a cold dread swept through me. Was I doomed to never be "who I really was" because I'd spent my life alongside my twin sister—being compared to her, vying for the same attention, never quite the center of focus? I'd always believed that Elli and I were stronger when we were together, but what if we weren't?

Who might I have become had we been separated at birth? I wondered. What if that hypothetical Sam was a better me, more focused, less wild, in total control of her life? Would she have succeeded where I failed? It was too depressing to consider.

Maybe instead of a childhood practicing how to be each other, we should have spent those years practicing how to be ourselves instead. Maybe that's where all of our problems began.

Maybe it wasn't too late to try.

33

SO. I HAD A kid.

Of course, this wasn't exactly news to me. I'd sold my eggs three times; the obvious conclusion would be the eggs that they scraped out of my ovaries had resulted in children. But I'd never really thought much more about it because what was the point? Those babies weren't in any way *mine,* even if we did happen to share some genetic material and a passing resemblance. I had far bigger things to fixate on, like my lost potential.

I never expected to meet any of those children. I certainly never expected to end up *taking care* of one.

There was a lot to take away from my sister's story. (She'd impersonated me in order to steal information from BioCal? I couldn't wrap my head around that one.) But this was the fact that my mind kept tripping over as we sat there in the bathroom, talking in whispers: Charlotte was my child. And yet not mine at all, either. What was I supposed to do with this news?

Then it crossed my mind that that little blond girl in Burbank who'd wanted to play—she was mine, too. That signed message I'd left for Michaela Blackwell: She must have recognized my name as her egg donor. I'd accepted a bonus of ten grand to let one of the recipient families have my name and photo (money I happily took—and later blew on oxy—with only a twinge of concern about relinquishing my anonymity); clearly, the Blackwells were that family. She must have assumed that I was trying to hunt down my biological child, a daughter I was calling Elli. *She's not Elli! How* dare *you name her?* No wonder she had sounded so panicked.

My legs had turned to jelly. I didn't think I could stand upright anymore so I slid to the floor of the bathroom and sat there, my back braced against the cool tile wall. Elli loomed above me, a pale figure in a white shroud.

"Well, you really made a mess of things, didn't you? I thought I was the fuckup twin but you showed me up." It was the only thing I could think to say.

She slid down the wall to sit beside me. The concrete floor of the bathroom was damp, the grout of the tile marked with ancient mold. It smelled like bleach.

"You were supposed to take her back," she said. Her eyes were fixed on the toilet stall opposite us, as if anticipating that someone might open the door and walk out adjusting their skirt.

"I was supposed to take Charlotte back to her real parents? Did I miss a text message from you or something? Because no one gave me that memo."

"I couldn't text you. I didn't have your number in my phone, and anyway they only let me have it back briefly to send a message to Mom about staying here longer. And they were watching me the whole time so my message to her had to be"—she squinted, remembering—"a little cryptic."

Sam will know what to do. Sam will get it. I recalled the text that I'd seen on my mother's phone. "Cryptic is an understatement, Elli. I'm your sister, not a mind reader."

"But you figured it out, didn't you? You figured out who she really is. I thought, if we had any connection at all anymore . . . you'd just know it. You'd see Charlotte and something in you would recognize her, that she was yours. Like, the instinct *I* felt when I saw her."

I laughed. "That's ridiculous. I didn't feel that at all. She just looked like a baby."

"You didn't?" She blinked, surprised. "Oh. Well, anyway. You still figured it out, right? Except that you weren't supposed to come *here*. I thought you'd take Charlotte back to Arizona."

"And how exactly did you think I would do that?" I imagined ringing the Gonzalezes' doorbell: *Here's your kid! See you later!*

"I don't know. I thought *you'd* figure that part out. I couldn't think straight." And she laughed a little, though her laugh was more hysterical than bemused. I reached over and put my arm around her shoulders and held her very tight, and pretty soon she *was* crying, great heaving sobs. "I fucked up, Sam. And now I don't know what to do."

"It's OK. I'll fix it," I said. Sitting there on the floor of the bathroom, in that decrepit summer camp, it was almost as if we were children again. I remembered what it felt like to be thirteen years old, and to feel my fate connected to my sister's, to know that I had the key to her happiness within my grasp.

Her shaved head rested against mine. I knew how the bare scalp beneath her stubble must feel, how naked and achingly sensitive, because I felt it, too. It was nice to know that for the first time in years, there was something we both shared.

There weren't many things that I missed about being an addict. Passing out in a puddle of vomit, say, or the constant bruises on my limbs from stumbling into walls and furniture, or that niggling feeling that there was something I needed to be ashamed about that I couldn't quite remember. Waking up to a regrettable one-night stand. Bar fights. Hangovers.

No, I didn't miss these at all.

But one thing that I did mourn, a year into this latest—and I hoped, forever—round of sobriety, was the end of mystery. I missed the sense of adventure that came from stepping out of your front door into the wide-open night, unsure what would happen next. The electric thrill of *what if* and *what now*. An accelerated pulse, the world ready to unfurl. The night could be a blast or it could be a disaster, and the excitement came from not knowing which it would be.

Sobriety required discipline, a constant metering out of days and hours and minutes. I planned everything in advance now, so that there was no chance of putting myself in the path of temptation. *I will go to dinner with my sponsor and drink a seltzer and lime. I will attend the AA meeting and then go straight to work. I will binge-watch six straight seasons of* Game of Thrones *to avoid leaving the house this weekend*. I was so careful. I was so safe. But sometimes—if I was totally honest—it made me feel dead inside.

For years, my life had been an exhausting roller-coaster ride, exhilarating highs followed by precipitous lows, and yes, I had been relieved to finally climb off it. To center myself, and finally find an even keel. And yet, as my sister and I marched out the door of that bathroom toward the lodge below, I recognized that I'd felt more alive in the last week than I had in the entire last year of sobriety. It wasn't just that I had a purpose again, something to work toward; it was that I'd rediscovered the unknown.

This wasn't only to be found at the bottom of a bottle, I saw now. It wasn't even about the thrill of adventure, though certainly there'd been plenty of that. It turned out that this—the precipitous adrenaline leap—came from giving your heart to someone, and not knowing what might happen next.

In order to love a little girl, Elli and I had no choice but to take her back where she belonged.

But first I had to spring my sister from a cult.

———

We'd heard people looking for Elli while we talked—voices on the stairs, a cabin door swinging open on its hinges, footsteps slapping across concrete. Someone had called Elli's name, an impatient woman's voice echoing through the oak trees. But by the time we finally left the bathroom, nearly an hour later, the hill was quiet again.

Dusk had settled over the camp, though it wasn't quite dark. Below, I could see the illuminated lodge, porch lined with fairy lights that twinkled through the scrubby woods. All of the women must have still been inside, because the rest of the campus was empty. As we stood there, listening carefully, I thought I heard the muffled sound of women's shouts coming from the lodge.

"They're doing Circle of Confidence," my sister murmured. "It was supposed to be my turn tonight."

I had no clue what this meant. I wasn't sure I wanted to know.

We gathered my sister's suitcase from her cabin and then headed down the stairs and crossed the meadow, our feet silent in the grass. At the back porch of the lodge, we stopped. Behind the door the voices were louder now, an angry chorus interrupted occasionally by a shriek of fury.

"How long do you think you need?" I whispered to Elli.

"I don't know. Five minutes, maybe? Ten?" She hesitated. "I'm not sure about this."

"I am. Go." I pushed her, gently, away from me. "Don't worry. I'll keep them occupied."

She lingered on the path. "But how?"

"Isn't it obvious?" I was surprised she didn't already know. "I'll be you."

A funny look crossed her face. She lifted one hand and made a slight gesture—just the barest twist of a wrist, a flattened palm turned sideways—that I hadn't seen in fifteen years. Then she smiled ruefully, turned, and left.

I watched her walk around the edge of the building, carrying the suitcase in her arms so it wouldn't clatter on the path. Then I climbed the porch steps, pushed the door open, and braced myself to face GenFem.

They sat in a circle, nearly two dozen women, on folding chairs and lumpy couches placed around the perimeter of a blue-carpeted lounge. Some women clutched mugs of tea and others sat cross-legged on the floor. The whole scene would have reminded me a bit of an NA meeting I used to attend in a rec center in Santa Monica if it weren't for the fact that all of the women were yelling.

Standing in the center of the room, her eyes closed, was Ruth. It appeared that they were yelling at *her*.

The cacophony in the room was overwhelming. It was so loud that I had to plug my ears with my fingers and still I could hear the insults that the women were flinging Ruth's way. "You're weak . . . you're useless . . . you are a terrible mother . . . you care too much what people think . . . you're vain . . . you're fat . . . you have no self-control . . . no wonder everyone you love leaves you!"

Ruth's face was the color of a fresh beet; her fists were clenched tightly against her side. She rocked back and forth on her heels, as if the abuse were a buffeting wind that threatened to knock her over, but her back remained ramrod straight. Over the chanting of the women, I could hear Ruth's own coarse, keening wail.

"I am strong! I am my own person! I don't care what you think of me! I am in control of my own life! I reject social norms!"

Surveying this savage scene, thin-lipped and contemptuous, was a slight woman with graying hair. She sat a little apart from the women in an upholstered armchair placed directly in front of the stone fireplace. In her hand was a steno notepad, on which she occasionally took notes with doctorly authority. I recognized her from the GenFem website: Dr. Cindy Medina.

She saw me standing in the doorway and the smile faded from

her face. She held up a hand for silence, and the shouting skittered to a stop. The women—flushed, out of breath—turned obediently to look at Dr. Medina, and then swiveled again to see what *she* was looking at.

Me.

I lifted a hand in greeting. "Hi."

Ruth, still panting, turned to face me. Her voice was dark with recrimination. "It was supposed to be *your* turn tonight," she said.

I sucked in my cheeks, dropped my shoulders, tried to sink into myself, to feel as gaunt as my sister looked. All eyes were on me; it felt impossible that someone wouldn't notice the ruse. Then again, I was a *professional*. "I'm sorry," I said, and smiled faintly.

On the other side of the room, leaning against the wall, I noticed the statuesque Black woman that Caleb and I had met at the GenFem center earlier in the week. The woman who had been in charge, the one who told me that she didn't know who my sister was. *Liar.* What was her name? Roni. She was looking at me with a strange expression on her face, as if seeing something that no one else had noticed. I quickly turned my profile to her.

Dr. Medina waved an encouraging hand at me. "Go ahead, then," she said. "You're here now, let's get you inside the circle."

I stepped into the center of the room, just under a dusty brass light fixture that emitted a dim glow over the room. Relieved, Ruth hustled to a folding chair on the edge of the circle and collapsed in it. She offered me a vulpine smile that appeared to be part commiseration, part vindictive glee.

I turned a slow circle, taking in the group. Two dozen women stared back at me. So many shaved heads, so many white dresses: The women's faces seemed to float above their bodies, their features in high relief, a strangely compelling effect.

Dr. Medina clapped her hands once, and the sound split the room. "OK, who's going to start. Suzy?"

Suzy jumped to attention, studied me. "You're so passive. You do whatever anyone tells you to do. Get a spine." Her eyes flicked to Dr. Medina for approval.

"That's a good start." Dr. Medina looked around. "Georgina?"

A striking Mediterranean woman with hawkish features and heavy makeup regarded me from the couch where she lounged. "You're a loser. A failure," she said flatly.

"Louder!" Dr. Medina commanded.

Georgina sat up straighter in her seat. "Loser!" she called out, in a voice already hoarse from the last confrontation. "Failure!"

Other voices began to chime in. "You're pathetic!" "You're too nice!" "Sucker!" "No one loves you!" "So naive!" The litany of insults grew in volume, the women shouting to be heard over one another. A dark electricity crackled through the room as the women gathered their energy together—collected all the pain and injury and petty grievances of their own lives—and hurled it at me. Or rather, not at me but at Elli.

Was this what the world thought of my sister? The cruelty in their observations was a kick in the gut. Even though it wasn't me they were describing—*boring, passive, pushover, forgettable*—I felt it as though it were. I became Elli, I let her pain be mine. I let all of the wounds she'd suffered pulse through me until it felt like every nerve was on fire. So this was what it was like to be my sister these days, I realized; it had been so long since I'd tried to climb inside her. And really, had I ever, truly, stopped to *be* her? Now that I was, it made me want to cry.

"Stop it," I said softly. But no one could hear me over the din. So I screamed: "You all need to shut the fuck up!"

The room went quiet. The women gazed uneasily at one another, unsure why I'd deviated from the script. From her folding chair, Ruth frowned at Dr. Medina. "That's not how it works," she complained. "She's supposed to defend herself. And we just barely got started. Mine was at least fifteen minutes."

I looked over at Dr. Medina. "I don't see the benefit of this exercise. I'm bowing out."

Dr. Medina was the one frowning now. "These exercises aren't *optional,* Eleanor." Her voice was low and even, unperturbable. "They're a critical part of the Method. They teach us how to stand up for ourselves in the face of a world that does its best to break down women's self-esteem. This is for your own empowerment."

"It doesn't *feel* like empowerment," I replied. "It *feels* like you're trying to break us down, so you can control us. You make us feel bad about ourselves and then you tell us that *you're* the only person who can help us feel better. And then we'll do anything you tell us to. Classic mind-control technique, right? You studied psychology; or at least, that's what you tell everyone. So, you would know. I mean, for fuck's sake, *I* learned the whole process with a simple search on Wikipedia."

I realized, belatedly, that this diatribe sounded nothing like Elli. Unfortunately, there were no second takes on this particular performance. I took a few steps back, trying to disappear into the perimeter of the circle, but it was too late. A leaden silence had fallen over the room.

Most of the women were gazing fixedly at their hands or the walls across from them, blank expressions on their faces, as if trying to purge their minds of what I had just suggested. But I noticed two twentysomething women catching each other's eyes across the circle, and exchanging a significant look that seemed to say, *See?* Georgina had arced one eyebrow in surprise, and was now casting her gaze around the room, as if waiting to gauge everyone else's reaction to this.

Ruth was staring at me in confusion. She tilted her head slightly and then gestured violently with her chin, as if to say, *Get back in the circle, stupid.* I shook my head, and she shrugged, as if there was no point in trying to argue with an insane person.

Dr. Medina was calmly reading her notes, but I could see that a vein at her temple had turned an angry shade of purple. She scribbled something on the notepad. "I'm not sure where this aggression is coming from, Eleanor. But perhaps you and I should go to one of the meeting rooms for a Reenactment. It sounds like you're stuck on something."

From her seat, one of the twentysomething women piped up. "I watched a documentary about that group Synanon last year? They had a similar ritual, they called it the Game?" Her sentences kept tailing off, as she tried to read the studiously empty faces around her. "I don't think things ended well for them?"

Dr. Medina whirled to look at her. "Aren't you forgetting your Sufferance, Alexis? You had two days of silence. And now you have three." Alexis closed her mouth and shrank back in her seat, but not before casting one more significant look at her friend.

How much time had passed? It felt like hours, but the clock on the wall said it had been less than ten minutes. I wasn't sure what to do with myself now, but I knew I couldn't go back inside that circle. Instead, I edged a step closer to the door and glanced through the window at the darkness beyond, willing my sister to hurry.

Across the room, Roni had pushed away from the wall. She was staring at me again, her eyes scanning my face. A sudden intake of breath, skin tightening over cheekbones, and I knew I'd been busted.

Somewhere, not so very far away, a car alarm was going off.

"You're not Eleanor." Roni's voice rang out across the room, flat and accusatory. "You're the sister."

All around me, women turned in their seats, half stood, craned their necks to get a better look at me. Suzy, cross-legged on the floor, looked left and right at the women around her, as if expecting someone to fill her in. Ruth stared at me, slack-jawed and glassy-eyed; I figured she must be mentally replaying our walk together, wondering how she missed the signs.

"Holy shit, it's the *twin*," I heard a woman say.

"I am the sister," I said agreeably, because really there was no point in pretending otherwise.

Dr. Medina looked across the room to where a wiry blond woman sat stiffly on a folding chair. She was wearing a yellow dress, just as Roni was, and didn't have a shaved head, which was how I knew that this must be Iona. "How did she get in?" Dr. Medina barked. Her question sliced through the room and made Iona flinch. "I thought you were monitoring the gate today."

Iona's face was ashen. "I was. But—how was I to tell? Just *look* at her."

Dr. Medina looked at me. She scanned me from head to toe, taking in the mourning dress and the haircut, and then she stood slowly from her chair. The notepad slid from her lap and lay, abandoned, on the floor. "I don't know what you're playing at, but you're not allowed to be here. This is supposed to be a safe space for our members. I'm going to have to ask you to leave."

"Great," I said. "That's exactly what I'd like to do."

"But where's Eleanor?" It was Suzy, the question not addressed to me but to the women sitting on either side and across from her. She repeated it again, her voice high-pitched and frantic—"Oh my God, what happened to *Eleanor*!"—as her head careened left and right. I wondered if she'd give herself whiplash.

"I'm right here." Behind me, the door to the lounge had opened and my sister now stood behind me, the handle of her rolling suitcase clutched in her fist. I could hear her breath, fast and strained, as if she'd just run a half-marathon. A slash of red was smeared across the otherwise pristine front of her white dress. Her hand on the suitcase handle was dripping blood from a cut. She was trembling.

I reached back and grasped the hand that wasn't bleeding. Squeezed it. Her cheeks were flushed and when her eyes met mine, I saw something bright and hard in them. Defiance, maybe? Or victory? She caught my look and smiled. It was a fragile smile, just this side of collapse, but it reassured me anyway.

We turned as one to face the room.

"Eleanor." Dr. Medina stood motionless with a hand on the back of her armchair. "This is a terrible idea. You aren't ready to leave."

"Is that a threat?" I shot.

Dr. Medina didn't look at me; I wasn't of interest to her at all. Behind her wire-rimmed glasses her eyes were fixed on my sister. "Eleanor, your sister is *toxic,*" she began. The words she spoke were slow and rhythmic, almost a metronome chant that seemed to slow the room around us. "She's an unreliable *addict,* you know she *doesn't* have your best interests in *mind,* she wants to keep you *small* so that she can feel *big,* she is *scared* that you will grow *past* her. Don't let her *sabotage* you. Don't leave. You're so *close* to achieving your fully realized *self.*"

Elli's eyes were wide and wild; she blinked fast, as if holding back tears. And for a moment, I hesitated, wondering if maybe I *was* toxic for my sister. I thought of that book I'd read years ago: *Identical twins must be raised separately if they are to truly become who they really are.* Maybe Dr. Medina was right in this regard, and my presence in Elli's life had kept her from being her true self. Maybe I was the reason she was here now. Maybe the best thing for her *was* to separate from me.

But Elli's hand tightened its grip on mine. "But what if I *want* to leave? You're not going to try to stop me?" she asked, her voice thick with disbelief. "You're not going to try to punish me?"

Dr. Medina shrugged, a noncommittal lift of her shoulders that didn't exactly inspire confidence. "Be my guest," she said coolly. "It's your own life you're ruining."

I heard my sister's sharp inhale and exhale. "OK, then. I'm going," she said. There was something new in her voice, something spikey and sharp, that she lobbed at Dr. Medina: "From now on, you leave me alone, and I'll leave you alone. Because maybe I know more about you than you think." And maybe it's just that I *wanted* to see Dr. Medina lose her grip on that icy self-possession, but for a split second, I could have sworn I saw her recoil.

And with that, Elli and I started to exit the lounge, but I paused just before the door and turned back to survey the women in the room. I couldn't help myself. Impulse control was never my strong suit.

"Just checking: You ladies know you joined a cult, right?" I thought I saw an electric pulse—a flinch of painful recognition—cross some of their faces. Those twentysomethings, maybe. At least I hoped that was what it was. "No? Think about it."

And, with that, we left.

Behind us, before the door slammed shut, I could hear the volume of the room slowly rising, voices growing hot and agitated, and then Dr. Medina barking out a single word: "Hush!"

Outside, night had finally fallen. A barn owl called out an alert as Elli and I scrambled down the path toward the front gate. The suitcase lumbered behind her, its wheels catching on the edges of the paving stones. Mosquitoes bit at our bare ankles.

I could hear voices behind us now. I knew that if I looked back I would see the women standing on the porch of the lodge, watching us leave. But no one tried to stop us; no one chased us down to force us back inside. I supposed they thought they didn't need to. They had other means with which to bind Elli to them. But those means, I hoped, were safely ensconced in the suitcase that now wobbled from side to side behind my sister, drunk with its burden.

"You OK?" I whispered.

She didn't answer. "Hurry," she said. "If someone goes into the front office, we're screwed."

We crossed the parking lot, where the cherry-red Land Rover gleamed in the dark. Its passenger-side window was smashed, a halo of safety glass glinting on the asphalt below. The axe that had once been lodged in the wooden *WigWam Woods* camp sign now lay abandoned nearby.

Through the parking lot, then, and down the pitted driveway, until the iron gate finally loomed up in front of us. Here I had a sudden bump of panic—would we need them to open it for us?—but Elli simply pressed a button by the entrance, and the gate groaned open on its track. Just like that, we were outside.

It wasn't until we were out on the road, the gate vibrating closed behind us, that we began to run. Down the hill and through the groves of oaks, past the quiet avocado farm and the chaparral scrub still blackened by the wildfires. Our sneakers slapped in the dust; our breath came fast in our chests. If I closed my eyes, I could almost imagine that we were children again, running down the trail from Rattlesnake Canyon, hand in hand, away from the rocky precipice that threatened certain doom and toward the safety of home.

Down we ran, my sister hysterically laughing, manic with her unexpected freedom, the white dress flying out like a sail behind her, and me, following in her steps for once, unsure exactly what I'd just done but praying that it was better than anything I'd done before.

LOOKING BACK AT OUR childhood, at those handful of years when Elli and I played at being each other, I see now that I always got the biggest thrill out of deceiving our mother. You could say I was a cruel little shit. Or that I was testing how little our mother saw and understood, for my own devious purposes. Or you could simply argue that *all* children grow by cutting their parents down to a manageable size. It's only once you recognize that they aren't superhuman, after all, that you start aspiring to evolve beyond them.

But that night, when our mother opened the door to her house and looked momentarily baffled by the sight of Elli and me standing on her front steps—her eyes flicking uncertainly from one of us to the other and back again—I felt no glee at all. Instead, I was relieved when it took her only half a beat to lock eyes with Elli and reach out a hand to draw her inside: "Good God, Elli, where on earth have you *been*? You said you'd be gone a *weekend*. It's been two *weeks*!"

It was just past nine, and she was already wearing a bathrobe that she clutched closed at her chest. From the living room I could hear the sound of the television, my father's snores intermingling with a comedy laugh track. Our mother made no comment on our matching outfits or our cultish haircuts or the blood smeared on my sister's dress; she simply stood aside as Elli made a beeline for Charlotte's room without answering her question. And for once I was thankful for my mother's fear of hearing about things that she didn't want to know. Because I didn't want to have to explain it at all. Not yet.

But she did grip my arm as I lingered in the doorway, waiting for Elli to return with the child. "Thank you," she said, bringing her mouth close to my ear. Her breath smelled of Riesling and popcorn. "Thank you for watching out for Elli. Thank you for bringing her back." Then she pulled me into a tight hug as I stood there, blinking in surprise. She made a little buzzing sound in her throat, her body hitching with her breath, and I realized that she was trying not to cry. I hoped that she wouldn't because if she did I was in danger of losing it entirely, too, and I didn't have that luxury. Not tonight, when there was so much still to do.

But it was also in that moment that I finally understood: She *did* see what Elli and I were up to, and she always had, even if she had her own reasons for pretending not to notice. I might never know what those were, but it didn't really matter, because they were hers and not mine, and so they weren't my burden to carry anymore. I didn't need to prove anything to her; the only person I had ever needed to convince of my value was me.

Elli reappeared in the hallway then, with Charlotte in her bunny pajamas dead asleep on her shoulder. Charlotte's curls were damp with sweat and her mouth worked drowsily at her thumb. She looked so content there in Elli's arms, and my heart was sick just watching them.

Elli spoke in a whisper. "Mom, you have to say goodbye to Charlotte now."

Our mother leaned over and kissed Charlotte's forehead, pruned lips yearning against soft flesh. "Maybe you could bring her over next weekend? I'm happy to watch her."

"I can't." Elli's voice was cracking. It was hard to hear. "I don't get to keep her anymore, Mom. She's not mine to keep. I'm so sorry."

"She was a foster this whole time?" My mom blinked, reading confirmation in my sister's silence. "*Elli*. Why didn't you tell me? I could have been prepared. I wouldn't have . . . I would have . . ." My mom closed her eyes. Her voice was phlegmy and thick. "Oh God. I don't know if I can do this." She placed a palm on the top of Charlotte's head, gazed intently at the child for a long minute, and then abruptly turned away. Her arthritic hip wobbled, threatening to send her tumbling down the steps to the living room, but then she righted herself, and was gone.

My sister turned to me, her broken face sticky with tears and hot with shame. "Let's go," she said.

I was the one who carried Charlotte back to the house on Joshua Tree Drive. At the last minute, Elli just couldn't make herself do it.

She sat in the front seat of my car, her feet half buried in the fast-food wrappers that I'd accumulated over the last week. We'd parked a few blocks over, as far from the streetlights as possible, but it wasn't well lit out here anyway. The desert spread out to our left, a dark ocean of invisible danger under a crescent moon and a sky shot with stars. It was 4:30 A.M., not a single light on in the houses that were scattered along the street.

"You're stronger than me," she said.

"She's not that heavy," I said. "It's only two blocks."

"That's not what I meant."

I knew that wasn't what she meant, but I liked hearing it from her anyway.

I climbed out of the car and then lifted Charlotte out of her car seat and rested her against my shoulder. She rustled once and then settled there, boneless and limp in my arms. Elli got out of the passenger seat and stood beside me, stroking Charlotte's cheek with the back of a finger, careful not to wake her. I'd changed into jeans and a black hoodie but Elli was still in the thin linen shift, and she shivered in the cold night air.

"I'm so sorry, Emma," she murmured into the little girl's ear, and then she kissed her, as soft as a whisper, and climbed back into the car. As I walked off into the desert, moving slowly so as not to disturb the child, I could hear my sister sobbing.

I moved silently through the dark landscape, hunting for an open path, tracing the edge of civilization. On my left, through the cacti and the desert scrub, I could see swimming pools and formal gardens, outdoor kitchens and patio furniture upholstered in all-weather fabric. To the right stretched miles of wilderness.

I could hear mice skittering away from my feet as I walked. Somewhere out in the dark, alarmingly close, a band of coyotes erupted in a chorus of yips and growls. On my shoulder, the little girl stirred, but she didn't wake up. I kept moving steadily through the desert, one step at a time, for what felt like hours, until the pink adobe house loomed up before me, and we were there.

I left her on a blanket on the grass of the Gonzalez home. Elli had suggested the front doorstep: "Don't you think it would be safer?" But I argued that it was more likely that we'd be caught by a neighbor's surveillance system if I approached from the front.

"You got insanely lucky the first time around," I pointed out. "What if they had cameras installed?"

And so I slipped out of the desert and across the backyard, praying that in my black jeans, with my hood pulled up, I was invisible. With each step, I expected a security system to trip—for floodlights to blink on and an alarm to blare the presence of an intruder—but nothing happened. There was just a pitch-black garden, and a house with curtains closed, and the chill that crept in off the desert with me.

She rustled once, when I placed her on the blanket, but she didn't wake up. I stood staring down at her, memorizing the way her face looked as she slept: my almost-child, my not-my-child

child, this human to which I was permanently bound by the powerful thread of DNA but to whom I still had no claim at all.

I wondered if Emma Gonzalez would ever wonder about me, her biological mom. I wondered if she would ask to see the Bio-Cal file when she turned eighteen, in order to learn more about me. Sixteen or twenty or thirty years from now, would she show up at my doorstep, never knowing that we'd met before, never knowing that I'd once changed her poopy diapers and kissed her sweaty head?

I hoped she would.

And so I left her there, but not before I banged on the back door of the house—pounded so loud that it felt like I would wake the entire neighborhood up. Then I darted back out into the desert until I was a safe distance away, concealed by a stand of cacti, and watched.

The lights in the house came on almost immediately, just seconds after Emma woke up and began to wail. I waited until I saw the figures silhouetted against the open doorway, and heard the mother's shriek of disbelief and the father's cry—"Oh Lord oh Lord, thank you Lord!"—before slipping out into the dark. I traced my way back, blinded by tears, weaving a perilous path between the saguaro and the prickly pear until I finally saw my car in the distance, and my sister standing there, her face pale with worry as she waited for me to come back to her.

"Did they find her?" she asked.

I nodded, for once finding myself incapable of speech.

"That's good." She gazed out over the desert for a long minute, her eyes fixed on the silver sliver of moon hanging low in the sky. "Then let's go home," she said.

35 IT MERITED ONLY A small story, on page four of the local news section of the *Santa Barbara Independent*. "Local Authorities Seek Former Psychologist Accused of Running Cult." Three columns, six hundred words. That was it.

Elli and I read it together, faces pressed close over the smudged newsprint, morning coffee still on our breath. My sister, in her florist coveralls, her hair smelling like shampoo, me in the sweats that I'd scavenged from the back of Elli's closet. Outside the kitchen window, the Mexican fan palms swayed in the Santa Ana winds. The sky was flat and tinged yellow with the smoke from inland wildfires.

> *Dr. Cindy Medina, a local psychologist and the founder of the women's self-help group GenFem, is being sought by local authorities after several former members came forth claiming that they were blackmailed into giving money to the organization against their will.*
>
> *The group, which set up shop in Santa Barbara three years ago, was founded by Medina under the guise of teaching its members how to "maximize their potential" and "free themselves of the artificial structures that have thwarted women's achievements." The organization claimed nearly five hundred members, all women, across*

four different centers in the United States and Canada. Members were encouraged to spend hundreds of thousands of dollars to rise up the "levels" of the organization. Medina claimed to have ninety-seven patents for "behavioral therapy breakthroughs"; however, a search by the Santa Barbara Independent *unearthed only four that had actually been granted, including one described as a "guidance system for addressing menopausal anxiety."*

Former members describe an environment of physical deprivation and psychological abuse. Women were manipulated into revealing deeply personal information, or even performing misdeeds, and then blackmailed for their secrets. A former summer camp in Ojai—property owned by Dr. Medina's family since 1954—served as a retreat where members were forced to participate in activities reminiscent of Synanon's controversial "The Game," according to member Alexis Latimer, one of the early whistleblowers. One senior member, a former lawyer who requested anonymity, suggested that Medina held multiple offshore bank accounts into which she had been secretly funneling the organization's funds.

The existence of GenFem came to light after member Ruth Hollenbach came forward earlier this fall. After being publicly named in a local college admission scandal, Hollenbach defended herself by saying that she was "brainwashed" by Medina into participating. Several other members have since come forward to corroborate Hollenbach's stories, although little hard evidence has been produced to support their claims so far.

Other members remain adamant that GenFem was simply a supportive self-help group for women, and that Dr. Medina is a victim of slander. "GenFem changed my life," says member Suzy Chan. "I owe everything to Dr. Medina. Every penny I spent on the program was worth it."

Medina appears to have drawn inspiration from New Age self-help methodology, experimental psychiatric practices, radical feminist theory, and the writings of Ayn Rand. A former practicing therapist in Connecticut, Medina had her credentials stripped in 2012 for "undue manipulation of a client" after three former patients claimed that she coerced them into signing interests in their businesses over to her. This didn't prevent Medina from reinventing herself as a "motivational counselor," eventually receiving invitations to speak at international women's conferences. Upon arriving in Santa Barbara, she was able to recruit scores of Santa Barbara women—many of them prominent and successful community leaders—into her growing organization.

After several former members agreed to speak to the Santa Barbara Independent, we reached out to Medina, but she declined to comment. Local authorities have launched an inquiry into the organization. However, Medina has not been seen in over a month, and is presumed to have fled the country. Without a paper trail to prove their claims, and their leader missing, GenFem's former members may have little legal recourse.

As of Tuesday, the retreat in Ojai was empty and shuttered. The GenFem offices in Santa Barbara have closed, and the remaining group leaders are refusing to speak to the press.

"That's it?" Elli sounded disappointed. "She just . . . left? She gets to live the rest of her life in Mexico, drinking mai tais with our money?"

I folded the newspaper closed. In the background the television played news footage of forests burning only twenty miles away, in between holiday ads for thousand-dollar television sets and personal drone systems. "Don't you think that's for the best?"

"Not really. It doesn't seem fair that she won't face any consequences. I mean, poor *Ruth*. Look at what's happened to her. I read she might have to serve time in jail."

I didn't want to remind my sister that *fair* would probably involve the FBI and drawn-out lawsuits and investigators who were far more skilled than the *Santa Barbara Independent* at digging into the regrettable behavior of former GenFem members. Better that the whole thing just fade into the woodwork. Better that the contents of Dr. Cindy Medina's laptop remained where they currently were: in Elli's basement, folded inside a garbage bag, at the bottom of a cardboard box full of back issues of *Real Simple* magazine.

It had been Elli's idea to steal the laptop, though that hadn't been the plan. The *plan* was just to steal the file folder, the one that we assumed held Elli's handwritten confession. We'd simply take back the blackmail material, so that GenFem would no longer have any leverage over Elli. It was the best option we could come up with, in those few stolen minutes in the summer camp bathroom.

And that had been easy enough. While I distracted the GenFem members in the lounge, Elli had snuck into the empty front office. The door wasn't even locked, GenFem leadership apparently assuming that their captive congregation was a passive herd that wouldn't have the temerity to demand their belongings back. For once, Dr. Cindy Medina made a bad psychological assessment.

The file cabinet in the front office was locked, but it was old, and a paper clip popped it right open. Elli took back her cellphone, her file folder, and then, for good measure, collected everyone else's folders, too. So that Dr. Cindy wouldn't be able to blackmail *anyone*. She shoved them all in her suitcase and prepared to come find me.

But then she hesitated. Because what if those weren't the only copies? In this digital age, it was a safe bet that everything had been scanned and duplicated and uploaded to the cloud for posterity. Nothing is ephemeral anymore; nothing can be truly destroyed. It wasn't enough to have stolen back only the original copy of her confession; she would need to locate and destroy them *all*. Which was, of course, impossible.

And even if she did somehow manage this, GenFem still knew what she had done. One anonymous phone call to the Scottsdale police department, or to the FBI, and her life would be over. Dr. Medina would *always* have that power over her, which meant that she could never truly escape her clutches.

No, she needed something stronger than a piece of paper, she needed—

"Collateral," she'd finished, as we raced back along the dark freeway toward Santa Barbara that night.

"Collateral?"

"Something we can wield over *them*. So that Dr. Cindy is too scared to seek revenge, because what we have on her is just as bad as what she has on me." Her eyes were wild; she'd managed to smear her face with the blood from her cut hand. She looked like a murderous nun. "So I smashed her car window with the axe and stole her laptop bag."

"And how do you know there's damaging material on the laptop?"

"I don't. But I gave them over four hundred thousand dollars, all told. And there are hundreds of members, also shelling out God knows how much money—maybe less than me, but maybe more. That's tens of millions of dollars, maybe *hundreds*. So where is it all going? It wasn't exactly paying for upgrades to the retreat." She shook her head. "Accounting isn't my forte, you know that. But it occurred to me that things couldn't be on the up-and-up. There has to be material on the laptop that we can use to our advantage. I mean, we don't *actually* have to use it. Dr. Cindy just has to be scared that we have it, and that we *might* give it to the authorities."

I laughed, understanding. "Leave me alone, and I'll leave you alone."

"Exactly. Between that and the file folders, we'll have everyone's dirty secrets." She stared out at the taillights of the cars on the 101, as traffic slowed to a crawl on the highway before us. We were almost back to Santa Barbara by then, and I could see her anxiety rising as we approached our parents' house. Her fingers tapped out a nervous scale on the dashboard. "Even the ones we don't want."

We didn't want them, and yet we had them; and when we did finally sit down to go through the stack of folders together, a few days after we returned from Scottsdale, it was clear we had so much more than we'd anticipated. Almost every folder contained a handwritten letter addressed to Dr. Cindy: cursives and block letters, some meticulous and others nearly illegible, occasionally written in ink that had been smudged with tears. One, composed by a New Jersey housewife named Missy, even had little stars dotting the *i*'s.

It was a depressing litany of confessions. Georgina had slept with her teenage son's best friend. He was seventeen, so it was statutory rape. Alexis had broken into her sister's home, stolen some family heirlooms she felt she'd been denied, and trashed the place. Lisa, after the end of an affair with her married boss, had skimmed a half-million dollars from the company accounts. A Canadian woman named Claire had fed her senile father peanuts, to which he was fatally allergic, so that she wouldn't have to spend another decade taking care of him.

Many of the pages admitted to illegal activities—major and minor—that could have potentially landed their perpetrators in jail. But others were more sad than sordid. Affairs with friends' husbands and slashed tires and addictions, sexual proclivities and small cruelties and petty acts of vengeance. Suzy had used her parents' credit card to go on a wild shopping spree, and then pretended that it was stolen. Kelly took revenge on a noisy neighbor by shooting his dog. Leecia spread lies that her ex-husband was a pedophile.

Maybe they wouldn't go to jail over these things, but the truth still had the potential to ruin lives, and Dr. Medina had orchestrated it all. She had manipulated these women to the edge, whispered in their ear until they jumped, and then leveraged the aftermath for her own benefit.

Elli didn't want to read the confessions. "I knew a lot of these women," she told me. "I *liked* them. It wouldn't feel right." But I was fascinated by them. I stayed up night after night, drinking coffee on the pullout couch in my sister's den, consumed by the handwritten missives. They made my own past misbehavior as an addict seem so benign by comparison, or at least measurable on a quantifiable scale. Would GenFem have been able to blackmail me, use my misdeeds as collateral to ensure my undying devotion while draining my bank accounts dry?

Probably not. I had already been my own worst enemy. I screwed up my family all by myself; I didn't need GenFem's help.

The confessions were accompanied by pages and pages of psychological analysis of each member on steno notepad paper in Dr. Medina's neat handwriting. They read exactly like the notes a therapist might jot down after a particularly insightful session, except for when they didn't. *Suzy has a classic case of insecure attachment and a reinforced positive response to authority due to emotionally abusive parents. Traumatic memories of mother withholding love after C+ report card; forced to clean toilets with toothbrush because she was "a piece of crap" herself. Responds well to enforced structure, not emotion. Use praise sparingly. Sufferance: Enemas.*

And so on.

Elli had disappeared with her own folder before I could read it; though honestly, I didn't want to anyway. I'd spent so much of my life longing to climb inside my sister's mind, wondering why we were no longer the same, but now that I could, I had no interest in knowing her truly secret thoughts. How much of her folder would be about me? The twin sister she'd blamed for ruining her life. I knew I was in there, but I didn't have to read the folder to know exactly how much damage I had done.

It felt like Elli and I had become the unwitting keepers of the GenFem members' secrets. We knew the innermost workings of their minds, their vulnerabilities and weaknesses, the things that might land them in jail. And we didn't want it, any of it.

We ended up burning the confessions in a trash barrel in my sister's backyard. Maybe Dr. Cindy still had copies of the confessions sitting on a hard drive somewhere, and our bonfire was pointless, but we didn't want to be responsible for anyone else's future. It was hard enough being responsible for our own.

There was another news article that I'd found on the internet, one that I hadn't shared with my sister, because we had an unspoken agreement not to speak about *her*. I knew that the wound was still too raw, and that it hurt my sister to even think about her. I knew because it also hurt me.

"Miracle Child Returns from the Dead."

That was the headline of the story that I found on Facebook, published by a Christian news service, one week after Emma's return.

> *Emma Gonzalez, missing since she disappeared from an Arizona garden last March, and presumed dead, reappeared at her parents' home last Sunday. Marco and Tiffany Gonzalez were awakened by a noise and found her, unharmed, in their yard. It is assumed that she was kidnapped and returned.*
>
> *Although the child is too young to explain her where-*

*abouts, police report that they are seeking leads on some-
one named "Mimi."*

*Meanwhile, her parents are overjoyed at her return,
which they describe as the work of God.*

*"It's a miracle," said Marco Gonzalez, father of the
missing child. "We prayed that she'd be returned to us,
and she was. She's healthy and she's smiling and laughing
and that's all that really matters. The Lord listened to us
and we thank Him for keeping her safe and bringing her
home."*

I showed Caleb the story, since he was the only person I knew
who might be able to put this in context.

"So who exactly is God in this scenario?" I asked. "Me? My
sister? Iona? Or maybe it was Dr. Medina, for setting the whole
thing in motion."

We were lying in bed in his apartment, naked in a beam of
late-summer sun, the damp sheets abandoned on the floor. He
slowly ran his palm over my bare head, back and forth across the
growing stubble, until my scalp was so exquisitely sensitive that I
had to grab his hand to stop it. He was a good lover, it turned
out—attentive and gentle, as if he'd broken people before by mistake but now knew better.

"None of those things, and all of them," he said. "You're still
missing the point. As I see it, God isn't necessarily the force that
makes things happen. It's the force that keeps you going *despite*
those things. It's just another word for hope."

Hope. Funny how, despite what had happened over the last
year, that word didn't sound like something from a foreign language anymore. I couldn't say why I was suddenly feeling it again,
hadn't yet found a name for the reason that kept me pushing forward against the forces that would push me back. It wasn't God,
or a belief system, or an organization or movement to which I
subscribed. It wasn't a person, not Elli or Caleb, although they

were both excellent reasons to wake up in the morning and face the bullshit of the day.

Maybe it was just that I'd finally caught a glimpse of something new inside myself, a seed that had the potential to grow. I was curious what it might become.

I turned and kissed Caleb. "Well, I *hope* that the parents are too busy thanking the Lord who brought their little girl back to spend a lot of time worrying about where she's been."

"I hope so, too," he said soberly, and kissed me back.

But of course the parents were going to worry; how could they not? And the truth was, even now—almost five months later—Elli and I still lived in a constant state of fear. Every time the doorbell rang unexpectedly, I would watch my sister turn ghostly white. And I would know exactly what she was thinking, because I would be thinking it, too: Was this finally it? Had the authorities figured out who kidnapped Emma? Maybe someone had finally dug up security camera footage that had led them to my sister's door. Maybe there was incriminating evidence that we'd left behind on the blanket with Emma: dead skin cells that they'd scraped out from under her fingernails, a stray eyelash that had come from my head, a tire tread, a footprint in the desert sand, the label on her fancy French footie PJs. *Something* would be the clue that would solve the case and land my sister—and, most likely, me—in jail.

But days passed, and then weeks, and then months; and no one had come. Maybe they never would. Still, we lived with this low buzz of anxiety, a new normal that Elli and I never actually discussed, just like we'd never discussed the fact that I'd moved into her house to help her get back on her feet, or that I was becoming the de facto partner in the florist business that I'd helped her resuscitate. Because what was there to say that we didn't already know? She needed me there, and I needed her, and that was just something we both understood.

We were doing that more often, now: knowing each other's minds. It was like picking up a rusty flute that you haven't played since you were young, lifting it to your lips, and seeing if you still remember how to blow. And maybe you do, at least a little, though a lot of the time you still get the notes all wrong.

She was her, and I was me; each utterly distinct. But there were still places where we blended together, where the boundaries got a little fuzzy. I liked it that way. It meant that I could be myself, fully individual, and yet still be part of an *us*. It meant that I would never be alone.

I put the newspaper in the recycling bin and took it out to the curb to join the others just as the recycling truck rumbled up the block. Outside, the winds were blowing in from the drought-parched hills, making the bougainvillea shudder and the neighborhood wind chimes peal out their alarm. There was fire in the air, a dusting of ash on the drive, the threat of unseen dangers just over the horizon. But we lived deep inside the city, insulated by miles of houses that would burn long before ours. We were, for now, safe. Whether or not we deserved to be.

I looked down the hill toward the sea, where the Santa Ana winds were blowing the breaking waves into perfect curls. A clutch of surfers bobbed patiently in the water: Someone else's disaster was proving their windfall.

The fires meant that the evening sunset would be brilliant, I realized. And maybe I should have felt more guilty about that—the balance of existence, shifting in my favor—but mostly I felt a strange peace, newly born and gossamer. Elli and I would watch the day end together; and together we would wait for the next to begin.

ACKNOWLEDGMENTS

I WROTE THIS BOOK PRIMARILY during the pandemic, a period that reminded me how much we need connection, friendship, and a sense of belonging. I owe so much to the people who helped keep me sane during this long, strange trip. I'm still in shock that I emerged on the other side with a novel in hand.

To Susan Golomb, a superlative agent and valued friend: I wouldn't be where I am without you. Raising a champagne toast to you.

To my amazing editor, Andrea Walker, whose discerning taste helped me elevate my prose, and whose sense of humor kept me from having a nervous breakdown in the process; and to the rest of my incredible team at Random House, including Avideh Bashirrad, Andy Ward, Michelle Jasmine, Barbara Fillon, Emma Caruso, Madison Dettlinger, and the indefatigable sales and design teams: I'm so happy to have found my literary home with you.

To the authors in my writing group, Angie Kim, Tim Weed,

Chris Bohjalian, and Danielle Trussoni: Your sharp insights and virtual company are invaluable to me.

To Jen Koziol and Jeremy Berg, Maureen Meyer and Nat Pastor, and Craig and Abbey DiGregorio: I would never have found the time to finish this book (nor would I have been cheerful enough to do it) without our pod. Thank God for you all.

To my Los Angeles fiction writers community, including Rufi Thorpe, Cynthia D'Aprix Sweeney, Jade Chang, Stephanie Danler, Edan Lepucki, Liska Jacobs, and Sara Sligar: Thank you for all the sage advice and strong cocktails.

To everyone at Suite 8: Our writing space was a haven during Covid; thank you for helping keep it alive. I promise I'll bring in more chocolate and LaCroix soon.

To Brooke Ehrlich, I am so fortunate to have you as my champion in Hollywood; as well as Alex Kohner, undoubtedly the best lawyer in town.

This book feels like it owes a huge debt to friendship, so I especially want to thank my girlfriends, whose presence in my life I value more than ever: Laura Millersmith. Colette Sandstedt. Dawn MacKeen. The Spa Queenz, whose prolific texts helped me survive 2020—Erica Rothschild, Carina Chocano, Lisa Daly, Scarlett Lacey, Rachel Samuels, Danielle Parsons, and Miranda Thompson. The (former) TT crew—Amy Davila, Myndy Christ, Rosie Johnston, Natasha Silver, Jen Koziol, and Cleo Murnane. Lena Wells. Miwa Okumura. Daniela Bleichmar, Nichola Walker, and Darby Saxbe, thanks for all those sourdough recipes. Keshni Kashyap. Rachel Neupert. Kristin Levy. Tula Jeng. Danielle Renfrew-Behrens. Guin Doner. Courtney Phillips. And a special mention to all the Ivanhoe moms whose company and commiseration were invaluable this last year. I'm lucky my bench runs so deep.

To my parents and sister, Dick, Pam, and Jodi: I am so grateful to have you as my family, and as my perpetual cheerleaders and publicity team.

I've spent way too much time on the internet lately, but one part I don't regret is the time I spend on Bookstagram. The Bookstagram community continues to awe and inspire me with its passion and creativity, and I truly value the connections—to both readers and authors—that I've made there. Thank you to everyone who read my books and then took the time to share them, whether on Instagram, Facebook, Twitter, TikTok, or some other platform I'm just not cool enough to be aware of yet.

And finally—and most critically—thank you to Greg, Auden, and Theo. Greg, I couldn't do this without your unwavering belief in me. Auden and Theo, you are why I get up every morning. If I was going to be stuck in a house for a year with anyone, I'm so glad it was you three. I love you, my darlings.

JANELLE BROWN is the *New York Times* bestselling author of *Pretty Things, Watch Me Disappear, All We Ever Wanted Was Everything,* and *This Is Where We Live.* An essayist and journalist, she has written for *Vogue, The New York Times, Elle, Wired, Self, Los Angeles Times, Salon,* and more. She lives in Los Angeles with her husband and their two children.

janellebrown.com
Twitter: @janelleb
Instagram: @janellebrownie

ABOUT THE TYPE

This book was set in Sabon, a typeface designed by the well-known German typographer Jan Tschichold (1902–74). Sabon's design is based upon the original letter forms of sixteenth-century French type designer Claude Garamond and was created specifically to be used for three sources: foundry type for hand composition, Linotype, and Monotype. Tschichold named his typeface for the famous Frankfurt typefounder Jacques Sabon (c. 1520–80).